Locks and Keys

With best wishes

P. McMaster

Also by Peter Arblaster

Blackcountrywoman

Locks and Keys

Peter Arblaster

Locks and Keys

ISBN 978-09572275-0-7

First Published 2012 by
Direct-POD,
part of the Lonsdale Direct Solutions Ltd. group.
Denington Estate, Wellingborough, Northamptonshire NN8 2RA

Distributed by Peter Arblaster
petethefeet1@btinternet.com

Printed and typeset in Great Britain by

www.direct.pod.com

Acknowledgements

I would like to thank my brother, Michael for his assiduous search for mistakes in the manuscript. This has been an easier 'write' than Blackcountrywoman but has had the complication of being both a sequel to the first book and a prequel to the third.

Front Cover

The clock shown on the front cover is known as The Doctor Tonks Memorial Clock and was erected, following his death at the age of thirty five, from public donations to commemorate his work in the community of Willenhall in the Black Country.

The lady shown on the front cover is Elizabeth Selina Darby, my Grandmother of New Invention, Willenhall, Wolverhampton and also of Hockley, Birmingham.

1. Tears in the Candlelight.
August 1914

Elsie sat there by the dying fire, crying in the candlelight, lines of strain cutting deep tracks across her forehead. Now she knew Dan; she understood him completely; Dan, her husband, who had been her unknowing saviour and proud of her fast moving pregnancy. That had been seven years ago. Now he was a Sergeant in the Staffordshire Regiment, and she had been left to survive or not survive regardless of what her circumstances became.

She had an allotment, the payment from her husband's Army pay for being the wife of a hero. She also had an income from Sam Jenkins the solicitor for collecting in his rents, and her own. She also had an income from her occasional work in the lock factory. She was lucky, she thought and then the thought came to her that she had created her own luck, her own income and her own worth by her years of applied study, learning every detail of what she had to do and fitting them all into her plan of being a secretly wealthy woman who could make things happen in the Black Country. She had developed a philosophy some years ago to refuse no possibility of earning honest money and it had worked for her.

She had done things to make her life easier eventually and make them easier for Tom. She had always loved her son. Tom, her first born had been sired by Stephen Stone, the master locksmith's son and Dan had never worked out that Tom had had an eight month pregnancy; he had just taken it as a sign of his virility. Tom had never suffered as a result of his birth. Both of his fathers loved him in their own way and so did his mother.

Elsie Barr, although born in Birmingham was a proud Black Country woman. Her progress in Wednesbury, the small Staffordshire town had been better than steady since she had arrived penniless with her father, James Stretton, after walking from Birmingham when he had lost his job in one of the great workshops of Hockley.

She and her father had been taken in by widow, Mary Bowyer and, after helping her brother, Jack to repair some faulty ironwork they had found employment at Stones' Locks where she had fallen in love with Stephen Stone, the son of the owner.

His life had been planned for him by his parents, Albert and Mildred Stone, to marry Mabel Elkins, the daughter of a specialist locksmith, to increase their share of the profits available. He had agreed to the plan before meeting Elsie and now the die was cast. He had married Mabel in spite of his love for Elsie. She had been heartbroken at the time but still loved him despite the pregnancy that had followed their lovemaking.

Life had not made sense until Dan proposed to her and freed her from the secret shame of a spinster's pregnancy. It's not always an asset, an intelligent man, she thought. Look at Stephen, bright as a button but can't be mine. What's clever about that?

Still, what's bright about me? I love one man and bear his child, then marry another and bear his. Am I a slut? I don't feel like one – not at this minute anyway, with a house to keep, and two children to rear. Elsie smiled and wiped the tears from her cheek. I've got to make the best of the situation, she thought. That's the truth on it! That's what we all do in the end, make the best on it! Dan's probably telling some Corporal off or telling some privates the best way to go over the top – don't!

She smoothed the long skirt, a black one, her favourite colour. Dan said she was just rehearsing for his funeral. It was a nice skirt, she thought, but ready for use for any purpose, not so short that it seemed cheeky and not so long that it looked something that a widow might wear. She stood and gave a cursory glance at her reflection in the mirror over the mantelpiece. She was attractive, she knew. Stephen was not the first man to tell her and without being too fond of herself she could look in the mirror and like what she saw. Her long - sleeved blouse in a shade of emerald green complimented her hair which hung long, blonde and auburn to her waist. Her short self - appraisal made her feel a little better about life.

Another tear hit the back of her hand, surprising her. She made up her mind again to make the best of things. She ought to have a cup of tea with Ruth, her best friend; her best friend who had lain with Dan between cups of tea, to who she had confided her secret affair with Stephen Stone.

How could she act in an accusing way to Ruth, now, after confessing her own sins? Still, the woman might fancy a cup of tea and a chat. Ruth seemed to have a versatile way of looking at things. She probably had a completely different way of looking at – the situation!

Ruth's husband, Jack was an alcoholic, a boozer, as Ruth called him. He didn't drink at all now, and he loved Ruth with every inch of his being. Ruth was attracted to Dan and he was attracted to her. They had each confessed in their own way to their shared infidelity.

Elsie had only confessed to Mary Bowyer and Mary was now dead. Ruth thought she knew about Stephen, Elsie thought, but she wasn't positive and without being definite she could not profit from the feeling that she thought she knew!

Ruth acted as if she was privy to an important piece of information though and Elsie found it unsettling. It was silly, really; she had more destructive information about either of them than Ruth could bring against her and if Ruth used what she speculated, she knew she would be in danger of losing her husband, her children and her home.

Elsie had saved her friend once, when she had been deep in arrears with her rent. Jack, her husband, had been given the sack for working drunk. He had pretended to go to work for some time after that but he could not produce the housekeeping money any more, nor the rent. The sorry state of affairs had been brought to the attention of Mister Jenkins, who had offered Jack a last opportunity as an assistant to Fred Stone, the blacksmith and he had been dry ever since.

Ruth was living a balancing act in her relationship with Elsie and she would find it easier now that Dan had volunteered for the Staffies. The two women had no one to turn to for comfort but

3

each other, Elsie realised and she had made the first move towards reconciliation. Ruth had welcomed the move with open arms and they had together formed an alliance against the evils that life brought to them, each often puzzling over what they thought the other might do in an imagined set of circumstances.

She had heard nothing from Dan for three months, and then it had just been a postcard saying "Miss you, love, Dan." She wondered if he, now being a Sergeant-Major, would be embarrassed to put how he really felt on a card that Ruth might see!

Dan didn't believe in the heroism of 'over the top.' He believed in survival, for himself first and then for his men. Not many survived an 'over the top' experience. He had told her of hundreds of bodies lying around piecemeal and the look in his eyes had told her more than the words in his mouth.

'Battles ain't won by getting yourself shot,' he'd said. He had no respect for officers, young or old. Young officers had a life of about six weeks. How could that win a war?

Dan seemed hard right through now and as good a survivor as it was possible to be but the empty look in his eyes belied the way he acted and spoke. He was still alive. She would have heard, else. It was time she had a bit o' that stew she'd put on, to warm her. Her depressed mood was leaving her now as she stood and ladled the stew into a dish; Tom had had his and was in bed. You couldn't beat a bit o' stew.

The front door scraped the floor; that would be Ruth after something. She sat up and spoke. 'Hello, Ruth,' she called. 'Is that you?'

She heard the chuckle as her friend came in. She pushed the poker deeper into the fire to give a bit more light and suddenly she noticed how tidy the little house was. Mary Bowyer had taught her that, everything in its place.

The kettle started to simmer with the increased heat and she threw the tea dregs onto the back of the fire. She reached for the brass caddy, took two teaspoonfuls of tea and settled back into her armchair.

It was nice to see Ruth even if she did wonder what the woman wanted and what she was there for. There didn't have to be something to be borrowed. Sometimes Ruth invented a borrowing cause, just for the pleasure of an hour's company. Ruth had managed better since Jack had come off the booze. They were a different couple since the help that Elsie had given them

'Hallo, Else, just thought you might want to share a cup o' tea. Jack's had a rise this week, tuppence an hour. That's a good rise, you know, eight an' a tanner a week. He does a lot o' work now that 'e dain't do before an' Fred Stone lets 'im! It's more sort of ordering things and managing now an Fred's bin talking about tekkin' on another bloke, a young chap they can train to do things their way, if they can find the right one.'

She looked proud as she sat telling her story and Elsie felt proud too, realising how she had played a part in the small story of determination that they shared. She knew that Ruth knew too. The two women knew so much about each other. They were always working out how they could help each other, or, if the cards fell that way, hinder. There always had to be a *something* between them.

'It must be very satisfying, so to speak, to see what you've done, bear fruit.' Ruth spoke with candour and sincerity. 'I was always ready to give you a good turn if the chance came. The first chance came when that Henry Wilkins thought 'e could beat up three women all by 'imself. Fat chance 'e had.'

The women laughed at the recollection of Wilkins, a worker at the hop picking, screaming when a saucepan, full of boiling eggs was thrown in his face when he had attempted to attack Elsie and her friends.

'Another cup?' Elsie asked, and poured at the nod of assent. A cup of tea was a great equaliser and bonding agent. She sat and waited; Ruth wasn't there for nothing; what was she there for? Ruth coughed and the words came tumbling out.

'Although Jack's had a rise, he's got to get a cowgown and

they cost twelve and a tanner.'

Elsie replied immediately. 'Well, If he's a manager or a foreman, he's entitled to order three warehouse coats on account and find out later who's responsible for payment. I can lend you twenty-five shillings if he'd rather pay for 'em 'imself, but it'd be better if the firm paid for 'em, wouldn't it?'

Ruth looked up, Elsie's words making sense to her. It was always that way. She worried and Elsie solved. She loved her friend for the way she always found a way of getting some little thing done more easily.

'You've done it again, you always do!' She pulled a little packet of biscuits out of her apron pocket. 'Here, have a short-bread'.

A nod of thanks passed and the two women settled to talk of the minor events of the day. Tom was still practising the arms drill, saluting, presenting arms and opening his rifle port for inspection. The time it took to make them eligible for Army Service would pass quickly. What changes will have occurred in those few years?

Would she be an Army widow? She was now, in a way but a knock at the door and a telegram could change her status from a frightened imagining to a bitter reality. Ruth had the best situation. Her husband, who could not enlist because of flat feet, earned good pay on Government contracts and if Dan came home, he was just as likely to be welcome at her friend's house as at his own.

Somehow, everything seemed backwards to how it should be, or at least sideways, as they said in the lock trade. How would her life turn out? Sometimes it seemed that whatever love life she had, only emanated from the odd hours she could get together with Stephen. Whatever happened, she knew she would always end up having to fight for the odd moments of happiness she had.

It all seemed a foolish waste of their lives but they had each accepted that there was no other way to get a small ration of the feeling they had when they were together. She wondered if Ruth had the same feelings about Dan. Probably not; she would expect her man to be able to offer her at least a small measure of security, and Dan wouldn't ever be able to do that. Willenhall was a small town and everybody knew everything about the home lives of the people who worked in the lock and key industry. Dan and Ruth would have to run away and start a new life somewhere else – and they could never bring themselves to do that; the strain on them would be too great.

Elsie felt a little more secure, with those thoughts behind her but she recalled when her suspicions had been first aroused. Dan had fallen from his bicycle in a bad winter and had hurt his ankle on the way down from the High Bullen. He had been laying there when she had found him and she had had to seek help from Fred Stone to get him home. Ruth had come over and seen him and started massaging his ankle while Elsie had gone to get some Friars Balsam. When she had returned, Ruth and Dan had been playing Nurses and Patients and obviously enjoying themselves. Elsie had been angry and had shown Ruth out of their little house but the damage had been done then, she was sure.

She had tried to ignore the feelings of the guilty pair and they had never been found in a compromising situation since but Elsie felt they still had feelings for each other. People were strange. The whole of society was bound up in the idea that a man and a woman should be devoted to each other and to each other only but the truth of the matter was that all sorts of behaviour occurred without drawing any strong attention to it.

Here they were, two good friends who would do anything to help each other and yet they were both breaking the most important rules of their society, even to the extent that one of them was having what was called an affair with her best friend's husband. What a name, an affair! It sounded like something from a lurid magazine. When an affair was described, it was nearly always some pair from high living people with position and money, never working class folk.

She picked up her cup and drained it. It was time to make another. She prepared the pot and poured boiling water into it. Ruth looked at her.

'What was going through your mind, my friend,' she said. 'You looked as if you were writing a book, then.'

Elsie smiled. 'No,' she said. 'I was just letting my mind drift around. It's surprising what daft thoughts go through your head, if you let them.'

They each reached for the cups. There wasn't any point in allowing private thoughts to become public.

Ruth was still looking at her. 'Is that a new blouse, Elsie? I don't think I've seen it before. Did Dan buy it?'

That was a dangerous question, Elsie thought. Whatever answer she gave, it could still cause trouble, either for her or Dan. Still, she could show her independence.

'No, I bought it myself. I have a few bob come in occasionally and when I do, I sometimes spend it on myself. Well, why not? I'd wait a long time before Dan bought me anything and I am sure I don't see all the money he earns so why should he see all that I earn?'

The two women fell silent for a minute, drinking their tea and then Ruth spoke again. 'I suppose I'd better go. Jack'll be home soon. He likes his dinner on the table when he comes in an' he'll be in soon. See you tomorrow, perhaps, eh?'

Elsie stood and spoke. 'Did you want to borrow that money then?'

She looked and saw from Ruth's shaking head that Ruth had decided to manage out of her own resources. That was a relief. Whenever you lent money to someone, there was always the problem of whether you would get it back. She leaned forward and gave her friend a kiss on the cheek and saw her out of the door. It was nice, in a way, to see someone becoming more self-reliant; they were more of a person, more real.

Well, at least she was in a better mood than she had been before her friend came to see her. That was a bonus. Jack was more real, too. He had come a long way from what his wife called a boozer to someone of real distinction, a junior manager. He might have the potential for more advancement yet. That would be nice for the Mallory family.

She looked round herself, mentally and listed the people who had tried and succeeded. There were a few but there were the others as well and she had no inclination to help the whole of mankind. Everyone had to grow in their own way.

She thought of her own mentor, Samuel Smiles, who had guided her actions since she had first read his book, *Self Help*, years ago. Now, she never made a serious decision without consulting his book. She had been given a copy when she first arrived in Willenhall, years ago and it had become almost her Bible. Her favourite saying from his book was *'Life will always be to a large extent what we ourselves make it'*.

She had made it her motto and had decided to make life how she wanted it to be. She would succeed; she could feel it in her bones. She had started as almost a vagrant when she had first arrived in Wednesbury but was now quite well off as she put it to herself. It gave her a small feeling of self-satisfaction which she did not regret. Why should she? She had earned every penny she now owned. She had been obliged to work long hours for every brick she owned in her small but expanding empire of Black Country properties.

Even Dan did not know anything of her life outside the world that he inhabited. She knew that if he ever found out her worth he would do everything in his power to deprive her of it. She could not and would not give him the satisfaction of what she had worked for.

2. Dan goes to war.
August, 1914

Sergeant Dan Barr leaned back against the carriage seat. He was going to war again! It was a thrilling thought and he relished it. He had always thought of himself as a tough sort of bird, and it had usually paid off. Some women loved him for it. Ruth did; she liked being taken, almost forcibly, being dominated by his sheer masculine strength. He recalled the first time; when he had fallen from his bike and she had been left in the house to comfort him while Elsie went out for help.

Ruth had let go of the bandages and moved her hands up his leg until he forgot all about the pain in his foot. She had offered her arms to him and he had accepted them, all over his body, as if she were worshipping him. The desire he felt had made him forget all about the possibility of being found out and he had turned her so that his body was on top of hers. She had smiled as she spoke to him.

'That won't get rid of your swelling, you know, Dan. Mind you, the swelling you have got is likely to make a girl forget any other.'

Dan had known then that her body was his for the asking. All he had to do was to take her with a little respect. He had lifted up her skirt to reveal no clothing underneath. She had made no comment. He had laid her back and pushed himself into her ready body. She had gasped and started to move with him, her body unable to keep still. They had both climaxed almost immediately; time being such a very valuable commodity. They had had to struggle with clothes; God knows what Elsie would have said if she had walked in. He loved his wife, Elsie, as much as he loved life but Ruth did something to him that he couldn't explain. It wasn't as if she was a raving beauty but she had large breasts and that aroused him more than anything. It wasn't as if she dressed like a beautiful woman, she was usually in an old jumper or blouse and a long skirt but he always knew that underneath her clothes there was a passionate and yielding woman who was always ready for him when he asked for her.

He brought himself back to the present. The assassination of Archduke Franz Ferdinand had delighted him. Not that he had anything against the man except that he was a foreigner but, because of the event, he was now going back to war, in charge of a large group of infantrymen. Promotion that had seemed slow, looked as if it could really speed up. In the month since Ferdinand's death the whole of Europe had started clashing swords and sabres and the war had started to gather uniforms and rifles, guns and coffins; boots and stripes; pips and crowns. How many men would be pleased at the thought of others dying, to gain promotion for them?

What a way to fill an afternoon. Where would it end? He knew instinctively that they were not the only members of the armed forces who were on the move; there must be hundreds of thousands moving around the British Isles. This train was just a tiny part of the move towards the front.

The air was full of the soot and the coal that was everywhere in the Black Country. The train was going over points; changing tracks. The vibration was affecting him. The distance from the countryside to the Black Country seemed like a thousand miles, or a few minutes on a train.

Dan knew exactly where they were going. It was to the regular training barracks at Whittington, where he had trained before, with the 1/5 South Staffordshire Regiment, Territorial Army, near Lichfield, but there were so many men on the move that they could be going anywhere. It looked as if they were going north; that was his best guess. The young soldier opposite him in the carriage was holding out his cigarettes again.

'No thanks; 'Dan said, 'I don't like to smoke too much. It's bad for your lungs and they won't be so easy to get when we get over there.'

It was pathetic, the way some of them tried to curry favour with anyone who had a stripe or two. He relented, mentally. The lad was probably frightened to death.

'Is this your first time away from home, son?'

Dan knew he looked fierce so he asked the question as kindly as he could. The recruit was almost shaking in his boots. Dan looked down. They were farm boots so that explained a lot. You didn't meet many people in the depths of Staffordshire. He looked up at the face in front of him. He hardly looked fit enough to be carrying a rifle. The recruit was nodding, to answer his question.

'Never mind; you'll soon get used to it. Before you know where you are, you'll be speaking French like a native.'

They both smiled at the jocular thought. Dan tried to imagine what the French would be like; tall and moustachioed the men; dark and curvy the women. Some hopes!

The Corporal in the furthest seat of the compartment winked at him and Dan acknowledged it. They each knew what Dan was doing, trying to give a bit of security and comfort to the young man.

They were going through a tunnel now. He reached out in the dark and touched the young man on the arm, then smiled. They came out of the tunnel to a clear blue sky. The other occupants of the carriage were all dozing, nearly all asleep. Dan stood and stepped out into the corridor. There were others there, getting a breath of fresh air. He walked along the corridor, pushing and squeezing past young men, showing his rank and status to teach them deference. He was one of the few in uniform. Everyone else was on the way to collect one.

Suddenly Dan was alert. There was a carriage just in front of him, first class, that was full of khaki uniforms; uniforms with Sam Browns! He wouldn't mind one of those, himself. They were issued to Warrant and Commissioned Officers, so he'd better watch his step. At least he knew they were there. Dan returned to the compartment and laid his head down. He had recognised the voice; Captain Brookes, the adjutant. He would keep away from that martinet. His son was probably with him; he must hate it, serving with his father. The Commanding Officer of the Regiment, Lieutenant Colonel R. Richmond Rayner was there too.

Another clatter of lines; they must be somewhere where there were a lot of tracks. He tried to recall but nothing came to mind. The train was slowing down. They must be coming to a station. He sat up, alert, and looked out of the window. It was a station and had no name but he knew it. It had obviously been painted out. As he jumped out, a voice shouted orders to the men in general and Dan, responding automatically, got the men organised into three ranks. In the next few minutes there was a lot of confusion as they left the train.

'Fall in!' Dan shouted into the crush and confusion. He stood silent for a moment as the men tried to sort their selves out then he took a deep breath and shouted. 'Come on, you lot; three ranks; tallest on the right, shortest on the left!'

At last there was a semblance of order as the men shuffled their feet, moving into rank and file. Captain Brookes appeared round the corner of the little station. He stood still as the crowd of civilians became three ranks. Dan, surprised that he was the only Senior NCO present, tried to maintain his dignity as he marched towards the officer and stopped as the officer indicated a position for him to stand.

'Platoon ready for inspection, sir!'

'That was well done, Sergeant Barr. I have no doubts about you. Come and help me to select a fighting platoon.' The Captain turned to the recruits and shouted. 'Do any of you men think you are fighting soldiers or are you just stand to attention soldiers? Where we are going, you are going to have to fight for your lives, and I want to be sure you can!'

There was silence among the ranks for a moment, then one of them said quietly, 'What do we have to do, sir?'

He was a tall man. He didn't seem anything special but he had a look in his eye that told you not to mess with him. The Captain looked him up and down.

'What's your name, private?'

The man stepped forward smartly, saluted and stood in front of the officer.

'Holyhead, sir; Private Fred Holyhead'

'Well, Private Fred Holyhead, you can see this young man here; well, you've got to take his stripes away from him. If you do you've got his rank, all right?'

'Yes sir!'

Dan saw the man advancing towards him up the slope and realised that he had got a small advantage over the recruit until he got to the top, then he would lose it. There was no point in waiting. He trotted and got to the top of the rise before Fred Holyhead. There was no room for doubt now. He lifted his fist and punched the man in the jaw and watched him roll back down and lie still for a moment, at the bottom. Dan turned to the captain and waited.

The Captain seemed to have got pleasure out of the encounter.

'Anyone else want Sergeant Barr's stripes?' He shouted. No one moved. 'Right, Sergeant; march them over there' He pointed to the collection of barracks behind them. 'The Corporal will put you right. Right, Corporal?' He turned to a stocky man. 'Show the Sergeant where to put his gear and then put this lot into billets!'

The Captain turned round and marched off to where the other officers were congregated. Dan looked at the Corporal.

'Right; let's get on with it; shall we? What's your name, Corporal?'

'Simkins, Sarge, Bill Simkins.' He was quite tall and looked as if he might be useful in a fight. 'What's yours, Sarge?'

'Barr, Sergeant Barr. Now come on; they'll want this lot sorted before they've had their first drink in the mess!' He marched and stood alongside the three ranks. He lifted his voice. 'Platoon will move to the left in threes; left turn! Quick, march!'

Some of the men knew what to do, having been in the Boy Scouts or the Boy's Life Brigade and the recruits marched off, slowly forming a uniform body of men. Dan turned to Simkins who was looking at him with a wry smile.

'Get to the front, Corporal. Somebody's got to show them the way. Left, right; left, right!'

Gradually the recruits came under control and a few minutes later they were alongside the group of brick built buildings. When they arrived, Dan shouted the order at them.

'Squad; squaaaad halt!' There was a clatter as the men stopped and looked around. 'Corporal! Come here. Have you got a list? Good; do a roll-call then.'

As the men answered their names, they were told which hut they were to go to. Inside, they sat on the beds that had no blankets. Dan relaxed and held his hand out for the list. He wanted to introduce himself in a way that would fix him in their memories. He walked briskly into the first hut, consulting his list.

'Allen, Asquith, Bentley, Brown.' He waited to hear from all of them. When he got to Fred Holyhead, he spoke to him.

'You learned a lesson today, son, didn't you?'

'Yes Sergeant?'

'What was that, son?'

'Never give the enemy a chance, Sergeant.'

Dan turned to the others.

'Did you hear that? Never give the enemy a chance! If you do, they'll kill you, so you might as well kill them first, mightn't you? What did you say? The answer is "yes Sergeant." Do you understand?'

There was a chorus of 'Yes Sergeant.' and then they fell silent again. Dan stood and surveyed his men. They were the usual mixture of young men, all looking quite fit, if not at all military.

'Right, now you're going to get your uniforms so that you will all look uniform, like soldiers should look. Try and make yourselves at home. You'll be on parade in about three minutes so keep awake.'

Dan turned and marched to the next hut and went round to each of the men, asking what they did before enlisting, which part of the country they were from and making notes. Then he lined them up to march to the stores. In two hours they had all been fitted with uniforms and issued with cutlery and housewives, boot brushes and Blanco, braces and boots.

Then they marched to the cookhouse and lined up for dinner. Some of them looked as if they had not eaten for a week, Dan thought. After dinner they were dismissed, after being told that there would be an inspection at eight o'clock. Dan kept them on the run until it was time for 'lights out' and then retired himself. There were three Lance-Corporals and Corporal Simkins, who was given orders to get Dan up at five o'clock. Dan was exhausted; he went to sleep immediately. He was a big man, over six feet but even he was tired from the sheer amount of movement they'd had to go through.

The next two weeks went by swiftly, with the NCOs teaching the recruits to march and counter-march, to stand at ease and at attention and to aim the Lee-Enfield, .303 Rifles that were the backbone of the British Army. Dan had thought that they were going to get six weeks at least, to get the recruits into shape but word came that they were expected to be moved in two week's time.

Before they knew it, they were on the train again, on the way south. Dan began to think how he might improve his chances of survival. Some men had shot off their trigger finger so that they couldn't be made to go into the firing line. What sort of mind would take that turn? The only thing he could think of was to be the best at whatever he was doing and hope for luck to help, as well. To get help in that direction he had to surround himself with others of like mind. To start with, he had a Corporal and three Lance Corporals. That wasn't enough. He would get them together when they stopped moving. Wherever they were going they would have to march. Information was important, now. He had to find out more from the officers. He thought about the Captain who had been in charge of them. Perhaps the officer was thinking along the same lines.

He would ask the Lieutenant. He marched up to the building that was called Company Headquarters. Lieutenant Urwin

Brookes, their Company Commander was standing outside, smoking. Dan marched smartly to him and saluted. Young officers ought to have better things to do than standing around, smoking.

'Good morning, sir. Sergeant Barr reporting for orders, sir. Are we staying or moving out, sir? So I can organise the Company, sir.'

Brookes stared at him as if he were a stranger, but welcome for all that.

'I don't know, Sergeant Barr. I'm awaiting orders myself. Just a mo'. I'll see if anyone else knows. If no one knows, you'd better get your platoon ready to bed down for the night. There may be news for you as well, Sergeant. I'll be back in a minute.'

The Lieutenant turned on his heel and went into the tent that served as shelter for the officers. Dan could hear murmurings from inside the tent. The Lieutenant came out and beckoned him. 'Come inside, Sergeant.'

Dan walked in, wondering what he was wanted for. The Lieutenant-Colonel was seated at the table, flanked by a Major and the Captain. The Lieutenant-Colonel looked up at him.

'Ah, Sergeant Barr. You're the one who wants to know what his orders are. Is that right? Yes, of course. Well, you won't always get orders. What you have to do, Sergeant, is to get and then keep, your platoon or your company, ready at all times. You will not get tents or billets from now on. *You* will have to take responsibility for finding somewhere for the men to sleep and eat. In fact, I would like to congratulate you. We have decided to give you the Company Sergeant Major's rank, so you will have to look after all of them! All I can say to you, and I should pass on this advice is, be ready for change and take advantage of it. Got it?'

Dan stood to attention. 'Yes Sir. Thank you, sir. I shall commence my duties now sir, with your permission?'

'Yes, carry on Sergeant- Major.'

The officer turned and started another conversation with the Major and Dan saluted, did an about turn and left the tent. He marched back to his sector and called Corporal Simkins.

'Listen, Simkins. There's a chance that you'll be given my job so keep yourself smart. You never know your luck. In this Army, you could be a Colonel in three months. We may not get tents tonight or any other night, so get the men as comfortable as you can and get them bedded down for the night. If we get orders to move, that's bad luck. In the meantime let them lie down as much as possible. Who knows what'll happen tomorrow? Right? I'll see you in the morning. Get a Lance-Jack made up to do your running around, the same as I do to you. Make sure you keep me informed of any developments and give me a shake at 0500. Right? Goodnight then.'

He went into a small tent and left Simkins to attend to things; he had to sew his Warrant Officer's crown onto his sleeve. He wondered how many others were carrying out a similar task. There were going to be a lot of promotions in this lot – and that was before the shooting started!

Next morning he was called and told that because of his superior experience he was being transferred to a Regular unit. He shrugged to himself. He had been told – and given promotion at the same time. Not a bad outcome, so far. The only thing was, he would be getting more experience, maybe more than he wanted.

He had to get his kit together quickly and catch a train back to the Midlands where he was put in charge of transporting a batch of recruits to France. His experience was quickly improved and he was moved to a holding sector, somewhere in France, where he and his men came under heavy fire to the extent that he was one of only a few survivors.

There were not sufficient men to form a unit so he was returned to Lichfield, taking on another batch. He was damaged mentally by the experience for a time but because of his strength of character he quickly resumed his duties as a Company Sergeant-Major in the Staffordshire Regiment. He was allowed to retain his rank and Regular status and soon found himself becoming expert at turning the young privates into skilled soldiers and cavalrymen.

He had difficulty in believing he had been through so much, in such a short time. He had been in the retreat from Mons and had been at the worst end of the fighting, losing most of the people he had joined up with. He had been a Private, a Corporal, a Sergeant and a Sergeant-Major in a matter of a few months. How could it be that he was still in the land of the living?

Sometimes he sat with his head in his hands, trying to make sense of the war. It had not changed his personal philosophy. He still did not respect officers and if they picked up that message from his demeanour and attitude, he could not care less. He knew he was quite capable of killing anyone who got in the way of what he wanted, officer or not. He was too valuable to be sent to prison for his attitude, though and he continued to hold the Battalion together in spite of the way his superiors planned for defence and attack.

The Battalion's commissioned strength now consisted mainly of young officers; most of whom were killed within two months of joining. Dan still found their loss too hard to live with. He knew that he ought to respect them but most of the time they died before being able to earn any respect.

On the other hand, he was respected and feared in equal measure by all he had to work with. He valued the fear he put into the recruits for the reason that he could give them a better chance than most, of staying alive. He seemed to have a miraculous way of avoiding bullets, either from the front or the rear. Many officers had been lost in battle from a bullet in the back. He was offered a commission but refused it, saying that he felt that not only did he have a better chance of staying alive as a Warrant Officer but he could also contribute more in his present rank.

Corporal Simkins, with whom he had joined at the start of his service, had been shot at Mons and sent far behind the lines to recuperate. Dan found it hard to reconcile this with his own expectation of surviving until the end of the conflict. He was quite sad about it. The expectations of promotion and victory had not come in as regular sort of way as he had thought. He had now known dozens of men who had joined with their own ambitions. Now, most of them were gone. Thousands of men had died in one day. It was ridiculous; they were being led by fools.

What could he do? It was a question that troubled him often. The best answer, as far as he was concerned was to be as good as you could be and then be lucky. It was all about luck and God, whoever that was. It didn't stop him praying though. Sometimes it was all you could do.

Every day he took his Company outside to train. It didn't matter what sort of training they did as long as they were active. They had to be got fit and kept fit. That way they had a better chance of surviving. All they needed after that was luck. He made sure that luck was all they needed. He would make sure he did the rest.

3. Stephen and Mabel.
August 1914

Mabel moved to one side as her husband slipped past her, his hands almost touching her breasts. If only he would, she thought. He didn't touch her like he used to, unless he'd had a drink. She knew what it was; it was that little hussy, Elsie Barr. It would get worse now Elsie's husband had gone off to do his duty. Sometimes she wished Stephen would volunteer, but he had shown no sign of it up to now. By all accounts there were two seeing Dan off. She had seen him in his uniform with the three stripes on the arm. Barr had looked like a real man. She wouldn't have minded if he had kissed *her* goodbye.

Mabel reached to pour Stephen's tea. He was going in to work early; there was a Government order that had to be completed as quickly as possible. His father would be there too, helping to get the locks out for the Army and the Navy. She wondered what old Albert Stone thought about his son not volunteering.

He was different to his son. There was no doubt that he would have gone to fight for his country. He was sexier - she didn't even like to think the word – than his son. She had felt Old Albert's arms around her before now. His hands could have slid onto her body, she knew. She had felt his hand almost cupping her breast, innocently of course, but still having an effect on her.

She wouldn't mind too much if Old Albert had his way with her. She knew he *put himself about a bit,* in the factory. She had stood in the back upstairs window and watched him feeling one of the young girls, and the sight had made her feel all funny. As the couple had parted, he had looked up and seen her in the window. There had been a quick nod and a wink, and then he had disappeared into the doorway after the young girl. Mabel had felt all funny for an hour after that.

Mabel put the cup in front of Stephen and filled his plate with breakfast. Perhaps her husband was just as sexy as his father but he *put himself about* more away than at home. She would have to do what she could to fight the attractions of elsewhere. Her hands slid over her body, sending small ripples of emotion through her. She gathered her thoughts. The children had to be got up; the house had to be cleaned and the washing done. How she would manage without Catherine Taylor, the maid, she didn't know. She was growing up, she had noticed. How long before her husband discovered her?

She put the plate in front of him. With a bit of luck she would fatten him up until he died! She wouldn't be the first to do that, she felt sure. Men were too lazy and too mean to refuse good food. They just got bigger and bigger until the strain on their heart was too much. It was a long-term plan but, combined with giving him all the wrong food, would make her a rich woman. How many women had got rich that way? She could still mourn for him at the wake and mean it, too.

Mabel smiled to herself as she watched him get up from the table. He smiled back at her. That was one thing about him. He was always smiling, whatever happened. She looked down; his plate was only half empty.

'That's a waste; you've left half your breakfast,' she admonished.

'Eat it yourself, then. I've had enough. You always put me more than I can eat. You should be more careful, with the way the war is going. There are bound to be shortages.' He took his jacket from the hook. 'I don't know what time I shall be in. I want to see if we can get this order completed today. I think if we do, we shall be asked to repeat it. That'll help us to beat the unemployment problem.' He put his arms around her and gave her a hurried kiss. 'I'll see you later, love.'

Mabel looked at the clock on the mantelpiece. It was six-thirty.

Stephen closed the door behind him and made his way along the entry that led to the small factory at the back of their home. Mabel was acting strange lately. Was she onto him? She bored him; she had always bored him, but their marriage had brought benefits to the combined firms that now existed, thanks to the marriage. He had never loved her, nor had it been necessary.

Mabel had wanted him and so had her parents. His father had known about Elsie but he had thought of her as not much more than a vagrant.

Elsie *had* been almost a beggar when he had first known her and her father but she had proved herself since, as had her father, before he died from lung disease. Elsie had got on with life and had made the best of their relationship when he had explained that his family wanted him to marry Mabel for business reasons. They had each accepted the way things were but had continued to love each other, spending time together when the opportunity arose.

Elsie was a well-off businesswoman now, and Stephen was one of the handful who knew it. She had gradually become a substantial landlady in the Wednesbury commercial circle. Not even Dan knew that she was more than just a rent collector. Aunt Mary had put her on the right road and guided her along it until her death from pneumonia. Now, Elsie had real power, the power to put people on the street if they didn't please her. Not that she would; it wasn't in her to act that way.

Dan going into the Army was going to make a lot of difference to them. They would be able to spend more time together. It was a wonderful thought. Would Dan ever return? Stephen didn't wish him any harm; he was a good man in his own way. It was just that he was in the way! What would he do if Dan died?

The factory was dark as he went in and he spent ten minutes going around lighting candles and oil lamps. He would turn them all off again soon. It was getting light now. The workers would be here soon. He took off his jacket and threw a few shovelfuls of 'breezes', the small cokes, onto the smithy fire which was the source of heating for the factory. Any other heating was supplied by the sweat on the brow of the workers. It was August and quite warm. He picked up a long strip of metal and started to feed it through a hand press just to get warm. He was pressing the front plate of a small padlock. He would soon get a gross of them done.

He heard a sound behind him and turned. It was Kate.

'Could you tell me where I can get some hot water to do the washing for Mrs Stone, please?'

Surely she knew! She had only started a few days ago and apparently didn't know her way round. She spent some time working at the house and some time helping in the factory. She had a room at the top of the house; the room that Elsie had had when she had first arrived from Wednesbury. He had spent some time in there, with Elsie, he remembered. The thought made him have another look at the young girl. She was shorter than him, wearing an overall that was burnished black by her oily hands constantly passing over front of it. It made her breasts seem as if they were illuminated.

'Why don't you wash your overall at the same time that you do the rest of the washing? Then it won't get all shiny like that.'

Kate looked down and appeared to realise that the oil on her overall isolated the shape of her breasts, making them stand out.

'Yes; I'm sorry, Mister Stephen. I suppose I don't look as often as you!'

She blushed as she said it but he felt that the blush wasn't all that sincere. He took hold of her.

'A sight like that could get you into trouble, you know. A man might want to touch as well as look.' He moved forward and put his hand onto her breasts. 'Do you see what I mean?' She didn't move so he slipped his hand inside her overall. 'Some man might want to touch you, there.'

He moved until his lips were on hers, teasing and insinuating them into her mouth. She suddenly pulled him closer and took hold of his hand, pressing it tighter onto her breast.

'I don't mind if you don't, Mister Stephen.'

Kate pulled his hand onto her again, more tightly, then lifted her breast out of her overall and pressed it into his mouth. He bit into her gently then squeezed her and sucked at the same time. She gasped.

'What are you doing to me, Mister Stephen? What are you doing? Oh! Oh!'

Kate seemed to buckle at the knees and Stephen had to place his arm around her to stop her falling. She cried out, softly.

'You make me go all weak at the knees, so I don't know what I am doing, you know. It's lovely. I've gone all soft.'

That's more than I have, Stephen thought. I'm as hard as ever. I wonder if she'll go all the way. He pulled the overall away from her body, revealing the contours and shadows of her figure. She was not beautiful but she was very voluptuous, and the way her long black hair framed her face, made her seem like the Mona Lisa. He was about to lift the last of her clothes away when he heard a sound. It was someone just entering the factory, on the way to work.

'Go and find yourself something to do, go on; get on with a job. Perhaps you'll have a bonus in your packet this week.'

Stephen turned away. He had more to think about than some stupid girl going weak at the knees. Somehow, his mind turned to the war and what was happening there. He felt a certain amount of guilt because he hadn't volunteered but when he tried to analyse the war, he couldn't find a good reason for fighting it.

He couldn't believe that huge Huns were waiting to ravish innocent English maidens. He had only met one or two Germans and they didn't seem very different from the English whom he'd had to do business with, apart from the language of course. It had all started because some insignificant Archduke and his wife had been shot in an alley which they had entered by accident. All the European states had immediately started rattling sabres at each other.

England hadn't wanted to enter the fray, he knew. It was all a matter of honouring our obligations to Belgium. France had set the seal on it by withdrawing their troops ten kilometres from the borders, virtually inviting the German Army to take advantage of it. They had done so, and that had ensured that England would honour her agreement to become an ally of France. How many

Englishmen would be killed to answer honour's call?

The trouble was, he thought, the die was cast now and all those flag-waving women would regret it before the year was out. If all those young men thought they would be able to shoot Germans without them firing back, they were in for a shock! At the back of his mind was the thought that he would be obliged to go to war eventually. He had no faith that it would all be over by Christmas.

One or two women had asked him when he was going to sign up but he hadn't given them the courtesy of an answer and he expected that one of them would eventually pin a white feather on him to try and brand him as a coward and a traitor. At the moment he was ignoring the stupidities but it would surely get worse.

In the meantime the firm was doing all right out of the war, completing government contracts as quickly as they could. He finished turning the lights on and returned to the office. He had plenty to do. He would have to do the office work that Dan Barr used to do. The thought made him miss the man. Six others had volunteered and there was no one to carry on with their work so the firm was recruiting what men and women they could. Some of them were all right too. He could do with Elsie to give a hand but she was busy with her work for old Jenkins the solicitor, and looking after young Tom. He would ask her but she would probably refuse because of the risk of Mabel spotting them in a compromising situation. Mabel would smell a rat straightaway. He turned his mind to the accounts again. If there was no one else to do them, he would have to them himself. The pen scratched and he noticed that the nib was crossed. There was always something! There was another in the small box that he always kept. He hated blotting the paper when he was doing the accounts.

Stephen's mind turned back to Kate. He had liked the feel of breasts on his lips and he would probably do it again if he got the chance. Where had she gone, anyway? He looked round and saw her sitting in the shadows. What was she doing there? Oh well; he might as well enjoy what was on offer. She looked very tempting, even if she was a danger to him. He stood up.

'Come here, Kate!'

Stephen spoke imperiously, as if he was a Caesar, and she looked up at him from the pile of stock clothes she was sitting on. Her face seemed to beam when he spoke like that to her. Some women enjoyed being dominated; she must be one of those.

'Come here, Kate!'

He raised his voice just a little. He very rarely raised his voice at all but his normal voice seemed to be enough for any of his workers to jump when they heard it. He peered into the darkness again, trying to see her. She was lying on her back now, he saw, and her hands were inside her overall, moving on her body. The sight stiffened him. He took a step forward and saw that her bosom was uncovered.

He bent and pulled her overall away from her body and he saw a sparkle of a smile on her face. She was obviously aroused by the situation; so was he! He took his coat off and knelt beside her, moving against her as he could. Kate's arms went round him again and the lust in her eyes was too much for him. He laid himself on top of her body, feeling the heat from their bodies combine to create a heat of passion that excluded any other feeling.

Stephen laughed to himself. Life was always worth a laugh. He could even laugh as his body combined with Kate's. Well, why not? It was very pleasant and you might as well laugh as not. He found himself pushing again; pushing harder and feeling the girl's body pushing back against him, like a dance, in time to some mesmerising melodious music, moving him. The words in his mind made him smile again.

He finished what he was doing and pulled away from her. It was not his function to create Heaven for the hired hands – hired hands? Another laugh, and then he walked away from the body on the sacks. There was always another one. He had other things to do. Workers were moving their numbered discs from one board to another to let him know they were on the premises.

Back in the office, Stephen made himself comfortable and reached for the daily newspaper that was delivered early. A cup of tea was on the desk; someone had put that there; who? Kate had been otherwise engaged. Oh well, it didn't matter, did it?

There was an advertisement for men to volunteer to join the British Expeditionary Force. Another half a million men were being called for. They must be balmy! All they could look forward to was a bullet in the body, somewhere in France. Would France be grateful? It was not likely; the French were much too proud to acknowledge the debt. Stephen felt that he was doing his part in the conflict, supplying items of military importance to the Army. How would they manage without firms like Stones keeping them in locks and other bits and pieces?

Stephen finished reading the newspaper and reached for his books. He just had to add a few figures to it and then he could go back into the works to spend some time on a hand press, doing the work that would normally have been done by one of the hands who had volunteered.

He liked presswork. Although it was boring, it had a quality about it that let him know that he was exercising his body. It was a heavy job, the one he was going to do, too heavy for a woman, really. Women were alright for those jobs where they just had to give a short sharp pull on the handle to pierce a hole in the front or back of the padlocks for a rivet to be put through when the innards had been assembled onto the back plate.

It was eight o'clock when he made his first pull on the long handle. A large metal ball had been fastened to the long handle, to give it some extra force when the handle was pulled. In an hour he was ready to stop for a change of activity. He liked a change every hour or so; it made the job more interesting and he told himself that he was doing six men's work.

Old Albert Stone watched him from the shadows. He had come in to help out. He had no need, now, financially, to be doing physical work but he felt that he was doing something to help to defeat the Germans. Stephen was quite a strong lad, able to swing that press handle like a professional. He was a professional, really, even if he had had his way with that Kate, first thing this morning! Why couldn't he just keep to his wife, like it said in the Bible?

Still, who was he to criticise? He would have had her himself, if young Stephen hadn't had her first. There were plenty of other young women now, among those they were taking on to fill the gaps left by those brave young men who were volunteering to go to France to fight for their King and Country. The more children that were born, the more troops that would be available in eighteen years time!

Old Albert felt that he would have gone if he had been young enough but he knew that he would have been turned down at the recruiting station and he didn't feel inclined to be laughed at. The thought came to him that perhaps they wouldn't have laughed at him and where would he have been then? He might have been among those young men, but struggling to keep up with them. Although his mind loved a challenge, he knew that he would have been in trouble, and that was before meeting the enemy, who would also be fit, young and wanting to kill him!

Why had it seemed such a good idea to marry Stephen off to Mabel? The idea had seemed financially sound at the time but it hadn't made his son any happier. Stephen still had some sort of alliance, or dalliance if that was a better description, with Elsie. She was a strange woman, somehow always seeming to be a bit better off than most, in spite of only being married to a locksmith, and he knew to a penny what a locksmith earned.

Elsie must surely be feeling the pinch now that Dan was away in the Staffies or whatever regiment he had joined. How did she manage? He knew that some Servicemen sent a part of their pay home each week but even then she couldn't live as well as she apparently did. She had a pony and trap, and quite a nice little house in Willenhall and he had heard that she had a place she used at Wednesbury as well.

Perhaps Stephen helped her out a bit; there was a thought. How could he find out? Perhaps he shouldn't try. Sometimes it was just as well to be deliberately ignorant. He had heard as well, that she did a bit of work for old Jenkins, at Wednesbury, and that was how she had got hold of the pony. She was a bit of a mystery woman, which was more than you could say for Mabel. She was just what you saw, and as plain as a pikestaff. She loved his son, though; that was plain enough, and it should be good enough for Stephen as well. Come to think on it, Mabel was looking broody, if that was the word to use. His forehead creased as he thought of the implications. That would be good news. How had Mabel managed to get herself pregnant? Stephen had always made out that he was bored with his wife. She must have made herself attractive some time.

4. Dan's new men.
September 1915

'Keep quiet, you men. Just listen, instead of wagging your chins, unless you want me to stop them wagging!'

The recruits knew by now that Sergeant-Major Barr was quite likely to carry out his threat. They were a rough bunch but the pick of the crop as far as Dan was concerned. A good proportion of the recruits he had had to deal with were so undernourished by their lives in their civilian roles that they were unfit for real soldiering.

A lot of them were uneducated too, and not likely to learn much. In his opinion they were just cannon fodder, just useful for going over the top and rushing forward as quickly as they could with bayonets poised in case they got as far as the German lines.

He had seen what an artillery barrage could do, at Mons. That would not happen to his men if he could help it. He had come to the opinion that the war was being run by idiots who were quite content to stay at the back of the field and order other men to give up their lives in hopeless causes. Now he was preparing a manual for his men, an unofficial and unwritten one that outlined the better ways to win. No more would he send his men blindly over the top. Instead, he would prepare traps for advancing German troops to blunder into. They would then be more easily slaughtered, he thought.

'Pick up your rifles and check them. I'll be round in a few minutes to see for myself. If I find any dirty rifles, I'll have you shot! I am not having any of you risking your comrade's lives by not taking good care of your weapons.'

He marched up and down the ranks, checking a rifle here and a bayonet there. He looked down at his watch. It was four o'clock. There would be food available for a short time. He hadn't better wait too long.

Whittington Barracks was a good sort of place for soldiering.

Since he had returned to England he had been on a crash course for regular senior NCOs and now he was training a better sort of recruit, a fitter, taller, heavier sort of man. These men wanted to learn how to win without losing their lives. He would show them what he had learned, plus a few tricks he had learned when he had been a bare-fist fighter. At the moment they were all as green as grass.

He called in his loudest voice. 'Come and sit around here, you men!' He shouted loud because he knew that he had to train his voice to be heard in the heat of battle. 'Come on; you're like a lot of pregnant penguins!'

He waited to commence until he had their attention and then he heard a Southerner speaking low. 'What does he know? Black Country bastard; what does he know?' The man turned and saw that he had been caught out. 'Well, its right ain't it? What do you know? You ain't seen much. Just a barrack square, that's all, I bet.'

He turned to his mates, completely ignoring Dan. The rest of them seemed to wonder what would happen now and stood instead of sitting. Dan decided that now was an appropriate time to establish his authority.

'Hey, you! You with the big mouth! I can see you have difficulty sitting down.'

He stepped forward and punched the man on the nose. The surprise was complete and the man sat down on the grass, his nose bleeding.

'Well, you seemed to have got the idea of sitting down; now it's time to see if you can stand up. What's your name, boy? Stand to attention when you talk to a Sergeant-Major.'

He stood back and waited for the man to stand but the man decided to have another go at Dan. He reached out to pull his legs from under him but Dan was quicker. He simply knocked the man's fingers with his stick and the man yelled.

'Have you got the idea of standing or are you still in the mood to sit down? Stand up, boy!'

He waited for a few seconds and the man started to get to his feet. Dan moved up close to him, thrusting his face into that of the recruit's.

'I asked you what your name is. Can you understand English or do you need help with that as well? What is your name?'

The man stood to attention and looked Dan in the eye. 'Larkin, Sir. Leonard Larkin. 802 Private Larkin, Sir!'

'Thank you, Larkin, Private Larkin. Now sit down with the rest of the recruits, Private Larkin. I'm going to show you how to kill a man with your bare hands before he kills you with his bare hands. You might find that the ability to do that is very useful and it may even save your life.'

Dan looked round the circle of men, all paying attention. Now they would start to learn. Now they would find out how easy it was to kill an enemy and how easy it was to be killed by an enemy. The men were all sitting now, unwilling to bear the brunt of Dan's anger. For an afternoon he lectured them on battle strategies, unarmed combat and the use of the bayonet. Larkin was paying attention. He looked to be one of the fitter men in the intake of recruits. He might prove very useful.

Dan stood them up and put them into three ranks. First he showed them the basic drill moves. Attention, at ease, easy, saluting at attention and on the move. Marching forward and backward across the square he marched them until they got the hang of the movements. Then he took them to the stores.

'Fall out and go into the stores and get yourselves issued with rifles, quickly. Come on lads. You've got to learn to march with rifles now. Hurry yourselves. The quicker you learn to use them, the quicker you'll be in France, firing at the enemy. The quicker you learn to do that, the quicker we shall get this bloody war done and finished with; right, Larkin?'

'Right, Sir. Right!'

Larkin replied quickly. The only way to get on in this mob was to do as you were told, as quickly as you could. He had learned one lesson, now he was going to learn more, as quickly as he could. Perhaps he could make it to Sergeant-Major!

While he was standing there in a complacent manner, Dan was watching him. It was obvious what was happening to the lad. He was learning!

The men were returning now, examining the Lee-Enfield .303s. The weapon was a strange piece of metal to most of them. It was quite a heavy piece of metal too, weighing in at over eight and a half pounds. They lined up again, in roughly the same order and stood facing the stores with their rifles butt down on the ground. Dan stood for a moment looking at the men, and then he started barking orders at them.

'Squad, squad attention!'

The men immediately put their feet together and put their rifles at their sides. Dan marched to the front of them and went through the whole range of drill movements, showing them what could be done.

'Now it's your turn. Let me see you stand to attention. Lift your right foot high and move it to the side of the left foot with a loud bang. Now stand at ease. Pick your right foot up and put it on the ground about fifteen inches from the left foot.' He waited while they carried out the order. 'Good. Now we shall see it done in a more professional manner.'

He put them through their paces, time after time until they could do each movement in an almost perfect manner. Then he marched them back to their billets.

'When I give you the word, fall out and get yourselves down to the cookhouse for a bite to eat. I want to see you outside your billet with your rifles at the port, ready for inspection, in an hour's time. The nice Corporal will show you a little drill first, and then you will learn to actually fire one of these things. Squad, squaad, dismiss!'

The men moved swiftly into the billet, putting their firearms away into their own bed-spaces. They had each been told to make a note of their weapon number in order to take responsibility if the rifle got lost. An hour later they were on parade again. This time they marched a mile to the range where they were instructed in the use of the various aspects of the butts and the signals that indicated the results of the last shot fired. They each had to take part in the running of the range, several men at a time making their way to the butts and taking hold of the long poles on which signalling discs were positioned. These were used to point out where the shot had hit the target.

Dan demonstrated the use of the Lee-Enfield, achieving a good score, and then others were allowed to try.

The Lee Enfield could reasonably expect to fire twenty to thirty rounds per minute. The rifle's use was a surprise to most of them, not having handled any sort of weapon before. They spent the evening cleaning the parts that they were allowed to take apart. They were issued with cleaning cloths and oil and told to clean the rifling in the barrels. Again, Dan was hard with his instructions.

'I shall be back later, to see if you've done the cleaning job as it should be done. If it's not as it should be, you'll all be on a charge for misuse of Government property! Now get on with it.'

Dan turned on his heel and marched away in his usual military style. He had heard that they were being shipped to France shortly and he wanted to meet his new son. He had been given permission to have a twenty-four hour pass, from midnight to midnight. He knew that he was one of the few, and that it was a sort of reward for returning to his unit, just as they had needed him, to train the recruits.

He wanted to know what was happening in the Black Country. The thoughts of home never left him and he would have given anything to be leaning on the bar of the Red Lion. He went to his own room and changed into civilian clothes, putting his cap on over his short hair. He had a lift to the railway station and was in Wednesbury by four o'clock in the morning.

The door was locked when he tried it and that was just as he wanted it. He had a key in his pocket and was in in less than ten seconds. As he blundered in, he felt a blow to his head and swore involuntarily.

'What the hell's that?' He tried to keep the noise low in case he woke the baby. 'Who's that?' He repeated the question and looked round. It was Tom, his son! 'Come here, Tom. Don't you know your own Dad?'

Tom looked at him closely and then recognised him by his silhouette.

'D,D,Dad,' he stuttered. 'I didn't know it was you, and I often keep watch in case we get broke into again.'

'What do you mean, broke into again? When was the house broke into?'

Dan sat down and listened to the story of the last break-in. He had never heard the story before. 'Did they ever find out who it was?'

'No, Dad, but they say there were two men; one from here and one from Hereford. They only say that because the man in the bar at the Red Lion recognised the way he spoke. Mom had a problem with a man from Herefordshire some time ago and I've wondered if it was him that was with the other man, from round here.'

Dan suddenly remembered Thurston and it all seemed to come together. He decided to say no more about it, telling Tom that it was time for both of them to be in bed.

They both crept up the narrow staircase, Tom laughing to himself. Dan had noticed that Tom often laughed. Dan pushed the door and saw Elsie, asleep on the bed. He crept across the cold floor and slid himself between the cotton sheets, shivering as he did so.

He reached across to Elsie turning her face to his. 'Hello, love. I hope you don't mind me dropping in!'

He kissed her on the lips, tenderly. He knew that she was a lover of tender ways; he had learned that in the past. He kissed her again and this time she responded to him.

'Dan?' She said, 'Dan, Have you deserted? You can get shot for that, you know.' Elsie was glad and shocked to see him. 'How did you manage to get a pass for a few hours? Are you going to France tomorrow? I bet you are, aren't you? Have you deserted?'

Elsie asked the questions again and he told her that he had been given permission. The way that he told his story convinced her that he was in legal order so she settled to what she knew would be his next move. She turned and lifted her arms so that her breasts were silhouetted against the sky.

'Dan; I know what you've come home for; let's get on with it, shall we?'

They both needed each other's body; there had been too much time since the last time. There was more lust than love, she thought, but that was a good place to start. Ten minutes later they each lay back, sated. For each, the experience had been as fulfilling as was possible. When Elsie woke again, he had gone.

It was frightening; he had been there and now he was gone. Was that the truth? She stretched and lay herself back down. He was probably making a cup of tea, she thought. A few minutes went by and she stretched again. Where was he?

She moved herself down the stairs; Tom was sitting there. 'Where's your father, Tom? Have you seen him?'

Tom looked up at her.

'He said he was going to have a look in the works; there wouldn't be any harm in doing that, would there?'

Neither of them seemed worried about Dan's absence.

*

Dan was looking for Ruth; that was his first priority. He had been home and done his duty but Ruth was the one who always held his imagination. When he lay in his bed in the headquarters, and when he had been in France, Ruth had been the one thing that had held not only his imagination but his dream of a sort of reality.

He knew that she would welcome him if she saw him and she would find or create an opportunity for them to make love in the inimitable way that they did. They just seemed to fit, as if they were two bookends, made for each other. She was not the only thing on his agenda, as he called it, but she was the main item. Dan made his way down the main road and left it to enter the little court. He turned into the second house on the right. There was a candle on the mantelpiece and Ruth started as soon as she saw the flame flutter. She turned her head and saw Dan and her face opened into a beaming smile.

'Dan; I thought I would never see you again. I thought I'd lost you!' She pulled him into her arms and held him as tight as she could. 'What are you doing here, anyway? You're a crafty bastard, Barr. I always knew you were. I'm glad to see you though! Have you seen your wife and kids yet?'

She was getting no answer from him. He was undressing her and she was undressing him. He looked down at her and noticed that she had put weight on.

'What's this then? Have you got another bun in the oven? Where's your old man then?'

He didn't seem to care, just kept on sliding his hands over her body and she didn't seem to want him to stop. An hour later he was home in bed again with Elsie. It was time for him to be making his way back to barracks. She was dozing as he left her and caught the train back to Lichfield.

At ten o'clock in the evening, he stepped silently into the first of the three barrack rooms he had under his responsibility.

'Come on you lot!' He shouted the words out and banged the first recruit out onto the floor. 'Let's be having you! Stand by your beds. Hands off cocks and pull on socks!' The recruits, who had been drilling all day, still managed to be outside at attention in a few seconds. 'I told you I'd be back to check on your rifles; where are they? Go and get 'em, Quick!'

The ranks broke as the recruits dashed back into the billets and emerged with their Lee-Enfields. In a minute they were all standing to attention, arms at their sides. Dan managed to stop himself smiling as he shouted them to form open order and then gave the order to port arms for inspection.

The first one to have his rifle inspected was Len Larkin; Dan made up his mind to give them a fair inspection. He had Larkin pull back the bolt to ensure that there were no rounds in the breech, and then looked up the rifle. He made no comment until he had emptied the magazine, refilling it when he had finished.

'Very good, Larkin. You are coming on well.'

He thrust the rifle back into Larkin's arms and moved on to the next man. He chose every third man to inspect and gave either praise or censure. In half an hour the inspection was over. He had been joined in the inspection by the Corporal. Each of the three billets had a Corporal, none of whom were all that experienced. He gave the task of inspecting the rest of the men to the Corporals and went to bed himself.

He was sent for the next morning by the adjutant, Lieutenant Brookes. After the usual report on strength and efficiency the Lieutenant started on the real business of the day.

'Sergeant-Major, we have been asked to form a special unit to harass the enemy, not in the usual way but to be given almost carte blanch to destroy what we can. We shall be given extra training facilities and specialists in certain skills. We shall also be given more equipment to carry out our missions, when we are given them. How does that appeal to you, so far, Sergeant-Major?' The Lieutenant leaned across the table and looked Dan in the face.

'I've been keeping an eye on your unit and you are making great strides with them, thanks to your Corporals and Sergeant. You yourself have been quite skilled in taking time off from your duties to spread your skills around the Black Country!'

He stopped for a moment, looking more keenly into Dan's eyes. 'You would never have been discovered except that I had given orders to one of the men with specialist skills to watch you twenty-four hours a day. He gave me a full verbatim report.'

Again he stopped. Dan wondered how he had managed the trailing of himself. He had thought that he was almost invisible. Why had he been watched, anyway? He had been given leave.

'I want a list of people who would be potential NCOs and those who would be useful if the NCOs were otherwise engaged, if you know what I mean. Thank you, Barr. I'll see you in the morning and I would like the new unit to be ready to travel on Saturday. We shall be going to Saffron Waldron, on the way to Portsmouth, with a couple of weeks extra training. Thank you.'

The interview was over and it was up to him how he got himself ready for Saturday. He went back to his quarters and sat himself down with a pad of paper. There was a lot to think about. Who was the one who had been given the task of trailing him and if he could find out, what should he do about it? Who should he select as potential NCOs for the small unit? Larkin was an obvious choice; he could see that. He decided to act on the impulse and called to Corporal Larkin. 'Henry!'

Larkin was in with him in seconds. He too was ambitious.

'Yes, Sir. I'm here, Sir.'

Dan indicated a seat and started to explain the idea behind the formation of a special unit to harass the enemy. The Corporal was enthusiastic.

'Sounds a good idea to me, Sir. I'd like to be considered for the unit, Sir. It would suit me down to the ground.'

'Well then, Henry. I want a list of people to be considered. The other thing is, do you know of any men who were missing over the last couple of days? I was given permission to go, but I think there was somebody else who went, and I want him. Don't tell him you know, just get back to me, right? I will see you with your list at 2100, right Corporal? Right, then. We shall have about 250 men including NCOs, and five officers so there will be plenty of chances at promotion for those willing to take a chance.'

He turned to his own pad of paper and started to add headings to it. When he looked up, Larkin had gone and the small room suddenly felt cooler and smaller. He felt more alone than he had ever felt. When he looked down he had a list of half a dozen men including his Corporal Larkin. Larkin was a dark horse and had come out of his shell quicker than anyone he had ever known. They moved out a few days later, by train arriving at Saffron Waldron at the beginning of October.

October went and the small camp was busy. It had been built

in a week. There were guards from other units ensuring the security of the personnel. They were a mixed lot with a collection of diverse skills to aid their first mission. The men had marched to strengthen their stamina and had practised with all the weapons of the most modern fighting men of the world. They had their own doctors and nurses, all 'attached' on a temporary basis. All the members of the unit were volunteers and were among the fittest men in the Army.

Newly promoted Captain Urwin Brookes was the CO, with a small group of others to assist. Dan Barr was in charge of putting the training theory into practise. He already had a list of potential replacement NCOs in case of deaths. A number of grenade teams were envisioned, with nine men in each; two carriers, two throwers, two bayonet men to act as defenders of the team, two spares in case of casualties, and an NCO in charge of the team. A machine gun team was also planned, without any set numbers as yet. Machine guns were in short supply, even for this elite team.

Dan was being allocated fifty men as a starting number; what happened after that was dependent on the results they achieved. It was quite frightening in a way, he realised, because if they were sent into a situation they could not handle, they could well end up being wiped out to a man. He put the thought behind him and concentrated on the way the training was going.

It was a strange unit. Some were from the Guards Regiments, some from the Staffordshire Regiment and some from the Marines. There were a few from the General Service Corps; they would be valuable for their mining and bridging experience. In the trenches, one of the hardest things to do was to get from one side of a trench to the other.

The whole unit would be about the size of a Company, with four platoons and a headquarters staff commanded by a subaltern, in this case the Captain. He would be responsible for signals up and down the line of command and the general running of the missions they were to be given.

The four platoons would be commanded by second Lieutenants, and Acting Sergeants would relay their orders as required. They would be referred to as 'D' Company. They would also have the use of other odd personnel; these would consist of a Drummer, Shoemaker, Transport, Signaller and Stretcher Bearers. Everyone seemed to be on a course, not always the same but always learning. The officers would have batmen. Dan was beginning to see the size of the unit now and realising what a large unit it was, compared to the other units he had been in charge of.

Very few of the recruits had ever seen a German and were surprised when Dan told them that they were not all six feet, six inches tall. Dan showed them pictures of the type of uniforms and equipment they could be expected to be seen wearing. There were soldiers from many nations and they all had different uniforms. Some had been killed by mistake by friendly allies firing in error and recruits had to learn quickly to avoid this happening either to them or by them.

The general dress for the German soldier at the front was field cloth in grey. Matching straps were used for the shoulders and a leather belt held six pouches with twenty rounds of ammunition in each. The ensemble was surmounted by a *pickelhaube*, a helmet topped by a brass spike.

Dan had pictures of these in each barrack room displayed in life size so that the recruits would become familiar with them. He had been told that they would be going home for embarkation leave in a week's time but it was not announced until the day before. The men all stood and cheered to be given the news; they had been training for a month and were heartily sick of it.

They had all been learning to dig trenches, fire rifles, fight hand-to-hand, cook in the field and how to make themselves become invisible in the field.

That night they were all polishing and shining their uniforms, showing how pleased they were to be getting the leave. The only undercurrent was that it was *embarkation* leave and that meant that they were to be that much closer to the battlefield. However, they were probably better trained than most and were therefore filled with more optimism. Instead of all being given travel warrants, they were told to make their own way home, the following morning, and to be back at the barracks by midnight on the following Saturday night.

Dan found himself a lift for most of the way and then jumped on a train to Wednesbury. He was outside his home by one o'clock in the afternoon and let himself into the house. There were small noises from the kitchen so he opened the door. Tom was standing to attention, imitating a soldier, and there was a small child looking up at him.

'Here you are, Private Ted. Stand to attention now, and you might get to be a Corporal one day. Come on now!'

Dan pushed his way in and saw Elsie sitting there, obviously joining in with the boys. At the same time, she saw him and jumped up.

'Dan, Oh Dan! You're home! Are you home for good or are you going back again?'

Elsie seemed to float across the room, into his arms and Dan was suddenly happy and at home again.

'And who is this little lad?' He asked the question although he knew as soon as he looked at the lad that he was the boy's father. 'What's your name, son?'

Tom jumped in response to the question, wanting to be seen.

'He is Ted, Dad. He is my brother. The doctor found him a few weeks ago when Mom sent me to find him and the midwife. Haven't you seen him before? He's not much fun, really, but Mom tells me he'll be more fun when he can walk about. He'll be able to march then.'

They start them young, thought Dan. From cradle to grave they teach them to fight for King and country. Just because a minor foreign Royal, nothing to do with us, was shot; He remembered that that was what Elsie had said to him. He looked at Tom.

'Yes, Tom. He will be a lot more fun when he starts to get around. You'll soon get bored with him then, looking after him just when one of your mates comes to call for you to go out to play.' It was nearly time to go again and he had only just got here.

'Come on, Tom. You can go out for an hour. Here's a penny; go and get yourself some bull's eyes.'

He thrust a penny into his son's hand. He needed half an hour with Elsie. The war would have to wait for a bit; he couldn't! A few minutes passed and the sunlight on the walls in the small bedroom seemed to move quickly as the couple coupled on the top of the bed. Half an hour saw them through and then they were struggling to find another subject that could be of interest to the other.

They said their goodbye on the step. A few neighbours looked across and waved to Dan as he drew himself up to his full height and displayed the crown on his sleeve. Again his thoughts were in Wednesbury, wondering if Ruth's husband would be at work if he went there. There was no point. He had to be sure of getting back to barracks first so that he could make sure of all his men as they returned.

The safety of his men would be a credit to the training he had handed out, but the proof was in the pudding. Would they all recognise a German when they saw one? Had he paid enough attention to the hand grenade training? Would his men recognise a German hand grenade when they saw one?

He had managed to save a few 'potatomashers', the *Stielhandgranate*. These stick grenades were favourites of the German soldiers. They sometimes exploded on impact but mostly had a five second fuse. This sometimes gave the recipient time to throw them back, if they were swift enough.

The ability to recognise all these otherwise mundane details was of the greatest importance to the serving soldier. Many had been killed by being just a little late in recognising the enemy when they appeared round a corner in a trench.

He sat silent all the way back to the barracks on the train, thinking over details. He knew he could never teach them everything but had he taught them all he knew? In the end, just before they arrived, he decided that he had done his best; what happened after they had left his training was not his responsibility. He fell into his bed and the next thing he knew was the rousing reveille.

He always liked Reveille. It sent a flush of excitement through him, waking him for the day in front. It was "Here we go again." He knew he would have to be wide awake to keep up with his own recruits. That was all part of it, and the pride of the Regiment. He would be helping to create the requirement for another Battle Honour, to be carried in front on ceremonial days. The Regiment had a long and noble history so far and if it was up to him, he would help to further enhance it.

He had practised with a large flag and found that the carrying was not as easy as he thought. He would practise more and become expert with it. Maybe he would be carrying it in front of the king.

Although he was the most experienced soldier in his company, his mind seemed to be always active, mentally working out what he would say to his men, teaching them of the hazards of warfare. There was always something new, not always what was in the service manuals but often what he had learned himself, during action.

Gradually his men became more proficient; smarter, more professional and fitter, moving in unison with each other. If there was any way they could be taught better, he did not know of it. They marched along, in step, their arms swinging together. Captain Brookes noticed too, and commented on the way it had been achieved.

'I think I would sooner be Officer Commanding of Barr's Company than any other,' he said to his father as they stood and surveyed the men at their drill and the Lieutenant-Colonel lost a little of the grim set to his face as he replied. 'Yes.'

5. The Hop Pickers.
August 1915

Young Tom Barr, now eight years old, was living a wonderful dream for a young English lad. His father was in the Army and had gone off to war, to fight the Germans. There could be nothing more thrilling than marching off to fight the foe. You had to be brave and pure of heart and fight with all your might against the instruments of evil, whatever they were. Dan had managed to make him a blunt bayonet and painted it with silver paint and Tom liked to fasten it to a piece of wood and practice charging.

Tom could imagine the soft impact the bayonet would make on the stomach of his sworn enemy, piercing the uniform first, and then into the flesh, with blood spurting out all over the place. It was only a dream, he knew, but his father, Sergeant Barr, was actually going to do it! Was doing it!

His father had described it to him, the lunge, the parry and the slice, if it were possible, to finish the enemy off. His father could beat anyone, he felt sure. They didn't know when they would all meet again, his father had told him.

'It's a big job son, ridding the world of evil. It could be a job that will take until after Christmas. You've got to be strong for your mother, son. You are the man of the house, now.'

Now his father was gone. They had seen him off on the train, all those people's arms waving wildly with little flags, all excited, and then it was quiet. The train had disappeared, its wheels making banging noises over the tracks at the curve of the line, and then he was left with his mother. They had stopped and spoken to Mrs Mallory, one of his Mom and Dad's friends. Her children had been left at home while she had come to see Dan off. Her husband was not going. He had too much to do at work, Mom said. He was very busy.

Tom practiced marching up and down in the garden with a paling stick from the fence as his rifle. He could slope arms and stand to attention and present arms to Majors and above, and salute to Captains and Lieutenants. His father had shown him how and he had practiced until he had got it perfectly. Mom wasn't very pleased to see him doing it. She made him stop.

'We've got enough with one soldier in the family without another,' she said. 'Just try to learn your lessons at school; that's your job, not practicing to kill people. Do you think that we have a quarrel with the ordinary Germans? We got a lot of work from them, making locks. Why should we start to kill them just because some Archduke gets himself shot? He wasn't shot by an Englishman so why should we go to war with them?'

It was no good asking him. He didn't know. His father must know why we were killing them instead of making locks for them. Otherwise he wouldn't have gone, would he? Grown ups did strange things at times. If his Dad could go away, why couldn't his Mom go away? We went away before, he thought. We went to a place called Bromyard when he was little. He decided to ask.

'Mommy, if Daddy can go away, why can't we go away? We went away before, to play in the fields. I bet the lady would let us come again, wouldn't she?'

Elsie started; she hadn't thought of Bromyard for a long time. Young Tom was right. The lady would like them to go again. It was August and they would be picking soon. They would be hard up for pickers now that a lot of them had gone for soldiers. The rent collecting could be done by asking the trades people to deposit their rents into the bank, and Luke at the office could collect the rest if all he had to do was to collect the domestic rents. She suddenly felt excited. Perhaps her old friends would like to come with her! She moved to her desk, picked out a sheet of paper and began to write. Three days later she had her answer.

Dear Elsie

Thank you for your letter which I found most exciting. We are desperate for pickers this year. A lot of our men have gone to be soldiers in the Worcestershire Regiment and this will leave us very short-handed. I will take as many as you can arrange to bring down, and I will pay you a finder's fee. On top of that, I am enclosing a cheque to pay for the rail fare for as many pickers as you like. I hope you are well, and that young scallywag, Tom who, I suppose is more grown up now.

God Bless,

Jenny Walker.

Immediately Elsie started sounding people out. Within a few days she had found eighty people who were willing to spend a month in Herefordshire, as a kind of working holiday. Betty and Ruth both said they were willing, especially if their fare was going to be paid for. Betty had lovely memories of when they had gone down, before.

On the first week-end in September, the train filled up with women and children, all ready to start their 'holidays'. The finders allowance had started Elsie off with enough cash to live on for the next month.

At five o'clock they were there, standing on the platform at Bromyard, waiting for the wagons to turn up to carry them all to Home Farm. The driver was a stranger to Elsie but he seemed to know the way and they were at the farm at half past six.

'Elsie! Elsie! It's lovely to see you. How many are you?'

Elsie looked up. It was Jenny Walker, looking only twelve months older than she had seen her before, six years ago. They each hugged and kissed the other until they were both crying. It was silly, the way women were, too sentimental by far. Still, it was nice to see her; that was for sure.

'Hello, Jenny; eighty; nearly all women and a few grown up children, if you know what I mean. They're all hungry as well. There's not as much food about as there used to be, you know. If you have any to spare, they'll all be grateful. I've an idea a lot of them will be grateful for whatever they get, money or food.'

'Well they'll all be fed here.' Jenny said, 'We have no problem with food at the moment. We've thought of asking the Army to provide some pickers. After all, they've taken most of ours! Oh, Elsie; it is lovely to see you. I think we are going to have a wonderful year at the picking. We still have some of our younger men, who are not old enough yet to volunteer, although, we've heard that some of them are lying about their ages. Anyway, most of the work has been done to get ready for the picking.'

Jenny hadn't changed, still chattering on as she always did, but Elsie felt that there was a dark side to her mood, somehow, and wondered what it was. Jenny suddenly saw Tom and immediately picked him up in her arms.

'Tom! My goodness it's a long time since I saw you! How long is it, Elsie?'

'It's six years, Jenny. He's a big lad, now, and ready to do a big lad's work, aren't you, Tom?'

She looked at her son and was suddenly proud of him. He was developing all the characteristics that she wanted for him. He was one minute a young soldier, the next he was a picker-up of heavy burdens and then the fastest racer he could think of. He wanted to be the best, the biggest, the strongest and the fastest. He might never be the cleverest, she thought, but he might beat the clever ones by his sheer determination and perseverance. It was perseverance that won the game, she thought. There were plenty of bright, idle men, plenty of well educated men without a plan for doing whatever it was they wanted to do with their lives. It was her intention to show her son that if he wanted to get on, he had to persevere through thick, thin and everything else, and have a plan. Any sort of plan.

In the meantime, they had hops to pick, and they would get good money for doing that, as well as getting food and board! It was a better sort of existence for these Black Country women than they knew at home, and they would make the most of it. Some of them had never been outside the Black Country. It was like emigrating for them, and they were silent and would be until they saw how the experienced ones acted.

They were all gradually getting used to having less to eat and they didn't know the first thing about living in the country. No doubt they would be scrumping the apples before the week was out. She would try to put a stop to that, if she could do so without appearing to be one of the bosses lackeys!

Elsie found herself walking at the side of Jenny Walker, listening to her instructions about where the cooking devils, the wrought-iron cooking tools that they all got used to using, had been put, and where they were all to sleep. The barn would accommodate thirty of them. They would all get used to climbing the rough stairs to the floor above the cow-stalls, and find spaces they could separate by hanging sacking curtains. This would be their bit of privacy. Some of the pickers would be sleeping in pigsties but as most of them had never seen a sty, they wouldn't come to any harm for their ignorance and the sties had been whitewashed anyway. They would find out when they had got used to it!

Agnes Ollerenshaw was an agreeable worker, she thought. Her house was always tidy when Elsie called for the rent and she sometimes worked in one of the local shops. Rough and ready but willing; that was the main thing.

Elsie recalled how she and Betty used to lie cuddled up together in the barn, to keep warm. It must have shown on her face because she looked up and saw Betty smiling at her. Betty had married Luke, the chief clerk at Jenkins the solicitors. Ruth had left her three children in the care of her eldest daughter, who was seventeen. She couldn't have brought the three of them so she had left all of them. It was a strange arrangement but then, all of them had to make do with strange arrangements when there was a war on.

Betty was showing Ruth how to hang the curtains to get the best bit of privacy.

'Do it like this.' she said, demonstrating. 'It's gainer that way. You don't always want prying eyes to see what you are doing, do you? You might want to invite a visitor for the night. If you do, you have to be able to rely on your friend's discretion and ask them to leave early in the morning!'

Elsie smiled to herself. Betty was making up stories, now, to impress the inexperienced. She would soon learn that Ruth was as clever as she was. Perhaps they would learn together! Betty had shown that she was not averse to a bit of female company so she would probably be making overtures to Ruth inside a week!

Ted was enjoying the change, never having seen a cow or a Shire horse before. He was soon imitating Tom, who was teaching him to moo.

The top floor of the barn was full of women making themselves at home. There were rumbles of discontent, especially when they saw the other occupants of the barn, below. Agnes was frightened to get too close to them. She had her daughter, Carol, with her and she was laughing at her mother's nervousness. Jenny Walker would soon organise them. Others were just trying to familiarise themselves with the new surroundings and smells they found themselves among and the children were constantly finding interesting places to explore. They had today to get themselves sorted, and then they would start work at seven o'clock the next morning. The experienced ones would show the others and they would all be seriously picking within three days.

Some of them would try live on as little as possible, letting the farm provide as much food as they could. A number had brought some supplies with them, tea and sugar and such, that wouldn't be supplied by the Walkers. The farmer and his wife had always opened their little shop to the pickers to save them the trouble of having to walk into Bromyard. There were always eggs and bacon and butter and lard. They were able to buy on credit, just signing their names and paying it off against their wages.

Elsie sat down on the narrow mattress, booking it for herself and lay back with her hands behind her head. What were the men doing now? It was frightening to let your imagination wander but she couldn't help it. For all she knew, Dan was lying in a trench with a leg missing, in agony. She took a grip on her mental wandering. For all she knew he was in charge of training at some little training camp that had been built in the south of England. It wouldn't be like him, she realised. He would want to be in the thick of it.

Her eyes closed; it had been a long day and she was not in as good a physical condition as she had been, the last time she had come down. She had managed to let Stephen know where she was, seeing him for a few minutes only, and then he had made his way to his wife's side, in the market at Willenhall. He would come to see her, she knew. He would be unable to resist the temptation of making love to her in the grass.

He would probably come down by pony and trap. He might even borrow Chalky, her Welsh Cob. Chalky would enjoy the long trot down from Willenhall. He seemed to have great stamina and had been very friendly when he had come down before, the local mares sniffing the air as he approached. What would his duty be in the war?

At the moment the Staffies were looking for large horses, Shires and Clydesdales, to pull the huge guns for the war, so Chalky was safe until some officer took a fancy to him.

Perhaps she was no different herself. It was just nature at work, keeping the species alive, taking chances of copulation where they could! She blushed at her own thoughts and opened her eyes, to find Betty looking into her face. Her blushes deepened as Betty bent and touched her breast.

'What are you thinking of, then? You look very suspicious to me.' She turned to Ruth who was standing at the side of her. 'There's more to Mrs Barr than meets the eye, you know, Ruth. You'll need to keep an eye on her, you know. If she can't get a bit of passion from one of the men, she'll be after you!'

Ruth was just as clever as Betty.

'Well how about you then, Betty? You're making all the running but I bet you've seen a bit of life in your time, such as it is! What's your skeleton in the cupboard?'

Betty shut up immediately and Elsie knew why. Betty had been habitually sexually abused by her father as a young girl. Elsie had seen to it that he had paid a bitter price for his abuse. Betty had never forgotten it. Elsie had never admitted it but Betty gave the impression that she knew Elsie had been involved in the affair. Ruth was looking at both of them. It was obvious that her mind was racing, trying to put things together. Ruth turned to Elsie.

'What's she worried about, Elsie? Look at her face; you can read half the story there; it just wants the other half to come tumbling out. Look at you as well! You know a lot more than you're letting on, don't you?'

'Yes, come on Mommy!' It was Tom. What was he doing? Was he really trying to pry a secret out of her, as Ruth was, or was he coming to her aid and just trying to give her a little respite by butting in? 'Are we going to play Truth, Dare or Promise?'

Truth Dare or Promise was a children's game that was usually played when there was a mixture of boys and girls to play. The one selected was offered the three choices. If they chose Truth, someone would ask them a silly, discerning question like, 'do you love Billy?' They had to tell the truth when they answered. If they chose Dare, they were given a task that began 'I dare you to...' This could be a dare to jump off the top of the mangle or some other task requiring a certain amount of courage. The Promise option was to Promise to carry out a task in the near future and was usually a Promise to kiss some person before the day was out, or a similar, romantic task.

Tom was still looking for an answer so she thought quickly.

'Yes. Tom, I suppose we're all playing a game, but there are no winners or losers. It's just a game and we can all play at finding out each other's secrets. Now it's time to go to bed. We've all got to go to work in the morning and we have to do as much work as we can so that we get paid a lot of money. The more work we do, the more we get paid. You can learn to pick as well, Tom. Come on; let's get you into bed. Here you are; tuck yourself into this big blanket. If you keep your eyes open you might see the cows lie down in the night when it gets cold.'

She threw the large blanket round him and lay him down into the mattress of straw that she had stuffed for him. He looked up at her and spoke.

'Shall I say my prayers, Mommy?'

'Yes, son, say a prayer for your Daddy and ask for him to be safe and ask for all the soldiers to be safe and come home safe and well. Say a prayer for yourself as well, Tom, and your Mommy of course.'

She looked up. Betty and Ruth were staring at her. Ruth was crying.

'What's the matter, Ruth?'

'Ask him to say a prayer for my three little ones as well, and my old man. He's a good man, even if he does like a drink occasionally.'

Elsie turned back to Tom but he was already whispering a prayer for Ruth's three. She sat at the side of Tom and gradually lay her head down on the pillow. It had been a long day, with so many things happening in it. Her eyes gradually closed. The other three women sat close to each other. Each of them was thinking about the prayers that young Tom had whispered on their behalf. Agnes was still worried about the cattle below so she would probably be praying she wouldn't get attacked by them.

Betty had had no experience of prayers other than her own when she had pleaded to be free from her father's embraces. There was something simple and innocent about the young boy's plea that had sent shivers down her back.

Ruth had gone through a similar experience when she he heard him praying for the safety of his father. Did the child know where Dan had gone? For all she knew, he was already being shot at in some trench in France.

The thought brought about an involuntary sob, wrung from her by the depth of her feelings for the man who, although he was the husband of one of her best friends, was also her lover. She looked across at Betty and saw that the thought she had was similar to her own. There was no point in dwelling on the sentiment, however.

Life had to be lived, regardless of the circumstances. Elsie lay back, dreaming of Dan and Stephen and their presence in her half-dreams helped her to sleep as she slowly relaxed and grew warmer in the barn as the combined body heat of the women warmed the air above the cattle. There was another face that came into her dreams, a frightening face, but she couldn't place it or recognise it. All that she knew was that it was filled with evil, disguised as a smile.

6. Wilkins in the Hopyards.
September 1915

Elsie lay asleep until her alarm woke her, bringing abuse to her from those who didn't like early risings. Elsie did; she had always liked the first rays of the sun on her face. She recalled how she had first experienced the sunrise, on her first visit to Bromyard, when Tom had been younger. It seemed different this time. She had had more experience of it, she supposed.

She looked round. The women were slowly rising, putting on their working clothes, if they hadn't slept in them. She looked down through the hole in the wall. Ruth was standing by the devil, cooking bacon as if she had been doing it all her life. She looked up and saw Elsie and waved.

'Come on, lazybones. I thought you were an early riser. I've fed half the farm!'

'Yes, I bet you have,' said Elsie. 'I've been watching you since five o'clock, wondering when you was going to start doing something instead of just standing there, smoking.'

They both burst into laughter. The thought of Ruth smoking was too ludicrous for words.

There was a movement at the end of the barn. It was Jenny Walker doing her rounds. It was unlikely that anyone would get up before she did. She waved cheerfully as she walked past. There were other pickers to get up in the other building, across the farmyard that was used to store the farm machinery and equipment. Everything had been moved to one end while the pickers were living there, to create as much space as could be provided.

A man walked out of the building and immediately walked back in. Who was he? Elsie felt that she should know him but for a moment she couldn't put an identity to the figure. Then she realised. It was Henry Wilkins! The thought somehow filled her with dread. How had he been able to get back into the good books of Albert Walker, the farmer? Surely Jenny would not have re-employed him. If he was working at the farm, what would be his attitude towards her? Elsie recalled the day she had whipped him and threatened to take out his eye with the whip. She had caught him attacking Albert Walker and had nearly killed him and she felt sure he would have done if she hadn't galloped up on Chalky and stopped him in no uncertain manner.

The thought came to her that she hadn't seen Mister Walker since she had arrived. Where was he? She determined to get to the bottom of things as soon as possible. She trotted down the steps to where Ruth was cooking. There was no sign of him to be seen. There was no reason to think anything untoward had happened but she just felt uneasy about her discovery. Elsie sat on a bale of hay and took a sandwich from Ruth.

'Thanks, Ruth. What got you up early? I suppose you're used to getting up with the kids, aren't you? Are you missing them?'

'Blimey, you're all questions ain't you? Are you on the trail of something, then?'

There was a sound of someone else trotting down the steps and as they turned in response they saw that it was Betty. Ruth called out to her.

'Here you are, Betty. There's a sandwich waiting for you, here. I had one and no sooner had I ate it than it was gone!'

Betty stopped and took it from the hand. She looked quite shaken.

'You'll never guess who I've just seen, Elsie. You'll never guess in a hundred years.'

Betty stood arms akimbo and waited for an answer.

'I bet you I can,' said Elsie. 'It's that mongrel who tried to kill the gaffer, Henry Wilkins. I'm sure there's something fishy going on; the missus would never take him back on after that lot.'

As she spoke, Wilkins came out of the building opposite where they slept. Instead of hiding, he walked straight over to them, his evil face smiling.

'Good morning, ladies, any chance of a sandwich? I don't seem to be very popular, today. Hello, Elsie. You don't seem so dangerous without your whip. Now if I had a whip, you would seem even less dangerous. Just think what I could do, then. Mister Walker is out of the way, fighting for his King and Country, so there would be nobody to stop me taking a terrible revenge.'

He stepped forward and looked as if he would carry out his threat but Ruth intervened to his surprise; he hadn't met her before.

'I wonder, Henry, if you would be as brave if three women tackled you.'

Ruth picked up the saucepan full of boiling eggs and threw it in his face.

'You bitch!' He screamed the words with pain and anger spicing them. 'You filthy bitch!'

Wilkins ran around in circles trying to get relief from the pain and as he did so, Betty put her foot out, tripping him up. He fell into a pool of mud and partially blinded himself. His anger was forgotten as he struggled to find relief from the pain. Again and again he tried to get up but the three women had his measure now and tripped him each time. Eventually he was able to get away from them and ran, shouting for help. He got to the farmhouse and one of the girls saw him and pulled him to one side where she could apply some salve to his scalds. The girl obviously did not know what had gone on.

The four women strolled over to see him get treated. When he came out, they just stood watching him, and he eventually wandered away from the farm. As he left through the gate, he stood and shook his fist at the trio. It was obvious that the affair was not over as far as he was concerned. They smiled and watched him go and then turned back towards the barn. Tom was watching through the high window.

'Mom, you're as brave as a man, and you Auntie Ruth. I heard that nasty man threatening you and I saw Auntie Ruth throw the eggs at him, and I saw him run away!'

The three women burst into laughter and then quieten as they saw Jenny Walker coming round the corner. They started getting ready for the picking. Some of the women had already started.

'Hello, ladies. It's good to see there's something to laugh at on this lovely sunshiny day. I must admit I do miss my Albert now he has gone away to fight. I don't even have a busheller now, and that idler, Wilkins is useless. I can't find him. Have any of you seen him?'

The women stood perfectly still and it was obvious that they were trying to think of the best lie to tell her. Elsie spoke up.

'Yes, Mrs Walker, I know where he is. He came threatening me, to get what he called his revenge for the day I whipped him, when he was trying to kill Mister Walker. He was saying that nobody could stop him now, and he got a saucepan of boiling eggs in his face for his trouble. He went into the farmhouse and one of the girls helped him, put some salve on his poor face, and then he went off. That's the truth Mrs Walker.'

Ruth interrupted. 'Well, Mrs Walker. I was taught that if somebody threatens you, you are entitled to believe them, and you should attack as soon as you can.'

Mrs Walker hardly seemed to listen to her.

'Oh dear, I don't know what I'm going to do. There were only two men left on the farm and Wilkins was one of them. I don't know why he hasn't joined up. I never did like him but there was no other choice. I had to have a fair busheller who the pickers would accept. The other man, Howard, is almost middle-aged and he's got some arthritis, so that was all I could do. If Wilkins doesn't come back, I shan't have a man for the kiln. I know Howard will do his best, but it needs more than one man to dry all the hops we are hoping to pick. I don't have time to do it myself. I shall have to close down the farm!'

She sobbed into her handkerchief. 'Wilkins came to me with a sob story, asking me to take him back on. He said he had learned his lesson and nothing like that incident would ever take place again. I can see now, that he hasn't changed at all. He'd be better off in the Army, like Albert who signed up the first day without giving a thought to how I would manage without him.'

Jenny seemed to collapse, tears springing into her eyes. It was obvious to Elsie that she was under severe strain. She stepped forward.

'Look, Mrs Walker. I think I could do the busheller's job, with a bit of training. Mostly, it's a matter of booking everything that's picked. I'm quite used to doing accounts for myself, so it would only be something similar, wouldn't it? I remember you telling me that what went round, came round, so perhaps it's all for the best. Wilkins can look after himself, now. I was amazed that you took him on, really I was.'

Jenny was thinking about it; that was obvious. The tears had left her eyes. And she was being a bit more rational. Jenny tried to answer Elsie's question.

'He came to see me a few days after Albert went to join his regiment. He said he was looking for work but no one would employ him because they had all heard how he had been sacked at Home Farm. He said he had seen the error of his ways and had thought about Home Farm with respect; they had given him a chance before and perhaps they would again.

'I had misgivings about taking him on but he seemed so sincere. The other thing was of course that when he came to see me I didn't know that you were going to get in touch with me. If I had known, I might not have taken him on. I wouldn't have wanted a second round of hostilities, so to speak, but I didn't know, so I gave him a chance.

'Wilkins seemed all right when he started. We had no pickers then, and he did the work of preparation quite well, really considering he hadn't worked in that capacity before. Just before the first pickers came down, he started throwing his weight about but I tried to ignore it; people who have just been promoted are often that way until they get used to handling the little bit of authority that it gives them.

'One of the local girls handed her notice in, saying she wasn't going to be treated as a bit of dirt by him or anyone else. I spoke to him about it and he went to see her. I thought he was going to apologise to her. She left anyway and I happened to see her in Bromyard and she told me that Wilkins had threatened her. She wouldn't take his threat, she said, and by then she had found a job at the Allen's farm. It was nearer to where she lived, and they still had quite a few men still working there and she felt quite secure, if you know what I mean.

'I've been thinking about what you suggested while I've been talking and I think I'll take you up on that idea, Elsie. If you come to the farmhouse when you are finished, tonight, I'll go over our system of bookkeeping with you. If you have experience, you'll soon pick it up. I always knew you were a one-off! At least I shall have a busheller and then I just need somebody to help with the drying.'

Jenny seemed much more cheerful now. If Wilkins came back, she would pay him off and give him as good a reference as she could. Whoever took him on would soon see what sort of man he was. Jenny became what she was born to be, a landowning farm employer.

'Now girls, I expect you to turn out a good day today. I think I might ask at the barracks to see if they have any soldiers who might like a bit of hop picking while they are awaiting a posting abroad.'

That was a good idea, thought Elsie. It seemed that Jenny was getting herself acclimatised to the new conditions created by the war. Everyone in the country was finding that nothing was the same as it used to be. She turned to her two friends.

'Come on then, you two. Betty; you and I can show Ruth how to do this work. She'll soon get it weighed up if I know her. She is able to take advantage of any situation, I can tell you!'

Ruth looked at her, her eyes flashing, but Elsie just smiled at her, and spoke to Betty.

'Look how she managed to make the best use of a few boiled

eggs, this morning. I suppose we had better find them and clean them off for when we have a bit of a break, later on. We've all had trouble with men, too much trouble considering how young we all are, but we've shown them what for, haven't we, girls? We don't have to say anything about this, filling mouths with gossip; just forget it as if nothing had happened.'

The other two women cheered, their arms going high in the air. They felt supreme, able to take care of any situation.

In the lane, Henry Wilkins was nursing his scalded face. This was the second time the Barr bitch had bested him. He'd make sure next time. He made up his mind. He would go to Jenny Walker shortly, saying that he didn't feel he could work there any longer; he would have his wages and a reference. She couldn't say he had been sacked because he had given up the job himself. He would make sure of her, that Black Country bitch, the next time. They'd be going home in a month or so. Then he would follow her and find a way to do away with her. He made his way back to the small bed sitting room that he rented from old Nellie Bellars the widow in Bromyard. She didn't know any of his business.

Wilkins kept himself to himself for the next few days. He had always thought it best if he was the only one who knew his business. He had a few pounds secreted away from his adventures, as he liked to call them. He would have done well in the Army, he thought. He could beat any gamekeeper at stalking and he could probably survive well over there, too. He had to think things out.

The following week he went to Home Farm early in the morning. Jenny Walker was up as usual. She was always one of the early risers. As soon as she saw him on her doorstep she looked at his face. There were still signs of the hot water. She immediately confronted him.

'I wondered when you would turn up. What do you want? I hope you don't want your job back.'

Wilkins smiled at her, his face set into a hypocritical, almost religious look.

'No thank you, Mrs Walker. I came to thank you for giving me a chance but if I had known that that Black Country thing was going to be here, I wouldn't have taken it. All I've come for is to ask you for any outstanding wages you might think I am entitled to, and a reference that won't run me down too much.'

Jenny smiled at him. 'Come in, Henry. I've been expecting you. I've prepared your money, and included anything you might expect in the way of compensation from your little escapade, and a reference that is as good as I can, under the circumstances. Here you are'

She handed over two envelopes, one containing his made up wages and the other his reference. He tried to mumble his thanks but she cut him short.

'I don't want your thanks. All I want from you is the sight of your back walking down the lane!' Jenny thrust the envelopes at him. 'Here! Take them and go. If you come round here again I'll set the dogs on you. Oh, and another thing; I wish you all that you wish others. That should keep you in bad luck for the rest of your life.'

Jenny pushed him out of the door and slammed it behind him. She walked off quickly, wanting to be away from the man. He looked round to see if he had been observed but there were no signs of life to be seen. It was six o'clock. He went round to the back of the stores, where she kept the money from the sales to the pickers. The door was latched but gave as he put his shoulder to it. He stepped quickly in.

The collie was there but Wilkins had got to know it well. He stroked her gently and she whimpered, expecting another stroke. He gently stroked her; she liked that, and as he did, he walked across to the cash box. It was no trouble to open with the screwdriver that had been left on the table. There were always tools left lying around in case they were needed! He put the sovereigns from the cash box into his jacket pocket quickly and the rest of the money into his trousers. It was time to go. He opened the door slightly, just enough to let him see out.

There was no one around so he slid along the wall, trying to keep his silhouette in with that of the wall. When he got to the path where he had to leave cover, he broke into a swift walk, trying to be as easy-looking as possible. In a few moments he was at the gate and into the lane. He was away! He broke into a gentle trot for a few hundred yards and then loped along until he got to the outskirts of Bromyard. Five minutes later he had hidden his booty under a stone and was on his way to his bed. He willed himself to relax and gradually drifted off to sleep. That was another good day's work done.

Now he was ready to start on his next plan – to get revenge on them women from the Black Country. They would never know what hit them. He put his working clothes together and put them in a large black bag. He had to face his landlady. He was up to date with his rent but wanted to keep things that way to serve as an addition to any alibi he might need.

He finally went downstairs at ten o'clock. His breakfast was waiting for him as usual, cheering him up. He looked down, smiling at the small figure of his landlady.

'G'morning, Mrs Bellars. How are you? I've got another job to go to for a few days and then I'll be back. It's only a small sort of job. They just need somebody to do some moving. You know; furniture and that. Here's my rent for a fortnight, just in case.'

Wilkins handed over the small amount she required. His eyes noted the glint in hers, as he swallowed the last slice of fried bread.

'Thanks Henry. That's very good of you. I wish all my boarders were as reliable as you.'

Nellie Bellars smiled at him, and he was satisfied he had created the right sort of impression. She sat on her armchair and took a pinch of snuff, placed it on the back of her hand and sniffed it in deeply.

'Well, I'll see you then. I've got my key, in case I come back late. I'm just going to catch the train to Worcester.'

He lifted his bag onto his back and went out of the door. As soon as he had gone she voiced her thoughts and feelings.

'Yes, I've got you weighed up, Henry Wilkins. You're up to something. You must think I come up the canal on a coal barge. Still, as long as I get mine, that's all that matters. So long, Henry.'

Nellie put the kettle on again. She was going to enjoy his absence, especially now he had paid her two weeks in advance. She could always say she was full when or if he came back.

'I wonder where you've gone, Henry. I think I'll keep my nose in the air and see what it finds in the wind. You're up to something, something I could be earning from, if not from you.'

Nellie stopped daydreaming and put her coat on. She was going to make a visit to Home Farm, where he was supposed to be working. The journey took her an hour on foot, and when she got there, there was no one to be seen. Mrs Walker had to be around somewhere so she walked into the farmhouse and sat herself down in front of the fire, dozing.

It was nearly an hour later when she was awoken by the door banging shut, but it was not Jenny Walker; it was a young woman who looked as if she owned the place.

She challenged Nellie. 'Hello, who are you? Are you looking for Mrs Walker?'

'I'm Nellie Bellars and I'd like a word with Jenny Walker if you know where she is.'

Elsie relaxed. It was obvious from her accent that the woman was a local.

'I'm Elsie Barr. I'm working here for a while. I'll try to find her for you. Would you like a cup of tea?'

The young woman poured a cup out of the pot she had just made and went to look for Jenny and found her almost immediately, in the barn.

'There is a lady waiting to see you, Jenny. She says she just wants a word with you. Her name is Nellie Bellars.' Elsie sounded as if it was a question.

Jenny smiled. 'Oh, I wonder what she wants.'

She walked swiftly round to the kitchen, surprising Elsie with her speed.

Elsie started for a second then recovered her equanimity. 'What is it, Jenny? Is there something wrong?'

'No, my dear, but I think it might be a good idea if you listened to what she has to say. She is Henry Wilkins's landlady. She lives in that little back street in Bromyard and lets rooms out to working men. Some of them are all right and some of them are not. I've had workers at the farm who have stayed with her for years. Like everywhere else now, most of them are in the process of joining up. Whatever she wants, its probably got to do with Henry. Let's go and hear her out.'

She led the way to the farmhouse kitchen and greeted Nellie in a friendly way.

'Hello, Nellie. It's not often I have the pleasure of your company. I see our young friend has given you a cup of tea. That's good. What can I do for you, Nellie? I'm not foolish enough to think that you came over just for the pleasure of my company. Whatever you have to say to me, Elsie can hear. We have no secrets.'

Jenny looked at Nellie in such a friendly way that Elsie wondered if she really meant it. Perhaps she did! Eventually Nellie seemed to gather her thoughts into one for she started speaking, trying to explain why she had made the long walk.

'As you know, Mrs Walker, one of your workers has stayed with me for some months now. Henry Wilkins, I'm talking about, of course. Well, he's packed his traps, as they say, and paid me two weeks rent in advance, something he doesn't often do. He told me he was going onto some other sort of work for a little while, removals or something. He said he would be back in a fortnight but he has left no clothes in his room so I don't know whether to believe him or not, and I wondered if you knew anything that I don't know?'

Jenny sat silent for a moment and then answered her.

'Nellie, I don't know anything. If I hear anything, I'll let you know. He came in here, this morning to be paid off. I won't go into details but I can't see him coming back here for work. What I do know is that I found my cash box broken into an hour after he left. It might be a coincidence but I don't think so. There were only a few pounds in it but a pound is a pound and if I find out that it was him, I shall get the police in.'

They sat silent for a minute, and then Nellie rose, nodded without commenting and went, leaving the mystery behind.

Jenny sat for a few moments thinking about the events of the day. Once again the young woman from the Black Country had surprised her with her ability to think and act. She had a feeling though, that the end of the conflict between Elsie and that evil man was not yet over. What would be the next act in the drama? Up till now, it looked as if the Blackcountry girl was quite able to handle most problems as they arose.

She felt lonely; her husband was in the Army and her son was in the newly-formed Flying Corps.

Would she ever see either of them again? Her son was such a dare-devil. You never knew what dare he would take up. That was what was needed, she supposed, young men with initiative, to solve the problems of warfare. The only trouble was that those brave young men had to take terrible risks in order to solve the problems of warfare. If she was lucky she would see her husband and son again. Would she be lucky?

7. Agnes and Howard.
September 1915

'I don't know whether to ask her myself or whether to let you put it to her. I know you've been getting on with her. What do you think, Howard?'

Jenny and Howard Humphries, the drier, were standing, talking about their current problem; that of getting the hops dried properly after they were gathered in. Whoever asked the woman they had in mind, it could only go one way or another. Jenny Walker waited for Howard's answer and saw him smile.

'You know, I wouldn't mind asking her. It'd be a bit of a dare, a challenge if you know what I mean. I'd have to explain that the drying of the hops is a twenty-four hour job. She might think I was offering more than a job, if you know what I mean!'

Jenny punched him on the shoulder, playfully. Howard Humphries had always had a sense of humour. She had known him for years and he had always been reliable. The trouble was he was only one man and she needed two to get the job done. It would be too much for the middle-aged man alone.

'Go on then, Howard; you ask her; but what will you do if she jumps at the chance?'

Howard started and a deep red blush crept up his neck and darkened his face.

'There's no need for that, Jenny Walker. You know I've never looked at another woman since my Tilly passed on. Anyway, she's out of my age range, if you know what I mean.'

'Yes, I know what you mean. She must be eight years younger than you, and with a daughter she can't wait to get rid of. It might suit her to get rid of her mother!'

She paused, thinking she had gone too far but Howard just smiled.

'Which one should I take on then, the daughter, the mother, or both on 'em?'

He was just playing word games, the same as she was. He shrugged and turned away. That was the end of the game. Impulsively he turned back.

'I will ask her then, Jenny, and see what happens. It's probably a lot of fuss about nothing.'

He turned again and walked into the barn where the Black Country girls slept.

'Agnes!' he shouted, 'Which on ya is Agnes?'

The barn went quiet and a middle-aged woman stood in front of Howard.

I'm Agnes Hollerenshaw. Is it me you want?'

She came up to Howard's shoulder and was quite well built. Her hair, black but with a hint of redness hung to her waist. She was not slim but she had shape; that was sure.

'Is there something I can do for you, mister? You only have to ask an' I'll do it.'

Once again Howard blushed. He was not used to speaking to womenfolk. He looked down at her and she looked up at him and blushed. He coughed and spoke.

'Well, Agnes, it's like this. Jenny Walker 'as suggested I ask you. The problem is I've got to look after the hops when they've been picked 'an pressed an' put in pockets. It's more than a full time job an' I have to have a bed in the kiln to sleep there.

'There's only me to do the job but it takes two men to do it, if you see what I mean, only there aren't two men to do it. Would you like to have a look at the job?' He paused for a moment. 'It's not like picking. It's got some skill. You have to get the hops in the kell, that's what we call the kiln, then spread 'em over the hair, that's the drying area, with a scuppet – that's a wooden shovel. Then they have to dry, but not too dry and you get so you can tell by the feel and the smell of 'em when they are just right. Sometimes we have to put sulphur on 'em to get them the right colour.

'The thing is, you have to keep 'em moving. It's spread, dry, press 'em into pockets as tight as you can, sew 'em up and paint the number on the pocket, with the weight and a number to tell you where they come from. Then all you have to do is stack 'em ready for market. The picking goes on for eight to ten hours a day but the drying goes on so long as there's any hops to dry and sell on the market. He stopped talking for a minute, seemingly thinking about the best way to put it to her.

'There's not enough men to do the job so it's up to the women to fill in the spaces an' it has to be a volunteer 'cos nobody'd stand for being told what to do. I suppose Jenny Walker had a look round for somebody who might have the brains and stamina to do the job and came up with you!'

Howard looked at Agnes and she looked at him and noticed he had a twinkle in his eye. It was the twinkle that carried the most weight in her mind. It was all very well having brains and stamina but life could be miserable without a twinkle in the eye. That settled it.

'I'll have a go an' do me best, Howard. That's all I can promise you. If we work out, I'll 'ave learned something very useful for the future. If not, well I'll 'ave tried me best; all right?'

She said nothing about the twinkle; it was best not to, worn't it? To Howard she was just a hard working Blackcountrywoman. No mention of any sort of relationship except that of work. She was volunteering; that was one good thing. He spoke.

'Alright, Agnes, if you don't mind me calling you Agnes, we'll give each other a try, eh? It might be a good idea to start in the morning, about eight o'clock, eh? You can come and have a look in the kell now, if you like, just so you know what it's like'

He stopped speaking and, beckoning, moved into the door in the wall of the building opposite the barn where Agnes and the other women slept. Agnes followed him, surprised at the darkness as they went in. The first thing she saw was the rough bed in the corner and she made to back out. Howard spoke gently to her.

'That's for one of us. It's always been mine, for fifteen years.

If you want a bed in here – and you might, because of the hours we work, especially when the hops are coming in fast and furious, I'll soon make you a bed up or you can carry on sleeping in the barn with your mates. I never thought of sharing a bed with you!' He blushed red again. 'I never thought asking anybody was going to be this hard.'

His sincerity was obvious and Agnes couldn't help but smile.

'Don't worry, Howard. I never thought you had evil intentions towards me!'

She laughed and set the mood for both of them. That was better. They were starting to feel at ease with each other now.

'This is where the hops come in,' he told her. 'They are brought from the hop-yard in green-sacks and stacked on the green-stage at the start of the picking. The drier, that's you or me, gets the fire going' an' keeps it going' til the end of the picking. It never stops; the drying. We work 'til late on Saturday then knock off 'til Monday morning, when we start an' work 'til the following week, snatching five minutes when we can, between spreading, pressing and sewing the pockets. Mrs Walker comes an' weighs 'em an' puts the kell mark on 'em an' the pocket's own number. With a bit o' luck we'll get an 'and with the green-sacks what 'ave just been picked an' are waiting' to be dried.' He looked at her face and smiled. 'I know, it seems a lot to remember but you'll soon get used to it. I know; I can see it in your eyes.'

Agnes answered straight away. 'All I can do is my best, Howard. If I do right, Jenny Walker will tell me. If not, she'll tell me. I suppose you can do it gainer'n me but I'll get better. Just say 'do this' an' 'do that' an' that's what I'll do. What do I do to start, Howard? Let's get on with it!'

Howard reached and touched her on the shoulder. 'Either get a clean hop pocket and fill it with straw or get the mattress you've been using out of the barn and bring it in here with your gear and put it in that corner, away from mine.'

He picked up a large broom and started sweeping the floor,

being quite careful in the way he did it. When Agnes returned an hour later with her mattress, the floor was very clean. She took a swift look around and dropped her mattress in the opposite corner, away from Howard's.

'Is that alright?' she asked. 'I don't want to seem forward.'

'That's fine, lass. I'll see you after bait in the morning an' we'll start. There's quite a few green-sacks being brought in from the yards, today, so we'll start in here, when the pickers start after bait, about half eleven. Thanks for volunteering, Agnes! You'll have to work all the hours God sends.' He stopped speaking for a moment. 'There is one important thing, though. You'll earn more money than your mates and when you know what you're doing, you'll have a job for life – if that's what you want, of course.' He paused again. 'An' you'll be in good company as well!'

He smiled and touched her on the shoulder, giving her a feeling she hadn't known for a long time but not an unsafe feeling, not at all, just nice.

Howard seemed quite pleased with the way things were turning out so she went to where Elsie's group was about to stop for a break. No one said a word when she arrived and Elsie just handed her a large mug of tea.

Agnes sat silent for a moment or two and then turned impulsively to Elsie.

'I'm training for the drying,' she said. 'Howard is showing me the ropes.'

'Well, that's a turn up, Agnes, said Elsie. 'It's a big job and a big responsibility. Have you told your daughter, yet?' Elsie thought about it and then continued. 'It's more than a part time job, you know, Agnes. It could be a job for life. This isn't the biggest hop-yard down here but it's more than enough for one dryer. You might have to think about moving down here. I've never heard of a woman drying but I suppose there's no reason they shouldn't, especially as we have a woman for a gaffer. It'd be unusual though, that's for certain! Still, who's making the guns and shells, eh? There are fewer men now, no matter how you look at it. I don't know if my husband's still alive. For all I know, I shall have to find another sort of job cos there ain't any men to do 'em.

'I know you probably think it's joke but a bit later into this terrible war and a lot of women will be left their husband's possessions which in some cases could be money, shares and property; so people like you and Howard might not be a joke but might, in some cases, suit both parties.'

The little group of women looked at Elsie in amazement but gradually took in that what she was saying could actually happen. They all started chattering except Agnes who just sat there thinking.

It was six years now since she had lost Ike from a stroke. He had tried to recover the use of his arm and speech but, a fortnight later, he had died in his sleep from another stroke. It was a kind way to go she had thought at the time. She had mourned him deeply, feeling the loss more than any loss before or since.

Slowly she had recovered and replaced the loss of Ike with a deep love for her daughter whom she had spoiled, she had realised since. Elsie had told her it was a mistake and she had changed her ways, bringing a more rigid rule to her house.

Hannah had responded well to the new way and was a great help now. She was working at Stones', assembling long-armed padlocks and was well thought of there and the money she brought in was useful too. Agnes was proud of her.

She was also worrying about the drying job. It was all very well for Elsie and Howard to say what a good job it was but, in the first place, could she cope with it? And in the second place, hop picking only took place in one month of the year. What would she do for a living for the other eleven months and, in the third place, if it was supposed to have some sort of permanence, where would she live? It was all very mysterious, castles in the air.

She made up her mind. She was going to have a word with Jenny Walker. Agnes felt she would be given good advice from her. She felt immediate relief and stood up.

'Where are you going, our Mom?' It was Hannah.' You sit there quiet for ten minutes and, all of a sudden, you're off like a whippet.'

Agnes nodded and gave her a short answer. I'm just popping in to see Mrs Walker about this drying job I'm supposed to be doin' I'll see you in a few minutes.'

She strode through the group quickly and went to the farmhouse entrance where Jenny was tidying her small shop.

'Hello, Agnes, I was sort of expecting you might be calling to see me. Is it about helping Howard with the drying? Let me tell you that there is no one I would sooner have than you. I have watched the way you work and I am sure you would make a good job of it. Have you got any questions about it? If so, just fire away!'

Agnes didn't know how to ask but thought she would be best asking just as the questions came to her mind. No sooner had she thought than she asked.

'Well, Mrs Walker, question number one is, how do I know I'll cope with the job? I've never done anything like it before'

She looked quite serious as she asked so Jenny Walker sat down and beckoned Agnes to sit opposite her. Then she smiled and answered the Black Country woman.

'Oh, Agnes, I hope you don't mind but I talked you over with Elsie and came to the conclusion that you are quite bright. It's quite skilled, the drying but it's not something you have to be born to. Howard will explain it to you as you go along, something like the way I expect your mother showed you how to do the housework, a bit at a time. The hops have too much water in 'em when they come to you, in green-sacks. You take 'em and tip 'em on the hair - that's the name we give the mesh floor that the warm air comes up through, to dry the hops. Sometimes we have to add a bit of sulphur; Howard will show you. When most of the water has been taken out of them, and the judgement of that is part of the skill, the hops are pressed into the long sacks, called pockets.

They are pressed very tight and then sewn up and weighed and a number is painted on the pocket to tell it from all others. Now, any more questions?'

The next one came straight away.

'Mrs Walker, Elsie mentioned to me that the drying could be more than just a part-time job but the hops are only picked for one month in the year, but that leaves eleven months when neither the drying nor the picking is done. I have to ask myself how I can earn a living for the other eleven months. The next an' last question is, if it's a permanent job, where do I live?'

She seemed so worried that Jenny wondered for a moment whether she had chosen the right person for the job, then she made up her mind to put Agnes at peace.

'Listen to me, Agnes', she said. 'In answer to your question, if you hadn't been offered the drying job, what would you do for the next eleven months? Maybe nothing, maybe whatever work you could find in the lock-making or what you call kay-mekking.

On the other hand, if you work out all right on the drying, at least you know what you'll be doing next September. The other thing is; a good dryer is too valuable to let go between seasons.' She paused. 'Why don't you just give it a good try and see how it turns out? We can take it from there and leave worrying about where you'll live between seasons. You've got a good little house, I believe?'

Agnes didn't know what to say. Jenny was suggesting a permanent job one minute then putting a decision into the future. Suddenly she felt more certain without a real reason.

'All right, Mrs Walker. I'll give it a go your way. What have I got to lose after all? I've still got to get through the year one way or another, ain't I?

Mrs Walker looked pleased and said so, in her own way.

'Agnes, I must say I'm grateful for that so perhaps we'll all get through the year, you, me and Howard! I notice you've moved your mattress. I am delighted!'

Jenny walked away, laughing. Agnes decided she wouldn't put thoughts of the future into Hannah's mind. The young madam might be quite pleased to take over her mother's house if she got wind of what might be going on. She walked round to the barn, picked up her clothes and bits and pieces and carried them to the kiln.

Howard was standing inside. When he saw what she was carrying, he smiled and started raking the hops on the hair until they were levelled at about a foot deep. He didn't look up at her again. She watched him though, as she put her hop box down and sat on it. He seemed to use two tools mostly, the rake to level and smooth the hops, and a scuppet, a tool made of wood in the shape of a giant sand shovel that a child might use on the beach. He used the scuppet to move piles of hops into the press where the top of a pocket was fastened to a ring firmly attached to the press.

He spun the press upward, away from the pocket then, using the scuppet, filled the pocket was hanging through the floor. When it was full, he spun the press and the round plate lowered into the pocket until the hops were firmly tight into the pocket. Then he spun the press again and pressed the hops again; each time he did, the pressed hops rose higher in the pocket.

Finally, Agnes could stand aside no longer. She took hold of the rake and as Howard spun the press, she raked the hops, filling the pocket in seconds. Howard reversed the press from the pocket swiftly and Agnes filled it immediately and as she did so Howard spun the press, ready to start the cycle over again. She was filling as fast as he was pressing, now and before she knew it, the pocket was full, tight to the top. He waved his hand for her to stop. Then he pressed past her with a long, curved needle and sewed the top tight. Then he picked up a long stencil, placed it on the sewn up pocket and painted the identifying number and weight on, using the stencil and pushed it against the wall. She looked at the weight. It was one hundred weight and sixty-four pounds, over one and a half hundredweight. How had he moved it? She'd never move anything that heavy!

'It's all right Agnes, I'll do the shifting until you get used to it.

You don't have to be particularly strong; it's just a knack and the way you lever it over your knee, see?'

He demonstrated the way he did it and she found she could lever them in the way he had described, after a few tries. Howard looked pleased again; he seemed to look pleased with her quite often.

He disappeared down the steps and when she looked down, he was putting coal on the small oven and poking it with a poker. The smell of sulphur hit her nose and she coughed. Howard laughed at her, up the steps.

'Have a drink o' cider', he said. 'It'll help to take the taste away.' He handed her a pewter mug and she lifted it to her lips swiftly. The sudden coolness and sheer exuberance of the drink shocked her as it hit her palette, taking away the acid taste of the sulphur. It was a beautiful, quenching sort of taste, born of apples and sugar.

'God! That's beautiful, Howard,' she said. 'I've never tasted anything so good.'

She put down the grey mug. Howard was looking at her again with that pleased look on his face. She was getting used to him now.

They kept bagging up the hops until the middle of the night, Howard switching to fire-stoking to keep its constant warmth coming up from the kell, as he called it, to dry the hops. At three o'clock in the morning, Howard suggested she have an hour's sleep while he carried on. He would wake her when she was needed. It only seemed like ten minutes later when he was gently shaking her at four o'clock.

'Come on, lass. They'll be starting in an hour or two an' there'll be green-sacks coming in at eleven o'clock, after they've finished their first bait.'

He turned his back as Agnes sat up on her palliasse and threw on a white blouse and long black skirt. She spun round and slipped her feet into her shoes dipped her hands into the large bowl of water, throwing it onto her face.

'Right, let's do it', she said. Just give us an 'and an' I'll be with you.'

That was the secret of it, she thought. Everything Howard did, Agnes copied. She got the hang of using the rake to smooth the over the hops to a level of about a foot deep all over. She got used to using the scuppet to move the hops round the hair and placing the six-foot sacks into the hole in the floor and fastening it onto the metal ring on the floor so that it would maintain its circular shape as it was filled. The hops were then pressed and then sewn up with string as tight as it could be.

She got used to the smell of sulphur and the colour of the hops as they absorbed it. She became accustomed to the odour of the hops and the odour of having another body close to hers and the feeling it gave her, and the wise cracks and the mock insults she took and gave until it was no shock to see the pleased look in Howard's eyes; she expected it. The taste of the rough cider became habitual and pleasant, very pleasant.

She got used to bearing responsibility for the small fire in the base of the kiln and keeping it just right so that the hops would dry out at the right speed.

She never considered that it was an unusual thing she was doing. Other women must have done the job at some time. It was only when Howard told her she was the first that she came to realise that Mrs Walker and Elsie Barr must have thoroughly thought through the idea of her doing the drying. Slowly she came to realise that she was an unusual person – and to accept it as other atypical women had to accept their rareness. Until then she had had no thoughts about herself. She had just grown up with the self-inflicted idea that she was just an ordinary Blackcountrywoman.

She gave the matter some thought and came to the conclusion that although there were hundreds of different occupations in the Black Country, there also hundreds of different things that Black Country people were interested in.

There were silversmiths, poets, painters, sculptors and writers, with all the variations of each. Agnes had never thought of herself as having an interest but her husband had been active as an amateur photographer and she still had his equipment. It might be interesting to take pictures of people as they were working. She made up her mind to sort out his camera and other gear. Perhaps she could take pictures with people carrying on their work. Anyway, she could do that when she got home, if ever she got home!

She had to go home sometime, even if it was only to pick up her belongings. If she never went home, Hannah could have her house, she supposed, if it could be arranged.

Elsie must be in the know about such things. She had heard that the woman had something to do with one of the local landlords. She could ask Ruth. Ruth seemed to be pretty thick with Elsie and it would save asking Elsie direct, wouldn't it?

She brought her mind back to her work on the drying. It was alright coming down for the picking. The weather was alright generally but she had no idea what she could do for the rest of the year – or even what had to be done with the hops. It was a nicer place to live than Wednesbury but you couldn't just pop in somewhere to put locks together, could you? And there weren't lists of house you could take your pick of, either. First you had to have money coming in to pay the rent an' the grocery and that meant getting a house and a job!

She seemed to going round in rings an' getting' nowhere. Well, at least she was doing well at the drying. One step at a time: another Sam Smiles saying. It was just that the things seemed bigger now and the step she had taken was a big one, even if it was only one. Carry on, Aggie, she said to herself; something'll turn up.

Three weeks went by before she realised, and the time for going home was fast approaching. She still found time to speak to her daughter, and have a chat with Elsie. Hannah was growing up fast; Agnes had seen her talking to one of the hands and smiling. Her time for a grown up life was very near, Agnes felt.

Agnes also dwelt on her own future occasionally, to the point where she found herself worrying about her daughter. How would Hannah be if she was left on her own? Would she have the sense of responsibility to cope with the small house on her own? It was possible that if she got herself a job, maybe in the lock trade, she could take over the house. That would be nice for her. All she had to do then, was to get somewhere for herself to live.

The thought of Howard came to mind He was the first man she'd had anything to do with since Ike had died.

They had not yet had any intimate dealings with each other. It was just the way he always seemed pleased with her and what she did, at the drying. Was that all it was or was she imagining more to it than there was. She knew she wouldn't mind too much, if at all, if she felt his arm round her shoulder.

She strolled round from the women's barn to the kell and sat on the stool she had found next to her bed, and tucked her face into her hands. Sometimes it seemed too much. She felt a tear running down her face.

Then she felt Howard's arm round her shoulder just as she had imagined it. For some reason she didn't want him to stop; it was so comforting, too comforting. Howard was a very private person; perhaps what he was doing was just as hard for him to do as it was for her to accept. She didn't move away from him, it was just as if she would rather snuggle down close to him.

The thought came to her that just accepting his arm round her might make him think she was a bit – easy. Somehow, she knew that that wasn't true. If Howard thought anything different about her, she was quite capable of stopping any further advances. She didn't want him to stop though; she wanted him to carry on. His arm seemed to tighten round her and she seemed to sink against him in response. She turned to face him and he gave her that pleased look again and she was pleased that he was pleased.

She couldn't recall, later, whether he kissed her or she kissed him. It just seemed the natural thing to do. They each heard a footstep; it was Jenny Walker. They had parted before she strode noisily into the kiln.

'Hello, Howard,' she said. 'I just wanted a quick word, with both of you, really.' It seemed she had just noticed that the two of them were there, together. 'Hello, Agnes. I'm sorry if I haven't spoken much to you about the drying. I've noticed the numbers are coming through all right so I assumed everything is going as it should.' She paused for a moment. 'Are you all right, Agnes? Howard hasn't spoken to me about how you're learning the drying so I suppose he must be satisfying with what you are doing.'

Howard looked at Jenny and gave her one of what Agnes called his pleased looks, with the corners of his mouth turned up and Jenny turned towards Agnes.

'He has his own way of talking to you. He gives you a special smile if he is happy with what you are doing. Have you noticed?'

Agnes smiled at Jenny in an imitation of Howard's pleased look and Jenny commented.

'Yes, you are doing all right. You're learning the language.' She smiled. 'We'll need to have another chat if you're staying on when the others go home, shan't we?'

She looked at the two dryers and they both gave her the pleased look and then turned to each other, smiling.

'Well, Jenny', Agnes said, 'I've still got a couple o' things to think about. If I stay on, after the others 'as gone, as you put it, where shall I stay?' The worried look came back to her face. 'An' not on'y that, I've got my Hannah to think about. Where's she supposed to live, even if she wants to? I am her mother you know an' I can't just let her go homeless, can I? I did wonder if Ruth and Elsie could speak for her, to the landlord, an' if they would keep an eye on her, for me. She's only just started growing up, if you know what I mean. Perhaps she could get a job at Stones'. Perhaps Elsie would speak for her; she seems to be well thought of, everywhere.

'Well, Aggie, the only way to find out is to speak to her.' Jenny was talking now. 'She has a way of dealing with problems. Some people seem to have a talent that way and she's one of 'em.'

'Who's one of them?' It was Elsie herself, walking into the

kiln. 'Who's one o'which? I thought I heard my name being used in vain!'

Agnes chuckled. 'We was talkin' about you, not to you.' She paused. 'To tell the truth, Elsie, I was hoping you could help me out.'

She explained the way the conversation had gone and finished with the idea that Elsie had the reputation of being a problem solver. 'We 'ad the idea you could help we. Can ya, Elsie? Can ya come up with anything, any idea at all, that you could put in my head so my Hannah 'as somewhere to live? An I want to live 'ere! It seems too good to be true I know, but why shouldn't I 'ave somewhere nice to live – an' somebody nice to live with, that's what I'd like to know'

Elsie, Jenny and Howard looked at each other and Howard seemed to have a very pleased look on his face, as if there was something he wanted to say to add to the conversation but couldn't because there were too many people there. There was a silence for a minute, a long minute and then Elsie coughed to bring the others to look at her.

'It seems to me,' she said, 'that it might be a good idea to solve your problems one at a time. Perhaps if each of us can solve one little bit of your problem, we can deal with most of it, eh? Now I might be able to help out with Hannah by either asking for a new house for her or acting as guarantor for your house, providing she wants to keep it. Is that any good to you, Aggie, or would you rather we got together; you, Hannah and myself to talk things over to come out with the best answer? We could do that and then move on to the next bit of the puzzle. What do you think?'

It seemed obvious that Agnes wanted to put her few words together now. She was beginning to move mentally towards a solution as they talked it over.

'Thanks very much, Elsie, if you can do either o' them things. I'll have a word with Hannah, tomorrow an' find out what she thinks.

'Mind you, it'd probably be best if she stayed in my old place.

She'll be used to it, havin' lived there all 'er life, an', to tell the truth, I'd be easier in my mind that way, just in case it don't work out with the landlord.'

Jenny then spoke ' That's one part o' the puzzle started on and if I can offer a suggestion, you've got enough work to last you two or three weeks Agnes, and maybe there'll be enough work to do, clearing up the hop-yards and one thing or another, to see you with enough work for some time. I'll talk it over with Howard and decide then. I can't really be fairer than that, can I? What do you think, Howard? Do you think we can find enough work for Agnes?'

The three women turned their attention to the middle-aged man and he acted as if there was a searchlight shining on him. His face reddened as it did when attention was forced on him. He was obliged to answer to the best of his ability and he did.

'What I was wondering, Mrs Walker, was how we would manage *without* Agnes, if she left and went home after the picking's finished? Usually we have Mister Walker and your son, Robin, God bless him, and a busheller or two to muck in and clear the yard but now, no offence Mrs Walker, we're very short handed. Now Agnes has a bed in the kell until the picking's finished, and it's quite warm. The problem is; where's she going to sleep during the winter season?'

Howard went silent, as if to hand over the puzzle to someone else and also to avoid facing other solutions, such as, he had a two bed-roomed cottage. They had, after all, only known each other for three weeks and under those conditions he couldn't offer Agnes the use of either of them, even if he did look pleased with her work. Jenny solved the problem. She had a four-bedroomed farmhouse, after all.

'Agnes can sleep in the house.' She said, just straight and plain. 'I don't know how long for, or when from, but I'm sure I could also find her work there as long as it suits both of us.'

Agnes thanked her nicely but it didn't somehow seem like a perfect solution to the puzzle. If they didn't get on, she could be given notice and replaced by a local man – or woman who might not have to be offered accommodation with the job. Still, it was a generous offer that showed how much Jenny Walker thought of her. She would accept the offer, with her own provisos.

'Yes, Mrs Walker,' she said. 'I'll be glad to accept a trial and see how it works out.'

It sounded as if she was giving control to Jenny Walker but in reality she was also letting them know that she was her own woman! She would see how it turned out for herself and Hannah. It was a benefit though, that she had learned that Barr had influence in Wednesbury. Perhaps it would pay her to explore Elsie Barr a bit more. She might learn something she could profit from. Time would tell, she'd see.

The two women and Howard looked at Agnes, weighing up what she'd replied to Jenny's offer. Howard had his pleased look written across his face. Jenny and Elsie each looked thoughtful, wondering how open Agnes was turning out to be. It didn't matter to the women which way Agnes responded; she was volunteering to do the work. Perhaps she would be an honest, hardworking workmate.

Howard had different feelings altogether about Agnes. She was an attractive woman who could bring useful skills to a couple. They weren't a couple yet but Howard had a feeling they were moving that way and he was pleased. She was a widow; he was a widower and there was a chance that they could recapture the pleasures of being a couple again – and why not?

He also felt they were fit enough to enjoy it. Not that he wanted the responsibility of children, nor did he want to take on Hannah. She was old enough to look after herself, and he could imagine the sort of problems that a twenty-year old could bring.

He looked at her quietly and she smiled as she often did when he looked at her in his quiet, pleased way. How could he make progress in his relationship with her? They were fortunate to have a large part of the week-end free providing they got rid of the green-sacks and, he supposed, that offered opportunities for spending time with each other but without anyone else.

Aggie would have to spend some time with her daughter, telling her of the new possibilities in her life. How she would respond to them was still to be seen. That young lady had matured a lot in the three years he had known her. He could see a lot of Aggie in her and that was pleasing of course but she still had her own personality and that brought her own way of looking at things.

He could not possibly estimate how she would take to the idea of looking after Agnes's house. Why should she, after all? For all he knew, she could be married and pregnant inside twelve months. It was more probable than possible at her age.

He didn't know how she felt about her mother working on the drying Aggie hadn't confided in him about that, not that she had told Hannah about having a bed in the kell with, well, not exactly with but close enough to him to make Hannah question the arrangement. He'd spoken to Hannah to say 'Good day', that sort of thing but she'd not acted any different from usual, just nodding and adding her 'Good day,' to his.

'What would she say if she knew how he felt about her mother? The question bothered him. If he couldn't get on with her, she could really spoil things between him and Aggie. The thought of that upset him. He had been a long time on his own but he hadn't really noticed the passage of time. He just knew he had been lonelier than he had ever been and it was only when he had got to know Aggie that the lonely feeling had gone away. Now it was possible that the feeling might return.

The best thing he could think of was to carry on as he had been. That way, he couldn't be accused of being devious. He relaxed and sat himself down on the side of his bed. The three women were sitting on Aggies bed, still chattering away. What they were chattering about completely escaped him, but it seemed to be serious stuff.

He leaned back and closed his eyes, forgetting all the questions that had been going through his mind. Aggie was lying on the bed beside him, her head lying on his chest and it was very pleasing.

There was a touch on his shoulders. It was Agnes. 'Come on, Howard. You've been sleeping while we've been solving problems. I know what I'm going to do. I'm going to carry on with the drying 'til it's all done and then I'm movin' into the farm an' Jenny'll find me work to do for a week or two. You'll move out about then, right? I shan't move until me an' our Hannah have had a good chat about my house in Wednesbury. She thinks it's great that I've got friends here an' she's looking forward to arranging the house, my house that is, to suit her taste.

'I might let her do it, an all,' she said, giving him a pleased look. 'Come an' sit by me, Howard. I think you an' me have got to 'ave a bit of a chat as well, don't you?'

Gently she took him by the hand and led him to her corner of the kiln, where her bed was made up. Ruth saw the move and nodded meaningfully to Jenny and Elsie. Quiet for once, the three women moved out of the door. Ruth quietly pulled the door to, darkening the interior. Ruth would swear, later on, that as the door closed, she saw Agnes with a pleased look right across her face and Howard had the same look.

Elsie was later deciding how she could help Agnes and Hannah without giving herself too much trouble. She heard from Agnes that she had had a discussion with Hannah about how she wanted the house looking after. Hannah was twenty-one in a month, just before Guy Fawkes Night. She was full of youthful enthusiasm about the whole situation, wanting to impress her mother that she would look after the little house in the same way that her mother had, while at the same time expounding her own ideas for improvements.

Both of them knew that Elsie came round for the rent on the property but neither of them knew that she owned it! Elsie had to go through the fiction of pretending she would ask Mister Jenkins, the solicitor if the plan could go ahead, and then quite seriously talk to Hannah and Agnes about their responsibilities for looking after the property.

Hannah could not have her name on the rent book as she was still not twenty-one years of age. Agnes was in the position of being the legal tenant and also the guarantor for the rent and the maintenance of the house. It was an unusual situation and Mister Jenkins had not been all that pleased about it.

'Just because you had the talent to take on responsibilities, it doesn't follow that this young woman will have the same ability,' he said on her return. 'What will you do if she falls behind with the rent? How can you give the blame to the girl when you were party to the arrangement?' He relented in a small way. 'You've always found your own way of solving problems. I just hope this works out for you.'

Sam Jenkins was quite elderly now, but his deep-set blue eyes still had the same piercing quality so it was a surprise when he suddenly smiled and she knew he would back her, fault or no fault. She had immediately felt more optimistic about the future. The girls wouldn't let her down. Her time in Bromyard had flown.

Before she had known it, she had been back at home for a fortnight and it was time to call on Hannah for the rent. She felt sure that Hannah was just as nervous as she did about their first encounter. She knocked the door of the little back-to-back and it swung open.

'Good morning, Mrs Barr,' Hannah said. 'It's a lovely morning. Come in.'

She stood back, encouraging Elsie to walk in. The small, pine table was drying white, showing that it had just been scrubbed, and the Welsh dresser was shining, the smell of it as evidence of polishing.

Hannah opened a drawer in the table and pulled out a rent book, made up to date and put it on the table with a half crown and a shilling on top of it. There was a fire glowing in the hearth. All was as it was supposed to be, thought Elsie. She gave a quick look round and signed the book for the rent. Hannah was house-proud. She could see that the little house was kept something like she would have kept it, herself. Hannah spoke

'Would you like a cup of tea, Mrs Barr?'

'No thank you, Hannah, not today. I'm trying to catch up with everything, another time perhaps. I still haven't caught up with all my work, yet. It's nice, the way you are keeping the place, a credit to you.' Hannah looked very pleased with herself and Elsie continued, 'Have you heard anything from your mother, Hannah?'

'Yes, Mrs Barr, I had a letter from her on Saturday. She said she's moving out of the kiln sometime this week, into the farmhouse, into a proper bedroom. That's better for her, I think, don't you, Elsie?' she said, becoming more intimate. 'I never did think it was right, her sleeping in the same place as that man. What do you think, Elsie?'

Elsie did not know what to say for the best but she had to reply.

'I don't think its right for me to have an opinion. Agnes is a very right and proper person. I'm sure she's got her head screwed on. As for Howard, now you're asking me, it's obvious he thinks a lot of your mom but he wouldn't do anything to ruin her reputation. He wouldn't get anywhere if he did. Your mom would soon put him in his place, wouldn't she? Let's say they've grown very fond of each other. They don't need to get anybody's permission, do they?

'They are both unmarried, you don't depend on Aggie for support of any kind. With a bit of luck I'll be able to give a good report to Sam Jenkins, who looks after this property on behalf of the owner, and if you are anything like normal, you will find yourself courting some young fellow and wanting a home jointly with him and you'll be in the unusual position of already having a home.

'Even so, it wouldn't be a bad idea if you started saving. If you kept that up, you could buy your home and never have to pay rent again, once your home was paid for!'

Suddenly, Elsie realised she was talking to Hannah in the same way that Mary Bowyer had spoken to her, years ago! Mary Bowyer had given her similar financial advice when she had first arrived in Wednesbury, as a girl in her teen years. She had walked with her father, from Birmingham, looking for a roof over their heads and for work, to pay for the roof. Mary had taken them in and had helped them find work, too. The lessons she had learned from Mary had enabled her to save and then to multiply her savings finally, to become a secretly rich property owner.

Did she have to take on the burden of teaching Hannah? Mary hadn't had to take her on, either, but something had inspired her to take in the two vagrants. She realised that Hannah was in a similar, if not worse position. Her father was dead and her mother was working to find herself a new life.

It was a shock, the realisation of the similarities between her life and that of Hannah. What should she do? For a start, she could help in a small way, as she was doing now, making sure the girl kept to her side of the rental bargain. She felt secure in her own way, knowing she had the last word as far as Hannah was concerned. However, there was also the problem of the girl's mother. Did she have any obligations to her? There was no easy way that Elsie could define a limit to the amount of help and resources the two women could take.

Hannah was looking at her now, waiting for an opportunity to speak. Elsie lifted her eyebrows and Hannah spoke, gently.

'I wish I had a relative like you, Elsie. Sometimes I feel as if I have no relatives, as if I'm all on my own. I know mom loves me but she seems to be getting further away every day, if you know what I mean.' She broke down, crying into a handkerchief, and Elsie was reminded that she, herself, had been doing the same thing not so long ago. Elsie moved to her, putting an arm around her in a comforting way. Then Hannah looked up at her, her eyes bright. 'I'm so grateful, Mrs Barr for the house, and the way you have trusted me with it and I shan't let you down. I'm trying for a job at Stone's, tomorrow and if I get it, I shall be able to afford the rent and everything out of my own wages, and get myself a new blouse or a pair of stockings, occasionally. I know it's a bit of a trip, to Willenhall but I'll soon get used to it.'

Elsie replied, her heart taking in the young woman. 'I think I will have a cup of tea with you Hannah and I'll tell you how I used to work at Stones' Locks.'

Elsie sat back down and in a few minutes a cup of tea and biscuits were placed on a little plate at the side of her cup. She looked up at Hannah. The girl was wearing a short length skirt, somewhere half way up her calf. Elsie felt old-fashioned for a change. Hannah was wearing a pale blue blouse with large sleeves. She had never seen a blouse of that design. She commented to Hannah.

'Hannah, that's a most unusual blouse, especially with sleeves like that. Where did you see that design?' Hannah looked somewhere between proud and shy as she answered. 'I made it, Mrs Barr. I saw a pattern in a shop and liked it so I decided to have a go. I quite like it, do you?' Hannah asked the question as if it was a sort of challenge, not wanting to hear the wrong answer, favourable or not.

'Yes, it's got a mind of its own, not like something out of Woolworths, for a tanner. I expect you could make one or two and sell them. You would get more than Woolworths, for them. Could you make one for me, not the same as yours but in a similar style?'

Elsie could see that the girl was delighted. 'Yes, of course I could. What I would like most of all is to have my own shop. If I could get a job at Stone's, I would make my own stock until the shop could afford to pay for itself.

'An idea hit Elsie. 'If I had a word with Mabel Stone, she might want to buy one or two things from you, to put in her window.'

'No thank you Mrs Barr. I would sooner not be beholden to anyone. I would sooner make and sell to myself, without involving anybody else.'

Of course she would, thought Elsie. Why should she take a risk, selling to the Stones, when she can do it all herself? The girl's got her head screwed on, like her mother. She wouldn't be surprised to find her looking to Elsie to find her a shop to rent, very soon. If she wasn't watched, she would be converting her mother's house into a shop!

She certainly had an eye for fashion and that could stand her in good stead. Women were becoming more open in the styles they wore, not just keeping to the styles their husbands liked. A thought came to her. 'Do you need to measure me for my blouse, Hannah I usually wear a thirty-six. That should suit me. What sort of material will you use to make it? I don't want to spend too much on material, you know.'

'Stand up, please, Mrs Barr.' Hannah reached into her apron and pulled out a tape measure. 'Just stand normal please.' She reached around Elsie with the tape. 'Yes, I think I know just what will suit you, nothing too ordinary, just a bit extraordinary.' She laughed and put the tape away. She pulled out a small notebook and wrote the details on it. 'It will be ready in a week, if I can get the material I want.'

She was all business now, Elsie noticed, just as she should be. She smiled to herself, recalling the difference between the girl and the way Mabel ran her shop, with a pile of older clothes in a pile on the floor waiting to be sold or not sold, depending on who walked into her shop. Mabel's daughters never seemed to buy anything from their own shop; not much of a recommendation!

It was time for her to move on. She had quite a few rents to collect in yet. Ruth was looking after Tom and Edward. She was useful that way, even if she had to be paid a little. She reached for her hat and moved out of the door. She would have to think about getting her hair cut; that was the coming fashion, especially now there were so many women working on factory work, where their hair could be pulled out by machinery. Skirt lengths had altered too, now being set at about half-way up the calf, this never being achieved before.

Perhaps it was because Dan was away, in France, and she did not have to please his eyes – or anyone else's.

The afternoon soon passed as she wandered in her thoughts but her feet took her round Wednesbury. There was too much to be done to be daydreaming. She had found two new friends and that alone was worth its weight in gold.

8. Henry Goes to Wednesbury.
September 1915

Henry Wilkins sat back in the railway carriage, smoking his Woodbine cigarette, the smoke curling up out of the tiny window, caught by the passage of the train through the countryside. He was looking forward to the end of this trip to the Black Country. Just for the moment he was daydreaming about the form his revenge would take on the three women who'd had the temerity to cross his path.

He enjoyed thinking in his own dramatic way, placing himself on a superior plane, as if he were immortal and others were just flotsam crossing his path from time to time, to be dealt with as he thought fit. He knew he would think of a punishment that would hurt each of them in a most appropriate way.

There was a different sound from the wheels of the train now, and a definite slowing down. The train pulled into Wolverhampton. He could get off there, change to a local train, catch a tram for part of the way or get a taxi. He decided to get a taxi and pump the driver about a cheap place to stop. He had found out that Elsie and Ruth were both living for the present in Wednesbury and Betty was living just outside the town. He thought about it and decided to find out the cheapest way to get to Wednesbury. He caught a local train after making his enquiries and got to Wednesbury just after lunch. He got off the train and after looking at the usual 'Station Hotel' sort of place, went into a public house. He sat himself down with a pint of ale and read his newspaper. He looked up at the barman who had served him.

'Do you serve any food at lunchtime, please?'

He was easy to please when it came to food. Anything would do.

'We've got cheese cobs, mate. How many do you want?'

The barman was standing with a meat plate full of cobs, partially covered by a linen towel.

'Two, my mon. Two's enough of them, I should think.'

Henry paid as he took them from the barman and the barman smiled to himself. Two's enough indeed. There was enough cheese and onion on one of the cobs to feed a family.

A man who had been standing by the bar came and sat nearby. 'Could I have a quick look at your paper, mate? I just want to check if my treble's come up.'

At a nod from Henry, the man picked up the paper and quickly scanned it.

'Oh well, two out of three's not bad, I suppose. I'll just go and pick it up. Do you want a refill?' At Henry's nod he winked at the barman. 'Here y'are Bill: two pints. I'll be back in a minute; I'm just going to see you know who.'

The barman smiled. Everyone knew who the local bookie was but he had no premises as such. He had to take his bets on the side, hoping that no police informers were about. In a few minutes the man was back, paid for the drinks happily and sat back down.

'Cheers mate,' said Henry. 'I was ready for that. I've been travelling all morning, from Bromyard, in Herefordshire. I've had a drink and sommat to eat. All I need now is somewhere to get me head down for a few nights while I carry out a bit o' business. Don't suppose you know anywhere, do you?' He looked at his new companion. 'It's a bit of a job, trying to find somewhere in a strange town, ain't it?'

The man nodded. 'I suppose it is. As a matter of fact, I might be able to point you the right way. I stay in digs most of the time and the old lady who runs the place where I'm at is looking for a new lodger. The last one left and didn't leave a forwarding address, if you know what I mean. Not that the old girl lost by it. You always have to be up front with her. I suppose you can't blame her, can you?'

Henry nodded his head. It sounded as if she was a bit like his landlady. He sank his ale and lifted his eyebrows to his companion. 'Ready for another one, er, what's your name?'

'Jack, Jack Thurston, bachelor of this parish for about four years. I used to live in Willenhall but I found it to be a bad luck sort of town. It was the women. There's nothing like a woman to bugger up your life. Have you noticed that, er, what's your name? Yes, I'll have another.'

'Henry, Henry Wilkins. You sound as if you've had the same sort of experience as I've had. What sort of woman would make you leave your own town, then? That takes a bit of believing.'

Wilkins pulled a wry face. 'Well they say it takes all sorts, and it sure takes all sorts of woman. Mind you, there's only one Elsie Barr. There couldn't be another as bad as her.'

Thurston started. 'Elsie Barr! That's the woman I would give anything to get me own back on. The bitch! I'd like to give her something, I would.'

The two men stared at each other in amazement. They had met another who'd had their life changed because of the same woman. It was not so amazing really. They had both crossed people close to her and she had taken up arms in defence. She had been successful, too. Wednesbury and Willenhall were both small towns and the residents often knew each other.

News from the hop-fields soon travelled the forty miles to the Black Country and got around once it had travelled. The news of the attack on Jack Thurston had been famous; everyone in the Black Country knew about it, but the news hadn't travelled the other way. People in Bromyard didn't get the news of Wednesbury in the same way that the news travelled the other way. Naturally the two men wondered what had happened to the other. Neither of them was particularly proud of their emergence from their conflict, nor the reason for it in the first place.

Wilkins was the first to enquire. 'What did she do to you then, Jack?'

Jack didn't want to be known as a child-molester so he brought out his stock excuse. 'My daughter, so called, if she was my daughter, kept climbing into my bed after her Mom had got up. I woke up one morning and the bitch was sitting on top of me! Her Mom threw her out of the bed. Oh, she knew what was going on. She said she tried to stop it but Betty, that's the daughter, kept on coming back for more, and when she was caught again, her Mom blamed me.

'They tried to make out I was a child molester but it worn't me. She was just like her mom, a bitch in heat. Have you ever tried to stop a bitch in heat? It's impossible, believe me. How would you behave if you woke up with a young woman in bed with you, trying to make you do it?' He picked up his glass and downed it all at once. After nodding again at the barman for two more drinks, he went on.

'I'm sure in my own mind that Betty met Elsie Barr down at the 'op picking. My wife sent her down there to clear the air a bit, probably because Betty was getting all the goodies and she wanted her share. Anyway, when they came back, that year, it was about five or six years ago, her and that Elsie Barr was as thick as thieves. One night I was coming home from a drink when I was attacked and castrated! Yes, that's what I said; castrated. The police were supposed to investigate but they never found anybody to own up to it and you know how people are. They always believe the woman.

'I was in hospital for nearly a month. I'm all right now, but I'm no good to a woman, even my missus, who's died, bless her. I found out a lot about that Elsie Barr. She works for that Jenkins down the High Street; she collects rent for him.

'A bloke named Luke Bryant works there and he has a lot to do with what they call the criminal fraternity and if you ask me, she asked him to get somebody to put a number on me. That's what happened, and I'm going to get my own sweet own back on her and 'im as soon as the chance comes up.'

They fell silent, each with his own thoughts about the secrets Jack Thurston had revealed. Wilkins had his own reservations about whether Thurston was telling the truth. He wouldn't mind waking up with that young Betty in bed with him. There was a thought. He hadn't been castrated; he had all his wedding tackle and liked nothing better than the chance to use it. There might be a chance, if he played his cards right. He could also ingratiate himself with Thurston. There could be money in this. In the meantime he had better show a certain amount of sympathy for Thurston's cause. He looked at the man sitting next to him. He was a proper country yokel and it looked as if he hadn't cleaned his boots for six months, or himself.

While he was musing, Thurston interrupted his thoughts. 'What have you got against her, then? You ain't been to bed with her, have you?'

'Oh, very funny! It worn't very funny at the time, I can tell you. Albert Walker, he's the farmer where I had just started, sacked me because of her. I thought I was on a good thing there. I had the chance to be a busheller if I kept me nose clean. If I'd been there now I would have been, especially now all the blokes are volunteering for France.

'Anyway, I was just having five minutes. You know; you can't work all the time, can you? He come down to me and started mouthing off. Some of them do, you know. Anyway, I went to land him one when this stupid Elsie Barr come trotting down in a trap. She had a whip and gave me a lashing with it. Said I was trying to kill Walker, as if I would. I tell you what; she can't half use a whip. I found out she learned how to in Wednesbury, from the bloke she works for, what's his name? Jenkins?

'Anyway, the upshot of it was, they sacked me, and two of his bushellers chucked me off the farm and nobody'd take me on since then. Then, when the blokes all volunteered for the war, I called round and sweet-talked Jenny Walker into giving me a job, daft as a brush. She dain't have much option, really, there weren't many blokes left.

I had my feet under the table almost until them daft women came down for the picking. I saw them cooking the first day they came, so I went and told her what I thought on her. Another one of Barr's cronies threw a pan of boiling water in my face and naturally Jenny Walker believed them. I got the sack and got scalded – the bitch! I'll get my own back; you believe me! There are three on 'em. Like witches, they are, all huddled up together.

If I had the chance, I know what I'd do.'

Jack Thurston didn't answer. He knew what Wilkins would most like to do. He would like to rape them! The desire for that had left Thurston since his attack, but he still wanted to take his revenge in the most painful and most degrading way. He hated women now, blaming all of them for his loss of virility. He had thought often about robbing them but didn't want to spend time in Winson Green prison. Perhaps he could persuade Wilkins to hurt the women in some way. It was worth thinking about. He raised his glass.

'Here's to you then, and I hope you realise your ambition. Are you having another?'

'No, I don't think so. I've got to find somewhere to get my head down. Is there anywhere you can recommend? I only popped in for a quick one. I never thought I would be this long in here.'

He looked at Thurston quizzically. It was early evening now, and he was feeling empty again.

'You can come and stop with me if you like, just for a couple of nights. I've told you that. You'll have to bung for your grub but that's fair enough, ain't it?'

'Thanks, Jack. You're a pal. I'll give you a quid for two nights. That should keep you sweet, shouldn't it?'

He suddenly noticed the broad man sitting on the table next to them. He seemed to be looking at him in a peculiar manner.

He turned to his companion. 'Eh, Jack; who's the bloke keeping an eye on us? Is he some sort of copper? He seems to be watching. There must be something he's interested in.'

Thurston turned and gave a quick look at the man that Wilkins indicated. It was Luke from the solicitors! He immediately turned to Wilkins. 'Come on; we've got to go. It's getting on and the old girl will want to see you before she takes you in. Come on.'

He spoke quite sharply and at last Wilkins got the message.

He stood and made for the door. Thurston followed him, pausing just long enough to have another look at Luke, who was still watching them. Luke sat for a minute when the two men had gone and then he nodded across the bar to a small man in a flat cap. The man came across and leaned close to hear what Luke had to say. "Just watch them two home, Bill. Make sure they don't get lost. I'll see you in the morning on my rounds.'

Luke stood and went out of the other door, making for Union Street. He had a suspicion that the two men were up to something that was connected with Elsie and he was going to make sure that whatever it was, it wouldn't come off. He had heard her name mentioned a couple of times and it had aroused his nose, as he said. If they were going anywhere near Union Street, he wanted to be there before them, just in case.

He turned into the small court and put his hand in his waistcoat pocket for the key to Elsie's house. He had slept there often, to keep it safe, He had no responsibility in that direction but he felt better for it, and Jenkins knew, in case he got pulled by the police and he needed a reference; not that he really needed one. He was well known to the local constabulary. The small, back-to-back was no different to the others in the court. It was different inside though, neater and tidier than most, probably because there was no one living there at the moment. He looked around; there was nothing out of place to show that an intruder might have been in. He strode up the stairs and looked round again. The bedroom was quite tidy. Elsie always seemed to have a sense of neatness, the bed had three blankets and an embroidered bedspread laid out on it.

Luke laid himself on the double bed and imagined he was not alone. Dan was in France by now, probably, and Luke wouldn't miss him. Ruth was in Bromyard with Elsie and Betty. He had heard her name mentioned in the bar, too. Perhaps there was something going on that was connected with her. Betty's father had been with the stranger.

He knew Thurston a lot better than he was known by him. He had been instrumental in arranging Thurston's 'punishment'. Not that he had meant the castration that had actually occurred. He had meant that he just got a beating but it had gone wrong. Perhaps it had been for the best though. He wouldn't rape anybody now; that was for certain.

Again he imagined that Elsie was with him. He had never let on how he felt for her. He had fallen for her; that was for sure as well. He knew that she had something going with Stephen Stone. Perhaps that had burned itself out. He hoped so. It would leave him with a chance if Danny Boy didn't come marching home. His eyes closed and he gradually found a sort of relaxation and peace. His mouth dropped and his eyes closed. The moon shone over Wednesbury, a cooler moon now that September was half through. October would be here soon, with its fog and the start of frost.

9. Portsmouth for Embarkation.
September/Oct 1915

Dan sat at the side of the glowing embers. He was cold. He could smell the horses nearby. They were giants, especially chosen to pull and guns and carts for supplies and limbers for ammunition, in wartime He stood and strode through the shed doors to where they were housed. He was always fascinated by the Clydesdales. They were so tall and strong and yet so gentle and intelligent. It was well known that they seemed to know what was required of them before their driver did.

They had been bred on the banks of the Clyde as a farm horse, to pull hay wagons or a plough, in the season. Most of them were bay or dark brown with white legs and to Dan they seemed to exude a spirit of strength that always moved him. He knew that many of them would die in the service of the Army and the thought filled him with a deep horror and a realisation of the implications of simply going to war.

He had felt like this since the first time he had been sent to France for a few weeks, to 'get some real experience'. He had seen men and animals torn apart by the shells and explosives used to win small skirmishes and he knew he had been affected by the experiences. Would he be able to inflict the same sort of madness on his German enemies? He recalled telling Elsie and Tom how he would but that was before. He could only wait until the time came and then madly, blindly do as he had been taught, and attack to win, with all the means at his disposal.

How could he even contemplate doing such a thing when he had two women and a son who loved him? He took a Woodbine from his packet and lit it. He leaned on the wall, allowing his memories, thoughts and emotions to flash past his perception. Overhead, the moon ignored him, moving across the sky as usual. The smoke curled up and disappeared into the air.

Eventually he seemed to have come to terms with his feelings. If any enemy had tried to harm any of his loved ones he knew he would attack in the most suitable way, to protect them. That was the answer, really. It was them or you. There was no other choice; if you couldn't make that choice you might as well just die, and that was no good to anyone.

He dropped the cigarette on the floor and ground it to nothing. There was just the sound of deep breathing from the horses. On impulse he stepped into the giant shed. There were rows of the horses, just standing in their allocated bays. He reached up and stroked the nearest one.

Suddenly he noticed the width of the horse. Would they be able to fit into the special devices aboard ship, supposedly designed to contain them in comfort for the trip across the Channel? Clydesdales were taller, longer and wider than most horses. He turned and strode back to his quarters. He took out his yardstick and went back to the shed. He held it across the back of the first horse. It took up most of the length of the yardstick. There could be a problem.

He reached into his pocket for the watch that Elsie had given him for their first Christmas. It was half past four. What should he do? It was only a thought, after all.

Still, it wouldn't do any harm to see if there was a Naval Duty Officer on duty, and tell him of his thoughts. It could save them a lot of trouble later. He reached to his neck and fastened his collar. He found his breathing was a little faster. Why did he feel like that, around gaffers? He would have to get rid of that feeling if he was ever to be a gaffer!

He would see if he could get aboard the ship first, to have a look at the size of the berths for himself. He strode out purposefully. He always felt better when he had a purpose. The ship was only a hundred yards away; he had taken a look at it earlier. He approached the gangway cautiously. The Officer of the Watch, or whatever they called him, might be around. There was a cough from the shadows.

'Can I help you, sir?'

The voice separated itself from the darkness. It was a Chief

Petty Officer, a rank roughly equivalent to his own. Neither man mixed very well with men from other services. Whatever he did now, he could be criticised for, later. Nevertheless, he thought, he was talking to the local expert so he might as well try to find out what he wanted to know.

'Yes, I think you might be just the bloke to help me.'

He tried to explain what his dilemma was and the CPO picked it up quickly. It was easy really. All you had to do was risk making an idiot of yourself and then, if you were listened to properly, something could be done. The CPO listened as Dan told him that he had responsibility for getting the horses safely aboard, then it was up to the Navy.

'It's the horses,' he said. 'They're not your usual size of horse. They are Clydesdales, a big horse, for pulling limbers and guns and ammunition to and fro from the Front. I don't know if the arrangements you've got on your ship include large horses, if you know what I mean.'

The CPO looked at him keenly and seemed to make up his mind about him.

'Come with me, what's your name? Dan Barr? You can see for your self what our 'arrangements' are, then.' He led the way along the gangway to the deck and turned to the stern. 'This is where the horses are slung onto the deck.' He indicated a place beneath a crane. 'Then, when they are un-slung here, they are led into these stalls and are left there until we arrive at the other side of the Channel. We feed them first thing in the morning and again at night. They have a nosebag on the outside of the stall so that they can feed themselves. That way, we hope to avoid them feeling too bad about the whole thing. Sometimes, horses feel so bad that they can die from a heart attack. Most of them are all right, though. What's your problem? Something to do with the size of your horses, wasn't it?'

He listened again as Dan explained that the Clydesdales were wider, higher and heavier than the ordinary size of horse, sometimes called light draught horses.

'These are not light draught horses; they are definitely heavy draught animals. They were chosen to carry out the heavy work of the Army, pulling guns and such. It's the width of the stalls that concerns me, not the height. Are the stalls adjustable?

The CPO smiled. 'It's not as bad as you think, you know. I would bet that we've got enough stalls to accommodate your horses – and the stalls can be adjusted for width, although it might mean we can't take as many as you thought. How many have you got? Two hundred? Yes we can do that easily, Sergeant Major. I like somebody who makes sure of everything first. It saves a lot of trouble in the end, don't it? Just ask for me in the morning, CPO Blake, Jim Blake.' The CPO shoved his hand forward. 'See you in the morning then.'

The CPO turned on his heel and disappeared into the darkness again. Dan stood for a minute or two, taking in the appearance of the ship. It was deep gray and the colour seemed to hide sides, corners and tops and bottoms, effectively getting rid of shape, contour and size. There was nothing personal about it. It was just a vast area of gray. He tried to imagine what it would be like in a swell, with waves breaking over the sides. How would the horses be when it was like that? He tried not to think about it but his mind took him to the imagined situation and he felt sick. Probably the Captain would want to be sure the weather was steady before he committed the horses to such an ordeal.

*

'Come on then! Move yourselves. You're like bloody pregnant penguins!'

Corporal Simkins moved along the line of beds. Most of the men were up and dressed. They all knew they were on the way to France today and they either got on with it or bore the brunt of the NCOs' displeasure.

The horse handlers had to wait for breakfast. Their charges came first and they were in their top coats already, moving out to form a small body of men outside the large sheds. The horses had to be fed and watered; they had about two and a half pounds of oats each and a bucket of water to drink. They would be left then until after breakfast then the horses would be slung, one at a time, aboard the ship.

Standing on one side, overseeing all the different tasks stood the Sergeant Major, stick held by both hands behind his back, apparently quite relaxed. He had seen Jim Blake and had been reassured about the arrangements. Now it was up to the Sergeants and Corporals to get things moving. Lieutenant Brookes was up and about. That was good.

The horses were fed in half an hour. That was good going. What effect would the slings have on their breakfast, he wondered? Time would tell. Most of the men had nothing at all to do with the horse loading. They had to help with moving the supplies and ammunition from the sheds to where they could be carried, box by box, up the gangways. The slings were for the horses.

The first of the horses were ready now, squealing with fright, kicking their hooves as they were lifted high above the wharf then swung aboard and dropped into the hold where they were caught and pushed into the wooden stalls. After a few minutes they seemed to recover and just stood, chewing on the little bagful of oats that had been put into their feed bags at the front of their stalls. They managed to load the horses one every minute. In four hours they were all aboard, including the men, swearing and sweating.

Dan pulled out his watch. Not bad at all! It was time to quieten down now. He decided to have a look around, just to be sure of everything. Corporal Larkin, now an Acting Sergeant was standing near his platoon, just watching every move they made. Every body was being watched by somebody. The thought came to him. Who was watching *him*? He looked round and saw Captain Brookes, also watching and he smiled, knowing that he, himself had been the prime mover of all this activity.

Everybody was getting promoted. It had to be that way. Leaders were soon separated from the followers. Fred Holyhead, the hard case he had punched on the nose was now a Lance Corporal. Most of the time the men chosen just accepted the extra responsibility and the small extra pay. He made his way up the gangway to where Jim Blake, the Chief Petty Officer was standing.

'Thanks for your help, Jim. To tell the truth I never thought it would all happen as easily as it did. I suppose you've done it before.'

The CPO smiled.

'It's always easier if everything is being checked and I could see you had it all under control. Fancy a wet?' The sailor pulled out a small flask. 'It'll warm you up a bit.'

Dan took a draught of the liquid. It was rum.

'God! Now I know why you join the Navy!' He handed the flask back. 'When are we going? Do you know?'

'You'll be told, same as us. It all depends on when your CO is satisfied with everything – and the tide and weather is right for the skipper. He don't tell everybody what he's going to do next, but you'll know, I can assure you!'

There was a shout from the bridge of the ship. The men at the mooring lines started to lift the heavy ropes from the bollards and the men at the gangway looked to the CPO. He winked at Dan.

'Come on, Sergeant Major, you'd better move yourself. We're on the move.'

All the men were aboard. It was time to go. How many would come back? He didn't usually think in such a way. His previous time in France must have affected him more than he thought. He reminisced for a moment and then took a grip on himself.

While he had been chatting to the sailor all the Staffies had marched past them, all organised and had put their equipment in the small spaces allotted to them. In a few hours they would be in France, shooting at and being shot at. Some of them would kill Germans and some of them would be killed by Germans. What a life!

The ship was moving now and the view of Portsmouth was beginning to blur. It was raining and suddenly Dan didn't feel like standing looking over the side. He turned, to find Corporal Simkins looking at him.

'Well? What do you want? Is everything all right?'

Simkins was standing to attention, obviously wanting to communicate something to him.

'Well?' He repeated.

'I just wondered how you felt, having been here before.' He hesitated for a second then went on. 'It's all very well, being brave and all that stuff but to tell the truth, Dan, I'm frightened to death and what's more, I think most people are. How do you see it, Dan?'

Dan stood in the pouring rain and thought about the question and how he was to answer it, not just to Simkins but to all the others who were likely to ask the same question in their own way.

'Well, the way I see it, if you must know is I'm shitting myself as much as anybody. The only thing is you can't do anything about the odds except try to be as good a fighting soldier as you can. That's what I've always tried to do. Probably half of us are going to die. You are more likely to die if you ain't no good at soldiering so it's best to be the best you can. Even then the odds against surviving without losin' a part of yourself can't be all that wonderful. I think it's always better to do something, no matter how little a thing it is.'

It was getting dark now and neither man could find anything else to say. Simkins straightened up and moved away. He had his own squad of new soldiers who would want words of wisdom from him. God help them. How Barr could stand it, he would never understand. Still, at least he'd said he was just as frightened as anybody else.

Two hours later the lights of Le Havre showed in the dark. There'd be more orders soon. There were other lights, too, the streaks and glows of an early morning bombardment in the distance. Men were being killed, there, although all that showed was just small, distant bonfire-night sights, little lights glowing in the dark.

'Come on then! You'd better move. The war is miles away, yet so it's too early to be shitting yourselves! There'll be plenty o' time for that when we get nearer, if we ever do, the way you're moving.'

Corporal Simpkins was in the mood now. There was a serious job to be done and he was the one selected to do it. If he didn't take charge, somebody else would. 'Listen to me now! If you don't do your best to do as you're told, the Germans will beat you to it an' it'll be no good sayin' it's time to start movin' then; you'll be dead! If you do your best you might get to be a corporal and have loads o' time on your hands, like me, so *move* it!'

The long line of men started moving then, moving down the gangplanks in an orderly fashion. Dan Barr, standing on one side smiled to himself. Simpkins was getting the idea now. He looked into the distance. There were lights, about eight miles away, he estimated. Three hours away but they would have to get themselves somewhere to sleep first. The officers would be getting their sleep to be sure they were in good condition for the performance in the morning.

Lieutenant Brookes was sitting at a small table in the rain, trying to make sense of the small map he had been given, to show where the battle in the distance was taking place. As far as he could see, it was at the side of the river Somme. As soon as the men had been rested he would have to make his way there to contribute his men to the death toll. He had no idea how many of them would survive or how many of them would not survive.

All he could do now was do his best, the same as the most ignorant of the infantrymen. He had heard that there were many thousands dying; tens of thousands. God, what was the point? Would he be any wiser if he was a Colonel? His father was supposed to be wiser but he suspected that he was no wiser either! There must be hundreds if not thousands of young officers, fit and intelligent, who had no idea what they could do to get the sort of result they dreamed of. He knew that the life expectation of a Lieutenant was about six weeks. So much for tradition, honour and class; so much too for the training they had been given. The whole thing was madness with no logic or reason. He found himself leaning on the table. Perhaps the best attitude was Barr's. He had heard him say that the best way was to be as good as you could be in the situation that you were put and then to be lucky Well, why not?

He stood up. He knew that he had done all he could to be as much of a good soldier and a good officer as he could. All he needed now was enough luck to see him through the conflict. He felt that it was not likely but he made up his mind to be as lucky as he could.

10. Hop Picking, Soldiers to Help.
September, 1915

The three women soon settled into the activities of the farm. Two of them had been there before, and Ruth was a quick, confident learner. She had been down in the area years ago and soon got back into the swing of things. They rapidly emerged as a good team, holding their own with any of the groups of women who had come down from the Black Country. Henry Wilkins was soon forgotten as they faced fresh problems of weather, soil and bine.

Elsie was accepted now, as a busheller, and another woman, Agnes Ollerenshaw, who originated from Birmingham, had been chosen for the position of hop dryer. The two women often found themselves discussing the problems of the day. Elsie asked Agnes questions about Birmingham and was surprised at the number of different trades that were carried on there.

Agnes lived near the centre of the city and loved it, telling Elsie of the Rag Market and the Bull Ring, where the traders threw their crockery into the air to attract attention, rattlers they called them. The Rag Market was where people sold second-hand goods; furniture and old clothes that still had a bit of life in them. Elsie still considered herself a Brummy, having been born in Birmingham. She had walked to the Black Country with her father, James, after her mother had died from a disease of the lungs. He had lived on for a time but he too had succumbed a few years later.

Elsie's earliest memories were of Hockley and Handsworth, in Birmingham, where her father had worked as an engineer in one of the great workshops. They had been given food and shelter by Mary Bowyer when they had arrived at Wednesbury and it was Mary too, who had found them their first work. Now Elsie was grown up and was making her own way, but was still willing to pick hops for the extra money it would give her. She said it was money she wouldn't otherwise have. She was quite skilled and was competent in other aspects of trade.

Elsie could keep books too, a profession she had learned in Wednesbury, at the firm of Jenkins, solicitors. They weren't just solicitors; they also invested in property and she had been employed as a rent collector as well as a bookkeeper. Her character had been formed by her experiences since she had made the long walk, as she called their march from Birmingham to Wednesbury, ten years ago.

The weather was holding good for the picking but there just weren't enough pickers. They would earn good money but it was no good if the hops were left on the bines. Jenny Walker had mentioned asking for help from the Army. That would be a novelty.

It was Sunday and the pickers had decided to work, an unusual thing, but it would give them all extra cash and also help Jenny Walker out. They were in the long field and had been picking since seven o'clock. The sun was shining, though it was quite cool. Jenny Walker was working alongside them; she would be going back to the farmhouse soon. She had prepared a stew, a firm favourite among the pickers. It was too much trouble to carry it to them so they would all be stopping for a break soon and joining her on the long benches they had set up.

Elsie looked up. Jenny was waving her hand to let them know that the meal was ready. She shouted to Agnes. 'Come on, Aggie!' She shouted. 'Come on, you lot! It's dinner time!'

Elsie looked round. What an impressive lot we are, she thought. Everyone had stopped and was walking briskly down the hill to where Jenny and two of the girls were scooping the food into large dishes. There was a good deal of friendly rivalry between the teams of pickers but it was all expressed in joking terms. They all sat along the long benches and the food was passed across the tables by anyone who felt like doing it. In half an hour, all the food was gone and the teams were all making their way back to the hops, each leaving one member of their team to help with the washing up. Within an hour it was all done. They would be finishing a little early today; the Church Army would be holding an Evensong service to celebrate the Harvest Festival. A few days later they would be holding a service for All Saints day. Elsie had missed going to church; she had always attended at Saint Mary's at Wednesbury.

As she picked the hops, Elsie's mind turned to her mother. She hadn't thought of her for some time now. She had been a pretty woman, petite in appearance but full of bursting activity when she had been in good health.

Suddenly her attention was caught by Agnes cocking her head. Elsie turned and listened. It was men, singing. She turned to the road. She could see a column of uniformed soldiers marching. Male voices had always caught at her emotions, making the tears flow. They were singing louder now, causing the tears to flow again. Elsie found her eyes pouring but determined not to show it. She stood still and listened.

'It's a long way, to Tipperary, it's a long way, to go.

It's a long way to Tipperary, to the sweetest girl I know.

Goodbye, Piccadilly, farewell Leicester Square

It's a long, long way to Tipperary, but my heart lies there.'

The column marched to the farm and then came to a halt. A Sergeant-Major stood the men at ease and made his way to the farmhouse door. Jenny was waiting for him and spoke to him easily. 'Good day, Sergeant-Major. A nice day for it, then.'

'Yes, Madam. The Captain will be along shortly, with the transport. If you please, madam, where would be a good place to set the tents? They are coming with the wagons.'

'Yes, that's a good question. I think the best place would be the field where the pickers are just finishing off. They won't be a nuisance there. By the time you're set up, my women will be out of your way. Have you anything to carry water with?'

'Yes, Madam; there will be a barrel wagon with the rest of the transport. It will all be good practice for when we get to France, if we ever do! Right then; we'll start getting to where we are going to pitch the tents. The wagons will see where we have gone and will follow us.'

The Sergeant-Major saluted and marched back to the head of the column. He led them round to the gate and then to the top of the hill before entering the field by the top gate. They appeared to be organised. Within five minutes they had broken ranks and were in small groups, cleaning the ground in circles, ready for the large bell-tents to arrive.

A few minutes later, the wagons rolled onto the field, the mules were unhitched and led to a line to which they were all hitched. There was no loud noise; they all just seemed to get on with their individual tasks.

The women now had no thought of hop-picking. The soldiers were too much of a feast for the eyes, especially for the country girls who had never seen a man in uniform. The soldiers too, were looking round, at the women. It was quite likely that they, in turn, had never seen such a large collection of young women. Elsie wandered over to the gate and leaned on it, watching the way everything was done.

'What are you doing here? Are you a German spy?' A voice spoke, close to her ear. 'You know what happens to spies, don't you?'

She turned round and found herself looking in the face of a young, broad-shouldered blonde man. He was trying unsuccessfully to look serious. His eyes twinkled as he spoke.

'Yes', she said, pretending to hold a cloak to cover her eyes. 'I am a German spy. I haf come to find out the secrets of beer-making. I know that if I can get the secret back to the Kaiser, Germany will win the war. You would haf no chance if we could get all the secrets.'

Elsie laughed. It was nice to be laughing again. There was too much of all this parting, going to war and people, men and women, dying. She deserved to laugh and smile just occasionally. She took another look at the young man. He was a Corporal. She smiled at him to put him at his ease. 'I see you are a non-commissioned Officer. My husband is a non-commissioned officer. He is on the way to France. If you should happen to see Sergeant-Major Barr, tell him I am missing him already'

'Yes, I should think that a pretty girl like you would have a high-ranking officer as a husband. I'd like to be going to France, to fight the foe, and all that stuff. We all serve, I suppose, whether in France or good old England. We're the Worcestershire Regiment, so I suppose its right that we should serve in Worcestershire. Where are you going to serve, at home or abroad?'

'Well, I'm from Birmingham and Staffordshire, so I could serve in the Warwicks or the Staffies. I think I shall do my duty wherever I serve. Where do you think my duty lies, Corporal?'

They seemed to be almost having one of those flirtatious double-meaning conversations that seemed like a lot of fun at the time but later, when you thought back to it, it seemed as you had said a lot of things you didn't really want to say; you certainly didn't mean what you said, not with any seriousness.

It was fun to say things you didn't mean. The trouble was that if you said them to young things, men or women, they might think you did mean them and their heart would be broken because you didn't mean them. Still, the fun was there to be had and you were as entitled to your bit of fun as anyone else. He was speaking to her again.

'What do you do when you're not picking hops, then?'

Now there was a question. It was obvious where it was leading as well. What you should say is something like I am looking after my husband's interests. Are you looking after your wife's interests? What you really said was,

'Well, we often go for a walk into Bromyard, to have a drink in the Lamb and Sceptre, usually on a Saturday night. Sometimes, when it is Peace, my husband comes down from Wednesbury to buy my drinks, '

Why she had said all that, she didn't know, she just wanted to chatter away, meaninglessly. What could she ask him? If she asked him questions he would have to answer her and then she would be able to ask him another question. He wasn't speaking at all, now so she spoke again. 'Why are you here instead of in France, being shot at? What have you been training to do, anyway?'

Elsie looked and he seemed to blush as if he were not completely happy with the answer he was about to give. Then he started, slowly at first and then he seemed to let go and try to get it all off his chest.

'What we have been training to do, young lady, is to march and run, salute officers and salute them with rifles in our hands. I wonder why we have to salute them with rifles in our hands.' He thought for a moment. 'What we have trained in is, Basic First Aid, so we can put a plaster on a leg that has been blown off a thigh. We have trained to mend broken arms as well. We have trained to make false injuries so we can blow each other up. We have trained to charge with bayonets in our hands. We have been trained to kill by the use of bullet, bayonet, grenade, shell, mortar, bomb, incendiary and bare hands. It is difficult to imagine what it would actually be like to kill someone with your bare hands but I suppose you get used to it. After all, it may get to the point that it is either you or him, if you see what I mean.' He hesitated for a moment and then went on. 'We have been trained to stand to attention, stand at ease and stand easy. We have been trained to polish our boots until they glitter, and paint our belts until they are blancoed white as snow. We know how to march at a hundred and forty paces every minute and how to charge as fast as we can, to stick our bayonets into the bellies of our enemies before they stick theirs into us.

'The sad thing is that if I had met him, the enemy I mean, I would have had no quarrel with him at all. I salute him because he is a man the same as I am, but I will kill him, given half a chance. Now that's enough of that. I'm here and now. That's all I know for certain; here and now! As for the rest, a bloke named Omar Kyam said, 'the moving finger writes, nor all your piety and wit can bring it back to cancel half a line.' I live for the here and now, now. That's me, take me or leave me.'

Elsie stared at him. It was obvious that he had thought a lot on the subject. Or had he? Was this a ploy to have as many girls as possible before embarking? What difference did it make to her, anyway? There was a cry from down the field and she looked to see what it was. It was Betty and standing at her side was Luke! How had he got down from Wednesbury? She was instantly jealous of her friend, thinking that it should be Stephen who was standing there. She heard a neigh and looked round, recognising the sound of her cob, instantly. It made her shout.

'Chalky! I can hear you, Chalky!'

Elsie looked in the direction of the sound and saw Stephen sitting in the trap. He was smiling at her, as he always did. She rushed forward and suddenly remembered that she was in a conversation with the soldier.

'Oh, oh', she stuttered. 'That's my man. I didn't know he was coming. I must go and speak to him. You'll have to excuse me.'

The soldier was laughing at her as he watched Elsie running through the grass towards Stephen. The Corporal was wishing someone was running through the grass towards him. Elsie caught up with the trap and stroked Chalky on the nose and was received with pleasure and a whinny. Then she lifted up her hand to be hoisted by her man into the trap. Before she had caught her breath she was being galloped across the field and out of the gate. A mile later they were slowing down and turning into a small field. She looked around, wondering where they were.

'What are you doing, Stephen? Where are we?'

He smiled at her again. This time he looked as if he was married to her instead of being her lover. Which was the best? She did not get chance to ruminate on the question. Stephen had tied Chalky to a post and was leading her, more like dragging her, along the path to a small cottage. Instead of knocking the door he pushed it open with his foot and pushed her in before him. 'This is where I am taking you, and this is where you are sleeping, tonight. Come and have a look at the bed. It's enormous, and there are two of them, one for us and for Betty and Luke. Which one do you want? You have the first choice. Do you want to try them both out, first?'

Her man stepped back from her. Elsie didn't want to ask him how he came to be there; she just wanted to enjoy him. She stepped forward, following him and threw her arms round his neck. 'I was just talking about you, to that soldier in the field. I was telling him that all I wanted to do was to love you.'

Elsie stopped, realising how she must sound, but he didn't seem to care. Stephen was just delighted to see her there, in front of him. 'Well, now's your chance; you're here and I'm here.'

She was suddenly reminded of the way the soldier had been talking to her. Here and now, he had said as if here and now was the most important thing in the world. It *is* the most important thing, Elsie thought. Your whole life is bound up by the never-ending here and now. She moved forward again, pushing her body forward until it was in contact with his. He could not deny her and if he felt the same, she could not deny him. All thoughts of who owned the cottage drifted away and she slid his jacket from his shoulders. It dropped onto the floor. 'Come on, then. Show me this enormous bed.'

Stephen took her hand to his lips and then pulled towards the little stairway, the sense of urgency apparent in the way he moved. Somehow they were at the top of the stairs. Somehow they were in the little bedroom. He undid the buttons on her skirt, letting it fall to the floor, making a little black pool of cotton. She stood, allowing him to get the best view of her body then she pulled at his remaining clothes until they were both naked.

Again they moved toward one another until they both became aroused with the desire of the moment. Neither of them wanted to do anything. The sheer pleasure and lust of the looking was enough, satisfying them for a small moment of time. Then the moment passed and they wanted to do everything to each other and they felt the skin on and of each other. It was the first contact and again, was enough for a second then that moment passed and they pulled at each other, trying to increase the tactile range of their movements.

Breast met breast. Thigh met thigh. Hand held hand. Hands touched thighs and they could not keep still. They fell onto the bed, the coolness of the sheets giving a small shock to her back, and then going as the heat of her body was submerged within the heat of *his* body.

'Elsie, Elsie. I want ...you!' He said the words loudly as if he wanted to let the words out like a bullet from a gun. 'I want you so much!'

'Stephen! Stephen!'

Elsie opened her legs and felt her own heat flood her body with the liquid of love. Immediately he was in her, moving until the moment was too much for either of them. Their combined climax surprised and shocked them both with its force and speed, making their bodies move in ways that they never had before, writhing and snaking about each other faster and faster until there was silence in the small bedroom. An eternity passed in a few seconds as the post-climatic exhaustion of satisfaction struck them. An hour seemed to pass as they gradually came back to earth, their hands seeming to come to contact each other and then touching other parts as if they were about to start again without the energy of the first time. They sighed and sighed as if that was enough communication, without the need for words.

They knew there would never be another time quite like this, and this might have to be enough, and it was, for now. What had she done? That was a useless question. She had made love with her lover, while her husband was, for all she knew, on his way to his death in France. She had made love with Dan on the night before he had joined the Regiment. She had found herself pregnant; now how would she know whose child it was? The thought was horrific and was also unlikely, she thought, so there was no use worrying about it. It was bad enough, knowing, or thought she knew, that Tom, her wonderful Tom, was the child of her lover.

Sometimes Elsie could look into Tom's face and see Stephen there, and that smile that seemed to be present most of the time. At other times, she thought she could see Dan in the way he held his head and the bulldog-like determination in his face. Tom certainly had something of her in his looks and character. She put the thoughts away from her consciousness. It was useless to dwell on such things.

The sunlight coming through the tiny window suddenly became darker. The clouds must be coming over the sky. What should she be doing? What was Betty doing? Had she too, been making love? If so, she was entitled to. She had been married to Luke for two years, now.

They had met at Elsie's house and had fallen for each other immediately. Luke had a secret from Betty that Elsie knew she had never been told. Luke had been involved in the punishment meted out unofficially to her father, who had been abusing her for years. She had asked Elsie what she could do about it and Elsie had seen Luke. He had been angry; angrier than she had ever seen him. A few nights later Jack Thurston, Betty's father had been attacked and castrated.

Thurston had recovered to a certain extent but he was not now able to abuse her in the same way. A few months later Luke and Betty had married and they were as happy as a couple could expect to be.

Jack Thurston had thrown his daughter out. Betty had stayed with friends for a while until Luke had provided her with a home. Like Elsie, Luke was far wealthier than was apparent and it was not hard for him to find Betty a home. Now they were here. How had that happened? Elsie knew that Stephen must have been at the back of it. He must have offered Luke a ride, to bring them to Bromyard and she knew they couldn't stay long. There was work awaiting both of them, in Willenhall and Wednesbury.

Elsie stretched her arms and found herself touching Stephen's body. Her hand lingered and found itself stroking him. She explored his body. He was quite relaxed and almost unaware of her attention. This would not do! She moved her hand to his most intimate parts and he instantly became erect in her hand. She leaned on him and lowered her lips. He moved her so that she was lying underneath him. He wanted to start again and Elsie opened herself to him and they became one loving unity again. Their loving was gentler this time and their climax was in a lower key. Nice, and not so frantic.

The time passed again. The sun rose to its highest and then started lowering. Elsie could hear a voice calling her. It was Ruth!

'Elsie! I know you're there. We've finished picking for the day. You are the busheller! We are waiting to book our hops in! Betty told me you would probably be here. Come on. D'you want me to come and fetch you?'

Naturally, Ruth would be angry with her. She had been in love with Dan and had even gone to the station to see him off. She had confessed to Elsie but Elsie had not confessed her misdemeanours to her. Ruth had found out for herself!

Elsie stood up and started dressing herself. It was alright for the men! Stephen was just lying back, relaxing. He could come and go as he pleased. No doubt he had given Mabel some cock and bull story to appease her over his absence.

She bent and dropped a quick kiss on his lips. There was no time, now, for playing around. When she walked out of the front door she thought she looked as fresh as a daisy. Ruth knew different as soon as she saw her but did not comment. As they went through the gate into the North field, where they had come out, the Corporal was still leaning on the gate.

'Hello love. It's a busy old life, ain't it? My blokes have all set up now.'

Elsie looked down into the field. There were rows of bell-tents all the way down. The soldiers were all looking smart but were in working uniforms. They had spread themselves among the women and were all busy picking into the same cribs. Elsie looked down at her watch. It was five o'clock. They didn't usually work this late on Sundays but they were all taking advantage of the soldier's labour to add their pickings to their own. They would have a good bonus for today! She smiled at the Corporal. 'You've done well, Corporal. I'll see you get some sort of bonus for this.'

Where was Jenny Walker? She would no doubt have been looking for Elsie. Where was Betty? Everything seemed to have got out of control. Then she saw her, stepping down the lane from the direction of the cottage. She must have been in there all the time that she and Stephen were … She found her cheeks were burning and she didn't want to face Betty. Or Luke! Luke had taken a liking to her, before she had introduced him to Betty. He had kissed her, and she had liked it! It might have gone further but somehow it hadn't worked out that way.

Betty caught up with her, acting as if *she* were the guilty one. 'I'm sorry, Elsie. I just got carried away with what I was doing; you know what I mean. Time just seemed to fly by. I suppose we'd better get back to the picking. It's time to finish isn't it?'

Betty was looking as if she had been used, thought Elsie. It didn't seem long since the thought of making love would have been abhorrent to her. Since her father had used her so violently. She was different now, radiant with happiness.

They made their way back to the lines of bines and started tidying up their area. Jenny Walker was walking up the slope, towards them.

'That was brilliant, merging the soldiers with the pickers. I don't mind paying the bonus out to them. The soldiers get another shilling a day, and that is paid out of their funds, not mine. I can see you're going to be a big help, Elsie.'

Elsie said nothing in reply, just carrying on with her tidying up and smiling as if she really had been there all day, picking with the rest of the women. Today had been what she called a golden day! Everything seemed to have worked out just right.

She was delighted that Chalky hadn't been called up for military service. She knew that men were going round buying horses for the Army, whether or not the owner wanted to sell them. How had Stephen got away with it then? She would ask him about it when she had a minute!

Elsie made up her mind to enjoy the rest of the day, wherever she ended up. Time was short. Life moved on whether you were sad, miserable or ecstatic with joy. There was a spring in her walk and she intended that the spring would continue, and she would put a spring in Stephen's step, too!

11. Howard and Agnes, Courting.
October 1915

The bedroom in the farmhouse was bigger and nicer than anything Agnes had ever known. The window, facing west, gave her the most wonderful view as the sun sank towards the horizon at sunset. She felt often that if she was able to paint, she would like to have her view on canvas, covering the window. It was a view that only existed in her imagination but it was as real as the view that she saw each evening.

Her work took her only about eight hours each day and then she helped Jenny Walker to prepare an evening meal for the two of them. They worked well together, more like friends than employer and member of staff, soon preparing the light sort of meal that each of them seemed to prefer.

She often found though, that she missed Howard's company and sometimes she went for a walk when the weather was clement and occasionally Howard seemed to turn up by accident. She knew from her experience of life that 'accidental' meetings were common phenomena of life when a man and woman were interested in each other.

She would walk round to the kell and sit on her homemade bed and occasionally she would hear his step on the mud of the farmyard and he would sit at her side and put his arm round her, giving her one of his 'pleased' looks. She would pretend that he was being too forward, move a little and take him to the kitchen and give him a cup of tea on the old oak table with a large slice of the cake she had cooked earlier.

They both enjoyed these times together but she also became increasingly frustrated as she began to feel the return of her sexual feelings without being offered any relief from them. She began to get annoyed with his shy ways, wishing he would be a bit more adventurous in the way he was with her. From time to time, she would smack him lightly on the cheek, playfully and kiss him, raising her eyebrows in a pointed sort of fashion to try to get a response to her.

It was an evening when Jenny was going to a meeting of her friends and he had come round to the farmhouse after Jenny had gone out. Somehow, Agnes felt it was going to be different. Howard was easy to please. She gave him a square of her bread pudding, covered with hot custard and he lifted it to his lips and cursed as the hot liquid touched him.

'Bloody hell! That was hot, Aggie. I've never had custard that hot. What are you trying to do, baste me with it?'

He stifled his curse and started to smile, the smile that told her that he was pleased with the food, hot or not. She took a cloth and started to wipe his lips, gently. 'What a fuss about a bit o' custard. Ain't you ever had custard before? You must have had a quiet life before I came along.'

He leaned towards her and she felt that what he was about to say was important. 'Yes, I did, for years, Aggie. I was too many years on my own, I suppose and I got used to the quiet life. In fact it would have filled me with horror if any woman had acted as if she might be attracted to me.' He gave her one of his pleased looks. 'You were quite a shock to me, you being such a fun kind of woman. You are, you know. I don't know how you ever wanted to know an old codger like me.'

'All I could think was that you were sorry for me, and that's the last thing I would ever want, somebody who was sorry for me. Do you know what I mean?'

Agnes answered quickly. 'Well, you're not the only one who's been on their own, Howard. I've been on my own for six years now. I suppose if he'd lived, he'd have been in the Army or waiting to be called up. There are going to be thousands of men and women who are losing their husbands and wives right now, maybe even as we are talking. I never thought I'd want to even talk to a man again. Women are luckier than men in a way. They have a way of getting on with each other if there are no men about, if you see what I mean.

'I suppose men are the same; they are alright together, in the

Army, as comrades an' all that stuff. It changes if there are one or two women. They all start struttin' about like stags, tryin' to show the herd who is the best! I've always thought that them who strut the most ain't necessarily the best for the job. I don't know where that leaves you, Howard. On that idea, you'd be the best o' the lot. Have you always been a quiet sort o' chap? I suppose it depends how you've been brought up. If your dad was strict, you probably got used to bein' quiet.'

They sat there exchanging thoughts and words. It was as if this was their way of getting to know one another; explaining their differences and how those differences came about. Howard lifted his spoonful of custard up, blew it gently and tried it. He smiled at her and Agnes found she liked it when he smiled at her. She tried the bread pudding and found she liked it more than usual. She looked at it a moment later and it was gone as so was Howard's.

'Do you want some more, Howard?' she asked, 'Or would you like to sit on the settee? It might be more comfortable than sitting on these dinin' chairs.' She blushed a little; it might seem as if she was trying to get him into a more seductive situation. He didn't seem to think anything of it, just got up and moved to the settee.

'That's better, Aggie; them chairs make my back ache sometimes. I made myself a couple of chairs years ago and I've got used to them now. I forgot, you've never been to my place, have you? You can come and have a look, sometime. Mind you might not find it as tidy as this place. I've never wanted to show it off before.' He paused as if he had said something wrong. You could come round and have a look, if you like. You never know, you might like it. I've never been what you women call house-proud but it ain't too bad if you don't look too close.'

'Yes, I think I'd like that, Howard, Flower. It hadn't better be too shiny you know, but I don't suppose it will be, you bein' a man and me bein' a woman.' She smiled. 'I'll come round after Church on Sunday, shall I?'

Howard gave her a nice look and it was settled. She knew that

Howard didn't go to Church very often and she had wondered why. She had got the impression that he was a religious sort of person but hadn't seen him there all that often.

'Why don't you go to Church, Howard?' she asked him. 'I've seen you there occasionally, I know.'

'I think everybody's religion is up to them, don't you, Aggie? To tell the truth, I'm always busy on one thing or another. The garden takes up a few hours, you know, and so does the housework. I'm always making some stick of furniture for the house as well. I've never bought anything for the house, I've always made my own; I prefer it that way. Shop bought furniture is never as good as what I've made myself. That's what I think, anyway. I like to grow my own vegetables as well. It's more work, I suppose but I like my stuff fresh out of the garden.'

Agnes looked at him, a little surprised. She knew, vaguely, that he was interested in wood work and had assumed, because he was a countryman, that he was interested in country crafts. He always brought his dog, Patch, with him to work but she had no idea how he spent his time outside work.

She stood as she heard Jenny Walker coming home. They had been talking until eleven o'clock! How could the time go so quickly? Jenny walked in.

'Hello, Agnes. Hello Howard. My goodness, the wind is getting up. I think we are going to have some rain.'

Howard looked at the time on his pocket watch. 'Oh dear, I never knew so much time had passed by. We must have talked about everything. I'd better go if I'm going to miss the rain.' He stood and put his coat on. 'I'll say goodnight then Agnes.' He turned to Jenny. 'Goodnight Mrs Walker, I'll see you both tomorrow.'

He passed through the door quickly and the two women stood and smiled at each other. Howard had reverted to his usual quiet style!

'He's really nice, isn't he?' Jenny said to Agnes.

'Yes, I never would have thought it of him but he is. Nice, I mean. I don't think I have ever met a nicer person.' She smiled again but excitedly. I'm going to his cottage on Sunday, after Church. He's invited me. I don't know if he's included a Sunday lunch but I've got no reason to expect one after all. Why should he go to that much trouble for someone who is more or less a stranger?'

Jenny smiled at her. 'If I were you, Agnes, I should be ready for anything. I think Howard has taken a real liking to you and may try to impress you on Sunday.' She changed the subject. 'We had a good turnout at our little meeting, twenty of us. There are always a good few at this time of the year the Autumn Equinox Its sort of half way through the Autumn, just past Harvest Time, and moving towards All Saints. The days are as long as the nights until the next day, when the nights take the length. Our people get quite excited you know, always wanting Spells for this and that and things to say for The Common Good. Anyway, we all had a good time. Perhaps you'll come with me, one of the days.' She looked at Agnes's face. 'No, I don't suppose so. Too fond of the Church of England's traditions, I expect.' She smiled in defeat. Sometimes you didn't exactly lose but you didn't win, either. One day, perhaps.

Agnes was too excited to be wondering what Jenny Walker had in mind. She was more concerned, after hearing Jenny's comments, about what Howard might have in mind. He was not coming to escort her to his cottage – how had he come to have a cottage? Did he own it or rent it? How could that affect her? The future suddenly seemed to be opening up. Come down to earth, girl, she thought to herself. Don't build castles in the air.

Sunday came and she started the mile-long walk to Howard's cottage. The sun was shining but it was cool enough to make the walk a pleasant stroll.

The cottage was easy to find. It had roses around the door just as she had envisioned. She tapped the door shyly and when there was no answer, she pushed it gently. She knocked the door, louder this time but not wanting to just march in. There was a scuffle from inside and then he was at the door, the pleased look on his face matching hers.

'Hello, Agnes.' He said. 'You're on time, but I expected that. Come in.'

He stood to one side and steered her towards a chair by the window. She looked out and was surprised at the amount of greenery in the garden. On the west side of the window was a typical cottage garden with Hollyhocks standing high among the many colourful annuals. On the other side there were rows of carrots and beetroot and closer, there were lettuce and radishes, with cucumber and tomatoes growing.

How on earth does he find the time, she thought. He must be very well organised. She looked at him the surprise showing on her face.

'Would you like a cup o' tea, Agnes?' He spoke quietly and shyly.

'Yes, thanks. It's been a warm walk, along the lane. I suppose you know. You do it every day, don't you?'

She laughed and suddenly felt more at ease. Howard as usual didn't reply but he did look pleased. It was one of the things, she realised, that endeared him to her, his transparent feeling were always reflected on his face with such honesty that she sometimes worried about what his face might look like if he were displeased. Still, he hadn't looked like that yet. A displeased look was still to be seen in the future.

She took the cup from him and looked round at the kitchen they were sat in. There was a table in the centre, with six chairs round it, all matching the dark oak of the table. Under the window alcove there was a low table with a vase on it, waiting for a bunch of flowers, she thought.

'I thought you might like to pick a bunch.' Howard was reading her thoughts and handed her a pair of scissors. 'I'll do us a bit o' peck while you pick what suits you. There's a few ready for picking now, and they'll remind me of you when you've gone.'

He smiled and her heart sped as she took the scissors from him and crossed to the back door. The scent of the blossoms was in the air as she opened the door and she started cutting the carnations immediately, her favourite flower. In a few minutes she had sufficient to fill the vase. She tidied the flowers and carried them back in with her. She placed them into the vase and sat down. As she did so, she noticed that the table was now full of food, with a plate of mixed salad in the middle and slices of fresh bread to accompany it.

'Oh, Howard, how lovely!' She exclaimed. She sat and started spreading the bread. 'I'm sorry to say I'm starving. I could eat a mouldy 'orse!'

Howard smiled again and sat opposite her, spreading butter on the bread before him. 'So am I. I didn't want to start without you but if you had been a few minutes longer, there would have been no food left. I've been in the garden all morning and I've worked up a bit of an appetite.'

They were both silent for the next few minutes, both finding things for their hands to do. Agnes was struck by the way they were both different from their working relationship. There was no hurry to get things done. They had all afternoon. She felt herself beginning to relax, feeling that if she said nothing or something, it wouldn't matter. They were just there together, enjoying each other's company. The minutes turned into an hour and the food disappeared, then they were just there.

'Would you like to have a look round, Agnes?' He surprised her. Of course she would! She just nodded and followed him as he rose and led the way up the flight of stairs. There were two bedrooms leading from the short landing, a small room at the back with a bed and a few boxes in the corner, and a large room at the front, overlooking the path to the gate. The window was open and she could smell the roses and carnations outside.

The bed was the largest bed she had ever seen, with a plain cover over it.

'I don't often sleep in that bed,' Howard murmured. 'It just seems too big for one.'

Agnes looked at him, thinking. It looks about right for two

though. Should I say something leading to him? I might as well. He's not going to say anything. She moved to the bed and sat on the edge, moving, to test it for lumps.

'It seems smooth enough for me. There's no lumps in it.'

She smoothed the bedcover with her hand, creating a space for him and he just moved into the space. She moved closer to him and leaned a little in his direction. 'I should think it's more comfortable than that palliasse in the kiln.'

She smiled at him and pulled him to her and he came closer, his arm seeming to naturally find a way around her shoulder as it had before, in the kiln. He leaned down to her and kissed her gently.

'Agnes, I just want to say something.'

Oh no, she thought. What have I done or said. He must think I'm a bit of a slut! Well, here goes. Let's have it out. I've had a bit of a good run with him. Perhaps it's been too good to be true.

'Come on then, Howard, say it. Put me out of my misery. I was just starting to think we might get on but if it's all too much for you, just say, and I'll go.' She found herself crying, sobbing into his shirt. 'I was getting to be so happy.'

She found herself being pulled down onto the bed and Howard's arms all the way round her. She pulled herself away.

'Come on then, say it, whatever you are going to say.'

'All right, I will, then. I will say it. What I want to say is I love you, Agnes. I never thought I would be lucky enough to love somebody again but here I am, loving you. The other thing I want to say is will you marry me? I know we haven't known each other very long but it seems long enough to me. I don't want to have to say goodbye to you, Agnes. I want to be your husband, if you'll have me.'

They pushed each other apart and stared at each other in deep surprise. Agnes gave a quick rub to rid her cheeks of the tears still finding their way down to her neck. She grabbed him and pulled him to her.

'Oh Howard. Of course I'll have you. I feel just the same about you as you do about me. The sooner the better eh? Let's tell people and just do it, eh?'

She pulled him again and although they were both enthusiastic about their embrace, Agnes felt that they shouldn't make love before they were married.

It was nice but there seemed to be so many things to think of. She separated them, noting that she seemed to be the one making the pace. She suddenly felt like saying lots of things to him.

'I've got to have a chat with Hannah. It'll be a shock to her. There's the girls at the pickin' to tell as well. They'll all have something to say about it. I don't think I'll surprise Jenny Walker though. Nothing seems to shock her; it's as if she knows in advance, sometimes. When do you think we should do it, Howard? You're the man and you know how these things work. Howard looked pleased again and spoke his thoughts softly.

'Well, the pickin's out the way so things on the farm will quieten down a bit now. I think if we went to see the vicar, we could put the banns in straight away. But I forgot; where do you want to get married? For all I know, you might want to get married in Birmingham or Willenhall or Wednesbury. I know you're a Brummy, born and bred.'

He went silent, awaiting her response.

'No, I don't want to go anywhere now, Howard. I'm at home if you don't mind. This is where I want to put my roots.'

Howard just looked at her and pulled her close to him again. For a moment she thought he was going to cry. Then he pulled her close again, as if he couldn't stop pulling her.

'Oh, Agnes, I love you and I couldn't be more delighted that you want to spend your life with me. Your daughter can come and stay with us any time you say. I don't want to close her out of your life. She will always be welcome.'

'That's nice of you, Howard but I'm sure she'll have ideas of her own. She may well want to take over my little house in Wednesbury. In fact, when she finds out about us getting married, I bet she won't want to wait before she gets her hands on my furniture'

Agnes sat up on the giant bed. This was very comfortable but it put too many ideas in your head. It would be a good idea if they moved. Did Howard wonder if she couldn't wait to get her hands on his furniture? She changed the subject.

'Which church will we get married at, then, Howard? You have to remember that I'm a stranger round here and don't know everywhere.'

'Saint Peters, in the middle of Bromyard, on top of the High Street; that's where we'll get married. I'll have to take you round a bit, introduce you to some of the people I know. It's because I feel as if I've known you for ever and I think everybody knows you like I do. You'll soon get used to people.'

'People are people wherever you are, Howard. There's always nice and nasty, fat and thin, little and tall.'

She laughed. She wasn't going to worry about meeting fat 'uns or thin 'uns. She'd met all sorts before and always got on alright. She moved off the bed. She wanted to see the rest of this nice little cottage before it got dark.

'Come on, Howard. Let's see what the cottage has got to offer a young bride. No secrets, eh?'

They moved back downstairs and he took her to the privy and explained what had to be done periodically, then showed her the narrow path that he used as a short cut to Bromyard.

'There's no point in going into Bromyard now; all the shops are shut today. Ask Jenny Walker if you can have a day off to be shown around the sights of Bromyard and I'll bring a trap to the farm for you.'

That was a surprise. She hadn't known he owned a trap and she said so. He led her round to the small stable at the side of the cottage and there was a small pony, chewing freshly cut grass. She gave him one of her pleased looks and he looked pleased about it.

It was time to be going now. She had been away from the farm for most of the day and Jenny might be wondering about her. She smiled to herself. She might be wondering but she wouldn't be worrying. They still hadn't arranged to meet the vicar but Howard would do that when he thought about it. She just hoped it wouldn't be too long.

There was still everybody to be told! They hadn't spoken to anyone since the proposal and acceptance. She smiled to herself. How posh that sounded; the proposal and acceptance! It had been a good many years since her last proposal, over thirty years. Ike came into her mind still but not as often. She supposed Howard's wife came to him as well but from the way Howard had spoken to her, she wouldn't interfere from beyond the grave. They had each lost their partners about six years ago and had got over the worst of the pain of loss. It was up to them now to make the most of their years they still had left.

She knew Howard was a good catch for her, with a cottage and garden and a pony and trap. She felt lucky. What had attracted him to her? Did he feel lucky? She only had a small rented house in the middle of the Black Country and although she loved it, she would be quite happy to swop for the cottage any day. There must have been some reason he had been attracted to her, attracted enough to propose after knowing her for just a few weeks.

How would she put it to Hannah, her daughter, her pride and joy who she loved with all her being? Would Hannah break her heart or would she be pleased for her? When Howard had asked her to marry him, everything had seemed simple and she had just felt happy but now all sorts of questions kept coming into her mind. Was it all too much, at her age? She could go home and get a job as a hand at Stones', she felt sure and she would live a reasonable life but she would miss the company of the middle-aged man who said he loved her. Why should she put herself through that pain?

The alternative to Howard was a life of almost loneliness. She would have Hannah's company but she would probably be married herself inside two years, if she was anything like the rest of the young uns. She still hadn't been introduced to the vicar, if that's what he was. He might be a rector or a deacon. She'd better go to church soon, to meet him, see if he liked her. He might have a few rules he wanted her to keep to. They would see soon enough.

Would he be taking her home or would he be embarrassed? She turned to him and he was right beside her, waiting for her to say something about going back to Home Farm.

He was holding her coat and smiling at her, as if he was letting her think her own thoughts but would be ready when she was. She felt lucky again. She turned her back to him and slipped her arms into the coat.

'Are you ready love? The trap is, when you are.'

He followed her out and helped her up into the trap and hopped up himself.

'Come on, walk on.'

The pony moved immediately and they made their way onto the long road that led back to the farm. They seemed to be there in a matter of a few minutes and he helped her down quickly. He was going to come in with her, to announce their engagement!

Howard knocked the door, his own knock which Jenny Walker would recognise at once. He waited for a second and then walked in. Jenny was sitting by the fire, a glass of wine in her hand. She looked up and saw the two of them standing in the half-light.

'Hello, Howard, Agnes. How nice of you to come in to see me as you brought Agnes home. You're later than I expected but it doesn't matter, does it? Come on in. Have a glass of this wine. I laid it down last year and it's just about ready for drinking. She turned and picked up two glasses and filled them. Here you are Agnes, and you Howard. It must be getting quite cool on the road at this time of the evening.' Jenny fell silent and looked at the couple; it was immediately obvious that they were a couple. 'You've got something to tell me, haven't you? I hope everything's all right. Come on then, tell me!'

Who should tell her? It would have to be Agnes. Howard was just standing there, that pleased look plastered all over his face.

Agnes took a deep breath. 'We, Howard and me, are betrothed, Jenny. He asked me this afternoon and I said yes. Well, what else could I say? We're getting married as soon as the banns can be called. I am so happy. I don't think I've ever been so happy in my life. Oh, we never thought about a ring. I didn't anyway.'

She looked at Howard and he lost that pleased look. He was so innocent.

'I never thought about a ring. How silly of me. We'll get one down the town when we go to see the vicar. I didn't know whether you were going to say yes, did I?'

He looked a little despondent so she put him at ease.

'Don't you be worrying, my dear. We've got plenty of time to be thinking about such little things. I'm sure we can marry, with or without an engagement ring. I'll be quite happy just to have a wedding ring. That's what counts, ain't it? You can put an end to an engagement but a marriage goes on for the rest of our lives together, as we both know, don't we, Howard?'

Howard had got that pleased look back on his face now and Jenny took the opportunity to propose a private toast, just between the three of them.

'Here's to the two of you and I hope you are as happy every day as you are today. You've each been on your own for over six years, now, and you deserve some more years of happiness.'

She raised her glass and then drained it all at once, to the amazement of the happy pair. Agnes could see no reason for restraint though and drained hers too, and Howard followed suit with a great show of enthusiasm.

They sat for a while then Jenny spoke.

'What are you going to do first, Agnes? There must be a few things you need to get organised?'

She looked questioningly at Agnes.

'Well, the first thing I have got to do is let my daughter know before anyone else. I would hate to think she finds out from some newspaper cutting. She's my daughter and I'm going to tell her face to face, as I should, regardless of other considerations. That's fair, ain't it? The other things, like seeing the vicar or whoever it is that will be marrying us and rings and such are a little way down the list of important things I have to do so, Jenny, if it's alright by you I would like to have a day or two off to go and try to explain things to Hannah, my daughter. When I've done that I'll be back, ready to get on with the rest of the arrangements, all right?'

Agnes looked at Jenny and Howard who both nodded assent at once, seeing that she was so determined to do things in what she thought was the correct order.

Howard was the first to speak. 'You must do whatever you think is the right thing, Agnes and I'll be with you all the way. Do you want me to come with you to see Hannah?'

'No, I don't think so, Howard, but thank you for asking. Hannah and me will have other things to think of such as what I shall be wearing for the wedding. She's a good hand with a needle and thread and I would like to think she might want to put her skills to good use, helping her mother to look her best on that day of all days.'

She paused for a moment and then went on.

'I hadn't better waste any time. I think, if it's alright with you both, I'd better make my way home to Wednesbury and get it all sorted out. When we know some dates for the wedding at Saint Peters, I'll be able to write the details to Hannah and anyone else who would like to come to see us married. Until then, we've just got to make the best on it.' She turned to Howard. 'You're not going to change your mind are you, Howard? It's all going to happen quite quickly, now we've made our minds up.'

Howard turned on one of his pleased looks and she felt everything was all right. 'Yes, I should have thought it would. There's a mountain of things to do and a crowd of people to see. I just know it will all work out if we just do things in the right order. You have to go and speak to Hannah and I have to go and speak to the Rector, to see that we get fair chance of the dates that will suit you and me. I do have one or two other things to do as well. I think it would be a good idea if we said goodnight now, don't you, Agnes. He led the way to the door and she kissed him quickly before he disappeared into the darkness. It was time for bed.

*

Howard pushed his feet out of bed. He had things to do that he had never thought he would have to do, or even want to. An hour later he was walking into the churchyard of Saint Peters, the Parish Church of Bromyard. Slowly he walked through the great gate and made his way along the sloping path that led to the door. He skirted it and continued the slow climb until he was almost at the top, then took a narrow path that led downward past a number of graves. Finally he stopped at a small stone and knelt there. He read the simple inscription.

O Lord now lettest thou thy servant depart in peace.

According to thy word.

Tilly Humphries

Beloved wife of Howard Humphries

Departed this life 4th April 1909

His lips moved slowly as he whispered the familiar lines.

'Our Father Who art in Heaven, Hallowed be thy name

Thy Kingdom come; thy will be done

On Earth as it is in Heaven...'

He blessed himself as he continued in prayer, finally saying. 'I am sorry, Tilly. The day we got married was the first day of my life as far as I was concerned. Now you have been gone for six years; six years when I have been faithful to you, but life is for the living and I need someone to be with me as I enter the mature years of my life. I have found someone else, Tilly. We both need someone to warm our beds as we grow older so I have to say goodbye. Our wedding day was the first day of my life but this is the last day of the life I shared with you. God bless you and keep you.'

I have tried to share with you since you passed on but I have to face my new wife in a few days time and say to her, 'For the rest of my life I shall think of this day as the first day. Amen.'

He started the walk back and watched from the large doorway as the parishioners came out of the Church. The Rector came out and saw him.

'Good morning, Howard. Nice to see you.'

G'morning, Rector. Nice to see you as well. I'd like a word with you when you get a bit o' free time.'

'Well the last of them are going now so if it's alright, we can have a chat in a minute or two.'

They stood there for a few minutes, watching the worshippers leaving the Churchyard. There were always one or two who stayed, just having a word with former relatives or friends who had died in the past. Finally, Howard spoke.

'It's like this, Rector. My Tilly has been gone for six years now and I need to not be on my own. I have met a lady, one of the women who came down from the Black Country. She has been training to be a dryer, same as myself, and we have come to like each other. I have asked her to marry me and she has agreed. She is Church of England, the same as myself and I want you to marry us when it becomes convenient, Rector.'

The Rector looked surprised for a moment then, recovering, spoke.

'Of course I will, Howard. You will just have to bring your future wife's details to me and I will read the first banns next Sunday. It would be nice if you were both there, of course.'

'Yes, Rector, I will bring them to you as soon as Agnes, that's my lady's name, had returned from Wednesbury, where she is staying with her daughter for a few days. Thank you very much for being so understanding. I shall bring her to Church of course and I am sure you will get on together.

*

Hannah was excited; her mother was coming home. That was nice, even if it was just for a visit. She had cleaned the small house again, even though she had polished it from attic to cellar, the day before. The brass number on the door had been polished until it shone like a soldier's brasses. Her father had been dead for six years but she knew he would be proud of her. He had died in an industrial accident; someone had mistimed the drop of the drop forge and her father had misjudged how close to the forge he should be. Then he was gone. She had cried for him as had her mother. They were used to it now but she still put flowers on his grave occasionally. Would her mother want to visit the little plot as she used to?

She had received the short letter warning her of her mother's impending arrival, yesterday. Not much notice. Why the haste? Oh well, she would know soon. The kettle was simmering over the fire. Everything was as her mother would like and expect it to be.

Would her mother be coming home for good, or was this just a short visit to make sure her house was in order? Elsie Barr had been round and had commented favourably on the way she had kept it, so there could have been no complaints from her.

She was meeting Joe later. Her mother hadn't met him but she would if she stayed more than a day or two. She had met him in the market and then in the library when she had been looking for something to entertain her long evenings. They had got to know each other quickly, not that it seemed to matter how long they had to get to know each other. He was nice and considerate and she was the same to him. She was pleased that he was a member of the library. She would hate to go out with someone who was semi-illiterate. Joe worked in the butcher's shop in Wednesbury so she got a bit of a discount on any meat or sausage she bought from there. She had some sausage ready for when her mother got home. Agnes liked pork sausage.

She leaned forward and poked some life into the fire, trying not to be impatient. There was a push at the door and then her mother was in the house, moving to embrace her. She stood quickly.

'Oh, Hello, Mom! How lovely to see you. I have missed you, you know. How're things at the farm? Everything ship shape? Everything is all right here Mrs Barr has been round twice for the rent and she said how nice your house looked, Mom. I've bought a sewing machine, Mom. It was in the second hand shop, only two pounds, and it works all right, ever so easy.'

Couldn't wait to tell me! That's my girl. I'm not surprised she bought one, though. She would be a natural. Agnes waited as Hannah started to speak again.

'I'm making Mrs Barr a blouse. She wanted something different so I've given her a design to look at. I think she'll like it. I told her she could have it for one and nine pence. Would you like to see it, Mom? No, of course not. You want a cup of tea, don't you? Sit yourself down, our Mom and I'll soon have your cup filled.'

The two women became silent for a few minutes and then Agnes spoke.

'It's a nice cup o' tea, Hannah, and I'm glad to see you're doing well. If you keep up like that, you'll not want a job. You'll be too busy to go to work. I might want something off you myself, soon. You never know. I'd expect a bit of a discount being family 'o course.'

Agnes felt a bit embarrassed about the something she might want so she changed the subject. She would raise that subject later on.

Hannah had noticed the light blush on her mother's cheeks though, and would not let the subject go. 'What's that, Mom? What do you need in the way of blouses and skirts? Anything you want, I'll make for you. You know that and never mind discounts. I'll make anything you want, no charge. Have you got anything in mind?' She waited for the answer but was still surprised when it came.

'Yes, I want a wedding dress!'

She waited and Hannah asked the obvious question.

'Yes, Who's it for?' This time Hannah knew the answer. 'It's for you, ain't it? You crafty old fox. You're going to marry Howard, ain't you?' Agnes had been expecting opposition but instead, her daughter put her arms around her neck and hugged her. 'Oh, Mom. I'm so happy for you. I did wonder but when I came to think about it, Elsie had already put me wise. She said you had the right to marry who you like and Howard is a good catch no matter which side you look at.' She let go of her mother and asked the question directly. 'Is he the one, our Mom? Are you going to marry him?'

'Yes, Hannah. He's the one and let me tell you. He is going to look after me like I've never been looked after before. He's got a cottage with two bedrooms that he owns and he made all the furniture for it as well – and he's got a pony and trap if I want to go anywhere. I know you missed your Dad but I have to tell you that I love Howard more than I have ever loved anybody, except you of course. I have always loved you as well you know. Now tell me what's been going on in your life, eh? It's about time you found yourself a chap. I bet you already have, ain't you?' She stood back and looked Hannah in the face. 'I can see it in your eyes; there is somebody.'

She turned and poured another cup of tea. There was no point in hurrying their greeting to each other, now. There were too many things to be discussed. Surely two people couldn't each find a loving relationship in the few weeks they had been apart; or could they? She had; Howard had; and now it seemed, Hannah had. Still, each was a justification for the other. If Howard could; why not she, and if she could, why not her daughter? Life was funny at times. She smiled to herself. It was no use either of them taking up a superior attitude towards the other and saying bad things about people they had not even met. Still, it was a mother's place to get her daughter to be cautious, wasn't it? You couldn't trust young men nowadays. She pulled herself up mentally. When could you trust them?

The facts were that her daughter was quite bright and was quite capable of taking advice when it made sense. She recalled how Elsie had had given her advice on how to be with Hannah and the advice had worked. That was the proof of the pudding –

it worked. She brought her attention back to her daughter. She still wanted to know who this young man was who was laying court to her daughter. She picked up her cup and sipped at it delicately. She had to be told; her daughter knew that so what was the hurry? She would change the subject and hope that Hannah would relax enough to tell her story.

'What sort of dress do you think I should have, Hannah? I know I could not really have a white dress. It wouldn't be seemly but I don't want to have one o' them military looking things, either. I don't think that would suit me.'

'Well, as I've only just heard about the wedding, you can't expect me to just reel a design off the end of my pencil. Give me a couple o' days and I think I might have something worth looking at. After all, you don't want one o' them things in Mabel Stone's window, do you?' She smiled at her mother. 'No, I think something nice and soft and pink would suit you. The last thing you want is to look like a widow! I'm sorry; I know you are a widow but why not look as young and pretty as you can? You want something that will put a pleased look on your husband's face.' She smiled at the startled look on Agnes's face, who hadn't known how the story of his 'pleased' look had spread among the hop pickers. Hannah continued her theme. 'Howard is a very smart, clean looking man and he will want a wife on his arm who matches him, if you know what I mean. Will he be having a new suit, or will he just be putting on his best working jacket? What will you be buying him for a wedding present? Has he got you an engagement ring, yet? When did you get engaged? I bet it was yesterday, wasn't it? And you wanted to tell me before anybody else? Yes, I thought so.'

She started to cry and Agnes put her arms around her again. 'You're quite right, my dear. I didn't want anybody to know before you. It was the least I could do. We do have a few things to talk over as you must have realised. The house, for a start; I sha'n't need two houses shall I? And I might as well make my mind up that I am going to make a go of it with Howard. No thinking to myself that if it don't work out, I can come home again. He's a lovely man and I have to tell you that I think he'll be a better husband than your father ever did, try as he did. It was the work that finished him; that and the booze, and you couldn't blame him for that. It finished a few off, that foundry did.

'Now, I am going to have a word with Elsie Barr, to try to get your place in my house as secure as possible but she is going to want to know what your prospects are, who your young man is, and whether he is the sort of young man that the owners of the house will give a lease to. Is he older than you? Do you expect me to hand over my tenancy to some young man who, at the moment, hasn't even got a name, never mind a prospect?

The other thing is, there might be one or two things that are of sentimental value to me and that I will expect you to hand over to me to be put in my spare room at the cottage or in the kitchen or the parlour, yes it's got a parlour. Whatever jewellery I've got, and I only have a few things, I will share with you. I'd sooner see your face when I give 'em to you than wait till I'm gone and you have to pick 'em up out of some little box.'

She became silent, waiting for Hannah to contribute her thoughts and feelings to the conversation. They were both still near to tears as they waited for the name to be forced, it seemed, out of Hannah's mouth, of the young man in her life.

'Oh, Mom, he's a nice young man. He has taken me out a few times, before you went away on the hop picking and we are regular now, if you know what I mean. His name is Joe Green. He is learning to be a butcher at the butchers on the high Street. He wants to buy his own shop as soon as he can. He is ever so pleasant. I know you will like him. You will give him a chance, won't you, Mom?'

She looked anxiously at her mother. It was obvious that her mother's judgement meant a lot to her.

'I do know Joe Green; at least I did a couple of years ago. He was working at the baker's then. He used to deliver the bread on one of those three-wheeler bikes and I noticed then how polite and courteous he was. I always used to give him a tip. I can't fault him in any way so if you'd like to bring him in, for my approval,

I don't mind. You shouldn't tell him he is being examined as a potential son-in-law of course; more of a casual visit might be more like it. If he calls for you and you're not ready, he could come in to wait for you, and then him and me could renew our friendship. How's that?'

She smiled. Her daughter caught on quickly! 'Yes, that'll do, Mom.'

Her mother rejoined rapidly. 'I don't want him to think he's got any rights to you though. I mean, you are not engaged or anything like that, are you?'

'No, he hasn't asked me any serious questions yet and I haven't been asked back to his mother's house for appraisal. They used to be Grocers but they're both retired now and I believe they are doing all right. I am seeing him tonight, Mom. He's taking me to the pictures. I don't know which one but he seems to like comic pictures. Mind you, they do make you laugh, don't they?'

She changed the subject again. Would you like to see my sewing machine? I can show you a few of the things it can do, in a couple of minutes.' She lifted the cloth covering the machine. 'It's so easy once you get it weighed up, see?'

Hannah sat and started to push the treadle with her feet and Agnes was fascinated as she watched the needle going up and down, hemming a small piece of cotton around the edge of what was obviously a handkerchief. Because it was treadle-operated, Hannah was able to use both hands to keep the cloth positioned just how she wanted it. In a few seconds the handkerchief was finished, just needing ironing.

Hannah gave it triumphantly to her mother. 'See how it gets the job done so quickly, Mom. I could soon get a wedding dress made up for you. You can buy patterns to make up now and there's quite a lot of choice. We could have a look and maybe you will see something that you like. When are you putting the banns up? Whenever it is, I shall still have about three weeks to get it done. I would have to see you to try it on of course but that doesn't take long. You could come home at the weekends and I would have it ready in about a fortnight, I should think. How would that suit you?'

She looked at her mother keenly. She was crying. Now what?

Agnes seemed to collapse into her arms. 'I never thought I would be as lucky as I am, to have another chance at happiness with a wonderful man, and a wonderful daughter to make my wedding dress for me herself. I shall feel like a princess, walking down the aisle.'

There was a knock at the door and the two women looked at each other, questioningly. Agnes strode across the small room and wrenched the door open. A young man stood there.

He looked at her in surprise. 'Why, hallo, Mrs Hollerenshaw. I thought you were down hop picking. I would like a word with your daughter, Hannah, if I may.'

Agnes stood back and made room for him to enter the small house. 'Of course you can have a word with her, Joe isn't it? I see you've lost your bike. I hope you've got a better one, now. Come in.'

He could see she was teasing him in the friendliest of manners and walked in.

'Hello, Hannah. I just wanted to say I might be a few minutes late for the pictures, tonight. I've had to work a bit later. It's a bit of a nuisance but we shouldn't miss any of the performance. Is that all right?' He turned to Agnes.

'I hope you don't mind me taking Hannah to the pictures, Mrs Hollerenshaw. I sha'n't bring her back late and I shall look after her properly.'

'No, that's perfectly alright, Joe. I know she won't come to any harm with you. How is your mother? Is she any better? The last I heard was that she had bad rheumatics in her back. Give her my regards, won't you? Are you just a casual friend of my daughter or does she mean something more than that to you?' She didn't wait for an answer but went straight into another question. Have you seen Hannah's sewing machine? She's been showing me what she can do on it. It's marvellous. She's going to sew a wedding dress on it.'

Joe's face went red. 'I didn't know she was getting married. Honest I didn't.'

Agnes laughed in his face. 'She's not getting married, as far as I know. I am the one getting wed. I am going to marry a friend of mine, Howard Humphries. Hannah is still available, if you are interested!' She laughed again. You fell for that, Joe! I'm sorry I didn't mean to play you up. It was just the way the words came out, that's all.'

Joe's face was still red but he wasn't going to be played with. 'As a matter of fact, I had an idea along those lines, myself but I don't really want to discuss that with anyone, at the moment. When I've got something to say, I'll say it. I really think I'd better go now, Mrs Hollerenshaw. I still have the front of the shop to sweep out. I have to do that. If it was my shop, I would want to leave it clean, eh? I may see you later then, Mrs Hollerenshaw and you, too, Hannah.'

He placed his hat on his head as he went out of the door. Agnes spoke to Hannah. 'It could be an exciting night then, daughter. You'd better get ready – and try to look your best!' She spoke in her slightly teasing manner that Hannah knew well, but there was a tone of seriousness behind her words.

Hannah looked at her mother with a mock careful tone. 'What was it like for you, Mom? How did Dad and Howard put the question to you? Did they get down on one knee and implore you to accept their hand?'

'No; it was nothing like that in either case. Your Dad just said, 'I suppose we'd better get wed, our wench. We've been courting for four years now so people will be expecting a wedding from us. What do you think?' 'There was nothing I could say, really so I just nodded at him and that was that settled. He was never one for show, was he?'

'And how about Howard, Mom? Was he romantic?'

'Well, yes, he was as a matter of fact. We were sitting on his bed, not that we were up to anything, he was just showing me round his cottage. We sat down to look out of the window when he just kissed me and told me he loved me and asked me to marry him. It was lovely, really. It was a real surprise but I wouldn't have wanted it to be any different.

'You'll see when it happens to you. It could be tonight but you never can tell. Your young man, I suppose we're talking about Joe, might get a bit nervous about asking you in the pictures but I bet there's lots of girls been proposed to there. Just be patient and he'll surprise you. Do you want to marry him? That's the thing. It's nice being proposed to and all that stuff but when you come to think about it, is he the one for you, the only one?'

'You've only got yourself to answer to, you know. As far as I am concerned, he is a nice young man and I would be pleased for you to marry him but if you don't want to, well, you can carry on living in my house on your own for as long as you like, working away on your sewing machine like a busy little bee. In that respect, do you think Joe would expect you to invite him into my house, although it will be yours as soon as you are twenty-one? The other thing is, do you think Joe would be one of those men who would expect you to give up any sort of work and just concentrate on being a good housewife?' She looked up at the clock. 'It's nearly time for him to come back. You'd better start getting ready for him. I shan't wait up for you. I've had a busy day, what with the travelling. I have things to think about as well, you know. I wonder what my Howard has been up to, today, while I have been coming here. I'll make meself another cup o' tay and then go to bed if you don't mind.'

She leaned forward and gave her daughter a kiss. It had been a long day for each of them and it might not be over yet. She was glad to be in bed although she knew her daughter might easily come crashing into her room with news that could change her life. She sipped her tea and put the cup down. It was time.

She went up the stairs feeling that the day, in a way, was only half over but she was so tired that she dropped off to sleep as she put her head on the pillow.

12. Howard's and Agnes's Wedding.
November 1915

The wedding was to be early in November. It was now late October and the banns had been read, Agnes had met the Rector and they had liked each other instantly.

Hannah has been proposed to by Joe and she had accepted. They were not to get married just yet, in order to avoid interfering with Agnes and Howard's wedding. Elsie had been consulted about Joe's suitability as a groom and, after investigating, had pronounced him to be in good standing with Mister Jenkins, who managed the property. Hannah will be twenty-one and a full tenant of the little house after Agnes has married. There has been no mention of Joe taking over the tenancy yet.

All the workers at Home Farm had been invited to the ceremony. To Jenny's delight her husband, Albert, came home for a few days leave, after being shot, in France. It was expected that he would soon recover, the wound being a small one in his shoulder, preventing him going into the front line for a short time. He was delighted to see how Jenny, with the help of her friends, had handled the problem of getting in the hops as he had been worrying, as a farmer does when he has insufficient labour to carry out his tasks.

The wedding reception is to be at the Hop Pole and a number of the soldiers who have helped with the hop picking, were invited.

The wedding dress had been designed and re-designed. It had been tacked together three times and taken apart for improvements. It is now a soft pink material with a skirt that extends halfway down her calf, making a pretty show of her ankles that will pull Howard's eyes to her. Her shoes have a three inch heel, accentuating the curve of her ankles.

Joe is coming to the wedding. His boss had given him the day off, providing he makes up the hours the following week. He has bought a new suit which he says he will only wear once before his own wedding which was going to be in Wednesbury. Hannah is quite pleased with the small, crossover diamond ring that he has given her. He has promised to buy her a bigger one when he comes into his own, whatever that means.

Hannah is attending in a dress that matches her mother's. She thinks it is the right thing to do. She is working on a white dress for herself, of course. She has also taken some orders for her work. Elsie has recommended her to a number of people and she is getting quite busy. It is taking her all her time to get her own wedding dress ready.

Joe doesn't want her to give up work. He doesn't believe in it. He feels that a family should advance by as many different ways as possible. He is saving towards his own shop. He doesn't quite have it all planned out yet but he will, when the time came. There is a possibility that his boss might want to sell, when his time for retirement comes, shortly.

The wedding is to be at eleven o'clock and will take about half an hour. That will leave time for everyone to have lunch at the Hop Pole. Howard and Agnes will ride to the church in their little trap, which Howard has painted in a nice pink colour to match Agnes's dress. They are praying for fine weather. Albert Walker in his Army uniform will be Howard's best man; Jenny Walker will be the Matron of Honour and Elsie Barr is coming as a special guest.

She is being escorted by Stephen Stone who, as a special favour, he says, is going to grace the event with his presence. He claims that the real reason he is coming is to give a lift to young Tom, whose father is somewhere in France.

Agnes and Howard are both up early. She has arranged to be waiting for Albert Walker at Home Farm at ten o'clock so that they will be ready at the Church and waiting for Howard. Howard has a few chores to do before he starts out but he will be there on time, waiting for his lady, as he now always calls her.

There are about fifty people on the left side of the church and about six on the Groom's side, on the right of the Church. It seems to be very quiet for a few minutes and then someone whispers the news that the Bride is coming and the organ starts to play.

Albert Walker peers round Howard and speaks softly to him. 'She's coming, Howard. Aren't you the lucky one?' Howard turns slightly, looks back at his bride and a very pleased look comes to his face. He colours slightly then gets himself under control as she draws level.

'Hello, my Lady,' he whispers. 'You look a picture. I'm glad it's me you are marrying. I'd be terrible jealous if it was anybody else.'

She smiles and stands next to him and the Rector starts the service. 'We are gathered together in the sight of God to witness the marriage of Howard and Agnes. This is an honourable state…'

The service seems to go quite quickly Howard thinks and he finds the singing of his favourite hymns a pleasure. He looks round at the church he has known since he was a boy. It has not changed much.

This is where he stood as a young man with Tilly, his first wife. He can't help thinking she is somehow aware of him, and doesn't mind, and is smiling benevolently. It is an old church, some of it of 13th Century. There are changes to come, he knows. The churchyard is closing soon and a new cemetery is being prepared. That is probably where he will lie. He never purchased a double grave so he will probably lie with Agnes instead of Tilly.

The choir stalls are of oak and are well made, with small Norman arches carved into them to let the light into the darker areas. The windows in the East transept were large and let the whole chancel flood with light. It has stopped him from dozing, a few times.

*

Almost before he knew it, the service was over and they were parading down the aisle. He has kissed Agnes to the delight of the congregation and herself. There was a crowd awaiting them as they emerged from the service and Joe had brought a camera to take pictures. They were all pushed and cajoled into place and told to smile at the camera and then it was time to move on to the Hop Pole. Albert Walker had the trap at the front, ready to receive them and a few minutes later they were being welcomed with wine by the landlord.

'Nice to see you, Howard, and this is your bride! My but she's beautiful. I bet she changes her clothes before she starts picking the beetroot out of that patch of yours. '

Everybody seemed to grin and smile at the joke and then they lifted their glasses again to welcome the guests who are coming along from the Church. In a few minutes the hotel was full of people jostling for drinks and food. The horses were led around to the back of the hotel and were looked after by a hosteller. There were mince pies in anticipation of Christmas and pork pies, beef sandwiches and hot food in the form of soup and stew, which was Agnes's idea because she likes stew.

Quite a few of the townspeople know Howard and one comments. 'You can tell he's pleased with himself. Look at the expression on his face!'

It is true. Howard really lets himself go, looking pleased at everyone he speaks to.

'Yes,' he said. 'I know she's beautiful but I saw her first. You will have to join the queue, after me!'

He reached and put his arm around her, possessively. He doesn't want to share her with anyone. He looked across the room and caught Hannah looking at him He looks back at her in his most pleased fashion and she strides over to him.

'I hope my husband looks at me like that on the day we get married, Howard. I hope you don't mind me calling you Howard. Stepfather seems too much of a mouthful and Howard is friendlier, don't you think? My Betrothed is looking around for ideas for our wedding. We'll never save enough to get married as quickly as you but by then I should think he'll have enough ideas for any sort of reception. There should be plenty of meat, anyway.' She smiled. 'You haven't really had much more than a quick introduction to my chap, have you, Howard?' She gave a quick gesture and Joe came over and spoke to Howard immediately.

'Hello, Mister Humphries. You look very pleased with yourself, as you should with such an attractive bride on your arm. I should like to offer my congratulations.' He held his hand out and Howard shook it vigorously.

'Thank you, young man. I just hope you are as happy as we are, on your day. How is your trade? I hear you are a butcher in the wings. That's our way of saying that you are a likely success story on the way. I'm sure you know what I mean, don't you?'

This time it was Joe's turn to have a pleased look on his face but he could not find a suitable response. Agnes spoke up then.

'He's not the only one to be a success story, either. Our Hannah's dress ideas have already fallen on rich ground today. Two of the ladies I have just been speaking to have made serious enquiries about my dress and I'm sure there must be others who will be as impressed. She smiled, a very happy look on her face. 'I suppose it would be nice if they could set up shop next door to each other on Bromyard High Street!'

They all laughed but Joe had a serious look on his face. 'I think I'll have to have a serious look around this town. There seems to be a certain amount of money here.'

The talk in the group moves from subject to subject and then suddenly it was time to go, for all of them.

Howard moved closer to Agnes. 'It's time we went, my lady. There are one or two things I'd like to talk to you about, when I get you on your own.' He blushed at his own double entendre but would not be put off. He put down his tankard with a crash that attracted everybody's attention but Albert Walker spoke first. 'Ladies and Gentlemen, I would like to draw your attention to the time. You've all enjoyed yourselves and now it's time for the speeches.' There was a shout of 'Shut up' but he continued. My old friend Howard has just had the luckiest day of his life and I would like you all to offer a toast as old as the hills – The Bride and Groom!'

Now the crowd really let rip with a roar and Howard grabbed Agnes again and led her out to the trap. He could not stand making speeches.

'Come on, Aggie. It's time we weren't here. They've all had their fun and now it's time for us.' He jumped up and took hold of the reins. 'Walk on.' The trap moved slowly forward, leaving the Hop Pole behind. Agnes looked over her shoulder at the crowd, who had followed them out. In front of them was Hannah, holding on to Joe's hand which was round her shoulder.

Agnes felt the first sense of loss since Howard had proposed to her and she realised that she and her daughter had each to go through this sense of loss together. She felt a tear on her cheek and wiped it away furtively. She did not want her new husband to think she had any regrets. She took hold of his free hand as the pony briskly took the two miles in its stride. In twenty minutes they were there.

Strangely she felt tired. She was now fifty-five, she thought, and after a day like today, she had every right to feel tired. Perhaps Howard was tired too. She did not feel like going to bed just yet. Perhaps a drink of that wine would help her to relax. She would feel happier waking up than going to sleep! Howard got down from the trap and opened their door and led her in.

'I'll be back in a minute,' he said and went back out to put the pony away.

She looked round the parlour and the fire was burning bright. A bottle of wine was on the small table. He must have arranged this before he started out, this morning. She suddenly understood, and she opened the wine and filled the two glasses. He came into the house in a hurry and she handed him a glass.

'I've looked forward to this,' he said and drank it in one movement. 'That's the first drink I've had since I got married!' He poured another and offered the bottle to Agnes. 'You'll have a drink with your husband?'

'Of course I will, any time you like, Mister Humphries, so long as you are not going to get drunk.'

She emulated his movements then, drinking the wine in one smooth movement. 'That's my first as well, since I got married. I thought the drinks were only for the guests; I never thought I would get round to having one. Now, I think I'll have another and then I'm going to bed if you don't mind, husband, I am absolutely shattered, I'm sorry.'

She took another drink, emptying her glass and then leaned forward and kissed Howard. 'I expect I'll see you later. Don't wake me up if I'm asleep.'

She smiled at him and made her way up the small stairs.

The room was warm, she noticed. There was a small fireplace and a fire had been laid by someone to warm the room. She pulled the sheets back and, stripping off her own clothes and donning her nightdress, jumped into the bed. The bed was cool, very cool but she was used to that feeling so she warmed up in a few minutes. She hoped Howard was not going to demand his rights. Oh well, she thought, if he does, he does!

She dozed off, not knowing whether to be excited or just to give in to the weariness that was overcoming her. She felt Howard get into bed beside her and his arm went round her as if it was born there.

'Goodnight, my Lady', she heard him say and then it was morning and the sun was shining through the windows. Howard was not there. Where was he? She hoped he was not out in the field already. Suddenly she wanted him near, very near.

She sat up in bed, ready to get dressed as he walked in the door. Suddenly she was shy.

'Good morning, my Lady. Here's a cup of tea for you. It is Sunday after all. I hope you don't expect this treatment every morning. I tried to sleep on but I just couldn't. It's habit I suppose. I am just used to being up and doing, not like you idle hop pickers, sleeping all the time.' He laughed quietly, letting her know he was not serious. 'Here you are then. Drink up.'

Agnes did not take the cup but reached for him and pulled

157

him down to the bed. Quickly he placed the cup on one side while his arms wrapped round her and he placed his lips on hers. Slowly, he moved his hand from her shoulder to her breast. She shivered as he did and she pulled him closer just enjoying the closeness. She undid her night dress and pulled him down to her, his lips biting gently into her nipple.

'Oh, Howard, I like that. Do it again.'

Howard pulled back the sheets and lifted her nightdress to uncover her body. 'And you.' She whispered. I want to see you like you can see me. Howard stood and let his clothes fall to the floor. Agnes reached for him and kissed him and he stumbled onto her, kissing her wherever he could. He found himself on top of her and her legs parted, making it easier for him to ease his way into the joining of their bodies. They forgot all their past and just moved into each other, their passion uniting them completely. Suddenly they climaxed together and sank into a calming disposition, enjoying that as much as the passion.

Later, they just came round and looked at each other in a pleased sort of way. Were they going to adopt the same vernacular? It didn't seem to matter if they did. Most married couples had their own way of communicating with each other.

'Howard,' she whispered, 'there's something I've always wanted and I did think you might have some but you haven't so could I get some for myself? I've got a few bob tucked away so I could buy them for myself. It's just that I would have to have somewhere to keep them.'

Howard leaned over and laughed. 'What on earth are you talking about, woman? You'll have to say what you want before I can even begin to think about it.'

'Well,' She said, 'I know there's different sorts but I don't know which are the best sort, do I?'

'Different sorts of what, Agnes? Different sorts of what? Say something; that's what you've got to do.'

'Chickens, Howard. I've always wanted to keep chickens but I ain't never been able to have some. Can I have some now?'

'Chickens? O' course you can have some chickens. You'll have to be the one who looks after em, though. I wouldn't have time to look after 'em. Anyway, what sort do you fancy? How many would you like? We've plenty of room for 'em. What would you do with the spare uns'? We could only eat so many you know and you would soon get bored with eggs for breakfast, every day.'

He looked pleased with her again and she knew he was happy with her idea. 'Have you got any idea what sort you would like? It all depends what you are going to do with them, you see. If you are going to eat the chickens as well as the eggs, it will be best to choose the heavier type of bird, so that you get more meat in it, see?'

They discussed the subject for a few more enlightening minutes, to make sure she knew what she was talking about and then they went back to what they had been doing before, and they each looked pleased about it.

13. The Fire.

1914

Jack Thurston walked as silently as possible towards the junction of the two main roads in Wednesbury. It was eleven o'clock and the public houses were turning out. He had arranged to meet Henry Wilkins but Henry hadn't turned up. Either something had turned up to stop him or he had got cold feet about the project. He decided to give him another five minutes. He lit a cigarette and just enjoyed the feeling of the Woodbine's smoke passing into his bloodstream.

There was a sound and he turned in alarm. He had never done anything like this. He mentally rehearsed what he would say if he was pulled up by some constable with more enthusiasm than sense. There was a silent shadow making its way towards him. It was Henry. He breathed a sigh of relief.

'You alright?'

'Yes; you?'

'Good. Let's get on with it then, shall we? Which house is hers?'

They both knew what he meant; the house of Elsie Barr, the one they wanted to get their own back on. They had planned this night for a week. Elsie was picking hops to augment her income. She would need more than that when they were finished with her.

They turned down Union Street and turned into a small court as the little squares of house were called. There was an even darker blackness about the area now they were off the main roads. The air smelled of factories and the chemicals that were used. There were no signs of life anywhere in the court.

'It's this one;' Thurston whispered. 'The one with the flower pot on the window sill.'

'Let me get at it, then. I'll be in, in a second if you keep out of my way.'

Thurston stood back as Henry moved forward, his pick-locks in his hand. A moment later they were in, moving silently through the small house. They could see quite well as the street light was shining through the window. It was the only one that had the benefit of a light. Elsewhere, everything was dark.

Henry moved to the fire, putting his hands to it for a joke and then moved back quickly. There was definite warmth from the coals. How had that come about when Elsie Barr was in Worcestershire? He motioned to Thurston to put his hands by the fire and frowned deeply to show he was puzzled. They immediately separated to explore the house for occupants. Henry crept quietly up the wooden stairs, which creaked almost inaudibly. He looked into the bedroom and saw that there was a man lying on the bed. Who was he? It didn't matter too much to him who he destroyed as long as he achieved his purpose.

Wilkins lifted his fist and struck down with all his might. The figure on the bed just slumped a little further and he decided that he no longer needed to be quiet.

'Hey, Jack! Who's this chap? I don't know him. He'll have to go up with the house.'

Thurston moved up the stairs quickly and shook his head in response to Henry's silent question. They searched him and the drawers in the room, taking a coin here and there.

'Come on then; let's do it. We should be out of here in a few minutes. He can stay or go; whatever he likes!'

They moved back down the stairs and piled the clothes and furniture into the centre of the room. They looked at each other.

'Right,' said Wilkins. 'Light it then.'

Jack Thurston took out a box of matches and was just about to strike it when a thought came to him.

'Have a look outside; see if there is anybody about.'

Henry crept to the door and peered outside. The court was still, silent and dark.

'There's nobody about, it's all right.'

Thurston struck the match and lit a piece of newspaper that he had left sticking out of the pile. There was a small flame at first and then it increased until the whole room was lit.

'Come on; that's alight now.'

Henry pulled at Thurston's arm. They both moved out of the front door as flames were beginning to leap from the pile in the middle of the room. They were just going out into the alley that led out of the court when someone shouted.

'Fire! Fire! Get the fire brigade, quick!'

The two men ran as fast as they could up to the top of the road and then slowed down to a walk.

'Light us a fag,' said Henry, 'I can't run so there's no point in tempting people to run after us, is there?'

They slowed to a gentle walk to take suspicion away from them. No one seemed to be taking much notice, anyway.

'I wonder who that bloke was that you killed,' said Thurston. 'I didn't know him at all, but it was too dark anyway. I know one thing; they'll be after us for murder!'

'What do you mean, us? The bloke I killed? I wasn't on my own you know; there was two on us!'

The two men realised that there was no point in arguing about the situation. The police would be trying to identify the man's assailants as soon as his charred body was recovered from the fire. The best thing they could do was to go to ground in some way. They carried on walking and then Henry Wilkins spoke.

'I'm going to go back to my digs, I think. Perhaps we shall meet up again; I don't know. I'll see you sometime.'

'Just you wait a minute, Henry. I seem to remember that you was going to be nice to my landlady for putting you up. You don't think I'm here to pay your bills, do you?'

Henry put his hand in his pocket and pulled out a few sovereigns. He didn't look as if he was all that grateful for being reminded. 'Here, have this; its five pounds. I couldn't get more generous than that, could I?'

He thrust the money into Jack Thurston's hand. Then he was gone, into the night. Jack Thurston there and then decided that that was the best thing he could do, too. He went back to his living quarters as fast as he could, but not without bumping into his landlady as he started to climb the stairs.

'Where you been, Mister Thurston? Where's your mate who was going to be generous because I was letting him stay for a night or two?'

'Hello, Maisie. That bloke decided that he had to get back to his missus. You know how these things work out. He said to tell you he was very grateful and he's left you four pounds. That was nice of him; worn't it?'

Jack put his hand into his pocket and pulled out a variety of change. All together it came to four pounds. Gently he placed it into her hand. She was delighted.

'He was nice then wasn't he? If you see him again, tell him he can say here anytime. At that rate I might let him have the best bed in the house – mine!'

Maisie laughed and passed through the hall into her own living room. Jack Thurston climbed up the stairs slowly, the seeds of worry already in his mind as he climbed into bed and thought about the happenings of the night. Where had Henry Wilkins come from, anyway? He seemed to know his way round Wednesbury but Jack had no idea where he had actually come from.

*

In the burning house, Luke was fighting for his life. He had awoken choking on smoke and fumes as he lay, semi-conscious, in the bed. His head ached from the force of the tremendous blow that Henry Wilkins had given him. His mind had begun to cope, to function to a certain extent when his throat had filled with smoke, forcing his cough reflex to function. As he woke up, he realised that someone had tried to kill him. From then on, the struggle was to stay alive. He managed to get to his feet. The stairway was full of flames and smoke, making that way down impossible. He thought; the window was the only other way out. He tried it and found it jammed. He picked up the great ewer from the dressing table and threw it against the window, shattering it. He leaned out. 'Help,' he shouted. 'Help!'

A face looked up. It was the small boy who occasionally looked after Chalky.

'Get me a ladder quickly or I shall die. The stairs are on fire.'

The small boy ran off immediately and returned in a few seconds with a man, the window cleaner. 'I'll have you down in a few seconds, sir. Just stay calm. I'm just going to get my ladder.'

The man turned and ran away, to disappear into an entry. There was a crash behind Luke. It was the staircase collapsing into a great wall of flames at the bottom of the stairwell. Flames were coming into the room, now. The heat was incredible; he could feel his skin almost frying; his body made him do something. Doing something was better than doing nothing.

He climbed out of the window and lowered himself until he was hanging by his fingertips on the window ledge. Vaguely, he was aware that the window cleaner had returned and was saying something to him. He knew that he had to let go of the window ledge but it seemed so natural to hold on as long as he could. He knew he was only about ten feet above the ground. His fingers were too hot to hold on. He let go.

There was a jolt and he went into blackness. The blackness lasted quite a time. He was in a hospital ward. A policeman was asking him questions but he found it difficult to answer him because of the coughing and choking.

'What were you doing in the house?'

'Where was the owner?'

'Who was the owner?'

'Who was the other person who had been seen running away from the house?'

'How did you get that nasty bruise on the side of your jaw?'

Eventually there was peace.

The sister covered his face with a sheet. Luke had put up a good fight but the smoke had suffocated him, and the fall had broken his back. It would have been a miracle if he had survived. His skin had separated from him and he had had no choice but to let go of the window-sill.

Luke had answered some of the questions that the constable had put to him. It seemed that he had overheard two men planning to break into a house, the owner's house, and damage it in some way, so Luke had gone there and opened it with a key that he always carried. He had intended to keep watch but he had been absolutely exhausted, travelling all day from Bromyard by pony cart with some other man, a Mister Stone, and then he had had a couple of drinks.

There was nothing wrong with having a couple of drinks but it had made him even more tired so Luke had laid his head down, just to rest his eyes. The men; it seemed there had been two, had seen him asleep and wanted to keep him that way so one of them had hit him to keep him quiet. The fire had been lit and they had run off, hoping that no one would see them. Fortunately, a boy had seen the flames from his bedroom window in one of the houses in the court, and had raised his parents. He had seen the men run off but it had been too dark to recognise them.

Now Luke was gone; just like a gaslight that had been turned off. The police were still making enquiries but they had got nowhere yet. Stephen Stone saw the report of the incident in the newspaper and hurried to Wednesbury to look for himself. He saw the Fire-Chief and asked him what he knew.

'It was arson, sir; no doubt about it.' The Fire-Chief looked as if the stress had been too much for him. 'The clothes and furniture were piled in the middle of the room. It was done to inflict the greatest amount of damage that could be done. Mister Bryant wouldn't have known a thing about it until he started to choke from the smoke. I'm not saying it was intended to murder him because they probably didn't know he was there until they discovered him asleep, upstairs, but it is obvious that somebody had really got it in for Mrs Barr!'

The appraisal by the Fire-chief had shocked Stephen. It was only a fortnight since her husband had joined his Regiment, and now this! He was not the only one who had taken advantage of her husband's absence! She had to have an enemy somewhere. He couldn't think who that could be; she was well-liked wherever she went.

Was there another reason for the arson? He couldn't think of anything. Her friends, Betty and Ruth had to be informed in case she was in any danger in Bromyard! The though struck him with another shock. He hurried to Jack Mallory's house a few doors from where the fire had taken place and put it to him.

'I can't think of anybody who has got it in for any of them, Mister Stone. It was a shock to all on us, I can tell you… If you're going down to Worcestershire, will you take a copy of the newspaper with you? They might be able to think of some sort of clue, between them. I hope they're all right down there but I can't see any connection between down there and up here, if you know what I mean.'

They parted and Stephen determined to go down again the following day, to make sure Elsie was still all right. He thought over what he knew and the only one who didn't like Elsie was Mabel! Still, he couldn't imagine Mabel taking any violent action against Elsie. She had heard the news of course, when he got home, and was quite upset. She knew Luke because she too, had had dealings with Sam Jenkins, Luke's employer.

'It's absolutely awful; Stephen. What was the man doing in that woman's house, anyway?'

He tried to explain that he wasn't in possession of all the facts, and that he had made enquiries at the hospital because Luke's wife was at Bromyard, hop picking.

'Really, I don't know why they do that. It must be awful, sleeping in the barns and pigsties. I would hate to do that for a holiday.'

There was no point in continuing the conversation on that tack so Stephen excused himself and went to bed. He had to get up early in the morning. There were contracts to fulfil for the Government.

*

The sky was blue and the women were up early. They were going to try for a record pick, today. It was Ruth's turn to cook the breakfast. Tom was going to help her. He liked cooking and he liked working with Ruth, as she liked working with him. He was nine years old and he reminded her of her own children. She had left them behind because she wouldn't have been able to make her mind up about which child to leave. In the end she had left all of them with her eldest daughter. Carol. Tom took their place and he was for ever doing things for her praise.

This morning he had been looking for eggs, not stealing them; just looking for spare eggs. He had found a dozen spare eggs today and they were all in the frying pan, cooking for breakfast. He was looking at the top end of the field, just looking for more eggs. If he found more, they could be saved for tomorrow.

Suddenly he heard the sound of wheels and hooves. He knew that sound. He had often been out in the trap with his mother. The neigh announcing his arrival confirmed that it was Chalky. It couldn't be his father because he was in the Army.

It was Mister Stone. Tom liked him as well. He nearly always gave Tom some sort of treat. Tom knew that it was his mother that Mister Stone had come to see, not him. He waved to him.

'Good morning Mister Stone. Can I have a ride, if you've come to see Mom?'

'Of course you can, Tom. Come on; jump up. Have you been egg scrumping?'

'You can't scrump eggs, Mister Stone. You scrump apples, not eggs. I found a few spare eggs; that's all, and Auntie Ruth is cooking them for breakfast.'

'What is your Auntie Betty doing, Tom? Is she working yet?'

'No; I think she is having what they call a lie in. She is tired this morning. I think she was up late on Sunday, when Uncle

Luke went home late. Did you take him home?'

'Yes Tom; he came home with me. I have to see your Auntie Betty by herself. I have got some news for her, so when I have told your mother, I think your mother will be the one to tell Betty. When I've finished, just try to keep out of the way for a little while, alright Tom?'

Tom nodded his head in assent as they neared the barn. His mother was standing looking at them, her arms akimbo, and her face glowing with pleasure. Tom suddenly realised that his mother liked Mister Stone more than she liked his father! The thought took and held his attention for a moment. Then he heard her call to the other women.

'Betty; Ruth; Stephen is here and he doesn't look too happy. Will you come over here please?'

The two women came out and stood alongside Elsie, as if they were going to try to protect her from some dread thing. Chalky stopped and his head turned towards Elsie. He always expected a treat or some sort of caress. Stephen was sitting in the trap and Tom was climbing down without any help.

'Hello, Elsie,' Stephen said, 'I've got some news. It's not for you, really; well it is, I suppose. Perhaps you had better see for yourself. It's for you, Betty. I am sorry. I really can't tell you how sorry I am. It's Luke. He was in an incident.' He turned back to Elsie. 'Your house, the one in Wednesbury, was on fire. Luke was in there. Somebody set fire to it. Luke tried to drop from the upstairs window and he broke his back.' He heard Betty gasp but went on. 'He woke up choking and then the fall hurt him. He was taken to hospital but he died during the night.'

He stopped as Betty keened her grief and shock into the cold air. A few minutes ago they had been laughing and joking and now, this. They all gathered round the young, newly widowed woman, attempting to share what she was feeling. Then they looked to Stephen for more information.

'I found out on Monday; it was in the papers. I went to the hospital and they told me what I've told you. Then I went to the

Fire Chief and he told me more. Apparently the furniture was piled in the middle of the downstairs room and all your clothes were piled on top of it. They, there were two of them, must have looked upstairs, the fireman told me and they were surprised to see him there. They hit him, knocking him unconscious, and he stayed that way until the smoke choked him.

'When I was talking to the sister on the ward, she told me that the police had interviewed Luke before he died and they said he told them quite a lot but not enough to identify the bastards, excuse my French. Apparently, when we got home on Sunday, Luke went for a drink and overheard them talking. He decided to sleep in your house and keep an eye on it. It was his bad luck that he dropped off and was knocked unconscious.'

Stephen stood there, his cap in his hand, not knowing what to say next. Young Tom suddenly started crying and everyone recalled how he had played with Luke. It was the first time anyone had considered Tom's feelings. Everyone just assumed that he would have no great feelings about the loss of Luke. Elsie suddenly recalled that Tom had been with her often when she had been rent collecting. She had always taken the rents back to the office and Luke had taken charge of it. He suddenly stopped and spoke. He had gone pale but Elsie knew there was something important on his mind and he was waiting to let it loose, as he always did.

She waited and after a moment Tom moved himself forward to make sure everyone heard the news he was about to disclose to them. The little group moved to let him get into the best position to speak. What was Tom about to tell them?

Once again the young lad was about to risk the wrath and laughter of his elders. Elsie looked at him seriously. He had shown before that he had a mind that thought in unusual ways. What was he going to tell them now?

14. Evil discovered.
1914

'It must have been that nasty man who was shouting at you, the other morning, Mommy. He didn't like you, did he?'

The young lad was quite clear in his mind and Stephen paid attention to him.

'What's this all about, Elsie? Who was shouting at you?'

Stephen looked so fierce that Elsie thought he was going to lose his temper with her. She answered quickly.

'It was that man, Henry Wilkins. He was that man who I caught trying to kill Albert Walker. I whipped him and threatened to take his eye out with the whip if he didn't go away. He went when two of the bushellers helped him out of the gate. That was six years ago! He was here the other day, threatening what he could do now that I hadn't a whip. Ruth sent him on his way with a saucepan of boiling water in his face.' She thought for a moment. 'He couldn't have done this thing, could he? He couldn't have covered the distance, never mind finding out where I lived *and* got an accomplice *and* got in *and* set fire to it. It's a bit far fetched, don't you think?'

Ruth spoke. 'Well, if you can get there in a pony and trap – twice in as many days, surely someone else could do it on the train! For all we know, he might not yet have got back. Shall we go and see?'

It was pie in the sky and they knew it, but it was just about possible. If they didn't investigate now, it would be too late. Wilkins could just say he had been there all the time. There was no point in taking that chance. They had to act now.

'I'll come with you!' It was Elsie. 'You stay and look after Betty,' she said to Ruth. 'I know him just as well as you. Between us, we'll make him think we know all about it. Come on then, let's be about it.' Elsie picked up her whip which was lying in the bottom of the trap, and snapped it in the air. 'Come on, Chalky, just one last effort for today!'

The pony responded to her bidding as if he sensed that this journey was more important than the other journeys he had made in the last few days. In a minute he was pulling them out of the gate, on the way to Bromyard.

'What's all the noise; and what's that mad woman driving like that for?'

It was Jenny Walker, walking to see the source of the noise. Other women had gathered and were listening to the events of the day. There was more and more discussion.

'Stop this!' Jenny was taking control, as she usually did. One of the bushellers had come on the scene and she grabbed him immediately. 'Come with me, Joe. I want to get the police onto this, as soon as we can. If the man is innocent, we can say sorry and slink away but if he's guilty, he'll have a job to get away from the police if they are there when he is being accused.'

The farm shire horses were harnessed to the wagon and all the pickers who could find room, jumped aboard. In half an hour they were in Bromyard and had caught up with Elsie, who was trying to find out where Henry Wilkins lived. She thought it might be an idea to look in the hotels and public houses so she tried all of them. No one knew where he was but one man knew where he lived.

'If you turn off just past The Falcon and look along the lane, you will see an old cottage. He lives there, with the old widow, Nellie Bellars. Just don't tell her that I told you. He'd cut my throat as soon as look at me!'

Elsie trotted Chalky round to The Falcon and took the turning. There was no one about that she could see. She stopped Chalky and climbed down to have a look round. The cottage had smoke coming out of the chimney so it seemed likely that there was some one there. She strode to the gate and went to open it. A noise made her turn round.

'What are you doing here? I thought I'd seen the last of you! Have you got your whip with you? Never mind, I've got mine.

172

Elsie started as the evil voice rang out and Henry Wilkins walked round the end of the little cottage. He reached into his bag and pulled out a long whip. 'Let's see how you like it.'

Crack! The whip caught her on the side of her back and she screamed with pain and tried to run away but he let fly again; Crack! This time she felt the pain like a red hot knife on the side of her face. She fell, and sprawled in the lane; her hand flew to her face and came away, scarlet. The need for flight became imperative.

She stood and ran, all in one breath, screaming as she did so. Chalky responded with a loud neigh and bounded towards her. He looked along the lane and saw Wilkins about to slash at her again.

The pony stood up in the shafts and his two front hooves flew at the man. He missed and Wilkins took the chance to cock his arm again. Crack again. This time the target was Chalky. 'Get out of my way you knacker's dinner. I'll soon sort you out when I've finished with her!'

The whip struck out towards the horse and Elsie took her chance. She threw herself at him, climbing onto his back and digging her nails into his face as deeply as she could. Wilkins pulled himself clear and raised his whip again.

'I'll get you like we got that Back Country bastard; you'll burn alongside him in hell, you bitch!'

Now was his chance, he thought. The whip started to descend but Chalky was quicker. He reared in the shafts again and his hoof struck Wilkins on the side of his leg. He immediately collapsed onto the ground, groaning. It was obvious that he wasn't badly hurt because he stood himself up quite quickly. Elsie spoke.

'Who shall I burn alongside, Henry? Why should I burn? You aren't man enough to make me burn in hell. You'll be there before me!'

'That Black Country bastard who was keeping watch when we went to burn you out; that's who! Now it's my chance to make sure I get the pair on ya!'

He once again raised the whip and was about to lash out at her again when a voice interrupted.

'No, Henry Wilkins, you are going to do nothing except come to the station and answer some questions about an incident in Wednesbury. Come on!'

A Police Sergeant and a constable walked out from behind the gate where they had been watching. Wilkins collapsed on the ground; his mental courage weakening as he saw a life behind bars in front of him. A cheer went up as Jenny and the pickers from the farm marched out and confronted Wilkins.

Ruth marched straight up to him. 'Even with a whip, you ain't much good, are you, Henry?' She turned to the police officers.

'Why don't you let me and the girls try him, Serge? We'd give him a fair trial, wouldn't we girls?'

She put her hands on her hips and twirled herself round, plainly teasing the man. The Sergeant seemed a little embarrassed as Ruth put herself forward so brazenly. He nodded to the constable and he stepped forward and put handcuffs on Wilkins's wrists.

'Move on, you', he said to the Black Country woman, 'before you get put in cuffs for lewd behaviour.'

He seemed to feel that Wilkins was being punished enough within the scope of the law, without being punished by a gang of women. The women seemed to get rid of their high spirits then, and just stood along the kerbside, watching Wilkins being taken away. Jenny put things under control and had them all back at the farm, working, within an hour. For the first time in his life, Stephen Stone had taken a back seat, being quite content to watch the Black Country women in action. He was very proud of the small group of friends and the way they had closed ranks, looking after each other's interests. He put his arm around the shoulder of Tom, explaining.

'That's what friends are for, Tom, to be helped when they need it and to help you when you need it.'

It was a day that Elsie never forgot, watching the murderer of her best friend being taken away. She had a deep personal satisfaction in being partly instrumental in bringing him to justice. Betty was deeply affected by the loss of her husband, and the arrest of his assailant brought her little comfort. The two friends were often crying in each other's arms.

Ruth was the only one who felt any triumph from the arrest. She had seen through Henry, she declared, and had been glad to see him go. He was a cowardly, skiving bastard. That was the only way she would describe him.

Stephen had been obliged to return home to his work, running his family's business and kept his small part in the affair under cover. Gradually the incident was forgotten and September and the picking season came to an end. The day came when they were all going home on the train. Most of the women had saved their pay until they were paid on their last day at the farm. The journey seemed to go more quickly now; they were getting used to it.

The Blowers Green station seemed very quiet when they got down from the train. Perhaps it was because the men were all in the Army. There were very few men around the station, anyway. Stephen was waiting for them, with Chalky. He was obviously taking a chance, as any of his employees might have told his wife where he was. They parted company, Betty to her lonely home, Ruth to her husband and Elsie to her little house in Wednesbury to look at the damage.

When she first entered the house, it looked as it had not suffered any damage but as she entered further, the burning of it became apparent. There was a terrible smell of burned flesh and wet but burned clothing, all mixed together. Elsie went back out of the door and heaved, her stomach emptying its contents. Stephen put his arm around her in an attempt to comfort her but she could not be consoled. In the end he knew he could only leave time to heal her loss of a good and rare friend who had loved her in his own way.

'I'll see you as soon as I can, my love.' He whispered. 'I have to go now'

He was in the cleft stick that every man finds himself in when he attempts to lead a complicated love life; he had to go and he had to stay. Elsie waved her hand weakly at him, giving him a signalled permission to go, and carry on with the other aspects of his life. He was bound by his love for Elsie to carry on, and he was bound by his love and duty to carry on living with his wife. No wonder it was called 'carrying on', he thought.

Betty was suffering too, of course. Luke had been a wonderful husband to her and they had looked forward to many happy years together. He had bought a small but modern house for himself and his wife, near Brunswick Park, not far from the centre of Wednesbury. Now she had it all to herself. The fact that his murderer had been caught and would almost certainly be sentenced to be hanged was no consolation to her. Now they all had to get on with their lives, making the best of them. That was what Elsie was thinking about.

Tom was sad, too. He had been fond of Luke, who he had called Uncle Luke. He was growing up, thinking all the time, now. It had been a remark from him that had set them on the trail of Luke's killer. There was something about the memory of the incident that kept bothering Elsie but she couldn't recall what it was. She dismissed it; it would come to her if it was of any importance. She turned to her son.

'Come on, Tom. I think we've finished here. I'll get a painter to sort this place out. It needs all the furniture throwing out into the yard, and then tidying and re-painting.'

Elsie took his arm and they walked out of the court, knowing that Ruth would keep an eye on the little house for her. It was Sunday, a day for praying so she went to church, recalling how Dan used to accompany her before they were married. Tom didn't like church all that much but he knew it pleased his mother if he went with her.

He did like the *Nunc Dimittis*, the psalm-like canticle that was chanted at the end of Evensong. The sound of the voices chanting 'O Lord now lettest thou thy servant depart in peace, according to thy Word' always filled him with a deep religious emotion that stayed with him. There was more comfort in that, he thought, than hanging killers, no matter how guilty they were.

Stephen had promised to leave Chalky for them when they came out of church and it was good to know that he had kept his word about that. Tom was thinking about events, too.

'Mom,' he said, as they were walking back to the court. 'Do you remember that he said something like, 'When we burnt you out.' If he meant it, when he said 'we', there must be an accomplice, mustn't there? I'm not sure enough to swear it but I think that was what he said.' He was silent for a moment. 'Is there another enemy around, somewhere? I remember that there was a time when Auntie Betty was very sad and then she became happy. What was that about, Mom? Could there be a connection?'

'Oh, Tom; you are always asking questions. Why do you keep all these things in your head? I don't know of any other enemies, I'm sure.'

She was getting annoyed with the lad, now. He was always thinking. There was no end to him. Still, he made her think. What he was putting forward was about the time when Betty had been getting attacked nightly, by her father. Could there be a connection? Tom had been younger at the time but he had never been sent out of the room as so many children were, to protect them from the 'effects' of adult conversation. Elsie had seen him, many times, sitting in a corner of the room with his head cocked on one side and she had wondered what he was making of the subjects they were talking about.

There was no way that she could think of Jack Thurston making any connection with Henry Wilkins. Tom was overtaxing his imagination again. They had thought that though, about Wilkins. She must try to keep an open mind about Tom's suggestions. He seemed to have a gift for putting this sort of thing together. Perhaps he was destined to become a policeman. The thought amused her but it seemed to be a family trait. She remembered her mother telling her to 'listen and try to put two and two together' when she had been young, and she had done it herself, making people think she had some sort of gift. Today he was just humming the *Nunc Dimmitis* under his breath, seemingly not taking much notice of anything.

The pony was waiting for them at the ostler's, where Stephen had left him and he neighed as soon as he heard them getting close. There seemed little else to discuss so they harnessed Chalky and drove home, to their house in Willenhall.

The thought of her house, burned inside to help in a murder made her determined to live there again as a fight against the evil behind the arson. It was her house and no one was going to take it away from her. She realised that she had no idea how Thurston spent his time, even whether he had a job or not. She would find that little man who Luke used to go to, to find out things. That was the way forward.

15. Bad News.

1915

Elsie awoke the next morning with terrible vomiting, the result, she thought, of too much driving and too much stress the day before. She arose and took some medicine to try to ease the pains and eventually they went. She should see Mister Jenkins today, to try to get her affairs in order. Strange how your mind still carries on arranging things while your belly aches, she thought. She made up her mind to see him. The painting and cleaning of the little house needed organising and Mister Jenkins would organise that, Elsie felt sure.

The elderly solicitor admitted her immediately when the new clerk announced that she was there. He was looking older now. His hair was grey but his eyes were just as searching when he looked her over.

'Good morning, Elsie.' He had long given up calling her Mrs Barr. 'You have had a nasty ordeal, I hear.' He waited for her to sit. 'I am glad you've called in. The fact is I need you to help with the rents. Now that you are spending so much time away from the business and Luke being…' He stopped for a moment. Luke had been like a son to him, she knew. 'I need more hands, if you know what I mean. Is it possible that you know of anyone that might be suitable for the work, male or female?'

Elsie's mind immediately fled to Betty. The girl had matured since she had married, and had no children to hold her back.

'Yes, I think I do know a suitable person. Luke's wife, Betty, could do the work, I am sure. She may need an income now that her husband has been taken from her. I know that she has helped Luke with his work, in the past, just to keep him company, and she is quite a bright sort of woman, clean and tidy. She can add up and take away and write the answer down neatly without dropping ink all over the account books. I also know she is as honest as the day is long and you will never have to worry about where the money is for the rents. It will always be either in her apron pocket or in the safe or the bank. Oh, Mister Jenkins, Betty ought to have a chance, if it's just to make up for the loss of her husband after he worked for you for all those years.'

Sam Jenkins sat and smiled. Elsie was just confirming what he had been thinking himself. He had decided already that that was what he needed to do. He had missed Elsie while she had been away on the hop picking, and Luke had had to help out to cover her absence. Now Luke would never be back to help out in so many ways. He had been a very useful man, knowing all sorts of people who would do any sort of dirty job that needed to be done.

Jenkins suspected that Luke had been involved in some way with the incident of Thurston, a few years back, but not a word of suspicion had ever attached itself to him. He had known that Betty had been abused by her father but he had never known that Elsie and Mary had asked Luke for help. It had been just a feeling, really. Little things, like not ever talking about the incident; that sort of thing made him suspicious. He had a theory that it wasn't what you said about something; it was what you would normally say, but weren't saying.

It was a pattern of speech that revealed that there was something to hide. He returned to the moment. 'Yes, well, I'll think on what you have said, Elsie. There are one or two others who I have to consider but if I decide, I will let you know. Now, there are rents to be collected and although most of what you are collecting will be your own, they won't collect themselves.'

Elsie smiled and went back to her own little office. He couldn't get out of the habit of playing his cards close to his chest! She would have bet that he would select Betty, just on her recommendation but he tried to retain the air of having some mysterious way of getting information about applicants. The truth was that he seemed to take a liking to the ones he chose. That was how he had come to a decision about *her* selection, Elsie felt sure. She put the subject out of her mind and got on with the work of the day. There was plenty to do.

It was a poor day to set off down the High Street, popping

into shops on the way, discretely collecting any owed rents. The weather was very cool and there was a dirty fog hiding the normally clear view of the shops. This was caused by the factories letting clouds of noxious fumes into the already misty atmosphere.

Some of their clients paid weekly, some monthly and some quarterly. It was only a few minutes walk to the bottom of the long sloping hill, and then she crossed over and started to make her way back up the other side of the street. It was a pity that they couldn't find a better, cleaner way of getting rid of the exhaust gases. It made her feel sick. She had been troubled by the sickness she seemed to have every day since she had been back in the Black Country. It was her private dream to move down to Bromyard on a permanent basis. The thought of that wonderful clean air made her long for it all the more, and increased her feeling of nausea.

It was a long walk up the long hill and then she turned off, into Union Street. As Elsie walked into the little court where she lived, she noticed that Peter Martin, the painter was supervising the removal of her furniture from the house. On impulse Elsie walked across to him.

'Good morning, Mister Martin. How are you getting on? You seem to be doing very well.' She knew him as Peter but there had been much publicity about a Peter the Painter, in London, and she knew he occasionally took a mild ribbing about his name. 'You've made a really quick start!'

Peter Martin turned and saw her, his honest face taking on a look of pleasure. 'Good morning, Mrs Barr. Yes, as a matter of fact I was glad of the work. It seems a bit tight, just lately. What would you like me to do with the furniture?'

Elsie looked at the slightly scorched furniture. 'As far as I am concerned, it all burned, so if you know anyone who needs scorched furniture, they are welcome to it. It's not that I can afford to throw it away, you understand, but I can't bear to think of them men walking into my house and handling it all. It makes you feel dirty, if you know what I mean. Just strip the house out and start from scratch. After all, I may want to rent it out again. It might as well be ready for whoever goes to live there.'

He received a quick smile, and then she walked into the house and picked up a few items that she was not able to think of throwing away; photographs and small presents from Dan. There were also a few toys belonging to Tom, which she decided to keep.

She put them in a corner and returned to Peter. 'I've put a few things on one side for keeping. I'll be back later for them,' she informed him. 'I'll talk over the colours with you, tomorrow.'

Elsie couldn't face making decisions about the house where she had spent so many happy days. This was where Dan had been brought when he had fallen from his bicycle. The thought made her think of Ruth who had taken an instant liking to Dan, that night. Elsie felt sure that they had had an affair since then. She turned and knocked on Ruth's door. It was time she had a cup of tea.

Ruth called her in immediately. 'Hello love. You didn't waste much time coming round. You're very welcome. Let's have a cuppa together.'

Ruth bustled into the tiny kitchen, preparing the makings for the tea. Elsie sat for a minute or two, patiently waiting. She seemed to spend so much time waiting around. No, she didn't, she argued with herself. She had been busy for the last six weeks and even now, she was trying to catch up on things she should have done and hadn't. She was beginning to get up to date with her collections. She knew which rents she should collect first, in case they spent it on food or drink, and which ones she could safely leave until it was convenient for her to call. Her mind wandered again, over the events of the last few weeks. What a lot had happened. Her husband was probably in France, now. Her best friend had died at the hands of a murderer, without having to wear a uniform.

Elsie had a lover, and she didn't care a damn how his wife Mabel was affected by it; she was going to live! Suddenly Elsie felt nauseous again and strode quickly to the front door. She managed to control it but she turned to Ruth, quickly.

'Have you got a bowl, Ruth? I'm sorry but I feel sick again. I'm sick of it!' She laughed. 'Thanks, love. It just comes on me some time. Must be something I've eaten.'

She sat herself by the fireplace, shivering. It wasn't cold. Why was she sick?

Ruth was speaking to her. 'Elsie; are you sick every morning?'

'Well, I suppose I have been the last few days. Why do you ask?'

Elsie thought; the answer was clear. It had been the night before he had left to join the Staffies. She had known then that she was pregnant, she had discovered that in August, when Dan was going away with the Army.

'Well, Jack ain't joined up; nor has he made a fortune, unless he's made it for your in-law, Fred Stone. It's about time Fred retired and let my Jack have the business. Jack could run that place with his eyes closed.'

Elsie was finding it hard to concentrate on what Ruth was saying. Something was on her mind again. It was what Tom had said. She broached the subject.

'Do you know what my Tom said, Ruth? He said that it must be Betty's dad, Jack Thurston, who was working with Henry to set fire to the house. I don't know where he gets his ideas from but he does have 'em.'

'Well why not, Elsie? I've always thought he was a bit bright. Not clever but with a different way of thinking, if you know what I mean. I don't really know how it could have been Jack. I don't think he's got it in him not now he's had the chop, so to speak, but you never know.'

Ruth fell silent, and Elsie started thinking of the ways that fate had affected them and brought them together. Theirs was an unlikely friendship but it had seemed to work out, each helping the other when help was needed. Had Ruth been in bed with Dan while she had been working, collecting rents?

There was one consolation. Neither Dan nor Ruth knew that Elsie actually owned property in Wednesbury. She owned the house that had been burned out and the house that Ruth lived in. She also owned the house in Willenhall that Dan had paid rent on as their family home, as well as a number of other properties. It was her secret and she would make sure that it was never revealed until after she died.

In the meantime, she would attempt to educate Tom in the ways of money. Tom was the most important being in her life. She had already seen that he had his own way of looking at situations and of coming to conclusions about them. It was Tom who had first deduced that it must have been Wilkins who had killed Luke. Now he was theorising about Jack Thurston and he could be right.

Before Luke had died, he would have been the one she would have turned to, to check on Jack Thurston. She had served a sort of apprenticeship with him, in her earlier property dealings. He had known all about Thurston and had played a part in protecting Betty against his advances, before they had married. Perhaps Thurston had had a suspicion about Luke's connection and was taking revenge. In that case, did he have any suspicions about her connections with the affair?

It was unlikely but there always seemed to be little wisps of information in the air, and if you picked them up, you could at least build a theory that might or not be true.

'Time for another?'

It was Ruth, breaking in on her thoughts. She was like that; nothing subtle. What you saw what you got, as they said.

'Yes, all right Ruth. That would be nice; then I'll have to move myself. I've a lot to do, today.'

'What have you got to do, then?'

There she was again; straight to the point. She was getting a bit nosy about things, thought Elsie.

'Oh; just this and that. I might go and see the doctor in Willenhall, when I have finished here. I might as well know how

I am; mightn't I?'

She wanted to see Betty first, to see how she was. The girl had been through a lot, and Elsie wanted to help her to make arrangements for the funeral, if she agreed. Elsie made her goodbye to Ruth and made her way to the fashionable home near Brunswick Park, where Betty lived. The bell rang noisily, making it sound as if the house was empty, but the door opened quite quickly and Betty, in black, welcomed her, although her face was drawn.

'Oh, I am glad to see you, Elsie. I've just rattled around in this house with nothing to do. I was hoping you'd call. There are so many things to do that I don't know where to start.'

Betty looked so forlorn that Elsie almost burst into tears. They were almost dripping down her cheeks. Elsie followed her as she turned her back and led the way into the front room of the house. Elsie decided to ask her questions before she had chance to evade them.

'Listen, Betty; I know you've had a difficult time but I'm trying to work out one or two things. In the first place, Tom has said to me that he thinks that it might have been your father who burned the house. That might not sound much but Tom usually, or unusually, take your choice, manages to isolate the cause of the incident. He has managed to say to me that he thinks that it is Jack that he suspects. He thinks that it might be Jack who is intent on destroying you – and me. I am sure Ruth was a target as well but that has probably gone now that Henry is inside, out of the way. I don't know how we can test the theory, do you?'

Betty was still shivering and Elsie could not see whether it was because of the cold, or for a more nervous reason. She poked at the fire, making if flare up and send a little more heat into the room. It was a cold day, anyway.

Suddenly Betty started. 'I wonder if it would be possible to trace the trail of Henry, after he came to Wednesbury. If we had a picture of him, we could follow his trail by asking people, in pubs for instance. If we found someone who had seen him, we could ask them if they remembered who he was with. I've got a picture of Dad, and we could ask anyone who saw Henry, if they also saw Jack!'

'I think it has the seed of a good way to proceed.' Elsie said, voicing her thoughts about it. 'The only possible flaw is that it might be hard for us to find somebody who would be willing to open up to a couple of women. It might be better if we could find a man who would be better able to go casually into the pubs. There is a man who Luke used to use for this sort of investigation. If you like, I'll ask him to have a go for us. What do you think?'

Betty's response was immediate. 'Yes, of course! That's a much better idea. If you can find that man to do the investigating and set him to work, we shall have the pair of them behind bars. Maybe, just maybe, they will never come out. They could be hung, and I'd pull the rope, even if he is my father!'

Elsie said goodbye to her friend and made her way to Mister Jenkins's office. She explained her theory to him and he saw the possible benefit behind the proposed surveillance. It was a small price to pay for the information it might reveal He promised to get something done along those lines as soon as he could. Elsie felt that the day had taken two, to pass. She made her way home to Willenhall and put Chalky away. Tom was ready for bed and so was she.

Bed was a blessing she had looked forward to for hours. She was asleep in seconds but it was a sleep troubled by thoughts and visions of the people in her life; Jack Thurston, Luke, Stephen and Dan and Tom. It was strange how they all got mixed up in her thoughts. Perhaps there was a meaning to dreams but if there was, she couldn't divine it. She had a theory of her own that your brain just got mixed up while you were asleep and that, therefore, dreams meant only what you made of them when you thought about them when you were awake.

It wasn't just herself that thought in that way. It was young Tom. He seemed to have a talent for thinking about events and a memory for things of significance. How had Tom known that anyone was about to come into the house in the middle of the night?

It looked as if whatever talent he had, it had been passed down from the female side of the family, herself and her mother. It might be a useful gift to have but it must be quite disconcerting for the lad to have these impulses about people and events. How could she help him to come to terms with his gift, if that was what it was?

Before she knew it, it was time to get up again and start on the business of the day.

16. Mabel's Loss.
1915

Mabel Stone was happy; she was pregnant again; another daughter, she felt sure. She liked daughters. Girls were that much brighter than boys, though they didn't ever realise it for years. Stephen had been coming to her bed in need since just after that Barr woman had gone down to Bromyard again. She couldn't bring herself to hate the girl but she was a nuisance, interfering in her married life.

Mabel knew that Stephen had only married her, and she had only married him, because of family pressures. She, herself, had wanted to marry one of the locksmiths, Harry Bunn, who had worked at her father's factory. He had tried to break her from the hold her family had over her but he'd had no chance. In the end he had left to form his own little, specialist locksmith's shop where he made locks to order, for special applications.

Mabel had seen him occasionally, by accident, and they had snatched a few moments sweet conversation but it could come to nothing so in the end they had both accepted the way things were. He hadn't had the courage or the wit to get what he wanted from her; neither had she, she later realised. Anyway, Stephen had been willing to sleep with her. He knew his place as the stud bull of the family and performed his duties with pleasure, regardless of the other woman occasionally in his life.

Men were like that, she thought, always willing to be put to stud. She couldn't bring herself to be like that. She only wanted one man, and that one, now, was Stephen.

Their son Stanley was an unknown quantity at the moment with little sign of any potential. Stephen had plans to enlarge the haberdashery shop, to create more trade to be shared by her and their girls.

Stephen climbed into the large bed that he had ordered for them, to 'provide space in case the children wanted to jump in with them.' The truth was that he took up a lot of space in bed, always moving around. He moved round now, his hands feeling for hers, and then moving onto her body. Mabel enjoyed this part of their day; the touch of his hands made her feel all tremulous, as she imagined a butterfly would, about to mate almost hesitantly with another.

Suddenly she took his hands impulsively and clasped them to her breasts. Sometimes she got brave and did things they hadn't done before, just to bring newness to their bed. She felt like that tonight. What could she do? She slid down the bed, touching him in that way, until her face came level with his loins. Stephen started and then moved urgently against her, pushing into her mouth.

They had never done this before and it was soon obvious that he was getting past the point where he was able to control himself. Instead of instinctively pulling away from the contact, she stayed with it. His climax wasn't as bad as she had anticipated. She felt her own surge and accepted it, accepting his climax as well, feeling his wonder and her own.

They separated for a while and then she cleaned herself off. She smiled. It didn't feel so terrible. She imagined what her mother would have said to her. She would have been horrified at the thought of sharing their most intimate intimacies in such a way.

Stephen lay back. He was amazed that Mabel was able to bring herself to take part in such sexual activities. He had never known such a feeling, even with Elsie but he would teach her. Perhaps it would be possible to reverse the roles. The thought was the father of the deed. He started by sliding down the bed and sliding her nightdress upward at the same time. He kissed her.

'Did you like that?'

He felt her head nodding and wanting to please her, lowered his head again. Her surge came again. He was amazed and found himself becoming proud again. His body slid upward again, unable to give without taking as well. He slid into her and as soon as he entered her, they both climaxed. It was the most wonderful sensation that either of them had ever known.

In a few moments the exhausted couple had fallen asleep, not in each other's arms but just sleeping where they lay, the needs of the night before, gone. They had been together but not altogether.

The next day, Stephen sat at his dinner, looking sourly at his wife. She was pregnant, a blasted nuisance. He wanted to walk round the corner to see his Elsie, to hold her in his arms, and comfort her. The three women had been through a terrible time at the farm and, due to his commitments to his formal family, he had not been able to influence any of the events that had arisen from them. He felt absolutely frustrated. He stood up, his meal finished.

'I'm going for a drink,' he announced, 'I'll see you later. Lock up; there are some strange men around just lately and I don't want to come home to a butchered family.'

He smiled at his joke as he put his large overcoat on. It was five minutes walk to where Elsie lived and he half-walked, half-ran the distance. She answered the door quickly when he knocked and pulled him in, pushed the door closed and threw her arms round him. He felt her body quivering next to his and his heart went out to her. It was clear how she was feeling. Was it through her experience with Dan or was it something else?

He pulled her close to him; wanting and needing the closeness to make him feel whole, as if she were the other half of himself. He had tried, and continued to try, to carry out his familial duties. He tried to put himself in Mabel's position and felt for her. She too, must feel the something that was missing from their relationship and he sympathised with her. Did she sympathise with his predicament?

Why did he think, this minute, when Elsie was in his arms, of Mabel's problem? Why had he been thinking of Elsie when he had been in the bosom of his family, five minutes ago? The whole situation was ridiculous and any man who called himself a man would have solved the problem by making a decision to discontinue the relationship with one of the women.

They had three children and now had another on the way.

There was something else worrying Elsie; he could sense it. He couldn't really ask her; she would have to tell him. He was beginning to enjoy the closeness and his body was responding to it. His lips moved from her lips to her neck, moving along to the centre of her body. Suddenly she stiffened.

'Is that all you think about, your body needs? Are all men the same? Am I just here to satisfy your wants?'

The strain of the situation was getting to her. She knew that she could not win him over to do what her heart wanted – and it was her heart that influencing her behaviour now. He knew that and although he thought of himself as a powerful man, he felt weak at the thought of doing those things to his wife and family that would put his and Elsie's relationship right in a formal way.

Divorce was frowned upon in business. You could do anything short of that, it seemed, but once you stepped over a certain line you would suffer censure from Church and Business alike. It was unthinkable.

He pulled his body away from hers. He had no right to be making demands. Her husband was serving the country and her loyalty should be to him, regardless of how she felt about any other man. He was not the only one with problems of the relationship. They had never faced up to the problems in a way that showed they intended to solve them. They never would. There were too many constraints. He voiced them.

'I'm sorry you think of me like that, Elsie; I really am. I think the world of you. It's just that so many people have so many expectations of the way I should behave. There isn't just you to consider, you know. There's my father and mother, who expect me to work in and expand their little factory and be proud of it. There is my wife's family who expect me to be a perfect son-in-law, bringing my skills and money to provide their fat daughter with a home and a handful of grandchildren to carry on their line.

There are my children, who, when they arrive, who will also have a right to expect me to be the perfect father, when I know, and I know you hadn't thought of this, I know, that my son is living with no knowledge of who his most proud father is! Then there is the woman whom I love more than anyone else in the world, who expects me to be both lover and husband – while her own husband is risking his life in the Staffies, fighting for King and Country, like a fool. Yes, that's what I think of this war. It's a war run by fools who are willing to give other people's lives away for some stupid principle.'

Stephen was suddenly silent, his voice choking and he started to cry. Elsie had never seen him cry. She had always thought of him as a laughing person, always full of joy and laughter. She wanted to console him as best she could. She had never realised the pressures he was under until he had just pointed them out to her. She had never thought either, that he was so certain about Tom; *their* son.

They had both let their hair down, allowing a brief freedom for their feelings to be allowed out. They had never done that before and it was a revelation to each of them. They suddenly saw for the first time the range of other people who could be affected by their activities. She knew she could not hold her latest news back from him.

'Stephen; I have something to tell you. Perhaps this isn't the best time for you, but it isn't the best time for me, either.' Elsie paused for a minute and he pulled her to him again, but she wouldn't allow closeness now; the news had to be given out. 'Stephen, I'm pregnant, about two months. The worst of it is that this time I don't know who the father is, you or Dan! I have never been able to deny Dan when he gets a wanting mood, although I do not encourage him, feeling about you as I do, but when he wants me, you know; he gets me!'

Again Elsie stepped back. This time it was his turn to put forward how he felt about things. The two unhappy lovers stood there almost drowning in the complications that held them in · thrall. Eventually, Elsie pulled Stephen along the corridor that led to her lounge. They were each getting cold and sitting in the warmth of the lounge would feel like a luxury.

Stephen moved after her, wondering if their life was just an unpleasant, confining dream. He followed Elsie to the lounge. He knew that this was a turning point that would alter how he thought about things for the rest of his life. He knew he couldn't just reach for her. She was not in the frame of mind to welcome him.

Elsie pushed him onto the couch and sat beside him. She put a hand to each of his cheeks and turned his face to hers and spoke.

'Look; I'm going to give this a try; I remember you saying to me that you would take life, and the best of it, whenever you could, so I say to you, Stephen, I am willing to have a go at anything that will give us the opportunity to enjoy each other's company, whether it's in bed or just walking through a field of wildflowers. I also know that although I don't need a job, I should be trying to get one, to avoid spending my capital and to be seen to be trying to support the country. The wage will come in handy as well! We are going to go through a patchy period of employment, with some doing well and others going bankrupt; I'm not going to be either of them!

'What I want is for you to give me some work, any sort of work. If you remember, I worked in your factory before you ever got to know me well, and I think I could fit in again. I might even be able to get to like Mabel and she maybe, to like me! Do you think you could do that for me?'

Elsie knew that what she was proposing was outrageous but it seemed to her, to be the only way she could have any sort of life. She moved along the settee away from him. It was up to him what he would or could do now. If he couldn't accept what she was offering, she would have to go back to Wednesbury and start another life without him. If he could accept, she would probably have to go back to Wednesbury, anyway, but in the meantime she and he would have a wonderful, if nerve-racking time.

Stephen was thinking about it; she could see that. She held her breath while he made his mind up. Eventually he moved closer to her and turned her face to his.

'I love you, and I'm going to love you whenever I get the chance, for as long as I get the chance, my darling. I shall hold tight to you, even when we fight and quarrel, especially when it's your fault!'

Elsie pulled him down to her and her lips moved on his, smoothly kissing away his worries. His hands found her breasts, fondling and stroking the smooth skin. His lips took over from his hands and he gently sucked at her nipples, teasing them into new height and hardness.

Their bodies gradually became closer until their clothes were too much trouble to be tolerated and they just threw them out of the way. He entered her, gently at first but with increasing speed and firmness. He felt that he was in control until she took over, sucking at his lips almost viciously and finding parts of him that had never been touched by human hand. The parts responded until the climax came for both of them in a giant thrust of feeling. They lay back then, relaxing until the evening sky disappeared into a scene of millions of stars.

Later, Elsie remembered her son, Tom, again. She had put him to bed early; she had been really frustrated at the time. She trotted up the stairs; he was fast asleep in his bed. Suddenly Elsie felt full of energy, willing and able to do whatever had to be done. The hell with the hypocrites! She would live all the time she had, to live!

She ran down the stairs and grabbed Stephen and he was perfectly amazed, asking her, 'What are you doing?'

She put a key in his hand. 'Come when you can; love me when you will. I will be here when I can.'

Her first thought for acquiring cash was Home Farm. She wrote to Jenny Walker who immediately offered her employment. A week later she was working for Jenny, Tom accompanying her to their delight. She was delighted to see Agnes and Howard again and they soon found her work to do, tending the hop bines. She came home a month later a few pounds better off and ready for another change. Her portfolio of properties increased slightly, as a result.

Stephen had left her feeling that they were entering a new

phase in their relationship. He went to work determined to find her something with which she could earn a living within his sphere of influence. It did not take long. She had worked in the factory before, and women were wanted, to make goods for the Government.

Within two weeks of her return from Bromyard, she had started and was employed as a trainer for the new women who were learning to perform the tasks formerly done by their husbands. Her size started to show but, to her surprise, the women admired her for her grit, even Mabel showing sympathy for this woman whose man was at war, protecting them.

'I'll say this,' she said at dinner, 'She starts work earlier than anyone else and stays later. She deserves everything she gets!'

Stephen, who was listening at the time, looked up sharply but the face that looked back at him was innocent of any double entendre. Mabel was pregnant now and Stephen expressed his wishes.

'I hope to God it's a boy.' He commented.'

Mabel hoped it was too. The new child would keep Stephen at home. He would not risk the possibility of the loss of his only son.

Albert Stone was getting old now and could not keep up with the work. He could still be seen paying too much attention to the new factory girls. He had always been that way. Mabel was just grateful that her husband did not follow his ways!

Still, thousands, maybe millions of men would return from the conflict to find their wives had had record-breaking pregnancies. The children would just be absorbed into the population with barely a mention and would grow up regarding their mother's husband as their father.

Elsie was unhappy when she heard that Mabel bore a son. She felt it was her job to supply the sons of the family; Mabel's to supply the girls.

Tom was growing, and wanted to start work as soon as he could get permission. Elsie tried to discourage him, telling him that his education was more important than his wages but he could not understand that, knowing that the wage was the only reason to go to work, for many people.

Nineteen-fifteen came but not his father. Tom was beginning to think that he must have been lost in action but no telegram came either. He had been home once, before their embarkation. Surely his father would write. Other families were getting letters, stories, even poetry from some. Then they had a short letter. It was only the second letter they had received from him and it told them nothing. She was frightened to open it for a minute and then she pulled Tom onto her lap, an intimacy that he only suffered occasionally. He looked at her askance and she pulled the few pages from her apron pocket.

'We've had a letter from your Dad, Tom. Let me read it to you.'

She read the letter out slowly and she saw a sort of comprehension come to his face. He was more mature now, due to his having to work things out for himself, without the sort of guidance he would normally have had from his father.

Dear Elsie and Tom,

I am writing to tell you that I am very well, although not often in a comfortable billet now. I am sorry I cannot write to you very often. The reason is that I am still doing this special work. It is not dangerous but I don't get to a post box you see. I will tell you all about it, one of these days. I hope you are both doing well.

Lots of love

Dan Barr, Sergeant-Major.

'Does it mean that he is a spy or something like that, Mom? I bet he is hiding in attics and all sorts of things, getting ready to jump on the Huns.'

He could be right, she thought. That sort of work would just suit Dan. She decided to agree with Tom. Her son needed his father to be some sort of hero, like thousands of other children.

'Yes, I should think that sort of work would be just up your father's alley. He was always a good fighter and now he has had training, he is probably the best man in the Regiment for it. I dread to think what those Huns are facing. I bet they would all be frightened to death if they knew.'

'Why is he a Sergeant-Major, Mom? He was a Sergeant, before. He must be ever so clever to get to go up in rank again.'

Elsie cuddled him a little closer. Sometimes she felt as if all she wanted to do was to pull her son closer to her, to feel him safe and without risk in his life. She knew that Stephen might be called up, to serve alongside the volunteer heroes. He could be sent away and be dead inside a week of going. It had happened to a neighbour's husband and it could happen again.

'A Sergeant-Major is what they call a sort of Warrant Officer. He is higher than Sergeants and Corporals; he is the one who tells them what to do. Very often the Captains and those other Commissioned Officers tell him what has got to be done and he is the one who makes sure it is done. It is a very important job.

Tom looked at her as if he was thinking that she might be being ironic. Then he decided that she meant it but was trying to shield him from some awful truth.

'I think he would be able to protect himself, don't you Mom? How many men do you think he would be able to fight, all at once, by himself?'

Elsie smiled at her son's hero-worshipping view of his father. 'I don't know the answer to that, son, but I should think it would be more than most men, don't you?'

The letter seemed to bring some sort of relief in one way but it also made them worry because of his admission of a special sort of work. This immediately made them imagine bombs and mines and incredibly complicated killing devices. In the end, Elsie just had to make up a story that would show him as being brave without taking too many risks.

'I think that what he is doing Tom, is finding the ranges for the big guns. You have to be very skilled to do that. You have to get a patrol up, crawl through into enemy territory and somehow signal to our gunners, without getting caught by the enemy and tell the gunners whether they have shot too far or not far enough.

Tom had to be content with that and Elsie was amused to see him crawling on his belly into the neighbour's yards and borrowing sticks to signal to his friends that the imaginary shot was 'over' or 'under'. Every so often, a telegram boy would walk into the court and knock on a door. Everyone would look round the curtains to see who was going to get the bad news.

Tom became a member of the local Boy Scouts and read *Scouting for Boys* by Baden Powell. He passed his tenderfoot badge and was proud of it. He was given charge of a patrol and proudly sewed his own Patrol Leader's stripes on. They were given messenger tasks to carry out in the National Interest and got occasionally mentioned in the newspapers. The novelty of the movement held Tom for some time but eventually he became more interested in girls. He always held to the laws of the Scouts though, and automatically took and carried a shopping bag that seemed too heavy for a lady.

No further news arrived from Dan for months and Elsie almost gave up hope for him. Her work at the lock factory took up most of her time although she still helped out with the rent collecting for Mister Jenkins. He looks older now and his son had started to take over many of the functions that his father used to carry out.

Most of the men who had collected rents in on behalf of the investors had volunteered for service in the Army so more women have been recruited for the task. Betty had proved quite adequate to the task and now was a useful assistant. She was aware of Elsie's financial situation and they shared much information that might be useful to each other.

Betty was not now able to carry a pregnancy to its fulfilment and probably never would but she shared Tom with Elsie and looked forward to the arrival of her new child.

17. Elsie's Second Child.
1915

Elsie felt as if she were carrying twins; the size and weight of her abdomen making her feel ugly. She knew she wasn't because of the way Stephen was with her. He always stopped whenever he saw her, to stroke her lump, as she called it. She had an idea that it was not his child but he seemed, if possible, to be even more attentive and caring than he had been when she had been expecting Tom. He had a way of showing affection that made her feel that his love was just for her, regardless of all the difficulties that were surrounding their relationship. This was a special feeling that she thought no one else would understand and she hugged it to herself all the time.

The date of her conception was most likely a few days before Dan had been posted. If that was the case, it was his. That, she thought, was just as it should be, the wife having the child of the husband; it was just that it didn't seem right. Even though she and Stephen weren't married, it would have seemed more natural if the child had been his. The thoughts she was having recently made her feel so sad that she was weepy a lot of the time.

Stephen did not seem to care who the father was. If it wasn't his, he would just laugh about it; if it was, he would still laugh. His wife wouldn't. She would be hurt, especially now she had miscarried. Elsie knew Mabel had been praying for a boy but she just had not been ready and fit for child-bearing. Maybe her time would come when she did something to improve her health. Elsie could only feel pity for her; she couldn't feel jealous, because Stephen was not Mabel's; he was hers, regardless of certificates and all that stuff.

Elsie was finding it harder to get to work, now and she knew she would have to give it up very shortly. Her weight was greater than it had ever been and her back ached. Christmas came and went. They had said the troops would be home before then but the fighting was harder now than ever. There had been a small, slight relief when the soldiers had stopped fighting for Christmas. The officers had not stood for that, for long. It wouldn't do, would it, for the opposing troops to be friendly? It might stop the war, and the killing, and you couldn't have that. Like Dan, Elsie had no respect for officers.

Elsie examined herself quite often in front of the mirror, keeping track of the changes within her body and trying to imagine how Stephen would see her. Ruth was helping with the housework. Elsie paid her well but she earned every penny.

Neither of them had to do anything for Tom, now. He was quite the mature boy, did not like playing with Ruth's daughters and was starting to show the first signs of manhood. How long would it be before he brought his first lady-friend home? The thought made her smile. A few downy chin-hairs did not make a philanderer! It would be sometime in the next twelve months, she felt sure. He occupied a lot of her thoughts; he was her man of the house now that Dan was away and unable to communicate with them.

It was the middle of the winter now, and the snow was six inches deep. At the end of February, her second son was born. There were just two witnesses; Ruth and herself. It was a time of pulling and pushing and pain that seemed to last for ever. There was no doctor immediately available; many of them had been taken into the Army and the weather made travel more difficult for them so the women managed as best they could, like so many others had over the years. Ruth had patiently bullied Elsie into pushing the tiny mite into the world.

The bawling had started almost straight away; as soon as he was born. He was quite heavy in her arms and moved for her breasts straight away. He pulled at them for a few minutes and then started bawling again. At first she had been distressed by the constant loud howling but she soon got used to it and then the child started wanted feeding all the time.

'There's not much the matter with him!' Ruth said. 'He just don't want to shut up! What are you going to call him?'

Elsie thought about it. Tom might have an idea. He was good

when she wanted a fresh mind thinking on a problem and he sometimes came up with a different solution from the obvious one.

'Tom!' she shouted down the stairs. 'You have a brother. Would you like to see him? What shall we call him?'

There was a clambering up the stairs and Tom's head appeared, shy and slightly puzzled at the sight of such a small child. He was almost scrunched up, as Elsie called it, feeling her pains as if by proxy and seemed frightened that she might die with the pain she had obviously gone through.

Tom sat at the side of the fireplace, just looking into the flames, not knowing whether to cry or to try to think of something to do that might help. He answered Elsie's question immediately though, obviously having already given the subject some thought.

'Name him after King Edward. He might be our second but he will be our Edward the First, won't he?'

'Here you are then, Tom. Hold your brother, Edward the First.'

Ruth thrust the baby into his arms and he was instantly frightened at the responsibility of holding such a small and fragile burden in his inexperienced arms but managed to contain his feelings. Ruth helped him by showing him how to lay the baby's head on his arm, to support it. She smiled at him, giving him confidence to pick Edward up a little higher.

Tom looked at Ruth and then at his mother. 'I think I shall call him Ted, if you don't mind, Mom. He looks like a Ted, don't you think?'

Elsie was frightened as soon as he spoke. She didn't know who he looked like! She hadn't thought of that idea, yet. She recovered quickly and pondered on the question he had asked her.

'No; I don't think I mind Ted, do you, Ruth?'

Ruth took on a serious countenance, examining the child minutely from top to toe. Then she put her finger in her cheek, thoughtfully, as if considering the question carefully.

'I am not sure, really', she said. 'I think there is a possibility that he is an Algernon or a Marmaduke. I can't make up my mind which. It would be awful if we gave him the wrong name, wouldn't it? He might turn round one day and say, 'I say you fellows; my name is Vernon. Why have you been calling me Ted all these years?' Do you see what I mean?'

They all burst out laughing at the expressions and voices she used. Tom spoke again.

'I suppose he could be a Dan or a Stephen or anything, couldn't he?'

His face was so lacking in guile that they laughed again. Was it just coincidence, thought Elsie? He was a little tease at times and you never could tell what he knew or what he didn't. He seemed to laugh a lot, like Stephen, but didn't always reveal what was making him laugh. For all she knew, it was false innocence. She would soon give him something to do, to take his mind off the possibilities that the question offered. She turned to him in a sharp manner and spoke imperatively.

'Tom, I've got a task for you. Just you go and tell the doctor that Edward the First has arrived then, and would like a certificate to prove it. Everybody has to have a Birth Certificate, don't they?'

Tom nodded and flew down the stairs, his heels clattering away as if he were on route to a sudden parade. He felt quite important; he didn't often get important tasks. He felt that a task was more important than a job. A task was what heroes undertook; a job was just something commonplace that had to be done. This was a task that he felt fitted for. He had the information to accomplish the task. He knew where to find the doctor. He would be in the quiet-looking house, where he lived with his wife. The doctor had taken over after the death of Doctor Tonks who had been something of a local hero because he didn't charge as much as other doctors. The locals had built a clock tower as a tribute to the unselfish man who had tried to improve the lot of his patients.

Tom ran half the distance, trying to release his energy with a controlled sort of style, as if he were emulating a child-hero from one of his books of Boy's Adventures. The doctor's wife was not at all surprised to see him. Perhaps boys were the best and most used sort of messengers.

'Hello,' she said. 'Who are you? Who have you come from? What is your mother's name? What is your address?'

In about a minute she had all the information she needed. Then she gave him a fresh task, apparently sensing that he was in the mood for tasks.

'Do you know where the midwife lives?'

He hadn't known, the information having no relevance to his experience but in another minute he was on the way again, to find her. On the way he wondered whether she would be in when he got there. She might be at another baby's house. She wasn't though, and she was on her way quickly and got home before him on her black, new-fangled bicycle. When he got there, they were all making funny noises to Ted, who didn't seem to take a lot of notice. Tom just stood there panting loudly, letting them know that he had arrived. Only Mom seemed to notice him.

'Oh, Tom, you did well, finding the doctor and the midwife. I'm very pleased with you!'

He had been thinking as he had run to the doctor's and the midwife's. 'I think we should call him Edward Dan. Do you think that would be alright, Mom?'

Elsie seemed to glare at him for a moment. She seemed to be thinking about things in a serious and complicated way. 'Yes, Edward Dan would be a perfect name for Ted, Tom.'

They all turned to look at him then, as if wondering why and he just went down- stairs quickly, to get away from the eyes. He went for a walk again in the darkened streets and on the way round the block, by the school, was met by Mister Stephen.

'Hello young Tom. You are out late. What are you doing out at this time?'

They looked at each other as if each were just getting used to the other. Neither had any responsibilities to offer, or authority and Tom knew it. He weighed what he was going to say. The news seemed as if it should be told with trumpets. He cooled himself down and prepared himself.

'Hello, Mister Stephen, I have been to tell the doctor that our new kid, Ted, that is, has arrived, and he is in there with the nurse, and they are all talking to him, and all he does is cry!'

Stephen started to laugh like he always did and Tom joined in. It was funny how they always laughed together. It was almost as if they were related. They stood there for a few minutes, talking about locks and keys, as they always did, and then Stephen spoke.

'I think I'll come home with you now, Tom. Do you mind?'

This was an admission from Stephen that he wasn't the Gaffer at that precise moment but Tom knew different. Tom couldn't mind really; Mister Stephen was the Gaffer, wasn't he? So Stephen and Tom arrived just after the midwife, and the doctor, who must have arrived while Tom was walking round the block, had gone, and Stephen walked up the stairs and Ruth Mallory didn't say a word except to smile at him. Stephen did, though. He knew Ruth and it was as if he was relying on her to keep what she knew, to herself.

'Hello, Mrs Barr. I found this young man wandering the streets alone and thought it would be a good idea to bring him home. Is that all right?' Elsie started to cry again and Stephen looked at the baby and picked him up and put a sovereign in his hand, without saying a word. The tiny hand seemed to clutch at the coin, tightly. Stephen turned to Tom, another hand held out. 'There's one for you as well, Tom. After all, you did most of the work, didn't you?'

He started laughing again and the two women joined in. Tom didn't think it was funny. After all; he really had done most of the work! He had even told Stephen how he had run, even telling him that he had run at Scout's pace; twenty paces running and twenty paces walking; now Stephen was telling the women all about it. He couldn't help laughing along with Stephen though, as he finished his story. There was always something to laugh about, even if it seemed slightly silly.

The time seemed to pass quickly from then. Tiny Ted grew into little Ted in no time. He was little Ted for years though. He did not see his father for some considerable time. Tom felt that he was extremely lucky, having a baby brother; not many of the neighbours had one.

Ted had to sleep in Tom's bedroom in Wednesbury, now it had been painted. After the fire damage had been cleared up, the house in Willenhall had been rented out, 'to bring in a few bob', Elsie said. He had been sleeping with Elsie for some time but when he was a few months old, she said it would be better if he slept apart from her, otherwise she would never get any sleep. Tom got used to looking at Ted, across the little room, in his crib at first and then in a cot. They lay there looking at each other for ages, both pairs of eyes locked into the other's as if afraid the other might disappear.

18. Tom Starts Work.
1915

Tom was ten, old enough to find a place at work. Elsie saw Stephen Stone and asked him to find Tom a job of some sort. He was delighted and interviewed Tom himself. He sent for the boy and saw him early in the morning, as he did most of his young men, to see if they got up in the morning. After motioning him to sit down, he started to question him. 'Do you know what we make at this factory, Tom?'

'Yes Mister Stephen. We make padlocks and other sorts of locks.'

Stephen was amazed at his proprietary use of words, as if he already owned the factory, and took him to meet his father.

'Tom, this is my father, Mister Albert Stone. He started this factory a long time ago. If I ask him to show you about locks, will you promise to keep the secrets of what you learn, to yourself?, You see, Tom, Everything we make here started in somebody's head and we don't want it to escape to the head of somebody outside our firm so they can make money with our ideas. Do you understand, Tom? '

Tom hadn't expected anything like this. It made him feel more important, as if he was about to be told things that hadn't been told to anyone else. Perhaps there was something else going on here that he should find out about. Of course he would keep the secrets!

'Yes Mister Albert; Mister Albert; I promise to keep any secrets that you let me know about.' He looked both of them in the eye. 'I have lots of secrets and if I get any more, they will still be secrets.'

He almost stood to attention as he announced his personal creed. This was a good job that fitted right in with his personal values of straightforwardness and honour. His mother had told him of how she had got her job with Mister Jenkins and had been told she had to be good at keeping secrets.

'Right then, 'Stephen said, 'Tom. I'm going to ask my father if he will teach you the skills of the engineering trade. Now, listen to what he has to say.' He turned to his father. 'Father, this is Tom Barr, the son of Dan Barr, who is in the Army fighting for us. Will you teach him all you know about locks and keys? Will you examine him to make sure he knows what he is talking about when he talks about the things that we make here?'

The older man looked serious as if he were considering carefully, then he answered. 'I will, son; I will. In a few years he will be as good a lock and key-smith as you can get. What you have to do now is come with me and learn how to make and to use the tools of your trade. I will teach you engineering as well as lock and key making. If you can use the tools of the trade in six months, you can go on to start making keys. By then, you should have made yourself a toolkit. Do you understand?'

Albert Stone was a big man and Tom was overwhelmed by him. He made up his mind that no bad reports would reach his mother.

'Have I seen this boy before, Stephen? He looks very familiar to me!' Old Albert stopped the boy, who was trying to keep up with the two men and turned him so that he was full face to him. 'What is your mother's name, Tom? Do I know your mother?'

'I don't know, Mister Stone. My mother's name is Barr; Mrs Elsie Barr.'

Albert stopped and looked at him again. 'Yes, I knew I had you placed. You look like your father; that is for sure. How old are you, boy?'

'I am ten years old Mister Albert. I'll soon be eleven. I don't know if I look like my father, sir. What do you think, Mister Stephen?'

He turned on inspiration to face Stephen as he asked the question. To his surprise, Stephen started to laugh, and to his own surprise, he started to laugh as well. In a moment the three of them were laughing, looking at each other and laughing again.

Eventually they stopped and Stephen looked at his father. Tom looked at both of them. He felt that he was suddenly privy to a world-beating secret.

'Is that the first secret, Mister Stone?'

He directed his question to both of the full-grown men and the older one suddenly became serious. 'Yes, son, that is the first secret. It is a big one so keep it to your self.' He turned to his son. 'That's that out of the bag! Talk about out of the mouths of babes and sucklings. I always had my suspicions; now I know!' He turned back to Tom. 'Here we go then. Come with me and we will get you the start of a tool kit. You will have to come to work on Saturdays and Sundays at first, and then start working in the week as well.'

Albert Stone walked off and Stephen ushered Tom in his wake. It reminded Stephen of the day that he had started, with Albert showing him around the small factory, half in darkness and half lit by the oil lamps and the glow of the fires in the hearths. It was obvious who the boy's father was. Had Albert seen the similarity? It seemed most likely from the way they had all been laughing, like a pack of baboons. Oh well, there were other things to do. Let Albert deal with it.

Albert strode swiftly through the quiet factory. He knew how Tom was feeling, having felt like it himself. The smell of suds oil and burning coke was forever in the air, to be imbibed with every breath. He loved it; it was his, smell and all. The other smells were the acrid tang of urine from the boshes, where the men had not had time to go to a lavatory, even if they had one. The smell flew up into your face when a hot length of metal was dipped into it. It was the ammonia that created the smell, of course. He turned round; Tom was right on his heels, another thing he remembered from his earlier days. He had refused to let anyone move more quickly than himself.

'You all right, Tom?' he enquired. 'It's only just down here.'

Albert didn't say what was just down here. He just kept walking into the dark. At last they arrived at a small workshop with no one working there. In the corner, Tom could discern an oil lamp. He looked round to see Albert lighting it with a match.

'It will be lighter later.' He laughed at his own little pun. What I want to do now is to give you a file. This is a file.' He lifted a slim piece of metal from the bench. It had a wooden handle on the end. 'This is for filing metal. They are quite costly so the way you use it is to put it on the metal you are going to file and then use as many of these tiny teeth as you can. You do that so that you don't blunt the middle of the file before the rest of it has chance to wear out.' He placed the front end of the file on a small strip of metal, held in a vice. 'Then you push it, nice and level, so that you use every bit of the blade up. Got it?'

He looked down at Tom, seeming like a giant of a man. 'Yes, Mister Albert. I've got it.'

Albert Stone slid the file forward across the strip of metal and the metal shone from the cutting. He slid it again and this time Tom could see that the edge of the metal had been taken a little lower. 'Here you are, Tom. You have a go, alright?'

He handed the file to Tom who looked at the height of the vice and at his own height. Albert saw the problem immediately. 'Here you are, Tom. Stand on this box and then you'll be able to do it.'

It did make a difference, Tom thought. Anyway, I shall soon be tall enough to file anything. He pushed the file back and forth, making a squealing noise as he did so.

'Look, if you file at a slight angle like this, it won't make so much noise.'

He heard Albert speaking to him and he adjusted his angle as he continued to file the metal. Now the filing was quieter and he could feel the file cutting. It was not as easy as he had thought it was going to be. The file, although it was not slippery, was moving around in his grip. He looked up at Albert. He was smiling again. His son smiled a lot, too. So do I, he thought, so what?

He was getting the hang of the job now, and the filings were coming fast and furious from the edge of the small strip. He was also getting warmer, although it was a cool morning.

'Right, Tom, that's the first of the skills you've got to master. There are others. You have got to be able to chisel left and right handed. You've got to be able to scrape and all manner of small hole-shaping. You had better get moving if you are ever going to master all the skills.

'Now, there are other jobs you'll be told to do that have nothing to do with engineering. You'll have to make tea, run errands and get the hot wash water ready for the men when they are finished. I suppose I should say men and women. There seem to be as many women as there are men, now they are all going off to war.

'You were right to call me Mister Albert as well, and Stephen will be Mister Stephen, all right?' Tom nodded and the older man went on. 'Is this the first job you've ever had, Tom?' He waited for a second. 'Good. Then I shall not have to un-teach you any tricks you might have picked elsewhere. For now, go to the hardware shop by the clock; you know the clock, Doctor Tonks's clock, don't you? Just ask for a dozen ten inch fine files. You won't have to take any money with you. Just tell them I want them on our account. Be back by four o'clock.'

Albert turned and went back along the dark alley that led to the front of the building. It was obvious where young Tom had come from but it wasn't so obvious where he was going! It was about time he had a word or two with young Stephen and spelled one or two things out for him. It might make him think, when he started to spread his seed about.

Stephen was thinking about things, too. It had been all too manifest that the three generations who had stood and had a good laugh together were related to each other. How many other connections were there, that he had not yet noticed? It made him more observant as he went about his daily tasks. Mabel seemed happy for a change. She had found out that Elsie was back, working in the factory. She herself did not wish to help out that way. Clothes were likely to be in short supply soon and she wanted to get as many around her as she could. There were always shortages in wartime – but not in her shop! She would make sure of that.

Mabel had always admired the way that Elsie worked, right from when she had first arrived with her father. The only problem was the way her husband looked at the newcomer. Mabel knew how her husband felt about Elsie. She could get rid of her by making a false accusation against her but if it came out, she would be shown in a bad light. She had got her parents to show Stephen the advantages of a union between the two firms to Old Mister Stone, and he had seen them immediately.

The only trouble was that Stephen had gone along with the plan his parents had put to him, to bring the advantages to his family, and had then continued to have a relationship with Elsie. Mabel had asked her parents to bring the matter to Stephen's parent's attention but it hadn't changed anything. Someone had pointed out to her that she had used sharp business practices to gain the business advantages of the union.

Now she had to live with the business gains she had made but without the love that she so desired. She couldn't have both. She would have to try to get him to love her, regardless of any material benefit. He was a merry person to live with, always finding the happy solution to a problem; always willing to laugh at the hard side of life. They were all the same, the Stones, always willing to have a good laugh.

Mabel wished at times that she had the gift of their laughter. Her own parents were dour by comparison. It was as if they did nothing without a balance sheet, trying to find the pros and cons of every situation, to turn a profit. She was learning that life wasn't like that. Profit wasn't the only reason for living.

She had seen Stephen's father in action with the factory girls, touching them where he shouldn't and laughing about it when he was repulsed by an angry word or gesture. He hadn't touched her where he shouldn't but there had been times when she had wished he would.

Albert was a big man, not over tall but big in every way. He had passed her in a doorway; she had been sure he had done it deliberately. Their bodies had brushed past each other, not exactly pressing against each other but just touching enough to know a sort of teasing thrill at the contact. He had seen her face redden, 'like a turkey cock's arse' and he had laughed as he had leaned forward and softly kissed her.

It had not been a kiss she could object to. It could have been described as a father to daughter kiss but she had known different. The next day she had seen him with his hand inside the overall of one of the factory girls. They were both obviously enjoying the contact and she had wished that it was her breast that he was holding.

He had looked over the girl's shoulder and had seen the expression on her face. He had taken his hand away from the girl slowly but had laughed about it, as if he had read her mind and body. It was so obvious that he felt no guilt about the incident. Later that day she had found her hand wandering over her own body in a self-caressing movement. She had felt guilt then.

Now Stephen's trollop was back, not exactly in her face but just being there was too much. She was a skilled and energetic worker; there was no doubt about that, and Mabel didn't want to lose her. The girl didn't need the job; she knew that. In fact, she looked as if she would have been better off at home, with a belly the size of a small horse. She had taken two weeks off to recover from the birth and then returned, with her neighbour looking after the child.

There was lots of work at home for Tom to do after that. He had had to go to work at Stone's and do shopping and clear the ashes out of the grate and do the black-leading and chop the firewood. Elsie could do nothing for some time; she was too ill. Tom was glad when it was bedtime, usually.

Things slowly improved and Ruth came in every day to help Elsie out. Stephen went to see Elsie and the baby every few days, but he stopped coming as often as the baby got older. It was as if he now felt less love for it.

Eventually Tom was able to go back to Stone's, part-time at first and then full time, to continue learning the trade. Mister Albert seemed to have taken a liking to him and gave him every chance to learn more. Tom also started learning things that

Stephen and Albert hadn't taught him. He learned to hang onto the shafts by his feet. He could do that better than anyone. It was because his boots were better than most, in good condition and with toe-boxes that curled just that little bit, giving him a start to curl round the shaft, which was about two inches in diameter.

There was a steam engine that worked the shafts and there was a main-shaft that ran down the centre of the factory and other shafts, lay-shafts; that were run from belts to them from the main-shaft. Some of the belts went from the main shafts through the windows before they connected up to the lay-shafts. It was an art, handling the belts, which ran on pulleys alongside each other, and the lay shaft could be speeded up or slowed down according to which pulleys had the belt on. Although the shaft was supposed to be stationary before the belt was changed over, most of the hands could just spin them from one pulley to the next while the whole thing was in motion. Sometimes they broke and, Tom was shown how to mend them. Whenever this happened, the belt naturally shortened, even though the break was usually at the end. There were a number of different ways to mend them and Tom had to learn all of them.

Most of the men were pleased to see Tom back at work as it was he who did the running of the errands and he had been missed while he'd had to spend more time at home. Tom was pleased too; he usually got a copper or two for running the errands and he saved this in a tin at home. Stephen had advised him to do this.

'You never know when it will be handy to have some cash around, Tom. I know that Mister Albert started this firm on the money he had managed to save and he taught me to do the same. Now I'm teaching you. Some people listen and some don't. It's up to you which sort of person you are going to be. That is another secret, you might say.'

Tom was always being taught secrets, he knew. Most of the workers went home on Friday nights, paid their wives an allowance to keep house with and then spent the rest on beer until their wages had all gone. He had been advised against that but he knew that when he was old enough he would like to go to the pub with his mates and buy a round, just to be able to say he had done it. At the back of his mind was the possibility that the novelty would soon wear off, especially if any of them expected him to pay all the time.

Ted was growing, now, and starting to move round the house under his own steam. Tom was too much older than him to feel any real affinity with him, especially after he had been asked to look after him a few times. 'Feed the babby, Tom. Take the babby for a walk, Tom. Hold the babby for me, Tom.'

The freshness of the activity soon wore off and Tom began to resent the babby. He began to disappear as much as he could, when he got home from work. Ruth seemed to understand and she tried to tell Elsie but Elsie was too depressed about everything to take a lot of notice.

'You will just have to be a bit understanding,' Ruth told Tom. Your Mom is going through a bad case of depression and it just has to be put up with. She'll get better when young Ted gets a bit bigger. You'll see.'

For Tom it seemed to take for ever but she did slowly improve and in the spring of 1916 they got another letter from Dan.

It was nice to hear from him, and Elsie was getting what they called an allotment from him, a small amount of money out of his Army pay each week. It was a help on top of Elsie's wages, Tom's wages and the rent on the property that Elsie owned. Stephen managed to sneak them some meat occasionally so they weren't doing badly, compared with many.

Tom started doing more hours at work. He was learning a lot from Mister Albert. He was shown how to make a variety of tools. He made screwdrivers, chisels, scrapers out of old files, a tap-wrench, parallel blocks, to hold pieces of work exactly level in the vice, for shaping on the shaping machine, and others. He also made 'holding down strips' for holding pieces of metal in the vice. Inside twelve months he had a full box of tools. The box was made for him by a cabinet-maker and was his pride and joy.

At the same time that he was learning to make the tools, he

was learning to use them and his skills moved along at a faster pace than most. Before he was thirteen he could use most of the machines in the factory, and was being employed on making locks and keys for most of the different orders they had to meet. Mister Stephen told him that it was better to be able to make machines than to use them; you had more idea of how they worked.

Elsie's health improved and she went out more in the evenings, leaving Tom or Ruth to look after the little one. Stephen was often waiting for her when she went out. It was as if she could not face the fact that Dan might not ever return. Stephen too, was living a life of ill-ease, unable to face a life without the comfort and warmth of Elsie's body and company.

Each of them was in a period of denial about Dan's position in their beleaguered lives. At times, Elsie wondered what Dan was doing; whether he was hurt and whether he was still alive. Tom was not as inhibited as the adults in his considerations. As far as he was concerned, Dan was a hero who could not be killed or wounded past a small graze, such as he suffered himself when playing war games. They heard that Dan was a Regimental Sergeant-Major now and they were proud of him; he was a Warrant Officer and that sort of separated him from the NCOs and made him that little closer to the Commissioned Officers. Who knows; he might be a Lieutenant one day soon?

There was only one other man who Tom had respect for and that was Mister Stephen. They each seemed to have the habit of laughing at all sorts of odd happenings, and the laughing brought them together. Tom knew how difficult it was to laugh when bad things were happening and so Stephen too, became a hero.

Tom could not fight as good as his father but he could hold his own, as some of the factory bullies found out. He would kick, punch, scratch or bite, as the need arose without trying to become a fair fighter. His father had told him how he thought about fighting.

'Tom, nobody asks whether he fought fair; they only want to know who won. If it is a fight to the death, the loser will get no satisfaction in dying fairly but the victor is the victor, however he won. No one asks if it's fair, or heroic, to shoot savages who only have spears to fight with, against our rifles and when you come to weigh it up, the savages have the most courage in that situation, don't they?'

Tom was learning that there was more than one way to look at a situation and that was part of his growing up. He was also looking at Mister Stephen with different eyes and wondering if the friendship he had with his mother was quite all right. He had nagging doubts about it but he did not feel inclined to say anything critical; he liked both of them, after all but he somehow thought that his father would not like the friendship.

His mother must be lonely, to be friends with a man who was not her husband. He could not bring himself to censure her; it was her life and he knew that he would not take kindly to anyone telling him who he should have as a friend. Anyway, Mister Stephen had been his friend before he had started working for him and he wasn't going to stop being his friend now.

19. Ready for France Again.
1917

The Company moved away from the ship in good order. The battle that they joined was not. They were attached to the old 38th, the 1st Battalion of the South Staffordshire Regiment, but were not part of them although they shared many of the same experiences.

The 1st Battalion had consisted of over a thousand officers and men. Now there were seventy-eight, not counting the attached troops, about which the Germans knew nothing. They had been involved in the second Battle of Ypres the previous year and had suffered severe losses then. For months since then, the war had been made up of struggling to stay alive in the trenches. The only real relief had come from the battles they were occasionally involved in at Neuvre, Chapelle, Festubert and Loos. None of these battles were particularly effective and the men were glad to be relieved, to be able to spend a little time in the small towns they were near. The battles were described by Lloyd George as 'the most gigantic, tenacious, grim, futile and bloody fights ever waged in the history of war'. Over these months, the British Army lost over 400,000 men.

Dan now had less than half the men he had started out with. Many of his special unit had been awarded medals, too many of them posthumously. Replacements had arrived slowly and were being trained in the realities of war. The war had continued right through 1916 with severe attrition on both sides. The American Declaration of War on the sixth of April 1917 was the trigger that signalled the coming end.

Assaults on enemy positions were a daily task now, harrying the opposing forces in ways not tried before, supporting the line regiment and supplying snipers in number to pick off the German officers.

Dan was part of these assaults, leading his men in the wake of the young officers who were almost all replacements. Captain

Brookes had died in a fighting charge over the top and Dan took his place until a Lieutenant could be found. The whole Battalion seemed to be going forward as one, in a long line. There was surprisingly little fire from the other side. Dan's Company all had fixed bayonets and were ready for anything when Dan was hit in the head by a sniper's bullet. His consciousness went and the next thing he knew, he was in hospital.

*

The contrast between the battlefield and the silent serenity of the field hospital was intense. As he woke and looked round, he could see faces that were familiar to him. Sergeant Larkin, newly promoted, was there with a silly grin on his face. Dan didn't feel like talking; he just wanted to close his eyes.

It was morning when he opened them again. There was the rattle of bedpans and trolleys being pushed around the ward. There was the scent of some sort of carbolic disinfectant and the sound of birds also. He looked round; there was a partly open window behind him and he could see birds in the large gardens. A voice spoke gently to him.

'Morning Sir. How are you now?'

Dan looked up. It was Larkin, out of bed now and seemingly alright. Dan looked him up and down.

'What you done, Larkin? Joined the Navy?'

Larkin was in the uniform of the wounded, the blue shirt and trousers signifying that he was going through a period of convalescence. He grinned back at Dan.

'No, sir. This is to show that I am a non-combatant. You'll be getting one of those soon instead of the nightshirt.'

Dan looked down and saw that he had pyjamas on. He suddenly felt foolish.

'You caught me there, Larkin. I suppose it's about time you got one over on me. Where are we? Is this France, or Blighty?'

He realised that he had no idea where he was or even what date it was. He sat up slowly and his head started to ache again.

He still wanted to know what was going on round him though. He looked at Larkin who was still smiling.

'What's that stupid grin for, Larkin?'

He felt like punching him again like he had the first time they had met.

'I'm grinning sir, because I think we shall miss the end. The Yanks are doing a great job now, and so are our lads with the Canadians and the Aussies. The Germans had mounted an offensive but we beat them back again. They lost thousands, and then the Yanks came! The Jerries had no chance. It looks as if they are surrendering all over the place. The Allies have just started another go and I have heard that over a quarter of a million Americans are in it with us. That'll take a bit o' beating sir.

'You had a bullet in the head; that's what you are doing here. They got it out all right, but we have all been just waiting to see if you wake up, and if you do, what you are like. I think I'll tell the Sister that you have died in the night and want to go back to your unit.'

Larkin walked away from Dan, leaving him feeling a bit stupid. Now he had no idea what was going on! He looked along the ward. There were about thirty beds, almost all of them filled. Why was that? Were they all seriously wounded? At the far end of the ward, one or two of the patients were sitting in chairs alongside their beds. As he looked, one of them turned and smiled at him.

Dan stood and tried out his legs. They seemed alright so he tried walking and that was alright too. He was just making progress down the ward when he saw a nurse coming towards him. She had a sort of exasperated look on her face and he felt that he was the cause of it.

'Good morning, er, Sister?'

The nurse looked like a Sister anyway, and had that air of authority that he liked to consider his own.

'What exactly do you think you are doing?'

223

She had a loud voice when she wanted to, by the sound of it. Perhaps she was different at other times. He didn't respond to people talking to him like that.

'Who exactly do you think you are talking to? And who are you exactly, to be shouting at me? People stopped doing that, years ago!'

The nurse stopped in her tracks as she replied, 'Who I am is Senior Nursing Sister in charge of this ward, Sergeant-Major and the reason I am shouting is to make sure you can hear me. For all I know, you might be deaf or stupid. The reason I asked you a question is to get an answer so in case you are deaf, I will ask you again. What exactly do you think you are doing?'

Dan had switched off. If people spoke to him without respect, he treated them the same way. He turned back towards his bed and started walking again. There was a small tallboy wardrobe at the side of it. He opened it. His clothes were there. He reached in and started to dress himself.

'You aren't thinking of leaving, are you, Sergeant-Major?'

It was the Nurse or Sister, or whatever she was. He was getting annoyed with her now. Ignoring her he continued with his dressing.

'Orderly, she called. 'Please make sure this man is back in his bed, quickly.'

A tall man came strolling along the ward. He looked as if he could handle himself, Dan thought. Well, we'll find out won't we?

The man came up to him and pushed his face into Dan's, his teeth bared as if he were going to bite him.

'Oy! You! Get yourself into bed before I put you there!'

The man waited to see what response he would get from Dan. Dan continued getting dressed. He completed his toilet and turned. The man was barring his way.

'Excuse me, please,' Dan said. 'I want to get past you.'

He waited and saw the man's arm move. Dan recognised the move and forestalled it. He grabbed the arm and put it in a lock on the floor.

'Please don't try to hit me again. You are likely to get hurt and it would deprive the lovely Sister of your services for a time. Do you understand me, Orderly?'

The Orderly nodded, his face filled with pain. Dan noticed that the Sister had disappeared. A few minutes later, two Military Policemen marched in with batons at the ready. Suddenly, Dan knew he could not match these men. He was hesitant about the next step. What should he do? He could not hope to win, in a conflict with these men. He could only be docile. He turned and walked away from the two Sergeants and got into bed as fast as he could. It looked as if he would only be safe in bed.

The Sister marched up the ward, flanked by her escorts, her face grim as she spoke. 'Sergeant-Major Barr, I want you to know that you need a good rest in a quiet place, so that is what I've arranged for you. You will be leaving here as soon as I am satisfied that you will do as you are told. You have had a bad time; you got a bullet in the head and it took a very good surgeon to remove it. Since then, for a week, you were shouting your head off all day and all night, though I expect you have forgotten it now. No one had any idea what your condition would be when you came to consciousness. You seem to be all right, though I have my doubts because of your little tantrum earlier.

'I shall ask the doctor to see you tomorrow morning and if he gives the word, you will be transferred to a convalescent home. From there, you will be discharged from the Army. The war is almost over now so there is no point in returning you to your unit. An officer has asked about you; he was the replacement for your commanding officer; he won't be coming back. I believe he has enough on his plate at the moment. Do you understand what I have told you?'

Dan nodded his head and the small party turned and marched down the ward. He was going home! It was a shock to think his unit could manage without him. Then he realised that there would be people who would be glad he was gone, in the same way that he had been glad when others had been wounded or killed because it had opened the road to his own promotion. He lay back and tried to organise his thoughts. The best thing he could do now was to just shut up, speak when he was spoken to and enjoy him self as much as he could. He had no responsibilities now!

The doctor, a dour Scotsman, came next morning to the side of his bed. He had a folder in his hands.

'Morning, Barr; let's have a look at you; sit up.' He examined the small wound in Dan's scalp and pronounced it clean and healing. 'Right then, the next thing is to get you on the way to a convalescent home. If you are seen to be mentally and physically stable, you will receive a discharge from your duties for the Country. Good luck and just remember to keep your nose clean. No one is going to stand for taking orders from a discharged Sergeant-Major, are they?' He smiled and reached out his hand. 'You've had a bad time but you're healthy and you should make a complete recovery before long. Goodbye, Barr.'

Dan looked around. He was not the only one to be invalided out. There were three others who were getting their clothes into kitbags. One of them had lost a leg. Dan went over to him. 'Is there anything I can do to help?'

'Yes, you can mind your own business and let me get on with mine, if you don't mind!'

Dan went to lift his hand in anger and then changed his mind. There was no point in rocking the boat. This man had obviously been through it as well! He turned and walked away. The man would have to come to his own reconciliation with his future.

He looked down the ward. The Sister was watching him. He smiled at her, went to his bed and started packing his clothes. An hour later he was on the way in a large car. The journey took him through an area where he had never been. The only thing he could tell was that it was south of the Midlands. There was a signpost saying that it was seventy miles to London. He suddenly realised that he must have been unconscious all the way from the battlefield to the hospital he had just left. He must have been seriously wounded!

They arrived, the soldier who Dan had spoken to remaining silent all the way. The other two had chatted to each other and he learned from their conversation that they had been in the same Company as himself, much to his surprise. He was used to knowing all his men. Things had changed; there were more and more replacements and probably no one would even remember him in a month's time.

The convalescent home, when they arrived was a complete shock. He had expected a place with accommodation for hundreds of troops but this was just a large house in Blackwell, just outside Bromsgrove in the Midlands. It seemed friendly, somehow, and this impression was borne out when the chubby Matron met them at the front door.

'Good afternoon, gentlemen,' she said. 'Welcome to the Uplands. There are no tight rules here or people to stand to attention for. All you have to do is relax and let nature do its work, and then you will get better. When you are recovered enough, you will be going to Whittington to get discharged. What you do after that is your business. Come on through and I'll show you around.' The Matron turned and led the way into the dining room where there was seating for about two dozen men, Dan estimated. 'Sit yourselves down and tea and biscuits will be on the way to you all.'

She sat and started checking the details of each of them. When she came to Dan, she seemed quite respectful. 'Oh, yes; Sergeant-Major Barr; quite a distinguished record. I believe you have been honoured with the Military Cross. You didn't know? Yes, here it is, signed by Captain Brookes.' She turned to the young woman who had brought drinks in. 'Thank you Jean.'

Dan was surprised. He had never thought much about medals and what you had to do to get them. She was carrying on reading details. Eventually she looked up at the four men. 'There we are; we know more about you all now. I expect you will want to get settled in as soon as you have finished your teas. I will see you in a little while.'

She bustled off to her office and the four men looked at each other, wondering how many beds there would be in their rooms. Dan stood and looked at the others.

'I'm ready when you are, lads. Let's get settled in, shall we?'

A nurse came in, hearing their voices. She was the one who had brought the cups of tea. She was slim but with enough weight to give her shape, blonde with shoulder-length hair and just about tall enough to reach to Dan's shoulder.

'Hello gentlemen; I am Nurse Jean Ireland and I shall be looking after you while you are here. I'm sure you're all going to enjoy your stay but if you need any help, just ask, and if I can help, I will do my best. Your rooms are on the ground floor and I expect you will be pleased about that.'

The nurse turned and led the way along a long corridor. To their surprise, each of them had a room of their own. There was a single bed in each, a wardrobe and a slim dressing table. On the dressing table there were a few books by well known authors. An orderly brought their kitbags and placed them in the room. Dan turned and spoke to the nurse.

'What do you do at night, Jean? Do you go home or do you live in?'

The nurse turned and looked at him.

'I can see you're not going to be here long, Sergeant-Major Barr. If you keep improving like this, you will be on your way home in a week or so. Where do you come from? You sound like a Black Countryman; are you?'

'Yes, I suppose I am. I come from Willenhall, a few miles north of West Bromwich. I can't wait to get back there. Oh, yes I know; everyone thinks it is a dirty place and I suppose it is but it's where I was brought up so I just think of it as home.'

He turned, the tears starting from his eyes. He had fallen into the trap of talking about the things that mattered to him. As soon as you did that, you felt the loss and it struck at you. He walked over to the window, looking at the view of the Malvern Hills, outside. It was, to him, sensational, the long line of hills with the drooping saddle in the middle. No wonder Elsie liked going hop-picking.

He made up his mind there and then that at the first chance, he was going hop-picking. It was going to be some time. It was only November but he could plan for it, couldn't he? He knew that Elsie and her friends had been for the whole of September. It would only cost the fare; the accommodation would be laid on, even if it was a bit primitive.

Perhaps he could go next year. He tried to envision himself picking the hops from the bines. The vision just wouldn't solidify in his mind. It just made him more determined, though. He would do it! He could imagine the journey down, with Elsie, Tom and the little one whatever he or she was called. The sun would be shining into the train carriage. All memories of the mud and blood of France would be forgotten.

He became more involved with his vision until he could almost feel it. The sun, shining over the hills warmed him through and he basked in it. It was autumn now and although it was cooler he knew that there was a lot of picking going on. Apples and pears were in their prime and were fetching good prices. He wondered if Elsie was among the women, picking the fruit.

He had a lot of catching up to do. His days of death and glory were over. He had to learn to cope with peace. His face gradually became less grim as he tried to envision how he could make the best of peacetime. He had not come into contact with any of the hundreds of thousands of Americans who were taking part in the European struggle.

He knew nothing of what was happening in Willenhall. For all he knew, Stones' Locks might no longer exist. His whole world seemed to be at risk in spite of the news from the front. What could expect when he got home?

20. Convalescence.
1917

He heard a cough behind him; it was the nurse, Jean.

'Is there anything else you want, Mister Barr?'

It was like déjà vu. She looked so innocent, standing there that he felt he could just grasp, hold of her and pull her to him. It was a tempting thought. He had done it before, in the battered village at the back of the lines, in France. He had wanted so badly to relieve himself that he had gone looking for a woman, any woman, and he had found one. The young Frenchwoman had been standing in the shelter of a doorway, sheltering from the rain. He had approached her cautiously.

'Bon jour, Mademoiselle. Do you speak any English?'

'Oui, Tommy, I speak a little. Do you speak any French? Is there anything you want?'

The question, so innocent, had caught at his mind. How was he supposed to answer? He had always had an honest way with him and mostly it worked.

'Oui, mademoiselle, there is something I want.'

The young woman had looked at him again and he had moved towards her as she had moved towards him. He had pulled her against his body, feeling every tiny bit of her pressing against him. He thrust her away just that little distance so that he could look in her eyes. There was the same look there that he knew was in his own. Again he pulled her, this time into the doorway, into the darkness.

His hand slid onto her breast, inside her lace blouse. He pulled the material away and pressed his lips against her. Inside a few minutes he was part of her and she was part of him. Ten minutes later it was all over. It was disappointing though momentarily satisfying. There had been no meeting of the minds or emotions of any depth. He had walked away, disgusted with himself.

Now this demure looking nurse had asked him the same question again. He didn't feel inclined to put himself through the same actions, leading to a lack of satisfaction, again. The trouble was that his body let him down sometimes. Keep your feelings to yourself, he thought. Then the feelings came pouring out.

'Yes, Jean. I want you!' The words, sticking in his mouth, still came out. 'I'm sorry but that is the answer to the question you asked me.' He moved forward as he had in France and put his hand on hers, holding her gently. 'Do you know what it is like to meet someone and to want them, not just a bit but passionately, against all reason? That is how I feel about you, Jean, and I have only known you for a quarter of an hour.'

His lips moved to take possession of her and hers moved to gently press against his. It was going to be all right. She moved away from him.

'I can't do this you know, Dan. I have a fiancé in France who is going to be coming home any day now. I believe in faithfulness, don't you?'

'Yes, Jean; I believe in faithfulness but I also believe in grabbing what I can in the day that I am. How could I sleep tonight, seeing you in my half-dreams? It's all very well bringing up such high morals and I am sure there is rightness to them but it doesn't stop how I feel. Should I go and see the Chaplain and ask him where the nearest brothel is? I want you; you, the woman in front of me!'

Dan moved again and this time she did not push him away. His hands moved to the back of her long skirt, sliding it up her legs and pushing her backwards until the bed tripped her onto the blanket lying on it. He followed her until he was atop her body. His hands moved to uncover himself and press himself into her hands. She started with a physical shock and so did he as her hand met him. He tugged at her underclothes until they came away in his hand and then he pushed her hand out of the way as he joined his body with hers. She gave a little shriek as his hot manhood slid into her and then she moved in time with him, helplessly slipping and sliding; attempting to get the most out of the nearness of him. A moment later she climaxed with a long sigh and slid down the bed in a faint.

Dan slid down with her and put his hand between Jean's legs, pushing deeply into her, bringing about another orgasm as she returned to normal consciousness from where she had been. She shook him by the shoulders and tried to hit him.

'You dirty bastard. Get off me! Look what you have done to me! How can I sleep tonight, knowing what you have done to me?'

The outburst was so comical to Dan that he burst out laughing. Instead of complying with her request he undid her blouse and took her breast into his mouth, nibbling gently upon it. He felt the blood returning to his spent member and bit into her until she cried out with pain. Then he plunged into her again, not as fiercely this time, but with such gentle firmness that she accepted the insertion as inevitable. Her breathing was getting faster now, and her grip on Dan's head got tighter and tighter until she suddenly arched her back and screamed.

They both realised what she had done and they lay there, wondering whether the scream had been heard. A minute, then another went past and they came to the conclusion that no one was aware of what they had been doing.

'You bastard!' she said, but this time she had a slight smile on her face. 'I want you again but not until tonight. I shall come and tuck you in later on.'

Jean moved away from him on the bed and replaced her clothes then she stood and moved to the door and looked out of it, down the long corridor. She turned and looked at him, a look that was something like a pleased glare! Dan smiled at her and beckoned her to come back for more, gesturing towards the bed.

'Bastard,' she whispered. 'I'll show you, later! Just you see!'

Jean vanished then and when he went to the door to look for her, she had vanished from the corridor. Dan went back to the window and looked outside. There she was, trotting along the gravel path like an antelope.

What had he done? He had always believed in one man, one woman. Now he had split a man from his woman; a man who was still fighting for king, country and his life! What could he do to put things right? He knew that he couldn't leave Elsie; he would remain faithful to her, even if he did sleep with another woman. There didn't seem to be any link between the two events.

He moved away from the window as Jean disappeared from his view. She was probably crying as she ran along that gravel path towards her home. He had forgotten what it was like to have a woman. Now he remembered and the sensation was intolerably addictive. He had to have her again. He had had the feeling before, in France, after he had been with the strange Frenchwoman. He had wanted her, night after night, but he had never seen her again. How could he overcome the longing he had in these situations?

Dan threw himself on the bed and allowed his body to arrange his thoughts into the sequences that he imagined he would most like to happen. Slowly he went to sleep, thinking of a composite female body and personality that suited him best.

*

The morning woke him up; the birds were singing and he could hear the cattle complaining as they were moved to the sheds for milking. There was no Reveille! That was the big difference between now and his recent experiences in France. He could easily recall the moment of the bullet hitting his head, and the fall from upright awake and then, later, waking into consciousness. He sat up and slid his shaving tackle under his arm. Where did he have to go? He looked round and saw a bowl on the dressing table. It was steaming!

Someone must have taken the trouble to get it ready for him. He had never been waited on before and it was a new experience. He dipped his finger into the bowl; it was quite hot so it couldn't have been there long. The shave was a double one; down first and then upwards, being careful not to allow his shaking hands to lose control over the razor. It was what they called a safety razor. Someone had taken away his cut-throat. They took no chances here! He had no intention of cutting his own throat; he had too much to live for!

He was early, one of the first to rise and he sat looking out of his window for some time, thinking about his 'event' as he called it, with Jean. He could not reconcile his activities with his morals. He had a faithful wife at home and a lover as a neighbour; both were missing him; were they able to replace him?

Breakfast was a subdued affair; there were only a few, less than a dozen men. Where were the others? He sat on a table by himself but a Scot came and joined him. There was not much conversation between them and they just nodded at the end of the meal as they each went their own ways.

There was no sign of Jean; perhaps she was not going to be on duty that day. Dan went into the garden and sat on a bench in the sun. It was a frightening feeling. He knew he should enjoy it but somehow it all seemed like a trap, as if a bullet was going to fly into the back of his head again. Gradually the feeling subsided and he felt his eyes close. A feeling of peace came over him and he drifted into the first really relaxed sleep he had had since he had left France. There was nothing in his mind; not Jean or Elsie or anyone else.

When he opened his eyes he was facing down a long slope towards the railway line that ran across the bottom of the field in which the house was built. There was a large child's swing halfway down the slope and he found himself attracted to it. He stood and walked to it and sat swinging backwards and forwards like a small boy. He pushed against the ground and found himself swinging higher. He enjoyed the feeling and pumped harder and harder. He was at the height of the cross-bar when he felt the hands on his back, giving him just a little more height. He looked round and saw Jean pushing him, a huge smile on her face. He measured his swinging motion and as he was almost at the zenith of the forward swing, he jumped, and as he landed, allowed himself to roll. He lay still until he felt her move his face and then he grabbed her and rolled the two of them behind a large laurel bush.

They stopped rolling with Dan on top and he took full advantage of his position. He pushed her away from him and laughed at her as she realised that he had not hurt himself.

'You bastard!'

'Is that all you can think of to call me, Jean? Every time you speak to me, it's to call me a bastard.'

She rolled back onto him and stroked the side of his face.

'I don't really think you are a bastard; I think you are lovely – even if you are a bastard!'

Jean moved against him, allowing her body to stroke against his. This was new. He felt like raping her.

'Have you practiced doing that?' he asked. 'I've never done that before.'

Dan went quiet as he felt the full effect of her hips moving against his. It was wonderful. He moved closer to her and started to emulate her movements, sliding his hips, too. He felt her close herself to him and he whispered in her ear.

'Bastard!'

She took hold of his head and pursed her lips to kiss him, then just touched his lips with hers and then moved them away so that the touch was so slight that it reminded him of a butterfly.

'Bastard!'

This time he learned quickly, moving his lips to just touch her on the tip of her breast, taking a little suck and then releasing her for a second and then taking a firmer grip, almost biting her but not quite. She lay back on the grass with her arms above her head, just allowing him to do as he would.

'Bastard!' This time it was Dan who uttered the expletive. 'You are just too much! I cannot stop wanting you. I want you!'

He slid his hands up the outside of her legs, taking her skirt with them. She was naked underneath her skirt and he thrust himself violently into her body. Her legs moved upwards and he felt himself held by them. She took over the control of his body, holding him with her thighs and surging backwards and forwards, as violently as he.

The climax was as different for him as it was for her. For Dan, it was a bringing to a head all the wanting in his body for a woman, any woman but especially this woman who had offered herself to him. For Jean, the encounter was the slow but accelerating feeling of a bringing together of all her emotions and teasing, tying and playing with her body to a crescendo of feelings that was as new as Spring. Her need was as deep as his; it just had a different emphasis; an emphasis that leaned towards the desire to bring about change in her body, the wellspring of life.

They lay back in the shade behind the laurel, holding onto each other, knowing that this was an encounter that might never be repeated, even though the memory of the desire would stay with them until the end of their days. Their hands met and were warmed by the sun as it passed overhead. The temptation to lie and doze off into a sleep was overwhelming and they were just drifting when they heard a bell ring.

'Oh, my God!' Jean was the first to become aware of what was happening. 'It's lunch time. They will be looking for us in a few minutes and if I'm found like this, I shall be dismissed and you will be put on a charge for conduct unbecoming...'

Jean was tidying herself up as she spoke; there was more urgency to the situation than just a need to hurry for lunch. The disgrace to Jean would be career-effecting and complete, and would bring to an end the peaceful convalescence that was so essential to Dan's recovery.

They stood and started walking, almost marching, towards the great house where he was billeted. A few minutes later they had passed into the shade of the building, Dan into his own room to look himself over in his mirror, and Jean into a corridor. He looked as smart as ever; it was only his feelings that had changed. He would never deny himself again; it was just too much of a strain on his emotions. It was true what they said. There were more regrets attached to not doing things than there ever were to doing things that you shouldn't do.

Dan made his way down to the dining room and silently ate his lunch. It was more like refuelling than enjoying a meal, a necessity rather than a pleasure. Slowly his mood returned to something like normal and he became aware of the conversations going on around him.

'Captain Alcock and Lieutenant Brown have flown the Atlantic Ocean in just over sixteen hours.'

There were so many changes he was hearing of, while at the Convalescent Home. This flight could affect the whole world.

'Two hundred men, sailors, have been drowned, in Stornaway Harbour.'

He hadn't heard about that, but he wouldn't; he had been otherwise engaged, but it was a terrible loss, especially as the young sailors were going home from the horror of war. The young Islanders had been on their way to their New Year celebrations. It made him feel lucky to be here, in Blackwell, so far from stress and horror.

He was suddenly filled with horror that he had survived when so many, more worthy young men had died. He started crying and didn't know what to do. Why should he be singled out to taste such pleasure as he had known, when there millions rotting in open graves? He leaned his head forward and lay on his arms amidst the chatter. The noise gradually stopped ands the room became silent. A hand touched him on the shoulder and a quiet voice led him from the table, back to his room. He lay on the hard bed and felt Jean lie beside him.

Peace came back to him then, and the horrific visions he had in his mind disappeared as he drifted into sleep. When he woke up there was no one there and he was under the blankets, feeling quite chilly. He recalled the girl who had been by him as he had seen those phantom figures of the young sailors, all drowning, and he wondered what she had thought of him.

Somehow, the deaths of those two hundred Scottish sailors, on their way to their homes, seemed worse and more tragic than those he had urged 'over the top.' He started crying again but this time there was no one there to lead him away and bring him peace. The air in the small room seemed full of tears for the whole of mankind.

When he woke again, it was morning and although the memories were still there, they didn't seem so bad. They were just memories, just records, without emotional content. 'Poor bastards', he thought, but didn't feel the loss this time. It was just a shame. It was funny how we say that, he thought, just a shame, but never feeling the shame. Did the officers at the top, who simply ordered hundreds to die, ever feel the shame? Did they really feel the responsibility of it all?

He became aware of the tiny wren warbling outside his window. This tiny bird, rarely seen, often made more noise than all the other birds put together. It made no difference between shameful death and death by old age. It still had to get on with the work of the day, to survive. He had to do the same; if a wren could do it, so could he! He supposed that some did and others couldn't care less.

He walked over to the ewer but it had not yet been filled with hot water. Hot water really made no difference to him; he had had many a shave in the trenches, without the comfort of hot water. It was only a few minutes later that he was dressed and leaning on the window sill, looking for the wren. He caught a glimpse of it, hopping from branch to branch of a large shrub growing there and it caused a smile to cross his face. The little wren had to cope with wind and rain, with the death of a mate, with lack of food, but it just got on with it. It had a loud cry; it had to because it was so small that it often could not be seen, even when it was chirruping. Somehow the wren reminded him of Elsie; she was like that, just getting on with life.

He had to do the same, act like a man, have a conscience; do the right thing, whatever that was. Gaffers did not care what the right thing was, only that it paid a profit. Kings did not care about the right thing; the only right thing was the thing that enlarged their personal empire. He had acted like a man with Jean, hadn't he? His body had demanded its rights, whatever rights were.

His thoughts were beginning to give him the germ of an idea. He needed a few more days of this little heaven though, to perfect it. Elsie did not know where he was, God bless her, and had not known since he had caught that last one in the head.

He wasn't going to write to her. He would just turn up on the doorstep, the returning hero. He could say he had lost his memory. In the meantime he would just enjoy himself at the Government's expense. How many of the others in this little hotel for injured soldiers were doing the same thing?

He returned to the little thought that had come to him. Why shouldn't he become a gaffer, owning his own firm, building on a small start to be like an oak before long? He had a few pounds that he could use to buy a hand-press and a few other things. An anvil would come in useful. You never knew, perhaps Elsie would help him to get started.

He had always felt that she had a few pounds salted away. He had looked in her drawer once and there had been three bank books, each with different titles, all to do with money. He had asked about them and she had said that they were the record of monies paid for rents in Wednesbury and that the monies were what she had to pay to old man Jenkins. She had seemed a bit embarrassed about it though, and he had never seen the books again. Perhaps there was a means there, to help to provide him with capital for his ideas.

Another thought came to his mind then. Even if he did get the equipment, he would have to have premises to manufacture whatever it was he was going to make, and who was going to buy the things, that was all he could call them for now, when he had made them? Would he have to make things better and cheaper than anyone else?

When he thought about it, most of the locks on the market were, to him, easily produced, with plenty of scope for profit undercutting. Perhaps he could specialise, just making parts for other manufacturers. It was a matter of finding a locksmith who had too much work who would be willing to pay him a decent cut, to make or assemble parts for him. There was a lot to think about. He would give himself a week to get it straight in his mind. In the meantime there were the birds to watch and Jean to enjoy, if he saw her again. He would do that.

21. Armistice.
1918

There had been no news from Dan for weeks, and Tom was almost convinced that his father had died in action although there had been no telegram telling of this. Many were in a similar situation even when the war had been over for twelve months. At first there had been a great joyous celebration when Kaiser Wilhelm abdicated and the Armistice was signed, at six o'clock on the morning of the eleventh of November, 1918. It was put into effect five hours later. The men had started returning home shortly after that.

That was all over now and there was a lot of unemployment with competition between women and men for the jobs that were available. Many women were widows and felt they had a right to the jobs that their husbands would have had if they had returned alive from the war. Others had demanded that they be kept on. They had been good enough to work for the bosses during the war why not continue? They were, after all, paid less and the bosses would make more profit out of the work they turned out.

Tom still wondered occasionally what had happened to his father but he had other interests now; he was starting to notice girls and found them attractive. He worked with a number of girls and after going through a shy stage, started to make overtures to them. He was growing taller and was becoming handsome and dark. He had a slightly receding hairline, something like a widow's peak but there was nothing feminine about him. His arms looked strong and they were, too. He was quite protective of his own employment prospects but felt that he was sufficiently well thought of by Mr Albert and Mister Stephen to feel secure at work.

The men had been slowly coming back from the Army, and were determined to demand their jobs back. Many men in the Black Country had been permanently injured and all they wanted was to fit into their old jobs. This created difficulties as the people who had been carrying out their functions during the war years seldom wanted to give up their skills and the wage that went with it. These people were usually more up to date with designs and newer working methods too, and consequently more profitable to employ as workers.

Then the influenza germ was released among the civilian population. It had started in Texas but had spread wherever the American Forces went. In weeks there were thousands of sick men and women in England. It became known as Spanish Flu but there was nothing Spanish about it. Millions died from it. Ted, now three years old was sick for most of the winter but survived.

Eventually Dan arrived home. He was thinner, having been sick with the flu. Tom barely recognised him when he saw him marching down the street, his kitbag over his shoulder. Dan hardly recognised Tom either. Tom had grown taller and at almost fourteen was as tall as his father. He stood for a few seconds watching the soldier moving smartly and then he darted into the house.

'Mom!' He shouted up the stairs. 'Mom! It's Dad! He's come home!'

Tom scrambled down the stairs again and stood by the front door as Dan marched up to the door. The soldier looked him up and down as if he were on parade and being inspected.

Then he seemed to recognise Tom, saying, 'Is it you, Tom?' Tom nodded. The soldier threw his kit bag on the ground and put his arms round Tom. 'I have missed you, Tom; don't you know me, Tom. I'm your Dad.'

'I know who you are, Dad. I've never forgotten you.'

Somehow, Tom didn't know what to say to this strange man. He looked like one of those killing types. It was all very well thinking of your Dad as a hero but when a real live Dad and hero combined into a swarthy killer-type man, with a curly moustache turned up, it wasn't likely that you could come up with any tender feelings. A rush of feelings came out.

'Dad, where have you been? We have written to you hundreds

of times and we've had no replies at all. Surely if you could get here, you could have written to let us know how you were!'

Tom felt the release that the words gave him, and he hesitated. Had his father been ill, or in a prison-of-war camp? Perhaps he had deserted. Perhaps he had lost his memory and it had only just returned. The possibilities were endless. Well, not endless; there could only be so many reasons why he had gone missing and then returned. No doubt he would be informed when his father thought it was the right time.

His father was looking at him strangely; it was as if he could not understand why his son would have the nerve to even bring any slight criticism against him. Dan suddenly took Tom by the throat and, half-strangling him, shouted directly into his face. 'Who the hell do you think you are, sonny boy, talking to me like that? Stand up straight when you speak to me!'

He stepped back and raised his hand as if to punch him in the face. It seemed to Tom that time stood still for a short period. Then a voice he recognised as his mother's rang out, 'Don't you dare raise your hand to my son, Dan Barr! You might have been a Sergeant-Major where you came from – and it looks to me that they've taken that rank away from you! I told you once that if you raised your hand in anger in the house, you could get out. Better make up your mind. We've managed all right without you for three years, without a letter or a word and without a hand being raised, and we can manage without you and your hand, for the rest of our lives without you!'

Dan stood stock still, apparently shocked by the anger and aggression in his wife's voice. It was a complete reverse of the welcome home he had been expecting. He had also got used to giving orders and telling men off, just as he thought, and a counter attack was the last thing he had anticipated. He looked up the stairs inside the house, to where Elsie was standing and saw her with her eyes flashing and her arms akimbo. He crumbled immediately, collapsing in a heap on the ground.

That was a shock for the two watching. Then they moved swiftly towards him. They too, had had expectations of the return of Dan and this pathetic figure was not part of the picture they had treasured. They stood and bent over him. Elsie turned and spoke to Tom.

'Tom, would you get him a drink of water please? He looks very pale. Perhaps he's been ill; go on, there's a dear.'

Tom darted through the house, not feeling at all sympathetic towards his father. Why should he wait on somebody who had been trying to bully him as though he were a dog? He brought the drink back to where his mother was cradling his father. Ruth was standing, watching. She had dashed into the house as soon as she had heard Tom's voice shouting out the news of his father's arrival. She stood for a second then turned on her heel and walked away, back to her own front door.

Dan had his eyes open, now, and was looking at both of them in turn. At last he opened his mouth, took a sip of the water and spoke.

'I say, I am sorry, my son. It was just such a shock, you know, seeing you like that, and then your mother. I have not been too well but I shall be alright now. I'm sorry I spoke to you like that. I hope I don't have to, again.'

Tom's temper caught at him; again? What was he saying? If his Dad thought he was going to give a repeat performance, he might as well put the boot in now! Dan looked all in and was lying back down in Elsie's arms and she was nursing him, tenderly. Grown ups were strange.

Elsie had got the idea that Dan was weak – ill – and lacking in strength. She looked from Tom to Dan. There was more information to be got from this poor hulk of a man. She would wait a little before she delivered her judgement. She drew herself up.

'Come on, Dan. You've just got home, from somewhere. Please don't let us spoil it already by quarrelling the minute you walk in the door. At least let's wait until you've got a decent meal inside you.' She sighed at the way both Tom and Dan still showed signs of hostility in their postures. 'Please yourselves then. Close the door, Tom, on your way out.' She smiled at his amazed look. 'Dan is my husband and he comes before my son, unless he shows signs of killing my son, in which case I will kill him. Come back in an hour. I need some time to speak to this man, my husband. I do have that right in my own house.'

It was the right thing to say to him. Tom said no more but turned on his heel and walked out, closing the door with pointed quietness. Elsie turned her attention back to Dan.

'Do you think you can make it to the settee, Dan?' She reached and helped him to his feet. 'It's just a little way now.'

Dan stood and seemed to take a grip on his resources. His hand, which he had seemed to hold out for support, took on a stiffness showing that it, like the rest of him, was still an independent item. He took a step, and then another, then he almost marched through the house as if he were taking possession. When she followed in his track, he was sitting on the settee.

Elsie walked straight past him, into the tiny kitchen and picked the kettle up. Turning, she carried it to the fireplace and hung it on the hook over the fire. Dan was still sitting there when she turned. She moved and lifted the hat from his head and the jacket from his shoulders.

'You don't need to be at attention, Dan; you're at home now. You can just be easy now. '

Her voice contained the forgiveness he needed and he lifted the hat he had worn all the time he hadn't been wearing his helmet. He placed it almost ceremoniously on the arm of the settee and he voiced his thought.

'I sha'n't need this again, ever. I've done enough now. I've had enough to do with death.'

The soldier turned civilian stood and removed his jacket and folded it carefully, placing it so that the medal ribbons were visible. He turned to face her.

'I've missed you, Elsie, and I've wanted you in the bottom of many a trench while I was waiting for orders to go over the top.'

Dan felt silly making such a confession but she made nothing of it.

'I have missed you as well; Dan Barr and I have wanted you when I have been walking round the market. I want you now.'

Elsie reached to him and, taking his hand, led him up the narrow staircase to their room. She had told him the truth when she had told him that she had missed him. It had nothing to do with the way she felt about Stephen. That was in a separate part of her life, a part that was almost a secret. Her husband was here now and she owed him the sort of homecoming that all returning husbands had a right to expect.

Her hands went to the back of his neck and she gently pressed the shape of herself into the shape of him. The two shapes merged on the bed and the sun shone through the dust of the afternoon onto the bodies lying there. Somehow Elsie felt that a great passion was not going to happen. What was more important was that they would lie next to each other, completing the meaning of the words they had spoken to each other in the little church.

In the street, Tom walked as far as he could; trying to get lost. He had often done this for his own amusement. He didn't really know if he was thinking about his father's return; he just felt that it was not such a happy event as he had expected. His father was not the hero either. Perhaps heroes got like that when they had had enough of killing. Perhaps the novelty wore off after a while.

Stephen, standing on the bridge over the canal, saw him walking along the tow-path and wondered what he was up to. He knew that Tom liked to be on his own sometimes but the lad looked a little cheerless, as if he had had bad news. Perhaps there had been bad news about his father. An un-asked for feeling of elation came over him. Shame for the feeling followed it, swiftly. He moved to the slope that led to the tow-path and waited until Tom turned up it to meet him at the top, with surprise showing on Tom's face.

'Hello, Tom; what are you doing here?'

Tom started. It sometimes seemed as if Mister Stephen always saw him when he was in the middle of some awful situation. How should he answer him? Honestly, he supposed. He made up his mind that this was the one person in the world he had to be honest with.

'I'm just going for a walk round, Mister Stephen. My Dad has just come home today, and he doesn't seem like the Dad I know, er, knew. He shouted at me and I think he was going to hit me but Mom shouted at him, and it stopped him in his tracks. She's a very good shouter you know; not a loud shouter but a quiet shouter that makes you do as you are told. Dad seems like a killer if you know what I mean; not at all like my Dad. I suppose you think somebody who looks like a killer ought to look tough, but he just fainted, right there in the street. Everybody was looking, even Mrs Mallory who knows him well, well I thought she did but she took a look at him and went back into her own house.

'We had to pick him up and get him into the house when he came to. Then Mom told me to go for a walk round for an hour, so here I am. It will be time for me to go back, soon. He said he was sorry for shouting at me but I think that if he got angry, he would shout again.'

Tom stood silent, having released all the emotion in a few minutes of talk with Stephen. He was almost crying as he let Stephen take all the turbulence of his troubled mind. He was dimly aware of an arm going round his shoulders and a feeling of comfort as if a load was being lifted from his back.

'Now look here, Tom. It is not all that easy going around killing people, you know. Some people go mentally ill! Just imagine if you have had to pick up bits of your best mate and try to separate them from the bits of other people. Your Dad has had to do that – and take prisoner the people who blew his best mates up!' Stephen saw the understanding suddenly appear in the youth's eyes. 'How do you think that would affect you then, Tom? Do you think you would still be normal after a few months of that? Your father needs special care for some time to come and you will have to make allowances for his behaviour.'

They had continued walking along the road by the canal and

were getting near to where the main road into Wednesbury turned. They stopped and Stephen again put his arm around the youth's shoulder. There seemed to be a rapport between them that was almost like love. It was as if the usual rivalry that exists between father and son was absent in this case. They stood and shook hands, Stephen going towards the livery stable and Tom towards Union Street.

In the small house a few doors from Elsie's, Ruth was crying. Her husband had been able to avoid conscription because he was engaged in war work, and therefore he had not been in the same stressful condition as Dan and thousands of other men. She had been glad because it meant that she was able to earn a few shillings working for Elsie Barr and her husband did well working for Fred Stone as a blacksmith, making hot forged items for the Army. Chisels and screwdrivers were turned out by the thousand, as well as specialist pieces of work.

Now Dan was back. She had seen him in Elsie's arms, lying outside their house when he had collapsed from nervous exhaustion, as she had thought of it to herself. She had had to walk away, unable to look at what seemed to be the wreck of a man she had known and loved. How would she face and talk to him when he inevitably came to meet her in mundane social circumstances? Would he break down and give away the truth of their affair?

Ruth had an idea that Elsie knew about it, anyway, but suspecting it and having it thrown in your face were two separate things. It was strange, the little things that could affect your future. Oh well, it was no good worrying about that. She could only cross that bridge when she came to it.

She didn't, after all, know how she was going to feel about him, herself. She had got used to her husband's ways now. Dan had been away for most of the war and although it had been thrilling to see him occasionally, he was only a passing thrill, not like her husband who had been a stabilising effect on her now that he had given up alcohol for good.

Perhaps she would have a last fling with him, perhaps she

would ask Elsie's permission; there would be a thing! She had never thought of that before. Just imagine; 'Hello Elsie, I wonder if I could borrow a cup of sugar and by the way, what are you doing with Dan tonight. If it's not too much trouble, could I have him for an hour or so just to get rid of this bloody need in my belly? No? That's not nice of you; after all you've got that Stone chap to see you through a bad patch, ain't ya?'

That would be a good way to lose a friend, wouldn't it? Oh well; that's life, as they say. She had enough kids, that was for sure and she wasn't really sure if one or two of them was Dan's. What a year this has been. A new organisation called the League of Nations had been called for by the President of the United States, Mister Woodrow Wilson. That would make the Germans sit up and take notice!

In the meantime, there were the kids and Jack to cook for and the house to be kept spick and span in case her friend came round for her rent and saw the house untidy. Elsie was a lucky woman. She had her own kids and her husband who would make love to her at the drop of a hat. How much power did she have with the solicitor? She had always done her best to look after Ruth and her husband, Jack, but was she in a position to actually arrange to have her evicted if she happened to fall out with her? It seemed unlikely. Elsie was an unusual person in many ways. She had managed to run three jobs quite successfully for some time, now. There was no point in worrying about what she might do when all she had ever done was to be a good friend.

22. Back to work.
1919

Now was the time to get up. Dan started, and looked up at the clock at the side of the bed. Six o'clock. He stirred his body and moved to the side of the bed before turning to put his feet on the cold floorboards. He would have to think about painting the boards. It didn't make them any warmer but would give the illusion of slight warmth rather than the cold appearance of pine. The other alternative was a square of linoleum. It wasn't very bright but it lasted.

Today was the day he was to start back to work. He knew it was not going to be easy, standing in the same place all day, moving his file backwards and forwards across a thin strip of metal until it was just right. He would probably get that Humpshire hump now. It was strange how he had been used to it, before he joined the Army. He had stood for hours at a time, pushing his file to shape the wards in the locks and then after more training, the keys for complicated mechanisms.

He had to get from Wednesbury to Willenhall. The house that he had admired so much in the street that led into the town was no longer theirs. He had thought that Elsie would have been able to keep up the rent on it; he had sent his allotment home quite automatically.

She had pointed out to him that the numbers he was using to convince himself of his own prosperity were at odds with the facts. Tom was forever growing and eating more. It was a fact of life. She had got him a job at Stone's and that had helped but at the start of the war he had only been seven and it was another two years before she would permit him to work. He had just not been old enough for the long hours that the adults worked. He had been willing enough, regarding himself as the man of the house, but his body was not that of a man. Even now, he was only fourteen, and he was working forty hours a week.

'What do you want from the lad, Dan?'

Elsie had been annoyed with him for expecting too much from Tom and she had let him know she was annoyed. Eventually he had come round to her way of thinking and it was now his turn to put his sweat where his mouth was!

Dan pulled on his trousers and tucked his shirt in. His socks were hanging over the fireguard, downstairs. They wouldn't be very warm yet but they would be warmer than his feet were now. The floor was cold but he ignored it. He had lived in worse conditions for months at a time in France. He had slept whilst keeping one eye open for rats nibbling at his feet. It had been worse for them, he supposed. Every hand, German, French and British, had been against rats.

Elsie was already cooking his breakfast, to his surprise. Their relationship had not been all that warm since his return. He had been to see Ruth and they had been able to have a few moments of pleasure but even she was not as welcoming as he had expected. The eggs were a rare treat for him and he knew they would not be repeated all that often; it was just a friendly send off. Tom had cleaned and oiled his bicycle for him, and it was leaning against the entry wall, ready for him to start out on the road to Willenhall.

Willenhall! The sound of the word made him feel strange. Not ashamed, exactly, but not exactly proud either, because before the War he had got used to living there in a nice posh house, better than this one, anyway. He dipped his bread in the yolk of the last egg in the house. That showed what a luxury they were.

At last, breakfast was out of the way and he could start out. It was unusual for a man to live so far away from his place of work. Mostly, men lived just round the corner from their foundry or wherever they worked.

The bicycle looked very smart and he scooted it for a few feet then cocked his leg over the saddle and started the slow, steady pedalling that would ensure that he got to work on time. There were other cyclists on the road, men and women. He made no attempt to link up with other riders, preferring to keep his own company. He knew he was not as fit as he had been; the bullet in his head had really laid him out and it would take some time yet before he was strong again. The work itself would tax his strength until his muscles had regained their ability.

He had dreamed about starting back to work, free from the discipline of army life, it had been an exciting goal, something to look forward to. Now it looked as if he might not like it all that much. After a few days it would just be another routine, different from the army but still a routine.

Tom had started out on his own bicycle, a few minutes before him, and Dan was glad. He had not wanted company on the long ride. He had always been a bit of a loner, being a bit dour by nature, he knew, and just accepted it. He wondered whether he would catch up with Tom on the journey. Other questions bothered him a little as he rode.

Would Stone make him welcome? It was usual for men to just turn up for their jobs when they returned from service in the forces and here he was, expecting his place to be ready for him, as if it could have been kept like that for over four years. The factory had been well used in the intervening years, making war materials, so someone had obviously used his vice, his place in the hierarchy of Stone, his seat in the sun when they stopped for lunch. Times would have changed; well, he would see about that when he got there. Any intruder into his space would soon be shouldered to one side, man or woman. He would not tolerate anyone in his way.

What would old man Stone say when he saw him? It would all be very interesting. You never knew; he might be offered a charge-hand or foreman's job. The bicycle ride was making him feel better, more optimistic. He was entering Willenhall, now and the sudden proximity of the confrontations he might have this day suddenly scared him. Elsie had said nothing about the sort of welcome he might have, and she had worked there for some time. You would think that she would have given him some sort of clue.

He was there! He suddenly skidded to a halt and lifted his leg over the saddle, turning into the alley that led to the works. As he passed the office window he saw Mabel Stone. Their eyes met and he thought he saw a friendly response. He had always liked Stephen's wife; she was always busy doing something in the shop. He hadn't noticed any of the daughters.

There were strange bikes leaning on the wall, lady's bikes as well as men's. He pulled up the brake and leaned the bike on a bare patch of wall. In a moment he was walking down the shop to his old vice. There was a key in it; a key type that he hadn't seen before. He would soon get used to it. As he walked along, a girl approached his vice and picked up a file. She began to work on the key, her arms moving back and forth as if she had been doing the job for years. Perhaps she had!

It was suddenly that he noticed how pretty she was and he found his body responding to her movements. Back and forth; back and forth. He found himself looking at her more closely. It was Laura. He had known her before he went in the Army. She was the eldest of the Stone's girls. What was she doing on his vice?

She seemed to sense that someone was watching her and she turned, seeing him standing there. Her face brightened and she smiled at him.

'Good morning, Mister Barr. I heard you would be coming back, soon. Father said if you were to turn up, you were to have your old vice back; you had earned it. I shall be able to go back to the shop, now. I'd rather work in the shop. It's nice to see you. Not all the men will be coming back, you know. You'll find out as you go along.'

The Stones' girls had always spoken a little better than the working girls. Mabel, their mother had made sure of that by setting them a good example herself. It was nice to see a friendly face. He hadn't really been made welcome by any of his family or neighbours.

'These are for a new lock we have been making for the Army.' Laura interrupted his thoughts. 'They have a slightly different mechanism and they are a bit awkward. You'll probably be able to do them much better than me.' She picked one up and showed him what was needed to make the key fit the lock that was lying on the bench, waiting to receive it. The idea was just a small variation on what had been used before. There was nothing difficult about it once you got the idea. 'Daddy said you were to go and see him as soon as you appeared,' Laura said. 'I think he's got a different sort of job in mind for you, if you want it.'

Laura didn't know what Stephen had in mind so he had better find out for himself. Perhaps he was going to get the sack before he started. Laura turned to the key and started filing it again. She knew what she was doing; that much was obvious. She seemed to lose interest in him.

Dan made his way through the workshop, noticing the number of women who were working. How would he fit into this lot? A number of the men gave him a handshake as he passed them and he tried to remember others who had been there, working with him before the war. There were more people there now; Stones' must be doing well.

He turned into the small workshop on the way, and noticed Tom. He was making locks and Dan suddenly felt proud of him. He had earned his place among these men who had many years experience between them. He must be pretty good! He caught his eye and they looked at each other, a sort of silent communication. A word or two wouldn't do any harm.

'All right Tom? How's it going?'

Tom stopped working for a moment and looked at his father.

'Yes, I'm fine, Dad. How are you? Are you going to see Mister Stone?'

'Yes, Laura said he wants to see me about something or other. I'll see you later, son.'

That was it, the limit of the conversations they had. There were too many years of absence between them. Tom had had to grow up under his mother's influence and felt himself independent of his father's control. Dan could see that Tom might very well resent being ordered about by his father. He might have regarded him as a hero at one stage but both of them felt differently about such things, now. Most of the heroes were dead. Dan had not only learned battlefield lore; he had been lucky and he knew it. He had seen many men of skill and expertise get killed just by a bit of bad luck.

Dan made his way to the office and knocked on the glass panel that allowed both of them to see each other. Stephen was sitting talking to his father. He looked up at the knock and beckoned him in. Both stood up. Stephen extended his hand and beckoned to a seat. Albert spoke first. 'Well, it's nice to see you back, safe and sound, Dan. We've heard about your exploits from time to time and we are very proud that one of our men has had the honour of the Military Cross. The Military Cross is next to the Victoria Cross, isn't it, Dan? Yes, I thought it was. I don't suppose you want to talk about it, do you?'

Dan didn't know how to respond to the question; he just wanted to be given a job, any sort of job, where he could earn a few bob to help keep his wife and kids. Stephen spoke up.

'Never mind that, Dan, I daresay that you want to know how or if you will fit into the firm now that you are back.'

Stephen looked into Dan's face and Dan just felt like nodding to anything he was asked to agree to.

'Yes Sir.' The habit of four years made him add the 'Sir' and he saw the two men smile but he went on. 'The truth is that I've got used to a different sort of work. Not that I expect I've lost any of my skills, but designs may have altered past recognition and it may take a little time to get used to them. I'm not sure where I'll fit in.'

Now was the time. Dan decided to remain silent. It was up to the gaffers what they did with him. The next words spoken would affect his life, he felt sure. He felt quite calm as he waited. He had had interviews with officers before; he was quite used to it; probably more than the two men who were talking to him. Stephen spoke.

'Right, well this is the situation, Dan. We are one of the lucky firms. We've had a lot of war work in the last few years and just because the war is over, the work hasn't dried up. We are doing well, Dan, and we need a supervisor who will take the place of the two men we had in mind but who died in battle. Although we know you were promoted, we don't know how you would get on, telling people in civilian life what to do. What do you think, Dan?'

Dan's mind seemed to get a different grip on things. This was his chance; it all depended on what he said now and he felt an inner surge of excitement as he put his thoughts in order.

'Well, Mister Stone,' He addressed them both at the same time. 'I was promoted, first to Lance-Corporal and then Corporal, quite quickly. My third stripe followed that and then all of a sudden I was a Warrant Officer. I don't know how much further I would have gone; a bullet in my head changed everything.

'I learned that the orders you give have to be shaped according to the person you are giving them to. It's alright, when you've got two hundred men lined on the parade ground, to shout at them and even to single them out for something they have done wrong, but if you are trying to teach men, or women I suppose, how to perform a task, you have to be a lot more sympathetic to them. That would apply to the work in the factory, and you get nowhere by shouting at them. Many men have been shouted at too much and would resent it.

'Most men just have to be asked to do something and they will help you as much as they can; that's the way I think things should be done, nowadays. If you give me a supervisor's position, this is the way I would work. Not that I would stand for any messing about; the job still has to be done, and done properly. If they can't or won't do it, they will have to be dismissed. It's as simple as that.'

Dan stood, almost at attention, awaiting the outcome. What would they say? Had they made their minds up before he had even walked into the factory a short time ago? His breathing, as he waited, became more relaxed.

Stephen suddenly reached out his hand. 'Congratulations, Dan. We knew before you came into the office that you would be the best man for the job and nothing you have said has changed our minds for us. We shall still expect you to do some work on the bench when you can but most of the time you will be checking batches of work through, and making sure that they meet the specification for the job. There is a desk outside. It's been waiting for you to come. Find yourself a little spot in the workshop and put it there; somewhere where you can see everything that's going on around you.'

Both of the men pumped his hand and then they walked out of the office, showing him that it was all over now and he just had to get on with the job.

He walked back into the long workshop and strode its length. The forge stood at the end, near the entrance, allowing materials, often in the form of long strips of metal, into the vicinity of the forge for ease of handling. There was a dull glow from the hearth of the forge. It had been lit but allowed to die down a little while the smith was away on other work. Dan looked along the wall at the side of the forge and saw that there was a bare part of the wall. That would be a good place to put his desk. There was plenty of light from the window next to it. Where was the smith now?

There was a loud bang and he saw that the smith was just coming in with his mate. He stayed where he was until they drew level with him. He knew the smith, Tommy Hefford, but he didn't know the other one. The smith recognised him at once.

'Good morning Dan,' he said, thrusting his hand forward. 'It's good to see that some of the old gang have come through this lot. I started back last week, in my old job. What are you doing?'

As he went to answer, the other man spoke up.

'I bet he's been given the gaffer's job, Tommy. He's got that look, ain't he?'

The two men looked at the third and Tommy Hefford answered.

'Don't take too much notice of him, Dan. It's just his sense of humour. He don't know any better. He thinks everybody who starts is going to be a gaffer. This is Bill Hawkins, Dan, striker and belt changer and he'll do anything and move anything from A to B if you ask him nicely.'

'Nice to meet you, Bill', Dan introduced himself. 'I'm the new gaffer. If I ask you nicely, will you bring in the desk that is standing in the rain, outside? I want it put in this place just here, where there is nothing else. That way, you can see me easy when you want to ask me for another job and I can see you when you are down at the side of the bosh, hiding from the gaffer, like I used to do.'

The two men stared for a moment and then burst out laughing at the way they had talked themselves into an awkward spot. Bill spoke up.

'Sorry, Dan; I didn't mean to catch you on the hop and it looks as if it was us that was hopping. Pleased to meet a gaffer who's got a sense of humour. We'll get your desk in right away.'

The two men bustled off and Dan looked round the spot he had chosen for himself. There was a block of wood between two of the bricks and he selected a new nail, picked up a hammer and knocked it in. The nail stood out about two inches. He slipped his coat off and hung it on the hook. This was going to be his home while he was at work! He suddenly thought: I haven't got a cowgown! It was tradition, in engineering, to wear a warehouse coat as a sign of rank. He walked to the next little workshop to where his son was working.

'Tom, go to the hardware shop and get me three warehouse coats, please. Put them on invoice and say they will be paid for at the end of the month, alright?'

Tom put his file down and nodded.

'Yes, Dad. Is there anything else? Do you want a teapot?'

'You are as bad as your mother; try to think of everything, don't you?'

Tom grinned and ran off to get the garments for his father. The desk and stool were brought in afterwards and Dan got down to his paperwork. He was familiar with the work methods used at Stone's and within an hour he knew the status of every batch that was on its way through the production process. Tom returned within an hour and Dan slipped the coat on with a sigh of satisfaction. The coat was a sign of his authority.

He had crossed the dividing line between those who gave orders and those who took them. That was the same step that he had taken in the Army. Who knows where he might go from there? This was not as large an organisation as the Army, but he might still go far. He had an idea that Elsie had money hidden away and he meant to get control of it. He might be able to start his own locksmith's company and get them another nice house in Willenhall, the same as they had lived in before!

His mind moved over the possibilities. He still had twenty-five pounds of Army pay that no one knew about apart from himself and he could see that a hundred pounds would buy a lot of tools and equipment. All he had to do was to find a small workshop, take his family with him when he left, undercut other firms on a few jobs and he would be made for life!

He might have to wait a year or two before he was able to achieve all he wanted but it would happen; he could feel it in his bones. Barr and Son. That sounded good to be painted over the doorway. Maybe it would be Barr and Sons! That sounded better still. Dan knew that Tom had had a good training at Stone's that would stand him in good stead wherever he worked so if Tom could be accommodated wherever Dan worked, he would be a good employee and earn good profits. Maybe the little one would be as talented.

It wasn't likely; Tom was talented. He had watched him in the last hour and had immediately seen that the lad had the way of standing and the way of moving that came from skilled practice. He might have other talents that would be useful to his family. It only took time to find out, didn't it?

Dan saw that he would have to be as good as the others; he walked across to an empty vice and picked up a lock and a file. He inserted the lock into the vice and started filing. He still had the latent skills, he knew, they just had to be brought back to the level he was at when he went away. It was a great relief. He looked around. No one seemed to be watching him. A good job as well' he would soon tell them where they got off.

23. To be his own Boss.
1919

No one queried the overalls he had asked for on invoice. He knew he should have paid for them himself but he did not want to spend his own money, nor let anybody know, even that he had a few shillings tucked away. He kept his attention on the job he was supposed to do and he soon found that he could cope quite easily with the work, delegating nearly all his work to someone else, as he had in the Army.

Many firms were closing down because of the economic conditions prevailing. There were many causes of closure. The influenza epidemic was killing off thousands and many people were even frightened to mix with others because of the risk. When this occurred, Dan tried to be at the sale or auction of premises and stock which naturally happened at these times. He picked up quite a few useful items for coppers; an anvil and almost the whole of the contents of the forge of one small firm on John Street.

He now had a problem with the storage of these things and looked around for somewhere cheap as a store-place. He had decided that he was going to have his small workshop in Willenhall as it was the centre of the lock industry, so he went to the agent whose advice had originally brought him to the house he had rented there. Dan was more mature now and looked something of a man about town as he stepped into the office.

There was a bell on the counter and he rang it twice to make sure that the proprietor paid attention to it. There was the sound of a movement from behind the screen that hid half of the office from view. Then a large man appeared; it was the same man that Dan had seen before. It was strange, he thought, how some people stuck in your memory.

'Yes; can I help you?' The man asked, respectfully, lowering his eyes as he recognised Dan. 'Hello, Mister Barr; it's a long time since we met.'

Dan looked at him. The man had an arm that was manufactured and he looked so strange with the way that he carried it rather than used it that Dan could not help but smile as he answered.

'Good morning; yourself. You look as if you've been through the mill, like myself but I'm lucky enough to have brought all my bits and pieces back with me. The only thing I added was a bullet in the head which I was lucky enough to have taken out.' He changed the subject. 'I'm looking for a small cheap, secure place to keep some locksmith's gear for the time being, until I'm ready to start on my own, and I want that kept confidential, right?'

The man nodded; he was used to confidentiality; it suited him and gained him respect. 'I'll just have a look to see if there is anything filed away; I don't recall anything at the moment but you never know your luck. Excuse me, Mister Barr.'

He disappeared again for a full minute then returned with a few pieces of paper. Most of them looked as if they had been in his care for some time, being creased and dog-eared. Dan was surprised that there was even a small selection of places to rent.

He slid his spectacles over his ears and looked through them at the sheets of paper. 'Here we are, Mister Barr. I've got three that might suit you. This one is a mile outside the town centre and its rent is cheap.' He handed the details to Dan. 'This one is not much more than a lavatory in size; it might do you if you don't have much to store.' He handed over the sheet with the details to Dan and that left him with one sheet of paper. 'This one is not really one of ours; it belongs to one of Mister Jenkins's clients, in Wednesbury. It is not in Wednesbury; it is here, just round the corner. It is a little costlier than the one I showed you just now but it is far superior as both a storage area and as a place to start up, if you were to start up in a small way. There is an office and a workshop, that's all – apart from the lavatory.'

He handed over the sheet of paper and pointed out the price. Dan recognised the heading at the top; he had seen it many times. S. Jenkins. Solicitor and Property Agent. The price was very reasonable and he was immediately tempted. He looked down the sheet and saw the code for the owner, EB. The implication was obvious. There couldn't be all that many people with those initials. It couldn't be Elsie, though. She might have a few shillings tucked away but she certainly didn't own any property, did she? He decided to ask. 'Who does it belong to? Do you think the owner might come down a bit in the price?'

He looked the agent directly in the face and the look demanded an answer. 'I don't know who the owner is, to tell the truth. What I do know is that Mister Jenkins Junior, as he is sometimes called, acts for a number of property owners, collecting the rent in for them and sometimes even investing it for them. Whether he will come down in price or not, I don't know. Not many people try that one but if you want to risk it, all you have to do is make an offer in writing. You can only be told yes or no, can't you?'

He looked at Dan with such a strange expression that Dan was left feeling that the man knew more than he was letting on. He put the details of all three properties in his pocket, tipped his cap and walked out of the little agency. He had a lot to think about. He could just ask Elsie's help. She ought to know the system at Jenkins's better than most. Even now that she had left their employment, after James's death, she still went in to see them, he knew. Was it possible that she actually owned property? He would try facing her with it, tonight.

Naturally she would want to know where he had got his information from and what he was doing, picking up information from agencies. Still, why shouldn't he? He had every right as a returning hero, to look for opportunities to start up a small business for himself and his family. He had a responsibility as well as the authority, to do his best for his family.

'Excuse me,' it was the agent calling him back. 'Your old house is back on the market, you know. I just wondered if you would be interested.'

It was more like a question than a comment and Dan decided quickly. After all, why should he cycle all the way from

Wednesbury, when he could live next door, so to speak, to his work? He handed over a deposit, the act bringing back memories and then made his way home.

It was half an hour before his wife and son came in. He had made a pot of tea. The family should be fairly prosperous, now, with three bread-earners. Ted was still at school and Ruth was cooking his tea. She came in sooner than Elsie; it was a chance for them to see each other. Dan immediately sent Ted upstairs and took hold of Ruth. She clung to him but not with the passion that she had shown before.

'Come on, Dan,' she said, 'We'll have plenty of time for that sort of thing. Just for now, try to behave yourself, there's a good boy.'

He slipped his hand onto her breast and she looked at him in a way that told him he wasn't wanted. It wasn't at all pleasant. It was enough to send him back to Blackwell, to Jean's arms. Perhaps he would! Sod 'em all! He walked away from Ruth and sat down, while Ruth took the hint and the hump, and walked out. Women were funny sometimes. Perhaps it was just a bad time for her.

Elsie walked in with Tom and he poured the tea for them. He prided himself that he knew exactly how she liked her tea and she sat and drank it without a word. Tom was going out but Dan had an idea that Tom could help him a little. 'Tom, could you just drop into the fish and chip shop and get us some supper, please? It would save your mother having to cook and I think she's done enough for today, don't you?' He didn't wait for an answer but put his hand in his pocket and pulled out two half crowns. 'That should be plenty; don't forget the change, my lad.'

He grinned. As if Tom would even dream of taking the change! He waited until Elsie had finished changing into her housework apron and decided to broach the subject on which he had been thinking. 'Elsie, there's a matter on which I think you could help me, please, love.'

She looked up at him and carried on placing the knives and forks for the fish and chips she had heard him ordering via Tom.

When she had finished she turned to him. 'What is the matter, Dan? Have you been up to something without telling me?'

Dan decided that a certain amount of honesty would help him. If his suspicions were correct, it was she who had been doing things without confiding in him!

'Well, it's like this. I've been thinking about starting my own business. You know, making locks and keys; making improvements where possible and making them at a lower price than Stone's could do them. I've bought some equipment with some of my Army pay that I had left over, and I have enough money to rent a small place to keep the stuff until I can rent a workshop. When I leave, I'll take both you and Tom with me and we shall be a family working unit. What do you think about that?'

Dan looked at her again and she just sat there silent for a minute. Then she started asking him questions.

'How much have you got towards the workshop? When would you want to move in? Do you have any orders for the goods you are going to make? That'll do for now but if you think I'm going to walk out of a job where I'm earning good money, into a job where I'm not earning money, you can think again.'

Elsie was looking at him in that way again, as if he hadn't a clue about what to do to set up in business. He would show her! He was about to stand and put on a fighting posture when Tom walked in with the fish and chips. He put them on the table and put down the change.

'There's your change. I've bought my own. I don't need anybody to buy my dinner; my housekeeping is in my Mom's hand every Friday, and I don't need your change either. I can get my own money, thanks, Dad!'

Dan rounded on him automatically. He wasn't going to let his wipper-snapper of a son to talk to him like that. He lifted his hand to cuff him and he was surprised when Tom just stood there. Dan could see that there would be more trouble than he bargained for if he struck him.

'I was only joking, son. I would never hit you. You shouldn't take too much notice of me. I've been in some rough company, you know, and the rough takes over you if you ain't careful. Sit down and have a few chips with us, and a cup of tea. That can't do any harm, can it?'

He moved and opened the newspaper that the chips were wrapped up in.

'Here you are Tom. Just take what you want. Here, Elsie. Where's that pot of tea, our wench?' He turned to face Tom. 'I was just starting to explain to your mother. I'm thinking of starting up on my own, making locks. I'm pretty sure I could make them cheaper than Stone's. It wouldn't be hard to undercut them, and then I could really make some cash. Not that I would want to do it on my own. What I want is to take you and your mother with me. We would be working as a family firm then, wouldn't we?'

Elsie walked in with the teapot and started to pour it out. As she did so, she was watching Dan. She seemed quite annoyed when she spoke to him.

'All right, Dan Go on then. Tell us the secret of how you can undercut Stone's and make a fortune. What secret have you got?'

Dan looked from Elsie to Tom. Neither of them seemed willing to listen with an open mind to what he had to say. '

'Now listen here. I know you both think I don't know what I am talking about but why shouldn't we start up on our own?' He realised that he was saying 'we' now, where he had been saying 'I', before. 'What has Stones' got that I can't give you?'

The gauntlet was down; how could they work for a stranger when they could be working for their husband and father? Where should their loyalties lie? Dan wasn't at all sure he wanted to know the answer to the questions that kept popping into his head. He might not like them.

The other thing that still lingered in his mind was Elsie's relationship with Stephen Stone. He had never actually caught them at anything they shouldn't be doing but he had always felt that there was something there; if not love or sexual attraction, there was a feeling that was more than just the respect that arose between a good employer and a good employee.

Tom too, liked Stephen; he knew that. Would that feeling prevent him joining a team devoted to undercutting the Stone family business? How was he going to promote his idea to the extent that that they would want to join with him in the effort to start up their own family business? Tom looked at his father and answered.

'Look Dad, I know you think that I should just leave Stones' and start to work for you out of family loyalty but there is more to it than you think. I think that I am probably one of the best trained locksmiths in the Black Country. That's not just a sign that I am big-headed about my ability; it's just facing the facts. I learned to make all my own tools when I first started, and there was no profit for Stone's in that, and not many apprentices get that sort of chance. When I started making locks, Mister Albert was always there to put me right, or show me a better way.

'That was a good preparation for a career in the trade, probably a better preparation than anybody else has ever had. Now you want me to show how much I appreciate the training by undercutting them! I can't say I feel like doing that. What sort of a bloke would that make me?

'The other thing to think about is this; you have been away for nearly all the length of the war, and your job was waiting for you when you came back. A lot of the sort of work that you were used to, has been discarded for better methods that were brought about by the need to do things faster and better.

'No one has blamed you for not knowing the new methods; you have been allowed to pick up the new methods in your own time, even though other people, including the women who filled your space while you were away, could have done the job better.

I don't know about Mom, but I am not about to be a traitor to a good gaffer! I'm sorry Dad, but I can't do it. I'll listen to what you have to say on the subject, and I suppose it would be nice to be a gaffer but I can live without it.'

Tom fell silent and picking up his cup, began drinking. Now

it was Elsie's turn, thought Dan. Tom had undermined his authority as head of the family. Would Elsie do the same? Would she support him or would she take the side of Stephen Stone? He turned to her, the question in his eyes.

Elsie put down her cup and looked straight back at him in the straightforward way she always did. He felt that everything was not going as he had envisioned it.

'I'm proud of the way Tom has thought about what you have asked us to do. He has tried to disagree with what you have proposed, but done it in a way that shows that he is still loyal to the family. I think that young Tom is a lad who just wants to do the right thing, and as you know as well as I do, its not always easy to do that.

'As far as I am concerned, you have heard how my Dad and me walked from Birmingham, looking for work, and it was the Stones' family all the way, who gave us the chance to earn a decent living, right up until the day that Dad died. They even paid for his funeral! How right would it be to show my thanks by setting up in opposition?

'I think you'd be better employing your time by doing your best to make sure that what skill you have is used to get better profits for the Stones. Perhaps they would repay you with promotion. After all, you are used to telling people what to do; you could use that ability at work.'

Dan was angry; he had been turned down by his own family! How could he get his own way? Young Ted was looking up from his breakfast, smiling at him. Dan snarled at him.

'Get on with your breakfast, you!' Was there anything he could do to force his opinion on his family? He thought about it. 'It's all very well to have the sort of loyalty that you obviously have to Stephen Stone, and I question whether you should have it; it's just that I think that your loyalty should be to your husband, not to some other bloke! People might think there was something going on!'

The moment he said it, he regretted it. Tom stood up and

glared at him.

'What do you mean by that, Dad?'

It was obvious that Tom had no real idea that what he had said was insulting at most, and sarcastic at least. He just knew that his father was being hostile and nasty to his mother, and he could not tolerate it. He did not reply to the question his son asked; Elsie was quite capable of defending herself and she did.

'Don't talk to me about loyalty, Dan Barr. I don't walk around with my eyes shut, you know. Ruth has been a good friend to me while you were away but a better friend to you, while you are at home! I wonder just how loyal you were to me while you were in France!'

It was now Dan's turn to become angry. He stood up and for a moment it looked as if he were going to strike her. Then he suddenly had a comprehension that if he did, he would have to leave the house, perhaps for ever. Elsie certainly wouldn't tolerate violence on his part; neither would his son. He would have no job; the truth about his business plans would emerge and they would soon get rid of him. Thinking about it, he saw that Elsie was surrounded by protective relationships. In any conflict he had been involved while in the Army, he'd had a clear field to impose his will on anyone he chose as a victim. He had better try to look more agreeable.

'Yes, you are probably right. It sometimes takes a conversation like this to help to get things in perspective. What you have to understand is that when I was in the Army, although we all had loyalties to our unit, and Regiment, there were many criminals too, and they had no loyalties unless they were more or less forced on them. You had to stand up for yourself against them and anyone else who tried to take advantage of you. I suppose I got to be good at it; that was one of the reasons I was promoted so quickly.

'I'll think over what you have both said to me and take it into account, but you also will have to see that it's not a crime for a man to want to better himself. That was how the Stones' got started and if they can, why not me?'

273

Dan sat and looked at them and they could see that he was right in some respects. Some people got on by inheriting money and land, others by careful investing and yet others by using their body and experience to carve a living out of whatever trade they felt they could.

There was no end to the discussion and no conclusion was drawn. It was just that at that particular time, they did not agree on the best way to get on in the world. Tom had listened though, and that discussion was to remain with him and influence his actions for many years but not to the extent that he would work against the Stone family who had given him so much.

The three participants looked at each other and the subject was closed. There was one thing that Dan was still curious about though, and he felt this would be a good time to ask directly.

'Elsie, there is one thing that I have wondered about. When I went looking for a small property to rent, I was offered a small place in Willenhall. It was one of Mister Jenkins's places. I asked the agent who the owner was, and he told me he did not know. He showed me the paper with all the details of the property and on the line for the name of the owner, it just said EB. Is that you, Elsie? I didn't think you owned any property'

He sat back and waited for her reply. Now we would see!

'Oh, Dan,' Elsie sighed. 'You are always looking for an easy way to make money. I used to collect rents on some business properties in Wednesbury and Willenhall as you know, and that was one of them. That was the reason it had my initials on the details.' She laughed and her laugh seemed genuine. 'Did you think you had a rich wife? You would have loved that wouldn't you? You could have retired then, and spent your days boozing. I am sorry, but I was just the rent-collector.'

Elsie stood and smoothed her skirt down. She had finished. She would answer no more of his questions. She had earned the money to gradually acquire the few bits of property that she owned; she wasn't going to hand them to him, on a plate, for him to pee up the wall!

Dan sat back. It was more than he had thought possible, for her to own property. She might be bright but not that bright! He had to decide what was to be done, now. She was right about one thing, though. If he couldn't start up on his own, his next best move would be to get himself well in with the Stones and try to get them to give him a job with more responsibility. He stood up.

'There is one other thing, love; I have put a deposit on our old house, in Willenhall. I think we can afford that now, don't you?' He saw the look of assent in her eyes. I'm going out for a drink; see you later.'

He closed the door behind him a little noisily, not enough to be accused of banging it on the way out, but enough to show his displeasure. He went up to the George; it was one of his favourite places in Wednesbury. It always had a warm fire and he more or less had his own seat there. The rest of the evening passed slowly. He was still thinking about how to make his life more bearable when they called time.

Elsie Barr smiled to herself. She had let the agent know that the house could be put back on the market but hadn't thought her husband would act so quickly. For once he had done the right thing, even if it was by accident. She put her arm around the shoulders of her son.

'Come on, Tom. Let's have a cup o' tea and a piece o' bread and jam. That'll cheer us up, won't it?'

She reached for the kettle. Another round had been fought and won. She still had her sons and Dan Barr would never take over them, whatever he tried! What would he try next?

24. The Foreman.
1920

Bert Stone was having a bad day. The gaffer had scolded him again. It wasn't very often, because Mister Barr liked him, even though he wasn't the brightest star in the heavens, as his father said. Finally, the gaffer, Dan Barr, spoke quietly to him.

'Look, Bert, Watch me do one; then you have a go, all right? First thing after you have hammered it to shape and filed and ground it to give it a respectable look, you have to harden the screwdriver and temper it. This is common hardening steel so the first thing you do is harden it.'

He picked the up the screwdriver blank and showed it to Bert.

'The way you do that is to heat it up in the hearth to a nice cherry sort of red, alright? See? There it is; a nice cherry red. Now you take hold of it with the tongs so that you don't burn your hands, and then you dip it in the bosh to harden it. Go on then, dip it in the bosh, about four inches of it. Good; that's right. Now you clean the surface, wait to make sure it's cold, and then you heat it up, but not at the end like you did when you were hardening it. You try to heat it up about three inches from the end; watch as I do it. Got it? Now watch the colour change, gradually. What you are looking for is for it to become straw-coloured, like that, see? Then you dip it in the bosh again. That is what we call tempering. If you don't harden it, the screwdriver will just buckle when you try to turn the screw; if you don't temper it, the steel will be too hard and then it will just snap because it will be too brittle.

'You've shaped the other end into a tapered square, so you can just tap it gently into a file handle and then it will be ready for you to use. That was easy enough, wasn't it, Bert? Good. Now what you need is a selection of shapes and sizes so that you can do or undo most sizes of screw. If you make three this afternoon, and show me what you've done, that should be enough for you to do this afternoon, and then you can ask your father if he has got anything for you do. Give me a shout when you are ready to start hardening, right? I'll see you later. The three extra screwdrivers will make your tool-kit more complete, see?'

Dan didn't know why but he always got a good feeling about helping Bert; he was not very clever but the lad really got a sense of achievement when he finally grasped a principle, or a way of doing a job that wasn't completely easy. He wondered why it was that some, in a family, were bright and others were thick. The other thing was that Bert seemed a much nicer person than his father. How could that have happened? Stephen Stone had always seemed bright so the idea that he could have a brother who was so inept seemed ludicrous and unlikely.

Dan also got that feeling of achievement when the lad got something. There was as much pleasure in teaching as doing. He thought it might be that he had been deprived of the opportunity of teaching his son, Tom, while he had been away in the Army. Old Albert had had that pleasure with Tom and had probably enjoyed every minute.

Bert was coming on though, and improving as he did so. All over the Midlands, young men were learning trade secrets. They called Birmingham the City of a thousand trades; if that was so, what would they call the Black Country? There were a myriad trades carried on here. Mining; leatherwork; saddle-work; locks and keys and all the associated trades, engineering and foundry work. Chain-making was an old established trade in the Black Country. There was even established china and glassmaking carried on. The canals carried other tradesmen, the men and women who lived and worked on the narrow-boats. There seemed to be no end to the groups who had their own skills and traditions. Dan himself had always been in the key and lock trade. He had started at eleven and had been in it ever since.

Now he was teaching others, but even he had had to learn other trades, soldiering, and professional killing when the King had needed him to put down uprisings from other States. It was surprising what you learned in a lifetime.

If there was one thing he wished he had more ability in, it was music. He had often wished he could play some musical instrument, even if it was only the harmonica. He had bought one, once, but he had never had the patience or the tuition to get to grips with it.

Perhaps teaching was his forte as they called it. He could certainly look at the work he had done with Bert, and feel satisfaction. What did the Stone family think about their son's progress? He suddenly realised that it was important to him what they thought. He had a need to be appreciated, even if what they saw was a rough and ready Black Countryman. Perhaps they would appreciate him enough to give him the Foreman's job, instead of a charge-hand's.

They were employing young girls, now, and he had been asked if he would be responsible for their training. He had accepted of course and they had put a few shillings more in his packet. Three girls were due to start work on Monday morning. He hadn't met them yet, much to his annoyance. Surely the one who was going to teach them should be the one to pick 'em!

He walked briskly along the narrow walkway that led round the workshop. He meant to have a hook for each of the girls to hang their coats on, along with a box seat to put their private things into. They would be making the long armed padlocks for Spain, to be used on their fishing fleet, to hold boxes of fish down on the decks. They had to be taught other skills of course. There was no guarantee that they would always be employed on just one sort of lock.

A fairly new girl, Molly, was sitting watching him as he knocked the screws in for the coat hooks. It was her break time. He had noticed her watching him before and it was getting under his skin. She was a good looking girl with long legs and an upright look to her posture which made her breasts jiggle. She smiled in response to his look.

'Hello, Mister Barr. You are always busy aren't you? You never seem to have time to sit down and have a chat, do you?'

Molly crossed her legs and he noticed that her skirt was quite short; it was the fashion now that the Twenties had started, but she was the first he had seen who was so willing for him to look at her. She had obviously seen that he was looking at her legs.

'Do you like looking at girl's legs, Mister Barr? You seem to, the way you look at mine!' She moved along the wooden bench and patted the seat next to her. 'Come along, Mister Barr, or do they call you Dan?'

He felt compelled by her audacity to sit next to her. He knew that if he made a false move now, he could be in trouble, but the false move was the one he was most tempted to make.

'What do you think of them now that you are closer to them, Mister Barr?' she said. 'You are not disappointed, are you?'

The girl took his hand and placed it on her leg and the small action took him past the point where he felt in control. He slid his hand along her leg until it arrived at the junction of her thighs. Surprisingly, she did not scream for help. She just took his hand in hers and kept it pressed against her pubic area. She was enjoying this, he thought. She slid under his grip and lay on the bench.

'Give me something to remember you by, Mister Barr, please.'

Suddenly, the words changed everything. She became trash in his eyes, just a slut whose feelings did not have to be considered. He pulled his hand away. God only knew what disease she might have. His change in attitude was made up of the fear of consequences and this helped him to rationalise it, and the application of the moral viewpoint that he had been brought up with. The thought came to him that if his mother were able to see him now, he would be ashamed, and so would she.

'You'd better get yourself back to work, Molly. Don't let me catch you playing around in working hours, again; right?' He stood and faced her, his face angry. 'I don't mind a bit of fun but I am not going to father some little bastard just for your pleasure. If I catch you again, you'll be out of the door without a reference. Do you understand?'

The coquettish look went from her face. It was obvious that she understood completely what he meant. It was a first and last warning. She nodded at him and he turned his back and walked away, furious. He would talk to Stephen Stone about the girl; Stephen would soon sort her out. In the meantime, he had other things to do. For a start, he had to decide what to do with the things he had bought in preparation for starting his own little business.

It was late but he always felt it was best to talk over any problem with the gaffer before he went. Stephen Stone was in his office with his mother. He nodded to Dan and he walked in.

Mabel turned and saw him and smiled. She had always had a soft spot for him, especially now he had taken Bert under his tutelage.

'Hello, Dan; how are you. We don't seem to see each other very often. You should come, with Elsie, to tea on Sunday. We shall expect you. It's actually been years since we had you to tea. Give my regards to her, won't you?'

Mabel turned away and Stephen raised his eyebrows.

How can I help you, Dan?'

That was one thing about the man, thought Dan. He was always ready to listen to you, even if he did laugh a lot. Stephen waved his hand at a chair and Dan sat down. 'It's about that new girl, Molly Cartwright.'

He lowered his voice to a pitch just above a whisper, trying to avoid letting Mabel hearing what he was saying. He gave an explicit account of what had happened on the bench in the workshop.

'What shall I do about her, Mister Stephen? I've given her a first and last warning but I'm concerned if she does something like that again, with someone else, perhaps.'

To his surprise, Mabel spoke first. He hadn't known she could hear that well.

'I think you have done quite enough, Dan. You have done everything necessary. It will all be recorded in the book, against her name. If you hear of any other infringement, she will be dismissed!'

Mabel walked out of the office and he was left with Stephen, to his relief. He hadn't known she had such good ears. He had turned his neck round in response to her voice. Now he turned it back so that he could face Stephen and waited for his answer. Unsurprisingly, Stephen laughed. He was well known for this response to any stressful situation, although he could usually come up with a good solution.

'Well, you heard Mother. If there are any other infringements she will be dismissed. That's that settled. Is there anything else?'

He still had the laughter in his eyes. Was that what had attracted him to Elsie, Dan wondered. Would Stephen really dismiss the girl, or would he take advantage of her, himself? Perhaps he would forewarn old Albert Stone. He still liked to mess around with the young ones. Still, the problem had been raised and a solution found, all in five minutes. Now he could go home.

The house was quiet when he walked in. That was unusual; Tom had not worked past the normal finishing time; surely he should be home by now. For a moment Dan wondered if he had got mixed up with Molly and stayed to satisfy her. Elsie wasn't at home either and his imagination caught at his mind again, visualising her with Stephen Stone on the same bench where he had lain with Molly. A few minutes later he heard noises upstairs ands looking up the stairs, he saw Tom.

'What's up Tom? Are you alright?'

Tom came down the stairs and spilled his story. Molly had asked him the same series of questions that had made Dan almost lose control of the situation. The difference was that Tom had almost gone all the way. Tom was very embarrassed as he told his father what had happened. She had sat on the bench, making comments on the way he was looking at her legs, and then had invited him to sit down. He had ended up with his hands up her knickers and his lips on her breasts. He had pulled himself away from her but she had begged him to stay and make love to her. He not only wouldn't but he couldn't. The offer of her body had been too blatant and he had felt more turned off than turned on.

Dan told Tom of his own experience with her, and included the warning he gave her, and the fact that her behaviour had been entered in the book, against her name. He told Tom that some women had a sort of illness that made them that way and it would be bad to take advantage of them. Anyone who did was quite likely to catch some disease that had been given to her by one of her lovers. Tom seemed impressed by the knowledge that his father was passing on to him, and it made him feel more mature to be even discussing such things.

Dan turned his mind to the problem of the items he had bought recently as part of his plan to form his own small firm. He had struggled down the stairs with the anvil, even though it was only a small one; God knows how he would get it back up again. The items that he had bought in the same lot as the anvil were all wrapped up, downstairs. He had bought punches and hot and cold sets to cut metal strips and a couple of fullers to increase the size of holes that had been bored in the metal that he was working on.

A thought came to him. Perhaps he could sell them to the Stone's family. They would never need to know that he had bought them as a means to set up in opposition to them! He would think about that. It was beginning to look as if he would have to give the whole idea up. Oh, well.

He suddenly thought of Molly and her legs and he felt a need for Elsie. Where was she? A panic came to him and he suddenly felt sad. It was bad enough if he was unfaithful but if she was, he felt as if the bottom would drop out of his world. He looked upstairs and found her tidying the clothes in the wardrobes. He felt a sudden, heavy sense of relief and he walked to her, putting his hands round her, cupping her breasts.

His wife never denied him and didn't this time. She turned and lay on the bed. 'Come on, Dan. Let's do it then.'

She reached to him and pulled his trousers down as she reached to take hold of his manhood, pulling on it and touching it with her tongue to help rouse him. The sensation was so intense that he could only push in response to her touch. He felt himself slip into her and touch her teeth. She didn't back away though; she took a firm hold of him with her gums and sucked him further in until the only response he could give was to ejaculate immediately. He had another sense of relief but this time it was combined with the sense of guilt that he had not been able to bring her the same pleasure that she brought to him.

'I'm sorry,' he said, feeling completely ineffectual as a lover. 'I just wanted you so much that I had to...you know.'

'Don't worry about it, Dan. It was nice, just being with you, no matter in what way. Perhaps it would be nice if you could make me come like that.'

She lay back and he thought, 'Now's the time to earn my keep, I suppose.' He bent and touched her most private parts with his hand and inserted his finger. He felt her get slippery straight away, and then he wondered if she had already been slippery from a previous encounter. He worked hard at the task of giving his wife an orgasm and he was rewarded by the sound of her heavier breathing as he moved his hand faster and faster. Suddenly he sensed her climax and relaxed. It was all over.

'Thank you, Dan,' she said. 'I needed that.'

Elsie lay back and he relaxed too, rapidly sinking into a deep sleep. Neither of them even thought of the feelings of their partner as they slept but Dan had dreams of Ruth and Molly, all mixed up, while Elsie felt in her deepest self, there should be a place where lovers could meet and make perfect love.

Tom and Ted were in the living room below, playing snakes and ladders. Tom was bored but there was nothing else to do, and he would only get into trouble if he went out and left Ted by himself.

He found himself thinking of Molly again. She was wonderful, with her long legs and beautiful bosom that moved and heaved, even while he was watching it. She had liked him; he knew that from the way she had touched him. She had said that his arms were lovely and she wished someone would put arms like them, around her. How could he have resisted her? It would have been quite impossible. While he had moved his hands along her legs, she had been undoing her blouse so that he could see and touch and kiss her breasts. The trouble started when she opened her mouth. She sounded like some slut who had no sort of values at all. It had made him feel awful, even though she had made him feel so good just before. He didn't even want to look at her, let alone touch her and do those things. His mother would have put him in his room for a week and slapped him silly, to boot.

He was going to have nothing to do with her after this. She was a bad woman, regardless of what his father had said about some sort of illness. Mind you, she had looked so wonderfully beautiful that if she offered herself to him again, he would go mad rather than leave her.

There was more to this faithfulness thing than met the eye. Sometimes you felt very faithful and the feeling was good; sometimes you felt wonderful, like he had with Molly, and it wasn't good at all. You were doing the wrong thing and you knew it. What about Dad, then? Was he always faithful? He had explained to Tom some of the sort of temptation that would almost certainly be put in his way, but maybe, just maybe, he had been tempted and hadn't told Tom!

Tom was almost asleep now, and so was Ted. Tom had to get up for work in the morning so he had better close his eyes He did that, then opened them again to blow the candle out. The moon shone through the window onto his youthful face. They couldn't come much more innocent than that.

In the next room, Elsie lay and thought of Stephen. If only he was with her now. Life was complicated.

25. Mabel.
1921

Mabel lifted the small skirt upward, out of the box. It was green, one of her favourite colours. Not too light and not too dark, a sort of sage green, not quite olive. There was a jumper somewhere that almost matched it. She knew there was because she had seen it, somewhere. She reached again and found the jumper. When she held it in the light to compare the two colours, they were as near as you could get to matching. Mary Billington would like that. The two items would just go with her auburn hair and green eyes. She often came in on a Monday.

Mabel gently slipped the jumper and skirt onto the mannequin that she sometimes used to model something that appealed to her. She hadn't got much of a window but it was often the fact that an item was the only thing shown that sold it. Most people liked to think that they had the original, and what they saw in the window was regarded as the original; that was what she thought, anyway.

Mabel picked up the mannequin and lifted it into the window space. That looked all right. She walked round the counter and out of the door, into the street. She turned around and viewed the mannequin. The sun shone on it; she couldn't leave it like that; the colours would fade. She walked back into the shop and picked up the long pole with the hook on the end. She hooked it into the blind and pulled. It was quite a strain to pull out and she could not quite manage it. There was a cough behind her and she turned in surprise.

It was Stephen. Somehow she hadn't been expecting him. She wouldn't have minded if it had been a younger, more handsome man. She smiled at her own clumsy attempt at fantasy. Trust him to turn up when he wasn't wanted!

'What do you want? Have you got nothing to do? Here, I'll find you something to do; grab hold o' this; make yourself useful!'

Stephen laughed as usual; he always laughed when he was

asked to do something, anything. She felt like hitting him; he never did anything right. Even that Dan Barr could do something useful. At least he could talk to their son. That was more than his father could do. Dan Barr was a nice quiet chap. He had been in to tell about that stupid Molly Cartwright. Really, he should have just sacked her, the little slut.

Mabel watched as Stephen pulled the blind into position and locked the sides down. Just because he had pulled the blind up, he probably thought he was wonderful. Why did he have to be so…?

Stephen pulled her to him and cradled her face in his hands. He knew there was something wrong but didn't know what it was. He kissed her full on the lips and felt her start to respond to him.

'You bloody fool! You can't behave like that in the middle of the street!'

'Who can't? You watch me, if I want to.'

He dragged her off the pavement, into the shop. Dan Barr was standing there, his face troubled.

'Hello, Dan, What can I do for you, now?'

'Nothing, Mister Stephen, it's alright. I'll see to it later on.'

Dan turned and headed out of the office. Stephen turned and saw Mabel standing, her face scarlet. He started to laugh and as he did, saw Mabel's face getting redder and angrier. He laughed again; he couldn't help himself. He knew that it was not a thing that made him feel better about himself; it was a thing that made him feel embarrassed and a subject of derision. He still laughed, though.

If only this stupid woman would just disappear, he could somehow get in touch with Elsie and let his feelings go. The thought made him want a woman, any woman. He grabbed hold of his wife, picked her up and laid her on top of the pile of clothes in the corner of the shop. Her skirt moved up easily and he was inside her in a few seconds. She responded vigorously and angrily. Pushing and pulling.

'Let me go you bastard. Who do you think you are, raping me in a public place?' She dragged her fingernails down his face, dragging blood with them. 'I'll let everybody see the sort of man you are, showing me up with that Barr woman. She's just as bad as you and she's married to a gentleman. He would never do anything like that to his wife; not that she would stop him. She'd let you take her in the middle of the office!'

That was it, thought Stephen. She's having some sort of fantasy. He bent and dragged her up from the pile of clothes and pulled her into the office. This time he stood her against the wall, lifted her skirt again and plunged into her. She collapsed into a heap on the floor and lay there in what seemed to be a faint. She had had enough. He reached and locked the front door and in the same movement turned the 'open' sign round. He was exhausted. He let himself slide down beside her and pulled her onto his shoulder. I love her, he thought. Even though she is such a miserable bitch, I love her.

Ten minutes later there was a knock at the shop door. Breathing to show his impatience, he stood and opened it. It was a youth.

'Yes!' He barked, 'What can I do for you, young man?'

The youth obviously expected to be let in.

'Please Mister Stone, is Laura in? My mother, Mrs Farthingale, wants to meet her. She says Laura is the prettiest girl in Willenhall, and I agree with her. I would leave home for her, Mister Stone. Is she in, please?'

Stephen looked and saw Mabel sitting against the wall, her eyes closed but starting to wake up. He smiled to himself. He could let the youth in, and let him see what married life was really like. He sighed; he knew he wouldn't really do that. He would be showing his wife up, and you just didn't do things like that.

'No; she isn't in! She went out an hour ago and God knows when she'll be back. Tell your mother that if she wants to see Laura, all she has to do is to walk into the shop and maybe look at something as if she were interested in buying it. Do you understand, son?'

The youth turned as he went out of the door.

'Yes Mister Stone. I'll tell her, Mister Stone.'

He disappeared and Stephen returned his attention to Mabel. She was still sitting there. She looked asleep, almost. If she hadn't blinked he would have believed it. He tried to get a response from her.

'Come on, Mabel. The children will be in from school soon. You don't want them to see you sitting on the floor like that, do you?'

'Well, come and sit by me then, Stephen. You don't mind having your way with me but it is too much trouble to sit by me afterwards. Is that too much trouble, Steve?'

She inched her way sideways so that there was room for him to sit at the side of her. It was ridiculous. One minute she was unconscious with post-coital relaxation and then she was chatting with him, encouraging him with her desire to fulfil some sort of adventure. It was a surprise to him.

Stephen had always known her to be what they called a 'nice quiet girl', and now she was like a roller-coaster, first quiet and then an explosive, passionate woman. If only she was like this all the time! She had always bored him, and that had made Elsie so attractive; her passionate, sometimes angry ways had lifted his spirits to new heights.

He made up his mind to make the most of the situation. He sat down beside her and reached for her breast. She went to push him away and then seemed to change her mind, grabbing hold of his hand and pulling him closer to her.

'Well, if you are going to do it again, do it! Don't just talk about it!'

Down she went, onto the floor, dragging him with her, her sheer physical strength astounding him. For some reason he could not define, he wanted her more and more. They seemed to come together for the first time in their married life, freely and generously acknowledging each other's appeal for the other one.

For no reason that they knew, they wanted to feel the ultimate thrill and stimulation. They did not know that they only needed to touch each other and the thrill would be theirs – if they let it. For this, first time, they discovered the reality of their type of sexual activity, the love-hate relationship. For this, first time, they each achieved what they wanted, in the measure that they needed.

Gone, for now, were the constraints of family and business. Gone were the intrusions of the invasion from other stimuli, other sexual attractions. They had everything they had never known they required. The moment of climax came and went, rarely to attend their moments of passion again but never quite forgotten either. The memory of this day would stay with them and keep them together despite Stephen's obsession with Elsie.

Stephen would use the excuse of his family commitment when Elsie tried to get any sort of pledge from him, and there was truth in it but it was this day that held him to Mabel, and the memory of the wonder of this single day of intense passion and love and the longing to recall it.

Time passed in the little shop, and they gradually returned to what Mabel thought of as the real world. They tidied themselves and put on a normal vista for the benefit of customers or their children if they happened to enter.

'I shall have to get on with this order for Germany.'

Stephen spoke, and it was the recognition that that their magical time had passed. She smiled at him.

'Yes, I suppose so; I've got other things to do as well!'

On impulse he pulled her body to his and kissed her; then he swung out of the door, to continue with his day's work. He had a lot to do; there was Laura to sort out. It was obvious that the youth, what was his name, Farthingale had been impressed by his daughter.

It was only natural that she would attract young men. He had noticed her growing beauty and poise; she was worth better than a Farthingale, whoever he was. There was also young Molly to put right. She had to be told that the only men she was allowed to play with at work were himself and old Albert, his father! If she didn't like it, she could go and peddle her wares elsewhere!

Mabel sat on the high stool in the shop. Her daughters would be coming in soon. She still felt the nice, sexual afterglow of her 'occasion' with Stephen. It had been a revelation to her. She hadn't known that between them they had such a range of emotions to bring to their encounter; love hate, respect, passion and raw animal lust.

She had liked Stephen more than she should, she recalled, when she had first met him, all those years ago. Even then, she had known that he had had a liking for Elsie Barr. Her mother and father had mentioned to her that a marriage into the Stone family would provide business advantages to them. Her father was as a good a locksmith as any of the Stones but they had the contacts; he didn't. She had never been able to work out just why that was. Perhaps, she thought, it was just the difference in the personalities of the men.

Someone said that the world would beat a path to the factory of anyone who made an improved version of anything, but it wasn't true. The one beating the path wasn't the world; it was the one who represented the person making the better version, letting the world know about it. Old Albert Stone used to travel all over the country, attending exhibitions and letting the trade know who was making the better items for them to use. It had stood them in good stead in the early days of the war. He had let the Government know where the innovations were, and who was making more, cheaper. Other firms had come on hard times but Stone and through them, her father's firm, had done well out of the war.

The Stones had liked her father and had let it be known that they would go along with a marriage of the Stone family with their business. She had no brothers and shortly after her marriage, her father had died. The Stones, of which she had become part, had taken possession of her father's small firm, using the few locksmiths who worked there, to carry on out of loyalty to her now widowed mother.

The dowager had been looked after ever since, becoming part of an extended family that the Stones were continually creating. She had a degree of experience that was slightly out of proportion to the capital that she brought to the joint enterprise and she was often consulted by Albert and Stephen about aspects of the trade. She had come from a long line of locksmiths herself, and her family was well known in Willenhall.

There was a clatter of shoes into the alley at the side of the shop. Her daughters had all been told that they should not enter the shop from the front door. They always looked in to see her as they passed along the alley, though. Laura, her eldest, was the first one in, chatty as usual.

'Hello, Mother. How are you? Busy as usual?'

Her eyes always seemed to take everything in as she swept in through the side door. Mabel felt herself blush, recalling the activities she had been engaged in, during the last hour. How or why should she blush in front of her own daughter? It was insufferable!

'Yes, daughter, I have been busy as usual – all day, since seven o'clock. How about you? Have you been busy? If so, you can get busy some more. We don't have a maid in the kitchen now, so the dinner needs cooking and you look like just the sort of growing up girl who could do something about that.' Her voice became sharp and a little angry as she continued. 'Your sisters should be busy as well. There is no excuse for them to sit around finding novels to read; there is work to be done. You can tell them what to do; you like taking up the superior position so take it up with them. Make sure you give them enough work to get the dinner done for the family, and make sure they do it. It won't do itself!'

It was Laura's turn to blush and she knew why. She confessed to herself that she did like to take over Mother's status. This time, Mother had caught her out. She lowered her eyes.

'Yes, Mother, I'll do that.'

She had a last look round the shop all the same. There was just something about it that seemed different. Maybe it was the slight smell. What was it? Whatever it was, she had never smelled it before. It was a sort of intimate smell. She passed out into the alley.

'Jean!,' she shouted at the retreating form. 'Mother wants you start on the potatoes, you have to check the meat; be sure it's not burnt. I'm going to start on the table setting.' She turned to the youth who had just entered the alley. 'Bert, I want you to go down to the grocer. It's only for a few things we need; a tin of pears and a bag of sugar. Here you are; here's the money. Get a tanner's worth o' cakes as well. Where's your brother?'

She looked for the younger son, Stanley but he had not yet come home.

'I don't know, Laura. The last time I saw him, he was talking to old Albert.'

Laura sighed; he was always talking to old Albert. Old Albert should be called Grandfather by right, as she knew. It was just that it was almost a tradition to call him old Albert. Stanley always had a query about a job, Bert never did; he had very rarely thought enough about a job to ask a question about it.

Stanley was talking to Old Albert. He was telling the elderly man about the new girl, Molly, and her legs and body. Old Albert was always interested in such things. He even had a go at getting his own way with some of them, depending on how he felt after investigating Stanley's claims about the girl in question.

'You ought to be finding something useful to do, never mind going round telling old men about the latest bit o' stuff in the works, our Stanley.'

Albert tried to sound serious but he knew that the young imp would soon see through him. Mind you, he could tell Mister Stanley a few tales about the times he had known there. He had even tried it on with Mabel! What would Stan think about that, then? Mabel had been a very flighty young thing a few years ago, before Stephen had made her his own. She had always been a comfortable shape, just the sort Albert had liked, but he should have known better than to try it on with her. She had given him an accidental swipe with her hand and he hadn't tried since.

'What about this young Molly then?' He hadn't been in the works for a few days so he hadn't seen the girl. Apparently she worked in the inspection department. It was a nice quiet part of the factory and whoever was in there, often worked on their own. It wouldn't be a bad idea to have a look at her. He found himself walking along the long alleyway that led through the production shop, into the Inspection Department. Finished locks were sent through to the Inspection Department to check that each lock had been assembled correctly, with the right components in the right order. The finish was also checked. Old Albert had been put in charge of the process because it was not a physically demanding task, but it needed a keen eye and the authority to stop production until whatever fault had been found, was corrected.

He had a small office there, and he determined to see that everything was correct; it would give him a chance to watch the few workers in there, to observe how they carried out their duties. He stepped smartly through the door into the department and looked round. There was only one girl there and she was bent over the bench in front of her, looking closely at the locks laid out for her inspection.

He liked what he saw, a girl really doing her job without supervision. The locks she was engaged in inspecting were export locks, for India. They had to be just right as they were for a rich merchant in Delhi and he wanted to be sure that if something was locked, it stayed locked. He walked over to the inspection bench and bent down, emulating her pose. He picked up a lock from under her gaze, and checked it over. She jumped as he did so, shocked at his sudden appearance.

'What do you think you are doing, cock? I was just checking that. What's it got to do with you?'

Albert pushed himself up off the bench and appraised the girl. She was about five feet, two inches and looked fit, he thought. I wouldn't mind, you know; I wouldn't mind.

'I am Albert Stone, the senior partner in this business. It's my job to ensure that everything that goes out of here is as near perfect as it is possible to make it. That means, young lady that I have to vet everybody who is involved with the inspection of the locks that we make for users all over the world. Now take this lock for instance. I think I can see a fault in the finish of this, and we do not stand for faults if they can be avoided. Does that answer your question Miss...?'

The girl backed off from her belligerent stance, her countenance falling.

'I'm sorry Mister Albert. I have heard about you of course, but I have never met you so I can't really be expected to recognise you, can I? I shall know you in future; that's for sure! My name is Molly; Molly Cartwright. My family has been in the lock trade a long time, as well as yours, and we are proud of it. Nobody is going to get a faulty lock past me, I can tell you, cock. I like this job and I'm going to make a go of it.'

They each stood back then, getting the measure of each other. He would try it on with her, she could tell, and she looked forward to it. She made up her mind to fire the opening salvo.

'What do you think, Mister Albert? Do you think I shall pass the gaffer's test? Am I good enough to be sent across the world without fault?'

She struck a pose, lifting her leg onto the bench that ran along the wall, showing a little of her thighs. Albert lifted his hand and put it on her thigh.

'There is a nice feel to this part of the lock. I wonder how hard it would be to open it.' He looked at it, over the top of his metal spectacles. Then he lifted his eyes until they met hers. 'What do you think, Miss Cartwright?'

'I think that with any lock, you have to have the right kay. I am sure that with the kay that fits, there would be no trouble at all.' She slid his hand higher up her stocking. 'Do you know where there is a kay that fits, Mister Albert?'

He turned and walked away. She was too hot for comfort! He

looked over his shoulder and snapped at her. 'You just get that job done, Miss Cartwright, and then we'll see what can be done about finding a kay for ya!'

Molly smiled to herself; he would be back. She didn't mind about his age. She just liked men and how they made her feel.

26. Old Albert and Dan and Tom's work.
1921

Albert Stone gathered his wits. It was a long time since a girl had made such an obvious pass at him. He was sixty five but still straight-backed and had good eyes as the girls knew. He seemed capable of finding a single fault in a bucket of components. It was just that his eyes were used to being set at a certain pattern and if any component was slightly different, his eye caught it and his hand followed, to pull the faulty lock or component out.

His thoughts and emotions returned to the girl, Molly, and the way she had deliberately set herself at him. Not that he minded but he wasn't so innocent that he thought he was wonderfully attractive to young women. Those days were gone, perhaps. What he wondered was why. He had been offered free love before and it had never turned out to be free. There had always been a price, not necessarily in pounds, shillings and pence but the cost had always intruded, making the offer seem expensive.

Even his wife had been gained at a price, not that he hadn't struggled against paying it. He had always been of an independent nature and Stephen had followed him. There was a boy! He had got his cake and ate it! He had made a success of his marriage to that chubby Mabel, making three children and had still found time or whatever it took, to get another from Elsie Barr. He now had four grand children!

It was obvious that young Tom was a Stone, regardless of what Dan Barr thought of it. The boy was growing tall now, and wide as well. Albert thought of the way he responded to what he and his son had taught young Tom. He was going to be a master locksmith one day soon. In fact, he thought, we could put him on man's rate soon, and that would confirm his status within the firm. It would be an unusual step but not unknown in a talented youth

Tom had surpassed any of the other apprentices except Stephen's younger son, Stanley. Stanley was another youthful prodigy; there weren't many of them in a generation. Bert, the other Stone's son, was the other end of the spectrum. He was just about what you might call normal. He could file; he was quite patient at that but he could not perform any task that had to be thought about. He didn't even know enough to ask a question.

Tom was anxious to get on, not necessarily in a lock or key manufacturing environment. He was a good engineering apprentice, never mind locksmith. Albert recalled when he had taught the boy how to scrape a slide, and decorate it with the feathery shapes cut into the surface being scraped, to provide a minute path for the oil to make its way across the slide, to lubricate it.

Tom had watched carefully how Albert had performed the task; rubbing a tiny amount of engineer's blue onto the slide and then rubbing the slide onto the master surface block to spread the blue around, highlighting the high spots on the slide. When the high spots were clear, Albert had picked up the old scraper he loved to use. He had carefully given the scraping surface a few rubs on an old oilstone to give the edge a final cutting surface.

He carefully laid the scraper onto the slide and gently pushed the scraper forward to remove each high spot. Then he repeated the whole sequence until the surface was almost perfectly level. He stood back, surveyed the slide and looked at Tom. Tom had looked the slide over and turning to Albert, nodded. Albert then picked up another scraper, the one he liked to use for finishing. He placed it on the surface and started the feathering process with a strange wobbling use of the scraper that left a curved marking in rows across the slide.

The feathering continued across the slide, gradually moving across the slide away from him until the whole surface was full of the little curling marks. He turned again to Tom and got the nod, as if the younger man was saying either, 'I've got the idea, now,' or, 'you did that well, Albert.'

Very few words were spoken: none were needed: a nod was as good as any words to convey meaning, and both understood the nods that were exchanged. The slide was put on one side and exchanged for another. This time it was Tom's turn to scrape and feather. The whole process took all afternoon, into the early evening. At six o'clock, Albert cleaned both slides until there was no sign of engineer's blue on either of them. Albert motioned Tom to stay still and walked away. He came back a few minutes later with Mister Stephen.

Stephen looked at the two slides, noting the decorative feathering and slid the master surface block onto the slides in turn. He rubbed each carefully, and the blue smeared the slides, putting an even pattern of spots across each. He examined each slide and then spoke.

'I can't tell who did either of them. Whoever did the scraping did a good job. I can't tell who should get the most or least wage for their effort. I think you should get another half a crown in your packet from Friday, Tom. Well done.'

Tom looked up at him, delighted, the pride of craftsmanship showing on his face. 'Thank you, Mister Stephen.' He seemed to think it over. 'I never thought I'd get the hang of it.'

Stephen shook his hand.

'There are not many who I even let have a go at this. Your Granddad was an engineer; you ask your Mother; she'll tell you. You seem to have it in your blood. You could get a job anywhere, now. Don't let your gift go to waste.'

He turned round and walked away, and Old Albert turned to Tom.

'He don't make a fuss but he thinks a lot, of you, you know. You should be grateful for that; he could disown you!'

Tom spent the next few minutes washing his hands in the bucket of hot water that had been brought for the men to get rid of the grease from their hands. It was half past six; time to go home. Tom was excited enough about his new status to want to hurry home to tell his mother. All of a sudden, he was being treated like a man. What should he do with the extra half a crown? Mom would know. There was no sign that his father would be able to find a use for the extra cash, except to piss it up the wall at the back of the pub.

He now had a status that not even the Stone's own son had achieved yet. The world was his to rule if he wanted to. All he had to do was to use his skills and employers everywhere would be anxious to pay him to use his skills to their profit. It sounded difficult but he knew he could do it. He was beginning to feel that he was at the end of an important phase in his life, with the next phase about to begin.

Perhaps this is what life is all about, the completion of an almost infinite number of phases, he thought, and when you get through the last phase, you die as an expression of your abilities and to show that there is nothing more to be learned, you leave your body, to get another one and start all over again. It was a tempting thought.

He dropped his overalls and hung them on the hook. He liked to keep them smart looking, as if they were the fore-runner of himself. He wanted to look smart as well as act and work smart. His coat was slung around his shoulders and he walked out of the building, whistling to himself.

Again he had the feeling that a phase of life had come to an end. In a way, a life was like a book with numerous chapters, all having different themes. How many chapters did he have left? He thought about it and the way his thoughts went along with Shakespeare's, the way he had moved from being a 'whining schoolboy'. According to Shakespeare, his next part would be a 'lover, sighing like furnace, with a woeful ballad made to his mistress' eyebrow.'

Tom smiled at the thought. He could not imagine himself composing love poetry to some factory girl. Mind you, the Stone's girls could make you raise something. Laura, the oldest, seemed to act in a superior sort of way, as if she wouldn't be seen with a common factory hand, even if he did fancy himself as a locksmith.

Jean was the one he liked the most. She was a bit chubbier, like her mother, but there was something about her that made him think that she might like him if the circumstances were right, whatever that meant. She had enormous breasts and carried them well. It was to be seen he thought, viewing himself as a mature spectator, what she would be like as she matured.

Then there was that Molly. Any one who didn't feel aroused at the sight of her working on the hand-press must be already dead. He only had to think of her to feel a strong erection coming on. It was a nuisance in a way, but a pleasant nuisance. What kind of girl would he end up with?

What had his mother been like when she was young? Had she had flirtations with the gaffer? Sometimes he wondered if she still did. It was obvious to him that Mister Stephen liked her a lot. His mind turned to his father. They didn't seem to see much of each other now. Dan was so cold in manner, now he was in charge and was standing there inspecting you all the time. Perhaps he would smile when he was told of the rise in pay that Tom was about to receive. Perhaps he would. He never seemed happy at all, as if something had happened to him while he was in the Army and it had left him permanently sad, or miserable.

Tom turned in at the court where the family now lived. Well, we would see now. He stopped whistling, listening as walked along the brick path. Now he would show his father. His father had had to he wait until he was twenty-one to get the journeyman's rate for the job. He started whistling again, *Look for the Silver Lining*. He was feeling happy. The door was open. He could hear his father shouting at his mother.

'I work hard for my money, woman, and I expect a decent meal every night when I get home, not scrag-end when you think you can get away with it!'

Dan's voice seemed to get louder and Tom moved to the shelter of the shed, near the door, his natural curiosity aroused. His mother was also shouting.

'I ain't trying to get away with anything, Dan Barr and you know that if you was honest enough to admit it!'

The suggestion that Dan was not honest seemed to inflame him. He slapped Elsie across the face and she dropped onto the rug in front of the fire. Tom walked in to the house trying to act as if nothing had happened, still whistling.

'Hello, Dad,' he said, and turned and saw Elsie lying there. 'What's the matter with you Mom?' He turned back to his father. 'What's happened to our Mom, then, Dad?'

Dan was still in a temper and it showed. He grabbed Tom by the shoulders, drew back a fist and punched him in the stomach. Tom groaned as the breath was forced out of his lungs. He could only just see his father standing over him, his face red with drink and temper.

'That'll teach you to question me, my lad. I'll show you who's the gaffer here. There's too many gaffer's boys thinking they are better than a man who's fought for his Country.

Tom collapsed on the floor and Dan prepared to kick him. There was a thud and Tom saw his father stagger and fall beside him. Elsie was standing there now. She had a poker in her hand and she had obviously just hit Dan. He was holding his shoulder as he tried to get to his feet.

'Look what you've done to me, you mad woman! You've broke me shoulder. Are you stupid or something?'

'I'm stupid? I'm stupid? We can all see who's stupid an' it ain't me. I've took the last blow from you, Dan Barr. And what have you done to Tom? What was his crime, eh? All he did was to ask why I was lying on the floor – and we both know why I was lying on the floor, don't we?' She hesitated but still stood there, the poker half raised. 'Don't you move, you brave man who has fought for his country. You are so brave you can try to kill your son. That's how brave you are. If you ever raise a fist or a hand to me or him again you are on your own, and you will be crippled, I'll make sure o' that before you go!'

Dan was beginning to see where he was now and he didn't like it. He was used to having his own way with soldiers and he couldn't understand how he had been bested. He turned to Tom, who was beginning to get the room in focus.

'Help me up, son. She's tried to kill me. I don't know why.'

Tom looked him in the eye.

'How do you think I'm feeling, Dad? You just downed me and then you want me to help you? You can get yourself up. You might have been a big man in the Army, Dad, but you ain't big here. You're just a bully. It's the last time you hit me, Dad. Next time I shall hit you back and you can see how you like it. I'm off. When you want me back you can come and ask me. Just keep out of my way at work. You do your job and I'll do mine.'

Tom stood and as his father tried to get up, Tom hit him on the chin.

'You ain't the only one who can hit, you know. I'm going to work. They'll let me stay there. My Granddad stayed there when he first came from Brummagem and he did all right.'

He turned and went up the stairs to gather a few things. He was down in a few minutes and when he returned he went to his mother. 'Let me know if he tries to bully you, Mom. I'll soon sort him out.'

Elsie looked at him and she seemed different somehow.

'Don't go, son,' she said, 'It'll shame us all. He don't mean it you know. It was the way he had to be, in the Army, to train them squaddies, to save their own lives. It's just that when he's in drink he goes a bit mad, son. Please don't shame us all with the Stone's. You can just imagine how that Mabel Stone would like to get something over us. She would laugh all over Willenhall. And another thing; how do you think Stephen Stone would treat your Dad, if he found out? Your Dad would have a lot of trouble trying to keep his job. Stephen would hound him out of it. Just think about it, son. It would make life very hard for us if you left.'

Elsie looked hard at her son, almost pleading. He thought about it, saying nothing, then he returned up the stairs and came back a moment later without his clothes. He moved to his mother and put his arms round her, telling her wordlessly that he would be there to protect her.

Elsie breathed a sigh of relief. Little did Tom or Dan know that the house they were living in was hers! If there had been any serious trouble, she could have had him evicted. She smiled to herself; the housekeeping that he had been reminding her about was just the icing on the cake! Dan bloody Barr was not half as prosperous as he thought.

Dan finished picking himself up and sat himself into his favourite armchair. What was the world coming to? All he was doing was complaining about the food. Then the world had changed. He had been drunk but not so drunk that he couldn't have worked out the outcome of his stupid outburst. He should never have hit Elsie, or his son.

Instead of him being able to hand out complaints and punishment, the tables had been turned. Elsie had given him a good one with the poker and his own son had punched him back. It just didn't seem right. He relaxed a little and tried to think things through. It looked as if Tom had changed his mind and was not leaving home. It would have been awkward to explain to the Stone's why their son had come to live in the factory. He could have tried to bully the lad out of it but he thought it probably would not work now. Elsie was clever in her own way; she had taken the heat out of the situation and persuaded Tom to stay.

Dan had been drunk again. He should really have known better. In fact he was thoroughly ashamed of himself. Elsie had shocked him, the way she had lashed out with the poker but he had asked for it. Tom had made the best of the situation, making sure he had got one in, and letting him know what could happen if he didn't toe the line.

He smiled to himself; always make the best of the situation, that was what he had told Tom, he recalled. Looks as if he had learned the lesson – better than his Dad! That's if I am his Dad. He had had his doubts, many a time. There was something about the lad that made him seem more like a Stone than a Barr. Well, it was no use dwelling on it; they say it's a wise child that knows its own father. There must be thousands in the same situation. You just have to get on with it.

It still rankled though, to think of Elsie and Stephen Stone in his bed while he was creeping across to the enemy lines and crawling along some bloody trench. The same thing must have happened to the Germans and the French. Perhaps to them little Ghurkhas as well, but somehow he didn't think it would happen to them; they all seemed so honourable.

It was going to be awkward now. How should he act towards Tom? It was no good acting normal; it was bound to affect the way they were towards each other. Tom was just the age when he would want to replace the old bull. That was one of the steps towards growing up. All Dan could do, really, was to try to improve the way he acted towards the lad, try to find something he could compliment him about.

What were Tom's interests and hobbies, now? He couldn't remember, probably because he was spending too much time in the pub. He felt that it might be suitable if he could offer to buy the lad a pint, now and then. Yes, perhaps that would do the trick; boys of that age liked to be taken for a drink. He wasn't legally old enough but that might add to the excitement, and he would get away with his age at the pub. Tom looked older than his years.

He would also have to mend his ways with Elsie. He couldn't expect to keep getting away with violence; she wouldn't stand for that! She was in the small kitchen now, rattling around with the crocks. She must be throwing his dinner away. Oh well. It was time to make an effort.

'Any chance of a cup o' tea, love?'

Dan stood and moved into the small space with her. He knew that the small space gave them an unusually private area of intimate possibilities and she would sometimes succumb to his needs. He took a mint from his waistcoat pocket and slipped it into his mouth; she didn't like the smell of beer on his breath. She looked up at him and spoke.

'Well, you've changed your tune haven't you? Knocking me about one minute and making advances to me the next.'

Nevertheless, she turned as she felt his body against hers. It didn't make sense but everything didn't have to make sense, did it? He slid his arms round to pull her buttocks close to him and felt the response in her. His lips touched hers with a hard sort of pressure that felt as if he was trying to get inside her. She pulled away.

'Do you have to be so bloody ferocious in everything you do, Dan? Why don't you try to be a bit gentle, for a change?'

Elsie slipped her hand down the front of his trousers and gently cupped his genitals. He responded immediately with an erection. Then she squeezed him until he pulled away in pain.

'Do you see what I mean, Dan? Some things are meant to be done gently, and it hurts if it isn't done tenderly; do you see what I mean?'

She changed back to a more gentle movement and he felt the difference straight away. He moved his lips back to hers again and gently touched them with his, and then took them away and returned them, all in a second. Elsie found herself becoming more intense in her response and undid the front of her blouse to allow him easier access. He moved his lips to gently touch her nipple, continuing the teasing, on and off type of pressure, until she found her body moving to a rhythm that matched the movements of his. She felt him slide his hands over the elastic of her bloomers and pull them down below her knees, where they dropped onto the floor. She kicked them on one side and pulled his trousers down. 'Everything seems to get in the way, sometimes,' she panted, 'get your shirt off, quick. I want to feel you all over.'

Dan slipped the shirt over his head and watched as it seemed to float down the cellar steps, to land in the coal dust, at the bottom. His body lunged to hers and they joined in a slippery instant. Their movements became more spasmodic until the climax came for both of them. They stood for a moment, almost unable to carry their own weight.

'Thank you, Dan, thank you.'

'Thank you, Else. You always give me more than I deserve. Thanks.'

The sound of the kettle whistling on the fire in the other room brought them back to present time instantly and they smiled at each other.

'Did you ask for a cup o' tea, a minute ago, Dan? You'd better let me go so I can go and make it. Otherwise the kettle'll bring the neighbours to see what the trouble is.'

Elsie moved away from him and picked up her bloomers.

'Passion killers, them are.'

He smiled. 'Well, they don't seem to have killed your passion, anyway.'

He stopped dressing,

'Yes you are right. Do you want to start again?' He slid his hand to her breast. How about it?

Elsie carried on moving away from him and into the living room. The kettle was still whistling. She put a small towel around her hand and lifted the kettle onto the top of the cast iron oven. The whistling slowed and she opened the caddy and put two spoonfuls of tea into the teapot then poured water in until the pot was full. Sometimes a cup of tea served to change a mood for the better. She smiled.

27. Family Troubles.
1921

'Here you are; what more could a bloke ask for? Nobody has it like you, and all you do is moan about the way I spend the bit o' money you give me to keep house on. I've a good mind to let you do the house keeping. It would save me the trouble. You seem to forget that I go to work as well as you, and I still have to find time for buying everything we need. You never volunteer to do the shopping, do you?'

Elsie spoke quietly as suited the occasion but Dan knew there was a challenge in her voice too. He thought about it. Yes, he would save a fortune if he did the shopping! Anybody could do the shopping.

'Yes, alright then, I'll do the shopping. I'm sure I can do it as good as a woman. Don't expect any housekeeping this week, on Friday!'

Once again his aggression has come to the fore, she thought. All he knows is that he has to be in control. If he ain't in control, he feels threatened; that's what it is. He's frightened! The realization overcame her. He was supposed to be brave and an ex-Sergeant Major, showing young lads how to fight the enemy with sheer courage! It wasn't like that at all.

She smiled. She would see how he got on!

'That's fine by me, Dan. It will give me a bit of time to myself, for a change. Perhaps I'll take myself to the pictures. I've got a bit left from this week's housekeeping. Unless you think you'll need it of course?'

She laughed to see if he would stand for it. Dan laughed too. As if he would need her few coppers left over from this week!

'No thanks, Elsie. I think I can manage to buy a bit o' grub without taking the money out of your hand. Whatever I manage on, you can have in future, to keep house on; that's fair enough, ain't it?'

Quickly Elsie reposted. 'Yes, that's fair enough, Dan. There's just one thing. What about if you can't manage? Will you give me the amount that you was short of? What about if you have to borrow to make ends meet, eh?'

Dan looked at her as if she was asking him some sort of catch question. He gave the question serious considering, and then conceded the point as if it were nothing. 'Well, that isn't likely to happen but if it does, you can have the extra few coppers to manage on after that.'

Elsie walked away. He had had his way with her. He was an animal with his randy ways. No finesse at all. Now he would be off to the pub. Nothing like Stephen; Stephen did everything just right for a girl. He was tender and gentle when that was called for, and hard and vigorous when that was called for. Dan tried; you had to give him that. It was just that he had no talent for love. It was a pity, really. He had had his way but what he didn't know was that she had had her way as well.

*

Tom was walking his temper off. It was what he usually did when he got worked up about something. His father had hit him, hit him in the guts as if they were enemies. It was awful. He tried to put it down to the drink but he couldn't completely go along with it. His father had hit his mother! He would never forgive him for that. His father had definitely taken advantage of him.

As he walked along, Tom was thinking all sorts of mixed up thoughts. Finally, he realised that although he could do little against his father's skill and strength in the ways of fighting, his father was getting older – and so was he! The difference was that his father was getting older and more out of condition; he himself was getting taller, stronger and fitter.

He started to run, slowly at first, and then quite quickly, not taxing his strength, just trotting along. He knew it would improve his breathing. He also needed, he felt, to improve his strength. He would exercise every day, until he was stronger than his father, and then... The thought gave him a kick and he put on a spurt for a while, then he started to worry about his mother. How was she?

Was she lying on the ground, injured?

Tom slowed down and then turned and started to trot in the direction of home. Was he going to be in time to save her? At last he came to the gate and pushed it. He stopped and listened. The house was quiet. He pushed the door and it opened silently.

*

Tom walked in. His mother was sitting near the fire. She looked up and smiled as she saw him. There was no sign of Ted or his father. He looked questioningly at Elsie. 'I don't know,' she said, 'He's probably gone to the pub.'

'Good; it's the best place for him. I hope he falls in the gutter. It's the best thing that could happen to him.'

'He don't mean it, you know. It's just the drink. He'll be right as rain in the morning. He's never late for work as you know. He's always said he wouldn't be late for parade.'

They sat in silence for a few minutes, and then Tom spoke. 'I'm being made a journeyman, next week. I shall get the full rate. Mister Stephen told me. Mister Albert made me scrape a slide and then sent for Mister Stephen. We did one each, Mister Albert and me. He couldn't tell the difference so he had to admit I was as good as him.'

Elsie swept him into her arms. 'Tom Barr; I am that proud of you. What you have done is very rare. Wait until your father hears about this. He is bound to be pleased for you.'

'No, he won't. He will say something to make it seem nothing. It isn't nothing; you know that and I know it but he will try to make it seem nothing. Anyway, our Mom, don't tell him. I don't want him to know. He'll find out the same as everybody else. It'll be on the board. I don't want to hear what he has to say about it!'

Elsie looked like starting to cry again. She had forgotten that she had made up the quarrel with Dan but Tom hadn't. What could she do to patch things up between them? Perhaps they would never forgive each other. Some families never forgave a quarrel they had with relatives. They just ignored the other, or moved away.

Her son had a cold look on his face that she had never seen before. She couldn't blame him. His father had been away for most of the years that the war had raged, and he had shown his love for his son by knocking him down.

It got him angry. 'I think I am going out for a walk. I may be some time. See you later Mom.'

Elsie gave him a little wave of her hand, as she always did but she felt that he was a different lad now. The passage to another stage in his life was being indicated by the look on her son's face. He was grim as he turned; he wasn't going to stand for his drunken father knocking him about for much longer.

Tom turned and walked out of the door, he had a lot to think about. There was his Dad and there were the girls, the girls he saw every day. The girls were the ones he saw at work and on the tram and just walking along the road. They all seemed to excite him to the same extent, lifting his responses to ever higher heights. Often it would happen when he was least able to control it.

He turned at the corner and started to walk at a really brisk pace. It was dark now and there were few people around. Most of the populace were either at home or were out enjoying themselves in the public houses dotted round the town.

There was a girl coming towards him. He didn't know her but he felt he had seen her before. It was strange how he thought things like that, without evidence. The girl had long legs and a short skirt. She was watching him out of the corner of her eye; he knew that. His eyes went to her legs and for a second he thought he might get away with holding her against him, feeling her body feel his. She seemed to have an amused look on her face as they finally passed each other. He had seen her before, he knew. It would come back to him.

If he turned and looked back at her, would she have done the same and would they meet each other's eyes with heightened emotions? Did they have feelings the same as men? Could they read his mind? It would be awful if they could. He looked back; she was still walking the same, head high and eyes on the horizon in front of her.

How would his father treat him now? Would he beat him up again? Well, he could do his share of beating up. He made his mind up; he had to beat his father up at least once, just to show him that it could be done. It was just a question of when.

Just then he saw him, coming out of a small grimy-looking pub. He was on his own and saw Tom straight away. He crossed the road and came to a halt in front of Tom. 'Come on, son. It's about time I bought you a pint. Come and share a bit o' company with your old man, Sergeant-Major Barr. How do you fancy that, eh?'

A drink with the old man! There was a thing. He had never been invited out by his Dad, before. He felt like telling him where to stick his pint but, instead, just nodded his head; he hadn't the heart to reject such an overture.

Dan led his son into the bar of the public house. It wasn't all that light, although a gas mantle was spluttering in the bracket that led down from the ceiling. The bar was 'L'-shaped and led towards another door at the rear of the room. There were a lot of men there, all jostling at the counter, either lifting their drinks or trying to get the barmaid's attention, to get another one.

Dan turned to Tom. 'What would you like, son; a pint o' mild?' At Tom's nod, he turned to the barman. 'Two pints o' mild, Jack; when you've got a minute.'

He planted his foot on the brass foot-rail and his elbow on the bar. The barman stared at him. 'I'll be with you as soon as I can, Danny Boy. Who's the sprog, yours?'

He nodded to Tom and started to pull the handle of the beer engine. A dark brown fluid came gushing out of the pump and the glass soon filled to the top and then poured over the top into the overflow bowl. He placed it on the counter and filled another glass, with the same effects. Dan just nodded at Tom and lifted his own glass. 'Cheers, our kid.'

'Cheers, Dad.'

A feeling something like love came over him. It would have

been soppy if it had really been love, but it was like it. Then he recalled seeing his mother lying on the floor, and the blow that had put her there. His face stiffened with the memory but he tried not to show how he felt. It was not suitable to let anyone who you intended to hurt, know how you felt.

Tom looked round the pub again. Most of the men there were working class, trying to forget the squalor of the life they were forced to live by the circumstances they found themselves. There was little else to do, if you hadn't the talent that took you away from it.

Among them there were writers, artists, poets and sculptors. There were men who played musical instruments and those who didn't, not having the wherewithal to buy any sort of device for making music. Bones and spoons were employed as percussion and penny whistles as woodwind. In spite of the difficulties of life, there were those who found a way to remove themselves, in imagination, to the orchestra of the mind.

Tom realised that he was lucky compared to many. He had talent; he knew that. That was why he was being made a journeyman; he was good at what he did. There was a tap on his shoulder; it was Mister Albert. Tom was shocked, although he had heard that the elderly man mixed with the hands, on occasion.

'Hello, Tom. Celebrating are you? Here; have one on me, and you, Dan.' He turned to the barman. 'Put these two on my tab, will you?'

The nod went in again. Dan looked shocked, too. He was very rarely treated by one of the gaffers.

'Cheers, Albert. What's this in aid of, then? What do you mean; celebrating?'

Albert seemed surprised. He raised his hand, the hand with the glass in it, to son and father. There was a moment's hesitation and then he spoke.

'Oh, it's nothing much. I just like to celebrate life occasionally. Drink up then; here's to you both. It'll probably be twelve months before I buy anybody a drink, again.'

He laughed and picking up another, smaller glass from the bar turned and made his way to a small table in the corner of the bar. There was a woman there. Tom looked and was shocked again. It was Molly! This had been a day for shocks. He found himself being pulled by her eyes. They were dark eyes; dark as night, that momentarily distracted him from her legs and breasts, but only momentarily. Her eyes called him again but so did Mister Albert's.

'Just you keep away and let an old man have a chance, Tom. There are plenty of others. She won't last long, anyway.' He winked. 'I'll keep your secret if you'll keep mine, alright?'

Albert wasn't going to let on about Tom's upgrading! That was what the wink was for. Tom winked back. This was turning out to be a good night, after all. His father didn't know everything. He looked round at his father. He too, was looking at Molly. Was everyone looking at her? If so, she was too much in the public eye for him. He couldn't stand to think that if he had a girl, everybody would be looking, and wishing and hoping.

Her eyes were full of wandering movements and that was probably how she would always be. In a way, it was a sign of having no commitment. He liked to think that if he had a girl, she would want to show that she was his only, not displaying her wares for other men to see and want. A woman could be good looking without flaunting her looks everywhere.

There were too many loose women about nowadays. He knew that the thought made him seem old-fashioned but he felt that his thinking processes were working sufficiently well to come to a common sense perception of the situation.

This was a funny year. The people who lived by their principles, like Ghandi, were put into prison while grave robbers like Howard Carter were applauded for stealing the historic contents surrounding an Egyptian dynasty's tombs. Would the Pope's grave be robbed one day, to be put in a museum somewhere? Would someone get high honours for doing it?

Tom seemed to be in two places at once, as the night passed. He wanted to be thrilled at the free drinks he was getting from his father and Mister Albert. The thought suddenly struck him that he might very well be Mister Albert's grandson. Then he dismissed the thought. How could he be? He looked up and saw that the table where Molly had been sitting was empty; they had gone.

'You want to sit down, Dad? There's an empty table there.'

'I shouldn't if I was you, our kid. They might be back in a minute and when he's declared his seat, that's his seat for the night. You have to respect his wishes you know.'

Dan turned back to the conversation he was having with the tall, dark man who was leaning on the bar alongside his father. Tom was left on his own again. The bar only had men in it now. There were not many that he knew. Most of them were five years or more, older than he. The youths who were his own age could not come into the pub.

There was a tap on his shoulder. It was Stanley Stone.

'Hello, Tom. I heard your news earlier. Well done. You should have heard Uncle Bert. He was really mad. He thinks he should be awarded every honour that's going, whether he deserves it or not. He's standing outside; he don't like coming into the pub. He's shy, you know. It's a shame but there it is. He could come in here if he wanted to, you know. He just ain't got the bottle. Did I see old Albert here, a minute ago? What was he after? Probably Molly, if I know him. I suppose I do talk a lot, don't I? She's a bit of a girl, isn't she? Mind you, I wouldn't mind if she liked me.'

Tom laughed; it was refreshing to hear someone talk who had something decent to say. He took another look at the young man who was standing next to him. He was younger than Tom, with intelligent blue eyes that seemed to keep moving and appraising everything that was going on.

'Dad told me earlier you'd been given the journeyman's status. Does your Dad know yet? He don't, does he? Why have you kept it a secret? Oh well, that's your business. Here I go again, never shut up. I suppose I might as well get a drink. Do you want one? No? Is this your first time in a pub? That's why you don't want a drink; you've already had too many, I suppose?' He turned back to the bar. 'A pint o' mild, please.'

Stanley signalled the barman with a lifting action of his wrist and stood and watched as it was drawn for him. Tom thought the liquid was revolting but he determined to get a taste for it. He pulled a half crown from his pocket and lifted his head to the barman. 'I'll pay for that, and two more, please.'

When the beer was drawn, he tapped his father on the back. 'Here you are, Dad, cheers.'

Dan turned and suddenly saw Stanley. 'Hello, Mister Stanley. I didn't know you were in here.'

He didn't seem to know what to say next so he turned back to his companion. Stanley and Tom were left standing silently, looking at each other. There was a speculative look on Stanley's face. It was as if he was working up to something. It was strange how he observed things. His mother had taught him to do that. She had told him that her mother always looked deeper than most, at any social situation, and had instilled the basic observation tendencies in him.

Tom decided to say nothing until Stanley had made up his mind whether to reveal his thoughts. As he stood there, he felt that there was a most important revelation to come.

He let his thoughts wander again, and they came back to Molly. Somehow she kept teasing her way into his mind. As he thought of her, his body started to react in that strange way, as if he was with her, pressing her against his body. He became conscious of his hand in his pocket, urgently trying to get relief for him, like a serious itch that needed scratching.

At last, he decided to push Stanley into saying what he obviously wanted to say.

28, Into the Open.
1921

'Have you got something on your mind, Stan? You're standing there like a tree trying to put roots into the ground.'

Stanley looked back at Tom and spoke. 'Yes, you're right, Tom. There is summat I wanted to ask you. I know it sounds daft but, are you and me related? Sometimes I look at you and I think you are like family. I've thought it for a long time but I really couldn't ask Mom, or Dad, could I? Especially as I know your Mom and Dad.'

Tom answered slowly, choosing his words carefully at first and then letting them pour out. This was the first time anyone else had raised the subject that had intrigued him for months.

'No, it's not been easy for me either, Stan. Of course I've noticed things as well. I think we are related but nobody is going to volunteer to tell us *how* we are related.' He took a deep breath and thought out his reply. 'I think your Dad and my Mom must have been lovers at one time, and no one ever found out. I think I must have been the result of that event. Whether it was a one-off, or a long-lasting affair, I have no idea. That's all I can think of to explain the resemblance between us. Perhaps, because my Dad was away in the Army, my Mom got lonely and their friendship became more than either of them bargained for. I don't know anything for certain anyway. I'm just surmising, trying to fit the pieces together like a jig-saw.' He coughed, to give himself time to think.

'I do know that your Dad gets on with me more than he gets on with the other apprentices. I know he thinks just as much of you, though I am not so sure about Bert. I know that your Dad and my Mom are good friends, though I could never know enough to accuse them of anything. I sort of half-worked it out in my head and then just accepted it. I thought it was you who did all the talking!'

Tom fell silent and waited for a response from the other youth.

Stanley was quite bright for his age and may have worked out the possibilities himself. Perhaps I've given away too many of my ideas, he thought. He felt that he had given away a dread secret.

Stanley was still working things out for himself. It was likely that he would not be able to believe what he had just been told. It was possible that he would go running to his Dad, or worse, his Mother, and tell what he had just been told by someone who was just one of the hands.

Tom might get the sack for even suggesting the story to Stanley. It was as if he was trying to create a rift between the families, and he wasn't. He was just responding to Stanley's questions. Anyway, he liked Stanley and didn't think he would immediately run to tell the tale. He was too bright to go that far without a good reason.

A thought just hit him. Perhaps there would, at some time, be a good reason. What about if Old Albert or Mister Stephen died? If the Stone family had any money at that time, would he have a right to claim any of it? Would he be mentioned in a will? Suddenly he felt vulnerable.

Tom knew he had the ability to apply for a position anywhere, as an engineer, but what about his parents? They too would be at risk following an exposure of his thoughts on his parentage. Mabel would probably be glad to get rid of him – and take the opportunity to have a dig at his Mom; especially if she thought there was a glimmer of truth in the story, which she would claim was just a sort of silly rumour, which poor people were always thinking up to take advantage of their betters.

'I think you may be right, Tom.' Stanley was replying to his thoughts. 'It seems the most likely thing to have happened, after all. There is no other way we could have got to have this likeness, is there? I don't mind, really. Somehow I think it might be nice to have a brother. Bert doesn't seem like a relation, somehow. He is always for himself, never thinking of anyone else.' Another thought seemed to cross his mind. 'I suppose, if what you say is true, your Ted would be my half-brother. I wonder what he would think about that.'

Tom didn't know whether he meant Ted or Bert. 'If you mean, what would Ted think about it, I don't know. If you meant, what would Bert think about it, you've got a better chance of knowing than I.' He smiled. 'It just gets too complicated for words, almost. I mean to say, what am I supposed to do if I fall in love with one of your sisters? I suppose I'd better decide that I can't do that!'

The two young men stood side by side drinking their mild ale, each immersed in their own thoughts. It finally got through to Tom that Dan might not be his father! What about that, then? Did his father, Dan, know, or suspect? Was that why he was so harsh with him? Did he think more of Ted than of him? He felt suddenly depressed. They say in the Bible that the sins of the fathers are visited on their children. It wasn't fair.

It seemed that the Stones would not accept him because he was born the wrong side of the blanket, and Dan Barr, his 'father', would not accept him for the same reason! Life was not fair: that was for sure.

'Will you have another one, Mister Barr?'

Stanley had already ordered two pints and was offering another. He must get a lot of pocket money! Idly, Tom picked up the glass. The taste definitely seemed better than the first one. He was feeling mellow now, as if the world had been put right simply by drinking the brown liquid. He knew that it was not true but it was nice to imagine it was so.

Was that why his father drank so much; because it made the world that little easier to get along with? There were so many sides to a question that the answers always seemed to breed more questions. He knew he couldn't belong to both families; he had to make up his mind which one he belonged to. He turned to Stanley.

'It's all very well speculating on such a question. In fact, there's only one family I can claim membership of. My name is Tom Barr. I cannot claim any other, although I feel that you and I have some sort of relationship. It would be better if we were just friends. My life would get harder, not easier, if I claimed to be a Stone. I would rather get on, on my own merits. So – here we are,

Stanley Stone and Tom Barr. Pleased to meet you, Stan.'

'Pleased to meet you, Tom.'

So it was decided between them. Tom was to be Tom Barr and no suggestion of being anything or anyone else. Tom decided then that as he had no relationship to anyone else – and certainly not to Dan – anything he achieved, he would have to achieve himself. He had already achieved more than most, and off his own wicket, than most youths of his age and social status.

When you are in that position, Tom thought, it is difficult to see more than one step ahead in the game of life, so Tom concentrated on living as much as he could. As Black Countrymen said, 'I am what I am and I cor be any ammer.'

This summed up what was to be his philosophical outlook for the foreseeable future, until he learned to see more than one step. One good thing seemed to have come out of the situation; he had lost a brother but gained a friend. For the moment, he decided to let his mother know of his decision and to let his father know nothing. Tom was learning to keep his own counsel. He returned home that night and told his mother of his decision. She was sanguine about it, realising it was just a sign of moving forward in ignorance and confidence. They sat there just gazing at the slowly failing embers in the fireplace. There was a scrape of boots at the door; Dan had arrived home. It was obvious when he walked in that he had heard of Tom's news.

'Eh, you! I hear you been creeping up the arse of the gaffer again. How do you manage it, eh?'

Dan laughed. It was obvious that he was not going to give Tom the credit for being given the journeyman's status; therefore he must have done something dishonest. That was his attitude. Tom stood up and suddenly it became apparent to those in the room that he was not going to tolerate this sort of accusation.

'Listen Dad,' he took hold of Dan's neckerchief wrapped round his neck, 'You have never known me tell you, or anybody else, a lie, nor have I. If you tell me that I have been awarded this status for any reason than true craftsmanship, just prove it; put up or shut up.' His voice suddenly became a little louder and harsher. 'You ain't in the Army now! You can't say what you like, like you did to your recruits. If you open your mouth to tell lies about me, I shall close it for you, so there! Do you understand me? Eh? Do you understand me?'

Tom flung his father away from him in an explosion of temper and let him fall hard on the settee. Dan looked up, amused. He had been knocked down before. His son had suddenly got some guts; that was the main thing. He smiled at Tom, suddenly proud of him. Tom was right of course; he shouldn't have taken a rise out of his son. Tom was always serious, a bit like himself, and he would not take kindly to anyone making denigrating remarks. He felt proud again. Tom had honestly acquired his new journeyman status; he wouldn't have been able to do it any other way. He was defending his honesty in the best way he could. Dan got to his feet and thrust out his hand to his son.

'Thanks for putting me right, Son. You were quite right to do it. I should have known better. Here's my hand on it.'

Dan reached out with his hand and Tom and his mother both looked at Dan in surprise. It wasn't very often that they had seen the ex-soldier back down. There must have been something about the way Tom had acted that had appealed to him. Tom tentatively put out his hand, as anxious as his father to end the quarrel. The two hands met and gripped; the hands of men in equal rank.

Elsie saw and started to cry. They, at least, were happy. She still had a divided love life, and financial secrets that she could not reveal. She would have to live her life as best she could, living and loving as the chance came, bobbing about, trying to get what she wanted and needed without hurting those around her.

She thought back again as she had so many times before, to the day she had met Stephen in the market and he had invited her to a ride in the country. The sun had shone; everything had been bright and exciting, and they had made love and Tom, in a little hollow just off the heath. If she had the chance to do it again, she would.

Tom and Dan were looking at her and it made her feel like blushing. Why were they looking at her in that way? She suddenly realised that it was because they were trying to think out how she was going to take their reconciliation. Elsie reached out her arms and encompassed both of them.

'I am so pleased for both of you. You are both good men and you should be on good terms with each other. I am absolutely delighted. Let this be a new start for both of you. Let's celebrate with a cup of tea, eh? Put the kettle on, Tom, there's a good man. Dan, you get the teapot ready while I cut us a bit o' cake.' She looked up at a fresh sound. 'Come on, Ted, you can join in with us. We are having a little party. Would you like a piece o' cake? Come on down to we, there's a good lad.'

Ted laughed, as he always did at his mother's Wednesbury way of talking. He loved her and all her ways. She was an anchor for him that was held by mighty chains of love. Like the chains that were forged in the dark, dirty workshops of the Black Country, they were unbreakable. He didn't understand all that had gone on before he came down the stairs, to be confronted by the small tableau, but he did know that he was loved by his mother and father ands he felt confident that they would look after him and protect him with all the resources at their disposal, until he was fit, mature and able to look after himself. It was a good life.

Tom felt as if he had passed another hurdle in the road of life. He had forced his father to accept him on equal terms. He was now certain that he was the son of Stephen Stone and he didn't mind at all. He was already feeling the benefits of the blood in his veins, but he also had the blood of his engineering grandfather in him. It had shown in the way he had been able to take to the trade he had been taught. Even Old Albert Stone had been impressed.

He had tried to trick Tom last year, giving him a six-inch length of one inch round shafting and asking him to fit it into a one inch square hole in a piece of plate. He had told Tom what he wanted and had walked away. Tom had seen what had to be done and had sawn off a piece of the shafting just over an inch long.

Then he had carefully filed it until it slipped into the square hole tightly. He had left the length of shafting on the bench top and had waited until Old Albert came past again. He had put the freshly filed piece in his pocket.

Old Albert had stood there whistling and filing a ward for a lock. Then he had spoken 'Where's that other job I gave you, young Tom? You know I wanted that doing before anything else.'

He had smiled as if he had caught Tom out. Tom replied. 'You never said there was any hurry, Mister Albert. If you had said, I would have got it done by now. Mind you, it looked like a tricky little job, trying to get a one inch round to fit tight into a one inch square.. Not that I wouldn't have got it done, somehow, in the end.'

He had tried to look forlorn, as if he was still trying to work out a solution for the puzzle. Old Albert had pounced on him in triumph. 'Here, let me show you how to do it. You'll never get the idea, the way you are going on.'

He bustled Tom out of the way and picked up the odd length of shafting and put it in the vice.

'This is the way you do it. You just saw off a piece just over an inch long and then you file it to fit. Couldn't you see that, young Tom? I don't know; you'll never be an engineer at this rate!'

Tom had looked at him as if in amazement. Then he slipped his hand into his pocket and pulled out the finished, one-inch length. He picked up the sheet of plate and gently pushed the shafting into the hole. He returned his gaze to Albert. 'It's still a bit tight I know, but will that do for now, Mister Albert?'

The elderly man had tried to cover his surprise. 'I should think so as well. What took you so long, young Barr?'

Albert had smiled to show he was pleased though, and Tom felt that he was making progress. Now he was a journeyman and equal to any of the other locksmiths around him. He had made a lock of his own, a showpiece lock, to show his skills to the best advantage. It had been a long-armed padlock, especially designed to hold large items down securely on the deck of a sea-going vessel. The lock was hanging on the wall now, and would not be moved until he left the firm, if he ever did.

There was a possibility of it. Old Albert had called him young Barr. It was the first time he had been called that and it surprised him a little. Was it a suggestion that he might have to leave the firm to get recognition? He thought about it and came to a realisation that if there was some position that he aspired to, he was totally responsible for making sure that he got it.

Whatever he wanted, he had to make sure that he paid in advance, by study, to be qualified for it. He had to study harder than anyone else, work harder than anyone else and be more suitable than anyone else for any position that he desired. He carried on thinking along the same lines. If he wanted more money than anyone else, he had to study money and its uses, and also save as hard as he could to build up a lump of capital that he could do something with. He didn't know what yet, but he would!

Tom also knew that although he had made a show of reconciliation with his father, they had not really come to an understanding of each other. He still hated Dan whenever he thought of him hitting his mother. Some day he would pay for that. For now he would say 'good morning' and all that stuff. He would not do his father any favours though; if his father wanted to borrow any money he would refuse him, it would be nicely, but still a refusal. It would be a regretful refusal of course. He would love to be able to help him out but just at the moment he was hard up himself! The fantasy was pleasant in his head.

*

Dan was thinking on the same problem. He never seemed to have any money to spare. Whatever he did, he never had any spare money. He only had to buy a couple of rounds of drinks and he was hard up for the rest of the week. It seemed to him that all his mates had plenty of money to spare for drinks. He had thought it might be because he gave Elsie too much house-keeping money. He had challenged her and this week he was going to test that out. He was going to do the shopping himself.

He would show her! Any bloke could do better than a woman when it came to brainwork. He hadn't worked out how he was going to do it yet, but it wouldn't take five minutes to come to a system.

He seemed to have come to a bit of a peace with Tom. The lad had taken the hand that been extended to him so he had conceded a point or two. Gradually, Dan felt, he would regain his place as man of the house. Tom would regret raising his hand to his father! The man of the house was the husband, not the son, no matter how cocky he thought he was, just because he had made a padlock! Dan had made hundreds of them, and had taught dozens of people how to make them. They seemed to have forgotten he had been away fighting for their freedom while the young ones had been free to do as they liked.

Even the gaffer had got away with it, playing the 'essential war work' card, skiving in the factory and working out deals with the Government to make both of them richer. He had also had his way with the women when he had felt like it. Dan had noticed how Stephen's eyes moved towards Elsie, whenever they met. You couldn't blame a man for looking at a woman and she was a bit special but it still made his blood boil to see a bloke eyeing his woman; that was only natural as well. For all he knew, the gaffer had held out his hat to Elsie while her husband had been risking his life. It was worth contemplating on!

29, More Open Than Ever.
1922

Stephen looked back on the time when Dan Barr had been away, with pleasure. He had made love with Elsie before her husband had volunteered, silly bugger! He had gone off with flags waving and one or two of the local women wanting him; had seen him as a hero, including that neighbour of Elsie's, Ruth something or other. He had seen Dan Barr with her on a night out, so he hadn't felt so bad about taking up with Elsie again, while the going was good.

Young Tom had been the result of their lovemaking, at the start of the war, and he had been in love with her ever since. She could not have any part of his other life, the life of family and business but, together, they had a life where no one else intruded. They had created a world entirely for themselves, where they could touch and whisper to each other of the things they wanted from the other.

Elsie was beautiful, with long blonde hair that had a hint of auburn in it that seemed to show off her hazel eyes. She was a little taller than the average but not as tall as Stephen. He loved the temper in her eyes when she was raised, and the passion there, too. The two sides of her temper seemed to match his more docile temperament.

When she sparkled with high red spots on her cheekbones, he found himself feeling so helpless that all he could do was laugh. All he could do was to take up some sort of defensive posture and beg her to stop whatever she was doing. When he did that, she stopped. He found he was laughing a lot of the time when she was round; he couldn't help it. If he had been forced to explain, he would have just said it was because he was happy when she was near, whether she was angry, sad or happy; it didn't make any difference which. There was nothing he could add to that. It was different with Mabel. He had tried to make her happy but with only a little success.

Mabel was wondering where he was. He had been out for hours. She often thought it was a good job she had the girls. They filled her life almost completely. From the moment she had first seen Laura, her eldest, she had loved her. The others had filled her glass of happiness until it spilled over. Stanley, her son was all that she would have wanted him to be; just like his father, he wanted to be the best at whatever he was doing at the time. He had a wonderful sense of humour, also like his father, but unlike his Uncle Bert. Bert was close to being below the usual run of intelligence. He really worked hard to do as he was told but always had difficulty with things.

Then there was Tom Barr. He was as like Stephen as he could be; it was obvious who his father was, but she couldn't bring herself to dislike the lad. Some day he would go off on his own, she knew. Maybe she would never see him again after that. The sooner that happened, the better she would feel.

Mabel thought back to the times when she had been offered love, or something like it, outside her marriage. Perhaps she would be again. She might enjoy it now that she was past child-bearing age. Maybe she could get her own back on Elsie Barr, and use her husband, just to see how she would like it. Maybe he was so staid that she knew he would be no good to her.

Perhaps someone else would turn up. In the meantime, she had work to do, to finish off for the day. That was her life – work. It filled her day; she liked it like that and it brought her a certain fulfilment. When her till rang up forty pounds or more, Mabel's day was happy: not because of the money but because of the achievement.

It was not likely that another man on the scene would make her any happier. Anyway, Stephen made her happy in his own way and certainly made her body feel complete. She recalled the afternoon, when he had taken her like an animal, and she had been an animal too. The children had nearly caught them in the act!

Of the family; Bert was the most trouble; not that he wanted to be any trouble. He always tried to please but usually unsuccessfully. The number of jobs he had scrapped through taking too much metal off them on a shaper or lathe was too many to count. The trouble was, he was beginning to grow up now and finding some of the girls exciting. That way certainly led to trouble and she knew that she would have to have a session with him, to explain the difficulties of being attracted to female factory hands if you were a gaffer. Not that he was a gaffer. He was, however, the son of a gaffer and that made the difference.

What about if his girl were to get with child? Bert wouldn't know what to do about that. He would just expect that he would have to get married and bring the child up. She had noticed the way the hands looked at the new girl, Molly, and she was a very attractive thing, with high breasts and enough of them. Bert would like to get his hands on them, she felt sure. She would make sure the girl left before that happened, even if she had to put some money in the girl's hand.

Yes, Molly would have to go. She would have a word with her mother, Ruth Elkins, in the other factory, to see if the girl could be eased into a job there. That might pacify Molly if she was to complain. That would leave a vacancy but that could soon be filled. No sooner had she thought of it than she decided to carry out her plan and called Molly into the office to explain the move to her. As soon as she did, Molly started crying, as if she was wondering what she had done while all the time, Mrs Stone was trying to congratulate her.

'It's a much better job you know; much more suitable for a young thing like yourself. If you don't want it, I can soon find someone else who would jump at the chance. Why are you crying, girl?'

Mabel knew why Molly was crying. It was because she was being taken away from a job where all the young chaps were constantly ogling her! Her father's firm was only half the size of Stone' and there weren't as many young men there. She tried to think of an incentive that would make the girl happier. Money might do it. She put it to Molly.

'I do believe my father wanted a young woman for the job

because it takes a bit of learning and he would expect to pay a bit more than the average, providing the girl had what it takes to get the job done right.'

Molly stopped crying and lifted her head. Money is a universal language, thought Mabel. It talks to most people in the friendliest of voices, if it is offered!

'I don't know if you are right sort of girl for this job after all. I would really expect an ambitious girl to be excited about it, not sitting crying and expecting sympathy. I have one or two others to see, to see if they are as suitable as you would have been.' She changed to the past tense, giving Molly the sense that she had been interviewed and found wanting because of her lack of determination. 'I must say I am a bit disappointed.'

Mabel paused to let the girl say something if she wanted to. Molly looked up slowly, as if the implications had only just occurred to her.

'I am sorry, Mrs Stone, I didn't mean you to think I wasn't grateful. It was just that I never had a chance like that before and it sort of upset me.'

Mabel smiled to herself. The girl was a quick thinker. She said nothing and waited. The girl was bound to say something in the way of acceptance, if she could, if she had that much cheek.

'If it's all right Mrs Stone, thank you for the chance to improve myself and I will start as soon as they are ready for me. What do I have to do now?'

Mabel sighed. That was it. It was all over. The girl was gone, or as good as gone. The Stone family was safe from a predator. The best time for Molly to go was now.

Mabel beckoned to her. 'Come with me, Molly. I'll show you the way and introduce you to my mother. She will show you what you have to do. You can start there in the morning, I believe. That will give you an hour, when you get back, to say your goodbyes to your friends here. If you like it there, and there are vacancies, you might recommend any of your friends, if you think they are suitable. Before you go, I will pay you any outstanding wages.

That'll save you any trouble you might have, in getting back here to collect it.'

That was as final as I could have put it, she thought. She had no excuse to come back here now. She reached for the drawer and pulled the pay packet out, handing it to Molly. 'There is an extra five pounds in it, to compensate you for any losses you might feel, Molly. You can keep your overall.' She reached out her hand. 'Well, congratulations. I'll see you outside the shop door in five minutes time.'

Mabel turned her back and started putting on her coat. Molly looked at her and surrendering, went out to get her clothes. Another episode in her life was over. Another was about to begin at the other factory; anything could happen. She had the idea she had been misled about something but she couldn't quite make out what it was. Still, she was to get more money; what more could she want? That was all she came to work for – and for the young men, of course. Perhaps there would be one at Elkin's she would like. She would have liked to attract the gaffer but he was an old man. The future might be better.

Molly marched through the factory, determined to leave with all flags flying. She had done nothing wrong. All it proved really was that Mabel Bloody Stone was jealous because her husband, Mister Bloody Stephen, had looked twice at her. Well, they had been forced to compensate her. It wasn't very often that she had won a battle with a gaffer. It had been worth it.

Old Albert stood by a doorway and watched Molly walk past. He smiled as he surmised what had happened in the office. Mabel had obviously decided the girl wasn't worth the candle, not like Elsie Barr. Strangely, she had never tried to get rid of that one. Mind you, he thought, that Molly was trouble. Perhaps she was being sent somewhere where she would be told to toe the line or else.

Out of curiosity he made his way to the office.

'What's happening with that young Molly then, Mabel?'

He stood waiting for an answer and she turned to him freely

as she had over the years he had known her.

'She is one o' them women that can't keep her body to herself. I know she's tried it on with Dan and probably young Tom as well. I just want to be rid on her. She'll probably die o' the pox and good riddance to her!'

'You are probably right, Mabel. She tried it on with me but I put her in her place. I could never take a risk to my life like she would be. I might flirt a bit but I have always been a one woman bloke, you know what I mean?'

Mabel smiled at him and made an excuse to get him out of her shop. He was as two-faced as they came. What would turn up next?

30. Selina.
1923

Selina Brown walked down the narrow street to where she and her mother lived in a little back-to-back house. It wasn't the only property in the family. Her mother, Edie Brown, rented a general shop just along the road and worked long hours there, to keep their heads above water, financially.

Sometimes, Selina dreaded going home to the bitter tongue of her mother who was often tired. Selina was an orphan, her father having died the previous year. She knew she would be looking for work soon; she had stayed away from school long enough; she had to find something to do to help with the family housekeeping problems. She walked into the little house expecting to find her mother there, but it was empty. Perhaps she had worked late. She did that occasionally if there was not enough trade to make it worth while to keep the shop open for just the normal hours.

The front door open and her mother walked in. Selina looked at her and smiled. 'Hello, our Mom; I wondered where you were. I thought you must have closed up early.'

'Never mind the shop. I've been down to see Mabel Stone. You know, that fat woman from Stones' Locks. It belongs to her husband. I had to close up early to go and make sure you got an interview. She came in the shop today and we got chatting. She said they've got a vacancy in the works for somebody to train up on the padlocks they make. I've got you an interview with the gaffer on Monday morning. Make sure you dress decent. You have to look as if you are worth training up. It's easy; really, you'll see when you get there. Just make sure you do whatever you have to do to get the job. If you don't get it, somebody else will. Try and act as if you've got two penno'th o' brains.'

Edie stopped talking and Selina looked at her. She had guessed that her mother might take some sort of action to get her into a job but had not suspected this. She could not complain, however; she felt it was her place to work to help with the household expenses.

'How much are the wages, Mom. Is it a good job?'

'Never mind how much the wages are, my girl. Just you get your arse down there and get the job. I'm fed up of working my guts out every day. You're twenty years younger than me.

'And another thing while we are at it; there's no reason why you shouldn't come down to the shop with me, on a Saturday and give me an 'and with the heavy things. You've had it easy up to now. I dain't want to upset you after your Dad had that accident and died, but it's been too much for me. I don't have any life at all! Well, it's going to change – and so are you, my young madam. You have to be there at eight o' clock in the mornings – and be ready to start straight away on Monday, if they want you to; all right?'

Selina was surprised but not shocked. She had expected something like this would happen. Any job was a coveted position, whatever it was, and a job learning to make locks, or at least a part of them could be quite interesting, and she would get paid. It wouldn't be much, she knew, but she would be allowed to keep some part of it, and she would also get a few coppers for helping in the shop on Saturdays. Perhaps she would be able to buy herself a few pretty clothes. The summer was on the way and it would be nice to wear something that showed herself off to advantage.

She caught sight of herself in the long mirror. She was about average height but that was the only thing that was average. Her face was a smiling face, a pretty face, even if she thought so herself. Her eyes were pretty too, even though she thought so herself!

Her hair was held in a tight bun for neatness and ease as much as for appearance and her waist was slim from walking. She knew that the way she walked seemed to attract looks from men. Men looked and women were looked at; that was what her mother had told her and it seemed to be true.

Her mother was speaking again. 'Here, here's an overall. I bought it for you at the market, just in case you get the job. If I was you, I should run an iron over it. You never know; you might have to wear it Monday!'

She thrust the overall into Selina's hands and walked off to start cooking the evening meal that Selina had prepared earlier. Selina lifted the smoothing iron out of the little cupboard and put it on the black, cast-iron fire range to get it hot enough to use. It was a matter of a few seconds for her to trot upstairs to take a blanket from her bed to spread on the table, to iron on. She didn't speak to her mother until the overall was smoothed all over, and then she called to her.

'Mom! What shall I wear to go to Stone's on Monday?'

'You can wear whatever you like, Selina. You can start buying your own clothes now, so it's up to you what you wear. Just try to remember, you won't be getting all that much, so look after it. I shan't have any money off you for two weeks, and I shall give you one and six for what you do on Saturdays, That should get you started, shouldn't it?'

'Thank you very much, Mom. Are you sure you can afford that? I don't mind giving you all my wages. I've never had any before so I wouldn't miss it now, would I?'

Edith Brown smiled. Selina had always been a good and loyal daughter; she was proving it now and she had always accepted her mother's judgement in deciding how much she had to spend, if anything. She had never felt that she had the right to anything without her mother's approval. The time would come soon when she would want to exercise more control over her own affairs but for now, she was the good, obedient daughter.

'Don't you worry, Selina. I shan't let you rob me and I shan't rob you either. Let's just let things run for a little while and see how we go. How's that overall; have you ironed it yet?' She poked her head round the door. You can wear your best coat if you like, Monday. It don't matter much about wearing a posh frock. If you wear your overall, a dress won't be seen and if you don't wear it, you won't be taking your coat off, right?'

They each smiled at Edith's way of putting things, then Selina asked her mother about the evening.

'Is Harry coming tonight, Mom?'

Harry was Edith's new man friend who used to work with her father before he had died in an industrial accident. Selina liked him and sometimes wished he was her friend, not her mother's. The way he looked at her, sometimes, made her think that he might feel the same. She smiled at her mother as she asked the question.

'Yes; he's taking me out tonight. You'll have the house to yourself, to get ready for this interview.'

The meal was ready and Selina thought as she ate. It might be a good idea to have an early night, tonight. She carefully ironed her coat after dinner, to try to make it look as smart as she could. She hung it on a hanger instead of on the nail in the door; that would help the smoothness to stay in. She would be working at her mother's little shop, on Saturday morning.

Harry came at seven o'clock. Selina let him in, turning to show off her shape.

'Well, it's the little un. Where are you off to, then? I'm afraid you can't come with us. Tonight is for grown ups only; another time, perhaps.'

Harry always looked smart, as if he were going to Buckingham Palace, as her mother sometimes said. What would it feel like if he had his arms round you? She decided to tease him.

'Well Mister Bossy Boots, if I'm not grown up enough for your taste, I shall have to look elsewhere, shan't I?'

Selina turned away from him but his arm, responding to her youthful challenge, went round her, capturing her. The sensation it gave was something strange but quite stimulating. He had caught hold of her from the back so his hand fell on her stomach. He moved it up until it was sliding up inside her blouse, almost onto her breast. She moved against him, feeling her buttocks taking hold of him. That was the only way she could think of it.

She looked round for her mother but Edie was still upstairs. Selina took hold of Harry's hand and moved it onto her breast, feeling his grip tighten. She had done that before; she knew he liked it. His body moved against her, tightly pushing, almost into her, she thought. There was something there that had shape and size and hardness and she knew what it was. The thought was frightening; she knew what men and women did but she could not let it happen to her while her mother was going out with this man.

Selina pulled herself away from him, moving to the table to pick up some crocks, almost as if the act would preserve her against further advances from him. She looked out of the corner of her eye; he too was moved by the unplanned intimacy of the small contact. There was no way of prolonging the contact for either of them. Harry looked up the stairs for her mother.

'Edith; are you ready love? We shall be late if we don't get the half past seven bus.'

There was a sound of the wardrobe door as her mother got a coat out.

'I'll be down when I'm ready, in a few seconds. It's only half past. The bus will be here at twenty to eight, the same as it always is.'

Harry turned to Selina.

'Is that right? We still have five minutes before the bus comes? Perhaps we could...'

He stopped and his hand moved to her body again, exciting her. She pulled away again, and her mother clip-clopped down from the landing, causing them to separate.

'Coming; ready or not!' Edie called out the childish words as she stepped off the last step of the stairs. 'Here I am; take me out to see the sights of Wolverhampton then, Harry.' She turned to Selina and kissed her cheek. 'Don't forget what I said; get a good night's sleep tonight.'

The courting couple swept out into the street as if they were celebrities but Selina noticed that Harry looked over his shoulder at her. She closed the door behind them and finished getting ready for bed.

Would Harry be attracted to her? The thought made her wonder how she could make him be as passionate with her as with her mother. He often came round to the house before her mother was home from her little shop. Perhaps she could persuade him, if that was the word, to make love to her in the same way that he had to her mother. She didn't want to steal him from Edie; she just wanted to borrow him for a little while. She would have to think carefully about it.

Selina's opportunity came the next day. Edith often worked late on Fridays; she liked to do a small stock check then in preparation for her order when the wholesaler's representative came in on Saturday. Selina lay back on the settee, trying to relax. Often she would walk down to meet her mother and give a hand with the counting. Not that she was short of energy; she felt that she could match Harry at any activity he liked to mention.

There was a knock at the door and she jumped. It could only be Harry. This was her chance. She took her time and answered the door. She had prepared for the occasion and was just wearing a dress. She knew her shape could be seen inside it. She slowly moved toward the door in expectation, hoping her desire was going to be met. Was it Harry? It was Harry.

'Yes? I think Mom will be home soon. Do you want to come in and wait for her?'

Of course he would, if he felt anything like she felt.

'Yes, I'll wait for her for a few minutes and if she hasn't come, I'll call on her another night. How would you like to make us a nice cup of tea?'

There was an atmosphere and they both knew it, she felt. How could he not feel how she felt?

'A cup of tea? Yes sir; how would you like it? Would you like it hot like you had it the other night? Or would you like to play games like you do with Mom? I know a nice game; we could play row the boat gently down the stream.'

Selina was playing word games with him again; but then she slipped onto his lap, facing him, and wrapped her legs round his waist, moving them together, back and forth. The action produced frustration and the frustration produced more action. She moved more insistently.

'Come on then, Harry; row the boat!'

Selina pulled herself tight against him, feeling her body pressing against his manhood, which she felt enlarging. Suddenly he slipped his hands under her dress and pushed it up and over her head, to be thrown somewhere, anywhere. Selina pulled at him and his clothes seemed to come off in her hands. His hand made for her dark passage and found it. She felt herself become wet as he put himself against and then into her. She screamed for a moment and then pulled herself closer still, her arms going round his neck.

He gorged himself on the feel of her breasts in his hands and took hold and put them into his mouth, sucking and biting them one at a time and then he could not wait any longer for the climax. She felt him shoot inside her like a hot spurt from a kettle and the feeling was so intense that she climaxed too. They lay back and he was the first to recover. He had to be; Edith might walk into the house any minute.

The childish game was the first of their sexual encounters in the front room of the little house. Selina's awakening sexual awareness came to full knowledge in the next few days. Edith never actually had the unfaithfulness of her lover thrown in her face. It would have been too much for the three of them.

31. The Meeting.
1923

Selina awoke with a bang; it was six o'clock! That was how it seemed on days like this, when she had fresh and exciting things to do. It was the day of her interview or, if she were lucky, the day she started as a trainee at Stone's Locks.

The firm of locksmiths made padlocks of special types, she knew, and she would train to make parts of them. She had often wondered what was inside a lock, to make it so special that it could only be opened by the correct key. The inside was a mystery to her. It must be a real jumble to be sure that it opened when you wanted it to, and wouldn't open with anything but the right key. Perhaps she would find out.

Her mother was already up; she must have had breakfast; there were two plates on the table. Selina picked them both up and took them into the kitchen where they wouldn't draw attention to themselves. There was a pot of porridge slowly bubbling on the range and she took a ladle down and helped herself to a dishful. She liked a drop of milk on it; it helped it down, she thought.

Half an hour later, she was ready to set out. There was no hurry; she didn't have to be there until eight o'clock. Her mother hadn't spoken to her since she had got up. Perhaps it was up to her to speak first.

'Morning, Mom.' Selina looked questioningly across the tiny room, at her mother. 'Are you alright, Mom?' Her mother was looking as if she had been crying. 'What's the matter, Mom?'

'Oh, it's nothing; nothing for you to worry your head about. I just wonder what the future holds for us, that's all. What use are men if they can't be faithful and loyal to you? They expect it from us, don't they?'

Edith stopped talking and Selina was shocked, realizing that Harry must have been unfaithful and had been caught out. What would her mother feel, if she found out how Harry had been unfaithful with her daughter? It was up to her to put her mother's mind at rest. She knew that she was going to get some revenge on Harry, but she would get some use out of him first! She put her arm around her mother's shoulders and gave her a quick hug.

'Don't you fret yourself, Mom. I don't suppose they are any different to women. Some are good; some are bad, some are thin; some are fat. All you have to do is find yourself one who ain't bad and ain't fat!'

Selina laughed and Edith couldn't help but join in. It was quite likely that her daughter was right! Women varied so why shouldn't men? Selina seemed to have a lot of common sense combined with a love for life that might lead her into strange places. The thought intrigued her, wondering why she had even had such a thought. What would Selina say if she knew that Harry and I did those things?

The moment she questioned herself Edith knew the answer; Selina would want to know more; she wouldn't be shocked at all. It would just be something new to her, and the girl would want to know more about, and would want to experience the thing, herself. Had she done so, already? Anger and jealousy hit her then, for a moment but it was useless to understand her daughter without using that understanding to guide her. It would stand some thinking about, that would.

Edith looked at the clock. 'Come on, child; it's time you were on the way. You don't want to be late for your interview, do you?'

Selina was putting on her coat as she moved though the little house. Her mother was still calling her 'child.' When would she realise that her daughter was fully grown, now? This was going to be a special day. It might be her first working day, the first day she would work and expect to get paid for it as an adult. Selina had worked in the little shop that her mother ran, and had got one and sixpence for her trouble but that was not the same as a proper paid job as a padlock maker, or whatever they called them.

She was getting to be grown up, now; that was the difference. How long would she work at Stone's? Selina knew that many men and women worked at a firm for most of their life, some even at the same bench, taking on the shape of the workshop as if they became a part of it, gradually developing the hump that came from long standing in a particular position. That wasn't going to happen to her; she would make sure of that! There must be more interesting things in the world than a little lock factory, whatever her mother thought.

Selina reached out to her mother again. It was like saying a permanent goodbye to her. She was a child setting off for an interview. She would be a young woman coming home, if she was offered the chance to start work immediately that would be a plus. There was a tear trickling down Edith's cheek as she tried to hug her without fuss.

'Off you go then; do your best; that's all you can do, ain't it? I'll see you later. I'll lock up. I'm off to work myself!'

As if to say you're not the only one going to work, Selina thought. Oh well. Ten minutes later, she was turning in at the side entrance alley that led to the lock-making section of the Stone's property. There was an office door that led to the shop at the front, so she went in and asked Mabel if she knew where she had to go.

'Yes, my dear. You go to the end, turn left and then go up the steps to Mister Albert's office. Just knock at his door. He is expecting you; you are Edith Brown's daughter aren't you?' Mabel waited for the nod and went on. 'He is an elderly man but he knows everything about this firm. He started it. Just be respectful to him. I am sure he will like you.'

Mabel smiled to herself. He would like her all right, the lecherous reprobate! The girl was beautiful without even trying. She would most likely cause just as much trouble as that Molly. There would be a few looking up at her legs as she mounted the steps! Oh well, she had seen and heard it all before. The girl seemed bright enough to take it in her stride.

Selina smiled back at Mabel and stepped back through the door. There were two youths at the foot of the steps and she swept past them without breaking her stride and climbed smartly up the steps, leaving the youths dazzled at the sight of her legs as she climbed. She tapped on the door at the top of the steps.

A voice answered. 'Come in!' She hesitated for a second and heard, 'Come on, if you're coming!'

Selina pushed the door and walked in. It was not a big office. There was a desk with two shelves fastened on the wall behind it. There were ledgers on the shelves, along with catalogues and papers. On the desk were pens and an inkwell set in a carved length of dark wood. The top of the desk was covered with lock parts; the jobs currently going through manufacture. Sitting at the desk was an older man.

From the back she could see that his hair was thinning but his shoulders were those of a young man, due to years of physical labour. He wore a short-sleeved, striped shirt that showed evidence of a little sweat under his arms. As she entered, he spun round on the chair and levelled his gaze into her face. The impact of his stare was as if he had hit her and she stepped back automatically. Then she pulled herself together; he was only a man, in any case, she thought. Her mother had taught her that, having spent many years of serving people of all kinds, in her little shop. She recalled her words. 'A man is only a man and a woman is only a woman in spite of what they sometimes think. Be sure you know that.' Selina reminded herself of the advice as she faced the slightly fierce look of her potential boss.

Selina placed a smile on her face and greeted the man 'Good morning.'

She waited as the man carefully surveyed her appearance. She was not going to be the next one to speak!

A minute passed then, 'Good morning; who are you? Are you Selina Brown? If you are, you're on time; I like that. You look good as well, so that takes us through the first part of this little conversation. We shall have to try you out, to see if you are likely to be any good at the job. Come on, follow me.'

That hadn't taken long! He stood, brushed past her and led the way back down the steps. Selina turned and followed him, her shoes clip-clopping down, the two youths scurrying away as they descended.

As she arrived at the bottom, he turned and looked at her feet. 'You ought to get something sturdier to work in, for your own safety. It's your own health, after all. It's up to you. If you fall over your feet, it will not be our fault; it will be on your own responsibility, right?'

Mister Albert didn't wait for her answer but marched off, disappearing into a doorway. Selina pushed it open to follow him in and became aware of a distinctive smell. It was suds oil; an oil that was used as a cutting lubricant, and was present in most workshops. The man, she assumed he was Mister Albert, was gaining ground and she wondered why he was walking so quickly. She found herself trotting to try to catch up with him, past a lathe with a young man working at it, and then a hand press with another young man standing by it.

'Hello; what's your name?' The young man said, looking at her admiringly.

'Selina. I can't stop. I've got to catch him up. He's almost running. I don't know why.'

The young woman was out of breath but stopped to have a look at the young man at the side of her.

He spoke. 'I'm Tom Barr. I expect I'll see you later. I hope so anyway. Away you go or you'll get lost and then you'll never get the job, will you? Gaffers always walk quickly, you know.'

He smiled at her and she knew that she would see him later. She hoped so too; he seemed nice. Mister Albert had stopped now and had turned round to look for her. 'Come on girl; I thought you'd got lost!'

Mister Albert didn't seem so fierce now, probably because that young man, Tom Barr, had nor seemed intimidated by the older man as he had walked past. She smiled at him and he suddenly seemed friendlier. She caught up with him and waited while he showed her the way by leading. The room they entered now was where the finished products were inspected and packed. It seemed a lot cleaner than the rest of the factory and somehow more homely with no machinery and less noise. Mister Albert turned again and spoke to her.

'This is where you might work – if you work out alright in the factory. You can't work in here straight away because you wouldn't know a good lock from a bad one. That's right, isn't it?'

Selina couldn't argue with him but she made up her mind then that she would do her best to learn about the other jobs, whatever they were, as quickly as she could. She just nodded her head to show her agreement with what he was asking her. She was being given a chance! That was enough for now. The future would take care of itself.

'Come on then, what's your name, Selina? That's a nice name.' Things were looking up. He seemed to have changed since she had been in his company, gradually becoming more human. 'Come on now and let me show you where you are going to work for the time being.'

Once again they walked the length of the small factory, Mister Albert, guiding her through what seemed to be a maze of machines.

'Here you are then. This is where you will start to learn the beginnings of the trade. Dan'll put you right.'

Mister Albert stepped forward and introduced the man. He had a military bearing and she felt that he had been a soldier; he was so straight-backed compared with the others she had seen in her tour of the small works.

'This is Dan, Dan Barr. He has worked here for a long time and he will show you anything you want to know. He will also be in charge of you for a while so take notice of what he tells you to do. If you don't, you will have to find another job; it's as simple as that. I'll probably see you later on, to find out how you have got on with the job. Do well and you'll have a job for life, my dear.'

The man had the same surname as the young man who had spoken to her earlier. Perhaps they were related, although they didn't seem to be much like each other.

'These are strips.' The man, Dan Barr, brought her back to the present with a jolt. 'We push them into this machine. It's called a hand press. They come in different sizes. What you do is push the strip into this tool here, until it comes up against this stop.' He was showing her as he spoke. 'Then you swing this arm as hard as you can and it crops off a piece of strip of just the right length. The piece you have cropped off falls into the bin here, and you do the same thing again and again. Have you got that?'

He didn't wait for her to even nod, just carried on talking. He must have given this lecture many times, she thought. He knows it by heart.

'When you've used up all the strip, give me a call and I will show you how to fill the spindle here with another roll of strip. Then you start all over again. If you think it's boring; you're right. When you get used to it, you can practically do it with your eyes closed and you sort of go somewhere else in your imagination. There you are then. It's your turn now. Let's see you do it. Do you think you'll be alright?'

It looked easy enough. Selina stepped forward, pushed the strip into the slot until it stopped at the stop and then she took hold of the handle of the long arm and pulled it to her. She watched as the arm came towards her and the tool turned as it lowered onto the strip and bounced off it. She felt the jar in her arm and looked at Dan in alarm, thinking she had broken something. He laughed.

'You have to pull the handle as if you mean it, you know. It's no good just farting about with it. Look, I'll show you.'

Dan stepped forward and took her place. Then he took hold of the arm and gave it a quick pull. The arm swung, nearly hitting her head as it flew round in an arc. The tool lowered into the bottom tool of the press, pushing straight through the strip which fell and clattered into the metal bin under the bench. He pushed the strip again and swung his arm; clatter; there was another one, then another and then another. It seemed so easy for him and so hard for her.

He stepped back with a mock attempt at gallantry and she stepped forward. This time she determined to conquer it. She planted her feet well and took hold of the handle, noticing that the part where she had to hold it was covered with a sort of cloth, and wondered why. She swung the arm round and felt a thrill of satisfaction as the top tool sliced through the strip and the arm bounced back towards the position where she could swing it again. The small length fell and clattered into the bin.

'Good; that's better; you only have to fill two bins of them to the top and you can go home. You'll do well; I can see that.'

Dan was laughing and she suddenly realised what a picture she must look. Her face had a determined appearance and her bust was pushing against the overall, showing her shape. Oh God, she thought, am I making a show of myself? She turned back to the press and started again. Dan watched her for a minute or two and then walked away, leaving her.

I've just got to get on with it, she thought, and steadied herself as she moved into position to try again. The next hour seemed to take forever as swing followed swing, then time seemed to speed up as she got used to the motion of her own body in relation to the machine. Her mind wandered and she found herself performing without having to think about it.

Selina looked round; there were about a dozen others in the room, all intent on what they were doing and also talking to each other. She couldn't understand at first, how they could hear each other with all the banging going on and then saw that they were lip-reading. She could see that what they also did was to over-emphasise the way their lips moved and also the expressions they displayed.

Before she knew it, it was lunch time and everyone stopped to eat sandwiches. The young man, Tom, who had spoken to her earlier, looked across and winked at her, giving her a funny feeling. She decided to go out for a walk, along to the small shop where there was a large pop bottle on the counter. The shop was similar to the one her mother ran.

'Halfpenny one, please.'

Selina indicated the bottle which was full of a red liquid. The woman nodded and turned a tap which allowed the drink to come out with a squishing noise. Selina walked back out of the shop and stood enjoying the June sunshine. When the cardboard cup was empty she took it back into the shop and strode back towards the factory.

As she walked through the alley that led to the factory, she could see that Tom was looking out of one of the windows, leaning on his folded arms. She felt instinctively that he was looking for her and this was confirmed as his face lit up when he saw her. Their eyes met and there was an instant understanding that they were going to be more than friends.

Selina walked towards him, her face showing her mood. She felt provocative. 'Hello, Tom. What are you doing, looking out of the window?'

Tom seemed a little nonplussed for a second then saw that she was playing with him. He tried to think of something to continue in the same vein.

'I just thought I would like to see if there is anything interesting around, but there isn't – as you can see!'

A moment of impulse seemed to take hold of her.

'Perhaps you are looking in the wrong places, Tom. If you looked with your eyes open, you might find something interesting to look at!'

Selina walked right up to the window and looked him full in the eye as her breasts seemed to settle on his folded arms on the window sill. She saw, for the first time in her life, the result of this action, saw Tom's sexual arousal become transparent on his face and she saw the longing for her in his look. The effect on her own feelings was like a physical blow and she stepped back quickly. She was completely lost for something to say. She felt her face redden and she turned and walked away, her head in the air. There was work to do!

Selina tackled the job, in the afternoon, as if there was something to prove. When she finally stopped for the day, her arm was starting to ache and she wondered what it would be like the next day. The memory of her first day would stay with her for the rest of her life.

The young woman walked out of the little factory with her head held up, as if she was emulating the walk of an old hand. As she strode out, she could hear footsteps behind her, keeping time with hers. She was about to turn round when she felt a hand take hold of hers. It was Tom. She went to pull it away and then thought better of it. It was nice, to have your hand held, after all. The two young people walked slowly from the factory without speaking for some time. Then Tom, wanting to be the one to lead the conversation, spoke.

'How do you like it then?'

Selina didn't know whether he was talking about the work, the factory or the feeling of having her hand held. She thought about it and decided not to tease him but to answer his question whichever way he meant it.

'The factory itself is dark and dull but the work is interesting, at first; then it grows boring. It's the same thing over and over again, that's the trouble. I'll say one thing; I found myself wandering away from work in my head, and I still managed to get a lot of cropping done. That's what they call it, isn't it; cropping? When you are doing the same thing all the time, you get so you can do it with your eyes shut. Is your work the same?'

Tom laughed to himself. He had worked on all the different tasks at the little factory and enjoyed them all. Even when the work was pure repetition, he had managed to keep his sanity by wandering, as Selina had called it. It was surprising what you could do when you were doing something else. Not all his work was production; some of it was to manufacture machine parts to use in the production process.

'No, Selina,' he answered. 'A lot of the work I do is not actually making locks; it is making bits of machines to make locks. Sometimes I make pieces of metal as part of a new machine, to try to find a better, or a quicker way to do something, so that it either makes locks quicker or cheaper. Sometimes I mend the machines if they break. It's more interesting, I suppose.'

32 Almost Lovers.
1923

'Sometimes we have to find just the right temperature to harden and temper things, so that the outcome is just the right hardness for that job. I think you give me just the right temperature.'

Tom was still holding Selina's hand and she showed no sign of removing it from his grasp. He slipped his hand from hers and put his arm round her shoulders. Still she did not demur so he pulled her close to him. Selina wanted him to carry on talking about the right temperature and hardness and things. He spoke again.

'I don't know why, but I like you, Selina. I even like the sound of your name. Where did you get the name from? Is it your mother's name?'

There was a question in his eyes but she was not sure if the question on his lips was the question in his eyes.

She decided to answer in the same way that he had asked.

'No, I don't know where I got it from, either. I like it anyway. There aren't all that many around, are there? To answer your other question, I like having my hand held.'

Selina slipped under his arm to be more comfortable and he pulled her a little closer again. They were going nowhere exactly, subconsciously looking for a place to be alone with each other. The sun had gone down now, and the gaslights were being lit. As they approached an alley, Tom pulled her into its shadow and pulled her body against his, feeling her shape merging with his own. He turned his face to hers and lowered his lips onto hers, pressing forcefully and finding a way to insert his tongue.

Selina pulled away sharply. 'You're a bit cheeky aren't you, Tom? I only met you today and look at you! Are you trying to do things to me that you shouldn't?'

He looked at her in a self-conscious sort of way. He had no

thoughts, only feelings! Was this the way things were? Thoughts were intellectual but feelings were emotional. Which was the right way to explore and discover new things about men and women?

'I don't know what I'm trying to do. I know I'm not clever; I just know I like you a lot and I love the way your body fits with mine and your lips fit mine. I know you like it as much as I do, or you wouldn't be standing here, holding me like I'm holding you. I know I will know you as long as I live and I know I shall never forget today.'

No one had spoken to her like that before and the words made her aware of him sexually, causing her to blush fiercely. He was entirely different to Harry, more natural, less mature but more *good*, she felt sure. They got closer to each other, finding innocent ways to feel more of the other, gradually getting bolder, touching and stroking, learning what the other responded to.

'Tom! Tom!'

Selina's voice called out as she reached the climax of her passion. He joined with her emotionally in response to her stroking and they collapsed against the wall. For Tom, it was the first orgasm he had experienced in response to an outside stimulus and was a totally new sensation. He looked at her in awe, expecting her to slap his face or carry out some sort of revenge but she just stood there trembling, as if she didn't know how to act.

'Selina,' he whispered, 'I don't know how to say this but I've never done this before.'

Selina smiled to herself. As if she didn't know! Tom felt as if he had grown ten years in experience in the few minutes they had been standing, caressing each other to the culmination of their desires; he never wanted to know another girl or woman ever, he was as sure of that as he could be. He also felt responsible for her, and for her future and felt that he would always be responsible for her. The young man tried to put it into words.

'Do you know; I never want to be or go with any other

woman, Selina? I suppose what I am trying to say is, I love you and I shall always love you, no matter how many other girls I meet. It doesn't make sense. I thought you had to get to know somebody well, to love them. I knew in one day, one minute!' He looked into her eyes and Selina felt that he was talking deep into her soul. 'As far as I am concerned, you are my girl. How do you feel about that?'

Selina hesitated before answering him. She had more experience than Tom in the field of love. She had been introduced to lovemaking by Harry, her mother's beau and it had been exciting but what she had experienced with Tom had more reality, more real love, more genuine feeling than anything she had ever felt before.

There was no doubt in her mind that Tom cared for her, and she cared for him, she knew. She took a breath and answered him.

'You're the one for me, Tom, and you'll always be the only one. I love you Tom Barr and I always shall. I never thought I would feel anything like this, for anyone. That tells you how I feel; Tom and I can't put it better any other way.'

Tom was standing, leaning with his back to the wall and she was leaning against him when the feeling came to him; the feeling that he was now complete. He hadn't known before but he had only been half a person; now he was two halves! Selina was talking to him.

'Come on, Tom, It's all very well but I've got to get home. My mother will be wondering where I've got to. This is my first day at work, this sort of work anyway, and she'll want to know all about it. I've been helping her in her little shop but I've never worked in a factory. You'd better leave me at the corner of the street or her chap, Harry, will start shouting. He likes to think he is my father, but he isn't! I shall tell him one of these days. I only put up with him for Mom's sake.

'She ought to get married again. Dad died last year and she's only just coming out of mourning. She deserves a bit of life; I just wish she had picked somebody a bit better than Harry. Anyway, come on. We've got a lifetime to get to know each other better.'

They carried on walking until they arrived at the street where she lived and then she turned to him.

'Please don't come any further, Tom. I shall only get into trouble with Harry. He gets so angry sometimes, and really he has no right to.'

Tom wanted to argue with her but felt that she had the right to make the rules of their courtship. Her stepfather could wait, whoever he thought he was. He could be sorted out in the future.

Tom started waiting for Selina after that first night, at the end of their shift and she expected him to. Neither of them wanted anything else; the way they were with each other seemed so natural.

Selina gradually got used to the work and she was occasionally given an hour or two inspecting a particular batch of locks. She walked into the Inspection and Packing Department the following Monday afternoon, after eating lunch with Tom, and found a strange woman there, inspecting the locks.

'Hello,' she said to the woman, 'How long have you been working here?'

Selina had started to regard the quiet little warehouse as her private domain and it was a shock to see someone else there. She looked at the woman. Whoever she was, she seemed to know what she was doing, separating the padlocks into types and then picking out the ones with small faults, putting them into a separate box to be rectified. The woman looked up.

'About twelve years, on and off. How about you? I'm Elsie,' she said, 'Elsie Barr.'

As soon as the woman told her name, Selina realised who she was. She must be Tom's mother! Is this a family concern, she thought? She knew she had to make a friend of the woman; there was every reason to; she wanted her on the same side as herself.

'Have you had any lunch?' Selina asked. 'I've got some

sandwiches left if you haven't.'

Selina sat down at the side of the woman and held out the lunch box. In a moment the woman started to eat the sandwiches. She must have had nothing all day. The woman wiped her lips. She didn't look particularly hungry; Selina thought. She must have had the sandwich more for my sake than for her own. There was a thought. The woman must be brighter than she had initially suspected.

'Thank you my dear,' the woman said. 'I enjoyed that bit o'peck. What's your name, my dear?'

'Selina, Selina Brown. I live with my Mom, Edith Brown. We live in one of the Courts, just down the street. You know, where the main road meets the High Street?

The woman answered quickly. 'Oh yes, I know, in Willenhall itself. I know Willenhall quite well but I come from Wednesbury.'

That was a long way to come, Selina thought. Tom must come with her. Did Dan come with her? Did the three of them come from Wednesbury, every day? It wasn't as simple as she thought, making friends with the Barrs.

Elsie was looking at Selina closely, as if trying to read her mind.

'My son and I come in the pony and trap, and my husband comes on his bike. My son has a bike as well so he comes on that, sometimes. I don't come here all that often. I just come when they need me to sort out a problem, like a batch of locks put together incorrectly or some other fault. Bert, that's the brother of Stephen Stone, sometimes gets things mixed up. He is a nice lad but he's a penny short of a shilling, if you know what I mean.'

Selina nodded, wondering as she listened, what could make three people come to work here when there was probably more work in Wednesbury than there was here, in Willenhall. There must be a story behind all this. She was always curious about people; her mother had taught her that, to try to divine from the clues given, to find out more about people she met. You never knew when that sort of information might come in handy, when you were making a judgement about someone, for instance. She responded to Elsie.

'It must be nice to have a pony and trap, to be able to get about and see things that other people never get to see.'

Selina was trying to keep the conversation going, to find out more. How could this woman and her family find the money to maintain a trap, and a pony? Elsie carried on drinking her tea for a moment, and then replied.

'Yes, it is nice, though I couldn't afford to keep Chalky, that's the pony, just for that. I do another job in Wednesbury and he helps me to get round, to do it. I just pop in here occasionally to help out. I started working here years ago but I left when the other job came up. I only work when they need me so it gives me time to do other things, like going out seeing things, as you said.' She changed the subject. 'Have you met my husband and son yet?'

This woman changes things to suit herself, thought Selina. Most people don't even bother to try to do that. They just carry on chatting, giving away all their lives. The fact that Elsie did change the subject revealed two things; that she had something to conceal that she thought was no business of Selina's, and that she might have another income that was also no business of anyone but herself. She was turning out to be the most interesting person she had met at work – except Tom of course! Selina decided to play the same game herself.

'Yes, I've met Dan, that's who you mean isn't it, Elsie? He looks a bit stern, as if he has been in the Army. Still I suppose thousands of men look like that now, don't they? Has he been in the Army?'

Selina shut up and waited for an answer. She had turned the question that Elsie had asked her, back against her. Now Elsie was being obliged to answer her questions.

'Yes, he was in the Staffies. He got to be a Sergeant-Major so he must have done something right. He worked here before he joined up. I think he was glad to get away from home to tell the truth. He always wanted to be in a position where he could tell people what to do, and he got it in the Staffies. Then, when he got out, he got promoted at work. He tells little girls what to do now.'

Elsie laughed and Selina joined in as the woman went on.

'My son, Tom, works here as well; you'll soon get to know him, I'm sure. He would have to be blind to miss seeing you, Selina. The other one you'll have to watch out for is the old man, Mister Albert. He might be getting on but you'll find he'll soon try to get his leg over yours. Don't say I never warned you.'

The horn sounded, calling them all back to work and Bert took it on himself to keep an eye on those not immediately restarting work. He found power in the activity.

Elsie pointed him out to Selina. 'Here he is, the creep; well he's not exactly a creep but it's as if he tries to act like a creep. Dan tries to put him right; tries to make him act like a responsible person but he doesn't seem to get the idea at all. Oh well; back to it.'

Elsie gave Selina a wave as they parted and went back to the inspecting, in the warehouse. The girl seemed quite astute for her age; she was only a child really, but she knew Tom better than she had let on. Elsie had seen the young couple, she realised that she was already thinking of them in that way, walking along the road. She had wondered why Tom was going to work on his bike; now she knew.

Elsie recalled what she had thought of Selina. She was very attractive, that was sure. Her breasts were very proud-looking and her back was very straight. It seemed to go with her hair, which was curled into a bun, very similar to her own. She had nice looking legs, too, and her short skirt showed them to advantage. She might be the one for her son. Elsie was glad the girl seemed bright; she would hate her son to be mixed up with someone who had no common sense.

Times were changing now, and the short skirt was a sign of it. There were changes all over the world. Even music was different and the theatre was putting on a different sort of show. Jazz was the new kind of popular music; loud and rowdy, it had been condemned in the United States by some members of the Church.

Even in Ireland, an old fashioned sort of country, change had come, splitting the whole country in two. The Southern part was to be called the Irish Free State; even now they were arguing about who was to be the Irish Prime Minister.

The afternoon soon passed in the warehouse for Selina and before she had finished thinking about all the new people coming into her life, the horn had sounded to allow them to go home. She felt as if she didn't want any more events to take place. Enough was plenty! Elsie had been a revelation and Selina wanted to think about her more. The woman might be her future mother-in-law after all, so she might as well make a friend of her. It would be nice if Tom and Edith could be friends but with Harry poking his oar in, it wasn't likely.

Selina worked her press less often now, spending more time on the inspection of the locks as she gained experience. There were about a dozen young men working at the firm, and most of them had made a pass at her before the first month was out. Even Bert, the gaffer's son had come over to her to talk about work.

'I've been brought up in the trade,' he explained, 'I suppose I know nearly everything about the locks we make.' He seemed to puff his chest out as he made the claim, giving the air of someone who knows everything about everything. 'If there's anything you want to know about locks, Selina, just you come to me and I'll soon put you right.'

Just then, Dan came over and interrupted them. Instead of admonishing Bert, he just asked about a particular item, sending the youth scurrying to get information for him. When he had gone, Dan spoke to Selina.

'Don't you stand any nonsense from him, you know, Selina. He don't know aye from a bull's foot.'

Selina laughed; Dan was nothing like his son! His son would have just come out with the words to start a fight, and if Bert hadn't liked it, it would have been too bad.

'It's all right, Dan. There was no harm done, and he didn't mean any, either. He was just showing off, that's all. All men do it, don't they, in their own way?'

Selina looked at him pointedly and he laughed. She had caught him out! This young girl was even smarter than she looked. Like Elsie, he had seen his son with Selina and had recognised that they were going through a natural process that could only lead to one thing.

Would that one thing be a good thing? Dan had a feeling that it might, but it was too early yet to say. For the time being, she ought to be back in the warehouse, putting locks right, or if she couldn't, putting them on one side for a locksmith to rectify. Dan spoke sharply.

'The Gaffer will be in soon, Selina, and he will be asking me why you are not doing the things you are supposed to be doing. I suggest you get yourself in the warehouse, and get stuck into inspecting them faulty locks.'

He turned on his heel and marched away, leaving her standing, looking after him as he moved back to his own workplace. A minute later he could be seen at his bench, his file moving backwards and forwards smoothly, automatically. Dan was like a machine, only taking time from his bench to carry out some small supervisory task. He found shelter and security in the movements his body made, shelter from the nightmare memories of the war that still disturbed him, and security from the stimuli of the young women's aromas that assaulted his senses in the confines of the small workshop.

In the warehouse, Elsie awaited the arrival of Stephen; he was bound to turn up sometime this afternoon. He always did when she worked there. Selina would be the only pair of eyes that would be able to pry on their time together. He would find some errand for the girl to carry out at the far end of town to keep her out of the way while they enjoyed the short time they could have together.

Without the satisfaction of physical union they were often frustrated but this also added to the pleasure they had in each other's company, often stimulating their desires until they quarrelled just to get relief; the quarrel, a short-lasting experience, acting as a safety valve to their emotions.

Neither Elsie nor Stephen could see a lasting solution coming about, the rules of decent behaviour keeping their formal relationships in check. They had too many other obligations to maintain. Time would solve it all, they seemed to feel. Time would see their children, the anchors of their marriages growing and maturing to the point where they would break from their parents and leave the lovers stranded as loveless couples, envying their own offspring. This feeling of frustration was one of the burdens they bore voluntarily, knowing there was no other course for them. Perhaps time and its events would do it for them.

The only trouble was of course that for things to be put into a 'convenient' situation something had to happen to one or both of their partners and neither Elsie nor Stephen could bring themselves to hope for that eventuality. They could not think of punishing either of their partners for just existing.

33. Looking for a Hops Holiday.
1923

Tom had had a good day. Mister Stephen was pleased with him. Tom knew that Stephen liked him though he did not quite know why, for certain. They had a strange relationship. Stephen had a son, Stanley and a brother, Bert but Tom didn't think much of the older one. It was hardly surprising; Bert was clumsy in everything he did. The Stone's girls could all work more efficiently than him at whatever they were given to do.

Tom felt a strange sort of sympathy for Bert, never mocking him as some of the younger hands did, behind his back. Tom often felt that he was taking the place of the elder brother in the family, showing Bert how to do various tasks and protecting him from the wicked mouths of the youths of the factory.

Tom was skilled as a locksmith and Mister Stephen had now given him a craftsman's wage and status. This was an unusual step to take and Tom hadn't mentioned the fact to any of the hands, in case they were jealous. It would be put up on the works notice board though and he would have to put up with a little ribbing.

Since Selina had started at Stone's they had become more conscious of each other as they passed each other at work. He had noted her slightly buoyant figure. She was of average height and had shapely legs which seemed to show when the opportunity arose. Tom could see her working on a hand press and his eyes were fascinated by the movements of her breasts. Stephen Stone commented on the fact.

'Tom, your eyes will come out on storks, like a crab's if you don't watch it. Mind you, I don't blame you. I wouldn't mind smoothing her blouse for her.'

Tom was tempted to say something vicious but saw the twinkle in Stephen's eyes. He had been caught! The thought though, made him examine her more closely. The shape of her breasts pressing against her plain white blouse did seem to signal to his hands. He watched her each morning as she took her coat off to put her overall on and the revelation made him sweat and tremble.

They had sought each other's company during the lunch period as if it was the most natural thing. When they were alone together, Selina had moved closer to him and allowed her breast to rest on his arm. She had left it there for a few seconds and then stood herself upright and blushed, as if shocked by her own actions. Then she had turned on her heel and marched away with the other girls to get ready to start work.

Now Tom could hardly work with the feelings that coursed through him. He tried to forget the sight and feel of her so that his body would have a little comfort but his body had its own rules of behaviour. The days seemed to pass like a fortnight and he couldn't wait to see her walking out of the gate. He always stepped out briskly and put his hand over hers, immediately telling her of how he felt. He was embarrassed to even speak in that way but felt somehow that it was important to let her know of his important feelings. They were feelings that he had never known before.

Selina didn't try to remove her hand from his grasp, just held to it lightly.

'Yes, I know what you mean. It's lovely. It just makes you want to... I don't know what, really. I suppose we'll know when the time is right, shan't we?'

They were just passing an entry and Tom decided to take the plunge. He gave her a slight pull, into the entry and they found themselves with their arms round each other. Tom could feel her breasts pressing against him and he could not resist. His hands went inside her coat and found her breast. She went to pull away but seemed to change her mind and just held onto him.

'Selina!'

The word was shouting its way out of his throat as Tom expressed how he felt. It wasn't the same for Selina; she had been introduced to the pleasures of sex some time ago. Harry had arrived on the doorstep one evening to see her mother. Selina had invited him in, and after giving him tea had shocked him by confessing that she had watched him and her mother making love. The confession had led to games that had seemed harmless at first but had led finally to full sexual activity and her delight in the movements that expressed their combined emotions.

Harry, her mother's beau, was also shocked at the feelings he was finding within himself. He knew that it could not last long and that he would be ostracised in the community if he was ever found out.

In the meantime, Selina had found Tom and he was a thrilling new man for her to revel in. She felt, quite rightly, that she was the more experienced in love, and she wanted to make him want her to the point that he would have no choice but to marry her. This, she felt, would be an ideal life, just the two of them, both at work, sharing the pleasures of their joint income and making love each night.

Tom seemed to have stopped making advances in their relationship, seemingly content with shared masturbation. The activity was pleasurable to Selina too, but she wanted to make a baby with Tom before she conceived a child of Harry's. Although she was going through a period when she was obsessed by the sexual activity, she was still able to stand back mentally and work out the likely consequences, maturing in outlook as she did so.

Not long after she started work, she was with a group of part-time girls in the factory who were discussing the possibility of going to Worcester or Herefordshire for the hop picking in September. Her mother had never been, as she had always been dedicated to her little shop and would never take time off for a holiday.

'Why don't you come with us, Selina?' One of the girls asked her. 'If you brought your Tom, we would be able to share him. Think of the times we would be able to have!'

'I'll not share him with the likes of you, Maisie. At least he knows where I've been.'

The conversation, which had started as a friendly discussion, was starting to turn to more bitter possibilities and that would get neither of them anywhere. Maisie knew that and adopted a more conciliatory tone.

'Yes, we know you are as pure as the driven snow. All we wanted to do was to share your bit of snow! Perhaps your Tom is too cold for you and that is why you are so pure.'

The thought of being in the country with him, working in the fields by day and lying in his arms at night pulled her towards the possibility and she decided to tackle her mother on the subject.

Her mother, Edith, was glad when the subject was broached. She had been waiting for an opportunity to take some time alone with Harry, her new beau, and Selina's absence for a month would almost certainly provide the conditions for more of an intimate relationship with him. They had made love but always with the slightly inhibiting close presence of Selina.

Edith knew that her daughter was attached to the young locksmith from Stones' and although it disturbed her in one way because of the dangers of pregnancy, it could provide a way out of the dilemma she found herself in. When Selina raised the subject, Edith pretended that she was shocked.

'Hop picking for a month? How dare you ask about such a thing?'

She turned to Harry, who was sitting with them.

'What do you think, Harry? Can you hear the young hussy? She wants to go into the country for a month with her young man! She is saying that she wouldn't be tempted to do things that should only be thought of by married folks – and I am supposed to believe her!'

Harry didn't know how to react to the news. He too, knew of Tom's interest in Selina and his first, jealous inclination, was to refuse permission, taking the moral high ground.

'Look here, Selina; you know you shouldn't even be thinking about such things at your age; it is not right. This young man, Tom, is bound to want to take liberties with you. He is from a different class to us, you know, and he will take advantage of you if he gets the chance. No, I couldn't countenance giving you permission for such a thing.'

Harry knew that if Selina was allowed to go, it would mean the end of his secret relationship with the girl. He knew that what he was saying to her could bring the possibility of a challenge from her that he would find indefensible. What would happen if she exposed him? How could he continue an affiliation with her mother if he won the argument? His link would be broken, and he would be at real threat of severe physical punishment from her relatives. In the Black Country, although there was the overcrowding of family living conditions that often led to incest, if he was found out, retribution would be swift and violent. He had to get out of this!

'How could we be sure that you would be a good girl if you were given permission?' He turned to Edith. 'The best thing to do is to think about it for a day or two and then come to a decision. Why don't we do that, Edie?'

The three of them breathed a sigh of relief. Power had been taken from Selina and put into the hands of Harry and her mother, but the door to progress for Selina had not been closed. She had a day or two to work on her mother; she wasn't really bothered what Harry thought, the hypocrite. He wanted to be able to have his cake and eat it as well!

Edith was pleased too. The argument had had the possibility of Selina defying her mother. That could have been awkward. At least Harry had made out that all they were concerned about as parents, was the morals of the idea of Selina going away with a young man. Harry had craftily cast himself in the role of father looking after the welfare of his daughter but without throwing his weight about.

The three of them moved on to other subjects, discussing how well business was doing in some parts of the country compared with others and what a surprise it was that Stanley Baldwin had been elected as Prime Minister.

Harry was still trying to get more promotion at work and he

did all the things that an advancing man did. He had a bicycle and went out on it, on Sunday mornings. It was meant to show that he was looking after himself physically but he knew that the reason he went was the possibility of finding a young girl. Like many men, he was attracted to the pre-pubescent appearance of fourteen and fifteen-year olds girls.

Sometimes he managed to steal a few minutes in the company of a pair of girls but he was rarely able to separate them so that he could advance his sexual cause. He could not help trying, however, and when Selina had acquiesced, to his delight, he had wanted no other. Now he was about to lose her! The last month had been the fulfilment of his life's desire and he had been completely obsessed by the liaison. Nothing in his life would ever seem the same but he had to face the fact that it could not continue. He had thought that Selina was as attracted by him as he was to her, but it was obvious that it was not that way.

The thought of her making love to the young, uncouth locksmith was hard to take. He would have to make do with Edith! She was very pretty but she was old, as old as he was, and that disqualified her from his fantasies. She was very useful though, as she provided a safe background for him to operate in, in his quest for young girls.

In the next few days, the three of them came to accept the idea that Selina was going to go hop picking, in the neighbourhood of Bromyard. The idea seemed to incubate like an egg. They were all a little nicer to each other, Selina allowing familiarities from Harry that she had been denying him for some time. In the end, Edith approached the subject with her daughter.

'Look, Sel, I don't think you're a bad girl. As a matter of fact, I've always been very proud of you. The thing is, you see; how would you decide if you were a mother of a beautiful young daughter, and she wanted to go away to work with a young man, no matter how nice or morally marvellous he was?'

Selina knew at that point that she was going to get permission. She turned to her mother, who seemed to be talking out of the corner of her face.

'Listen to me, Mom. You know I wouldn't let you down. I've always thought you were marvellous, much better than some of the women round here, and I couldn't let you down. How could I face you for the rest of my life, knowing what I knew? It would be the same as if you were going to bed with Harry. I know you don't. I know you won't until you are married, if you ever decide to get married again, that is.' Selina stopped and they both blushed for some reason. 'What I want Mom, is for you to be at my side when I walk down the aisle, when I get married. I wouldn't mind if we had a double wedding, but I know that it will be longer before I get married than when you and Harry do it.'

Again she blushed in time with her mother although neither of them seemed to know what they were blushing about.

*

Edith was working late at her little shop. Selina would be at home now, and Harry might be calling before she got there. Something about that made her feel insecure. Not that Selina was likely to do anything she shouldn't with Harry; she wasn't that old yet, although Harry might be interested.

Edith had met Harry a few days after her husband had died in an accident at work. Harry had been a foreman at Mister Corbett's factory in Dudley. He had called to bring her five pounds from Mister Corbett, to help to pay for the funeral. It had been a devastating time and she had been glad of any help she could get. Her husband had had no insurance so the money sent from Mister Corbett and the four pounds, six shilling from the collection among his mates had seen her through the worst.

She had her own little shop to sustain her and she got her food at wholesale prices. Because she was in business, wholesalers were willing to give her trade discounts on clothes and household goods and furnishings, so she bought goods for sale from their collections, and watched her turnover increase by a significant amount.

Edith had hoped that Selina would take over and increase the worth of the little shop but it seemed the girl would rather make padlocks and flirt with the young locksmiths. She had seen Selina with that young Tommy Barr recently and had wondered where that was leading. In the long term, the sooner her daughter left to be wed to some young chap, the better. She would be able to settle down then, with Harry, then. He was very courteous, too courteous at times, as if he didn't do it naturally but was just putting it on.

Harry had been very kind to Selina; so kind that her daughter had taken a shine to him, climbing onto his lap as if she was a little girl. Sometimes he gave her a penny or two, although Edith didn't encourage that. Once or twice, Edith had come home and found him already there, waiting for her. Somehow she didn't like him doing that.

Edith had done enough in the shop; she could lock up now and get her self home. She felt tired. Harry would make her forget her tiredness, she knew. She looked down at the little cash box she had just put the takings in. She had taken three pounds, tens shillings. Not wonderful but better than some shops she knew.

The floorboard lifted easily and she slid the small collection of coins into the hiding place below. She had another place too, where she kept her savings. She had always believed in saving and was teaching Selina the same way. The girl now had over five pounds and was delighted. Edith was proud of her.

The key slid out of the lock and she put it into her handbag. It was only a few minutes walk along the dark streets to where she lived. Edith had never been nervous about the possibility of an attack; such things were rare. There was an unwritten law in the Black Country, that you didn't rob your own, not that it would do them much good, thought Edith; no one had much to be robbed of!

The other aspect of that was that robberies were usually carried out by young men, and there weren't all that many young men about now; they were nearly all still in the Army. She pushed open the front door of her house and listened. She could hear Selina giggling in the back room. It was obvious that Harry was with her. His overcoat was hung on one of the hooks fastened to the wall in the little space between the front and back rooms.

'Hello,' she called. 'Hello!'

Selina came bouncing out of the front room to meet her. They had loved and sustained each other after the loss of her father, last year.

'Hello, Mom. Look what the cat's dragged in.'

She pulled Edith into the back room where Harry was sat, ensconced on the settee with a cup of tea and a biscuit. He looked up and smiled at her.

'Hello Edie. Have you had a good day at the shop? I suppose the better the day you have, the more tired you will be.'

It sounded almost like a challenge.

'I'll give you tired, my lad. I'll show you how tired I am.' She picked up a cushion and advanced towards him, lifting the cushion to a position where she could hit him. She let fly and he tried to duck but still caught the full force.

The cushion hit him on the top of the head and he yelled.

'Oy, you! What do you think you are doing? How would you like it?'

He pulled her down across his lap and smacked her buttocks, making her scream loudly.

'Help; he's killing me. Murder'

Selina was delighted and wanted to join in. She jumped on his back and pulled him away from her mother. Harry turned and let her fall onto the settee at the side of Edith, banging her buttocks as she did so. As she slid, he slid his hands so that he had an arm around Edith and Selina.

'Now I've got you both! Let me see you get out of that, then!'

He pulled them both to him and kissed Edith roundly on her cheek and then he turned to Selina and pecked her on the cheek. She immediately pushed him away and they all seemed to quieten down.

'Here you are, Mom,' Selina said. 'Have a nice cup of tea and a slice of cake.'

Selina went into the small kitchen and made tea, bringing it in with cakes that Edith had brought home from her shop. Everything was very friendly. Selina was getting quite attached to Harry and this pleased Edith. He would make a good step-father with a little guidance. She enjoyed their games together. It made her feel young. Not that Harry was any younger than she; it was just nice, that was all.

Edith could see that Harry might be attractive to a young girl like Selina but there couldn't be any harm in it. He had never married so it would probably be a bit strange to him, to have a daughter in her teen years. The best thing for Selina was to find a young man of her own, not just keep borrowing hers!

Harry was still sitting with an arm round each of them. Which attracted him the most? He couldn't be one of those men who liked little girls could he? She put the thought away from her mind and concentrated on enjoying his closeness. He was very warm and nice to be close to.

Selina was feeling the experience quite differently. The closeness of him was making her feel strange, as if she had never felt the closeness of a man before. His hand on her hip was hot and she could feel the blood moving round her body as if it was being pumped. Silly, it *was* being pumped. His hand slid across her hip joint and she felt as if she would faint from the pleasure of it. He slid his hand inside the waistband of her skirt and she could feel the heat from his hand on her buttock as he slid it backward and forward. He moved over and his fingers seemed to enter the space between her thighs. She could stand it no longer.

'Come on, Mom,' she said. 'Your tea's getting cold. Have a piece of cake.' She looked at Harry's plate. 'You haven't eaten yours either, Harry. Come on. You've got to go to work in the morning.'

Almost reluctantly Harry withdrew his hand from her back and picked up the cup in front of him.

'It seems warm enough for me, anyway. How's yours Selina? Is yours hot enough?'

Selina felt that little thrill she received when she knew he was saying one thing and meaning another and she couldn't resist answering him in the same vein.

'Mine's hot enough, thank you, Harry. I wouldn't like it to be much hotter, anyway.'

Selina smiled to herself. This was a good way to have fun! She was brought back to earth a moment later as her mother rounded on her.

'Come on, Selina, my girl. Its time you were in bed now. Say goodnight to Harry and get yourself into your bed. You've got to get up for work in the morning. I've to get to the shop early to open up for the man from the market with the vegetables.'

Selina leaned and kissed Harry on the cheek in an innocent sort of fashion, and then she kissed her mother. She slipped up the stairs noisily to prove she was not sleepy, and then she put a pillow under where her head would have been if she wasn't sneaking out of her own bedroom and ducking into her mother's wardrobe and closing it almost to, then sitting down on the floor of the wardrobe to ease her legs.

It was almost an hour before her mother came up the stairs. Selina heard her push the door to her bedroom and then go back to the head of the stairs.

'Harry, Harry', she whispered, 'She's fast asleep in her own bed. You can come up now.'

Selina crouched down in the wardrobe, hardly breathing. If she was caught in the act of voyeurism, it would mean disgrace for a long time to come. It might mean that Harry would stop calling on her mother and that would mean a good dose of her mother's anger for a long time to come, if not for the rest of her life. Harry was her mother's lifeline, the only way back into a slightly more affluent section of society.

She could hear Harry climbing the stairs, cautiously, not wanting to be found out in this almost illicit act of lovemaking with the widow. She could see him through the ever so slightly open door. He was removing his shirt; he had a good body, thought the young girl. I wish he was doing it with me!

The notion frightened her and thrilled her at the same time and she found her hand trying to give herself relief as she crouched in discomfort to find out the secret of love and lust. She had never known such a feeling before. It seemed to be engulfing her.

Harry was removing his trousers now. She wanted to smile at him; he looked so comical in his socks without shoes and a pair of white underpants. She saw her mother reach up and pull at his underpants. 'Come here, Harry; you don't need them things on. They just get in the way!'

Edith gave the pants a good tug and they came down, to settle at his ankles. Selina gasped as she saw his manhood rearing towards her. She felt that if she put her hand out she could take hold of it. The thought made her feel all wet and weak at the knees.

Harry was sliding his hand across her mother's breasts and she was calling his name, as if she were in a passionate fit.

'Harry, I want you, Harry. Come on, let's put it in.'

Edith reached and took hold of him and opening her legs, placed Harry into the dark patch at the top of her thighs. He pushed, Selina could see that he was trying to push slowly but he could not help pushing harder and harder. Her mother was holding onto him, pulling at him and kissing him. They each slid and pulled at each other until they seemed to reach a point of exhaustion when they both pushed as if it was the last push they could manage. Then, the two lovers collapsed on the bed panting, almost as if they had been working hard.

Selina had to let her weight take her down to the floor of the wardrobe. She too felt as if she had been working hard. She wanted to take part! That was the only thing she had learned from the experience. She had used her mother and her lover for a surrogate experience; now she wanted the experience to be her own! She was ashamed of the voyeurism she had exhibited but certainly not enough to confess.

34. To Bromyard.
August 1923

Tom walked into work feeling nervous. He knew that this year would be the last one he could possibly be spending at the hop fields. His father wasn't in charge of him, Stephen Stone was, and Tom felt he would get permission to go to Bromyard for a month.

It was the last time he would ever ask. He was a journeyman now and had responsibilities. Still, the prospect seemed exciting to him and he felt he would do anything for this once in a lifetime chance.

He recalled with pleasure the earlier years he had spent hop picking, but this time it was different. The difference was Selina! He had lusted after many young women since he had entered his teen years. He used to sit on the tram or train, just looking out of the windows at them.

He even counted them, giving himself a score for the journey. He had got up to eighty-three in a day, last year. Eighty-three young women, on a hot summer day, although most of them had been girls, who he would have liked doing it with. He knew what 'it' was but had not yet tried 'it' out with anyone, not even Selina, although they had come close to it.

He would, he expected, spend the rest of his life working in Willenhall. Tom loved the little town with its smells and noises and thousands of locks being produced each week. It was only three miles from Walsall or Wolverhampton if he wanted to use the bright lights of a large town to turn the head of a girl.

The work he did in Willenhall was likely to continue to be available into the distant future as far as he could tell. Their goods went all over the world and were known to be the best although new firms were springing up all the time.

He turned into the alley that led past the Works Office towards the factory. Laura gave him a smile through the Office window and he smiled back. Was it possible that he could make a successful attempt there?

Tom marched on, into the factory and hung up his jacket on the nail he had knocked into the wall. He was feeling nervous about bringing up the subject of hop picking with Stephen. After all, the man was a businessman and had to show a profit. He wondered again how Mister Stephen would respond. How would Selina go about it? She too, had to ask for the time off.

He picked up the small metal blank, inserted it into the vice and started to file the intricate shape of the wards into the key so that it would open the lock for which it had been made. His mind wandered; he could perform this task without thinking and he often did. After a minute or two a young boy came to him with a mug of tea. Tom paid him a few coppers each week to perform this service, as did the other journeymen. The tea was hot as he sipped it while looking round the workshop.

Stephen Stone was walking down the walkway between the benches, saying good morning to each locksmith as he did.

'Good morning, Tom.' Stephen stopped for a moment. The two had a special sort of relationship born of the fact that that they were natural father and son, although it was not generally known or recognised. 'How are you doing?'

'Alright, Mister Stephen, but there's something I want to ask you.' Tom stopped, almost begging for Stephen to prompt him. When Stephen just waited for him to continue, he went on. 'I would like a week or two off, to go to Bromyard for the hop picking. I would do extra hours when I come back to make up for the time I lose from the job.'

He couldn't think of anything else to say. It was up to Stephen now. It just showed how much power the gaffer had. The only way round it, to get the same sort of power, was to become a gaffer himself. In the meantime he was subject to whatever decision his gaffer made. Stephen looked at him, his face serious. Then he seemed to brighten, as he always did, his serious demeanour turning to a laughing face.

'I suppose we can manage without you for a month, Tom, but it won't happen again. I hope you realise that. You have responsibilities to the firm now, especially as we've put you on full pay. You can go to Bromyard on the first of September but I shall expect you back four weeks on, at the most. Do you understand? While we are at it, Selina Brown has also asked for the time off. Is there any connection? Never mind; just enjoy yourselves. It'll be the last chance in your working life 'cos I'm expecting a lot from you, in the future – and you'll have to pull back the time you lose!'

Stephen smiled and walked off, nodding and having a word here and there to the other locksmiths as he did. Tom felt as if a great load had been lifted from his back. He couldn't wait to tell Selina but he had to look as if the most important thing in his life was the key in the vice in front of him. He returned to his stance, left foot forward and his hands on the small file, his excitement slowly subsiding. He was going to Bromyard!

Had Selina got permission? Oh, well, he would have to wait, now. He looked in the direction that Stephen had taken but the manager was not in sight now. Suddenly he realised; Stephen had said 'enjoy your selves!' He had given permission to both of them!

Tom tried the key, put it with the lock and picked up another blank. I'm like a key-blank, he thought. I'm being shaped by the gaffer and all the things that life brings to bear on me. Life is like a file, wearing away at my childhood, leaving only the bits that are any use to the gaffers. Why can't I find a way to shape myself - to suit myself? Why can't I find a way to shape my parts so that I will fit any lock that suits me, like a master key? That's the move! I will make a master-key of myself. No one else needs to know. All I have to do is to decide the shape and temper of the key that I want to be, and work at it. The thought of shaping himself intrigued him and he worked and thought about it all afternoon.

Before he knew it, it was time to go home. He now had to face his mother and father. There was no reason he could think of that would prevent him going. His mother would be glad for him. His father would sulk and pull a face but could not stop him if the gaffer had given him leave. After all, he wouldn't be taking food from the house; he would be earning his keep at Bromyard.

Neither of his parents showed any sign of surprise when he revealed his intention. The only comment was from his father.

'You'll not get away with that game, again, my lad.' He turned to Elsie. 'I'm surprised that Mister Stephen let him away for a month. I would never have got away with it, in my time.'

Elsie spoke up, sharply. 'I suppose you wouldn't have let him go, would you, Dan? I bet you've got away with a few things in your time, eh? He'll not get the chance again so don't moan out of jealousy. You didn't mind coming down to Bromyard, did you, Dan?' She turned to Tom. 'You'll have to get your hop box ready yourself. I'm too busy. You'll have to get some gloves as well. Them bines'll have the skin off the back o' your hands. It'll be Sunday morning I suppose, when you go? I'll lend you a few bob to go with and I shall want it back when you get home. Don't go wasting it on that young Selina, d'you hear?'

Elsie had no great expectations that he would keep to that rule. The month in Bromyard would grow him up this year. He was going as a callow youth, just beginning to shape himself. When he came back, he would be a man. She recalled the times they had spent among the bines, in Herefordshire. It would be good if he grew up as bright as Stephen. Stephen was a problem solver and that seemed to be the difference between him and Dan. Dan, although he had had ambition to get on when he was in the forces was only interested in next week's wages now, and how much of it he could grab, to spend on ale.

The only time he had shown much initiative was when he had been messing about with Ruth Mallory. He had done all sorts of things then, to provide opportunities to be with her, to satisfy his sexual need. Ruth had come out of her affair well, with her husband completely ignorant of his wife's infidelity.

In a way, Elsie thought, women were brighter than men. They had to be; they were smaller and weaker, and lived in a male dominated society. Their time would come, she felt sure, and the world would be a better place for it. The best of them would tie up with the best of men and between them, they would rule and the world would be a better place. In the meantime her son had to be taught to be one of the best. Selina would be the one to teach him and he would be the one to teach Selina.

In the office, Mabel watched as Stephen gave permission to young Barr to have time off. If she had had her way, she would have made use of the lad's father but he didn't have the initiative of Stephen. Elsie Barr might think she was clever but Mabel knew she had had the best of Stephen herself and could still have, whenever she gave him her body to play with.

At the small house, Elsie sighed and then smiled. She had made enough sacrifices for love; perhaps Tom would have better luck and better judgement. She still had her own love problems to solve. Stephen would still have to use his problem solving abilities but with luck they would enjoy many hours of shared intimacy in the years ahead.

It was wonderful, in a way, to see your seed flourish and come to the flowering. She had flowered; now it was her eldest son's turn. The time in Bromyard this year would be a journey from childhood to manhood, and his life would flower. Life was wonderful. She couldn't afford the time off this year as she had in the past. She must remember to write to Jenny Walker and Agnes Humphries. How was she, she wondered? She recalled their marriage, the same year that Dan had gone into the Forces. Were they as happy now as they had been that day? What a wonderful day that had been.

Later, she would let Tom know some of the financial secrets she had access to, but not just yet. She would see how things worked out with young Selina. She seemed a nice enough young woman. Perhaps she would be a good wife to him. She had better be! Elsie had a lot of power now and could soon make life very awkward to anyone who crossed her. She was becoming quite wealthy now and the trend was that she would continue to increase her assets.

Selina was elated, more than just elated; she was thrilled at every thought of the hop picking that was to come. She was going to put her mark on Tom, her man, though he didn't know it yet, and make him happy to be marked! She would start her move away from her mother and Harry, towards her own independence. She would be the lock, Tom would be the key! Tom would pick her lock and would be her key-smith for the rest of her life!